Praise for Cherie Priest

"Cherie Priest is our new queen of darkness, folks. Time
to kneel before her, lest she take our heads."

—Chuck Wendig

"With *Maplecroft*, Cherie Priest delivers her most terrifying
vision yet—a genuinely scary, deliciously claustrophobic,
and dreadfully captivating historical thriller with both
heart and cosmic horror. A mesmerizing absolute must-
read."

—Brian Keene

"One of the best Lovecraftian stories I've ever read."

—*io9* on *Maplecroft*

"There are few writers I'd rather have keep me up half the
night than Cherie Priest."

—John Scalzi

TOR BOOKS BY CHERIE PRIEST

The Eden Moore Books

Four and Twenty Blackbirds

Wings to the Kingdom

Not Flesh Nor Feathers

The Clockwork Century Novels

Boneshaker

Dreadnought

Ganymede

The Inexplicables

Fiddlehead

Fathom

The Family Plot

The Toll

THE
TOLL

CHERIE PRIEST

TOR

A TOM DOHERTY ASSOCIATES BOOK

NEW YORK

THE TOLL

Copyright © 2019 by Cherie Priest

A Tor Book
Published by Tom Doherty Associates
175 Fifth Avenue
New York, NY 10010

www.tor-forge.com

Tor® is a registered trademark of Macmillan Publishing Group, LLC.

Library of Congress Cataloging-in-Publication Data

Names: Priest, Cherie, author.
Title: The toll / Cherie Priest.
Description: First Edition. | New York : Tor, 2019. | "A Tom Doherty
    Associates Book."
Identifiers: LCCN 2018055936 | ISBN 9780765378231 (trade pbk.) |
    ISBN 9781466860629 (ebook)
Subjects: | GSAFD: Mystery fiction.
Classification: LCC PS3616.R537 T65 2019 | DDC 813/.6—dc23
LC record available at https://lccn.loc.gov/2018055936

Our books may be purchased in bulk for promotional,
educational, or business use. Please contact your local bookseller
or the Macmillan Corporate and Premium Sales Department at
1-800-221-7945, extension 5442, or by email at
MacmillanSpecialMarkets@macmillan.com.

First Edition: July 2019

Printed in the United States of America

0 9 8 7 6 5 4 3 2

This book is dedicated to Dr. Linda Jack, who is presently running for the Florida House of Representatives. By the time this book is published, she'll either be fighting the good fight in Tallahassee on behalf of Pasco County (36th district, represent!) . . . or fighting it closer to home as a private citizen, as the case may be. Her courage, patience, and fortitude have been a bright bit of hope in a time without much hope in it. Win or lose, this book is for her.

THE
TOLL

1

STAYWATER, GEORGIA

"What nobody ever tells you about gardening is . . . how many things you have to kill if you want to do it right." Daisy Spratford jammed her spade into the earth, slicing a worm in two. She used the small shovel to toss one half toward the bird feeder, and the other toward the water fountain full of murky green water and the fish that somehow survived there, in the overgrown backyard of a house called Hazelhurst. "No one says how many bugs, how many beetles . . . how many naked pink things that might be voles, or might be mice. I don't know the difference, when they're little like that. They all look the same until they get some hair."

"It don't matter anyway," said her cousin Claire. She didn't look up from her knitting. She didn't change the tempo of her foot, which leaned back and forth from heel to toe and back again, rocking her chair in time to the clicking of her needles.

"It matters to the crows, and the cats. It matters to Freddie, over there. It's a service I provide them. It's a kindness, is what it is."

"Not if you're a mouse." Cameron sat on the porch's edge, his feet maybe dangling right in front of Freddie, the resident king snake, for all he knew. He wasn't bothered by Freddie, and he wasn't particularly bothered by the thought of doomed pink rodents, writhing on his godmother's spade. But he liked to be contrary. He shrugged at both old ladies. "Or a vole, or whatever. I was just saying, it's all a matter of perspective."

They gave him a flash of stink eye.

"*Perspective.*" Daisy's drawl made the echo sound like a sneer. "*My* perspective is, I like having tomatoes come summer—and squash and cucumbers, too. My perspective is, I got pests enough without letting the stub-tailed pinkies grow up to be long-tailed brownies and breeding more of their kind. They don't stay in the garden, you know. They duck under the house, and get inside the walls."

"And inside Freddie," Claire added, lifting a needle for emphasis.

Daisy shook her head. "Not enough of them." She stabbed something else with her spade, but it might've only been a root, or a clump of clay. "We'd need an army of Freddies to get them all."

Cameron didn't look. He wasn't squeamish, but he didn't care what Daisy was killing this time. He liked summer tomatoes, too, and he didn't know anything about gardening—except for what Daisy told him, when she offered up her weird lessons while he looked on, sipping lemonade he'd mixed up with a splash of Jack.

His godmothers, each one past eighty years of age, surely knew about the Jack. They knew about everything else that went on within a hundred miles, so the whiskey wouldn't come as any surprise; but they didn't hide the bottle, so that was as good as permission.

The ladies had no trouble putting down their tiny feet when the fancy struck them.

Seventeen was plenty old enough to drink, in Cam's opinion. Seventeen was almost old enough to vote. Almost old enough to go to war. Neither activity sounded like something he'd go out of his way to do, but some people placed a lot of importance upon such things. Cam placed most of his importance upon clandestine sips of Jack.

Daisy adjusted her sun hat and shook a bag of seeds. A smattering sprinkled into her canvas-gloved palm.

Claire's needles tapped together, full speed ahead. "It's gonna rain."

"So what if it does?" Daisy wiped a smear of sweat from her forehead, though it wasn't very warm. Certainly not as warm as it'd be in a month, or in another month after that. Hell, the mosquitos were barely even out. It was barely even spring.

She glanced at Cam. "When the rain comes, I'll need help getting inside."

"You know I'll take care of you, Miss Claire. You feel the first sprinkle," he vowed, "and I'll whisk you off to the parlor."

"That's a good boy. Mostly." She peered down at the project dangling from the needles. It was finally taking shape—green and gray. Not a mitten or a scarf. Not a blanket for a baby. It was already too warm for any of those things, anyway.

The town of Staywater was always both too warm, and not warm enough.

Cameron wondered if it was just him, or if everybody felt that

way. Hazelhurst had air-conditioning units in half its windows and gas heat that came up from the floors, but he couldn't remember the last time he'd heard either one of those systems running. God only knew if they even still worked.

His swinging feet picked up a rhythm. Claire's needles followed along, unless it was the other way around.

One-two. One-two. One-two.

If this weather was some kind of sweet spot, it could stand to be sweeter. He thought about taking off his shirt—a striped button-up with long sleeves, rolled up his forearms. He thought about going inside and getting a sweater.

He thought about.

The needles pulled the yarn, loop by loop. Claire's foot leaned.

"He's wandering again," Daisy murmured.

Claire murmured back, "He's bored."

"It's a boring town for a boy his age. In another few years, he'll kill time down at Dave's place—whatever they call it now—and he won't have to reach into the cabinet, feeling good about stealing. He *does* feel good about it, you know."

"He kills plenty of time at Dave's already, but I don't think they serve him. He goes down there to see that woman."

Daisy clucked her tongue. "She's trouble. Anyway, she's too old for him."

"She agrees about that, so it's one thing we got in common. Someday, we should tell him who she is, and what she's done. He might not believe us, but then again, he might. Might make it easier for him to leave, when the time comes for that."

Daisy snapped, "You hush your mouth."

Cam stared into space. His feet kept time with Claire's lone foot, pumping against the weight of the rocker; but Cam's heels knocked against the lattice that screened off the porch's underside. It was thin with dry rot, and flaky with old lead paint. It cracked under the percussion of his heels, but he didn't stop.

"We may as well get used to the idea," Claire said. "He's growing up, and he might not stay. It'd be best if he didn't. You know it as well as anybody."

"But they always *do*. Now that it's safe."

She shook her head. "No. They don't." Her needles knotted the yarn, row upon row. "And you don't know that it's safe."

Daisy's spade cut the garden dirt, row upon row. "They *usually* do," she amended her conviction. "And it *mostly* is. Besides, where else would he go?"

"Forto. The swamp park. Somewhere farther off than that. Anywhere he wants, I guess." Claire peered over her shoulder. Cam's feet bumped up and down, back and forth. The lattice held just fine. If Freddie was under there, he held just fine, too. Probably, he'd taken off already—retreating to some quieter corner under the front steps, where bigger things than pinkies burrowed.

"Cameron wouldn't leave us here, all by ourselves."

"We won't live forever. Hell, we won't live that much longer."

"No, we won't." Daisy clenched her jaw, and squeezed her spade. She bore down on a cricket until it was nothing but damp black chunks that squirmed, then stopped. "But as long as he knows the rules, and knows to follow them when it counts . . . he can stay right here with us."

Claire didn't feel like fighting, or else she was losing track of her rhythm because Cam cleared his throat. "You thirsty, baby?" she asked him. "Maybe go on inside, and get yourself another glass of lemonade."

"I'm . . . I'm all right for now."

He still had half a glass. Dwindling cubes of ice clattered together when he spun it in his hand. Condensation soaked between his fingers, and dribbled down his wrist. He took another swallow—a long one that burned this time—and with two more just like it, he'd finished off the glass. He held it up and wiggled it; the ice cubes crunched against each other, and melted into slush.

"Would you like another one?" Daisy asked.

"No, ma'am, that'll be enough. And would you look at that, the very first drops of rain are just coming down. You were right about the weather, Miss Claire. I probably ought to help you get inside."

"It's only a sprinkle," she replied with a squint at the sky. "But it'll get worse, before it goes away. All right, hand me my knitting bag. If there's any breeze at all, I'll get soaked up here."

He stood up and stretched, then picked up the cotton satchel full of needles, balls of yarn, and whatever else old women toted around when they planned to make something, or acted like they were going to. He slung it across his chest and bent down to help Claire, who was a little fat and very arthritic, and maybe didn't need as much help as she pretended—but he didn't mind, just in case she did. Her cane was beside the knitting bag, but she always said how getting up and down was hard without a hand like Cameron's.

Daisy was on her own, and that was just how she liked it. But he called back to her: "Would you like me to come help? When I've got Miss Claire sorted out?"

She shook her head. "I'm all right. It's hardly damp at all, and there isn't much to put away."

He took her at her word, and assisted godmother number one

to her favorite chair by the lamp with a shade she insisted was a valuable piece of Tiffany, but was more likely a plastic piece from Woolworth's. The sky was overcast and the house's interior was dark, though it wasn't late and wasn't early—so Cam turned it on for her, figuring she'd go back to the knitting, or else to one of the books she kept within reach of her preferred perch.

Daisy had told him not to bother helping her pick up the gardening, but he went back out there regardless. Besides, he'd left his glass on the porch, right by the rail. If she saw it, he'd never hear the end of it.

He watched her, thin and hunkered, but stronger than she looked. She pulled a wagon with a seat on it, and all her gardening tools loaded up inside; she drew it toward the storage shed with a roof so rusted it hardly gave any shelter at all—but technically, it was better than nothing. Her hat sagged and bounced with every step.

He retrieved his lemonade glass and tossed the mushy ice into the yard.

The rain wasn't coming down any harder, and he didn't believe that Claire was right when she'd predicted that the weather would get worse. He poked his head back into the house. "I think I might go into town, if it's all the same to you," he announced.

"Wait for Daisy to . . ." Claire began, but stopped when she heard her cousin's footsteps on the porch. The boards creaked and stretched beneath her, and the handrail strained.

"Wait for Daisy to what?" she called as she climbed.

"I was going to say, he should wait for you to come back inside . . ." Claire hollered. She dropped her voice when Daisy appeared in the doorway.

"You're getting paranoid in your old age."

"What if you fell? What if you broke a hip out there, and Cameron was halfway to the square? I wouldn't be any help at all."

Cam chimed in. "You've got your cell phone."

"I can hardly use that thing."

He grinned. "You used it just fine when you wanted pizza last Friday."

Daisy sighed loudly and shut the screen door behind herself. She leaned against the frame and picked dirt from under her nails. "I've got mine in my apron pocket, and I'm not afraid of the buttons anymore. Don't worry about us," she said to Cam. "We're fine, same as always."

"Same as always," he echoed.

Everything in Staywater, always the same as always.

He swiped a light jacket from the coatrack, in case he needed it. He pushed the screen door open again and saw himself out, then latched it back into place. If the ladies had wanted him to close the front door, one of them would've said so. Then the other would've argued. Then they would've bickered about it so long, by the time they'd come to some agreement, it'd be the middle of the night and Cam would still be standing there, waiting for them to reach a consensus.

Just like always.

Cameron Spratford had lived with Claire and Daisy since he was a toddler. His parents had left him there at Hazelhurst one day, leashed to the front door's knob like a puppy abandoned at the pound.

Unless it wasn't his parents who'd dropped him off in a ding-dong-ditch. Really, it could've been anyone.

And it could have been worse. When he was especially bored, he would consider the alternatives in great and terrible detail, imagining his small self the victim of vast, unspeakable horrors.

He could've been leashed to a canoe and set adrift in the nearby swamp. He might've been swaddled and dumped in one of the many abandoned buildings that Staywater boasted, now that its heyday had long ago passed. Someone might have even left him in the south Georgia woods, tethered to a tree, waiting for wolves.

Did they have wolves in Georgia?

He paused, and stared thoughtfully at the sky. A faint mist dampened his face. He swiped it away with the back of his fore-arm.

Probably not, he concluded.

Coyotes, then. He might've been raised by coyotes, or deer, or whatever else might be big enough to manhandle a toddler. Wouldn't that have been weird? It might've been fun, or it might've been awful. He'd never know for certain, because instead of a wildlife upbringing or hasty devouring, he'd received the Spratford cousins, doting and batty—but no more batty than anyone else within the city limits, he had to admit.

He strolled down the dirt-and-gravel drive that ran almost half a mile to the main road, swinging a black umbrella by the U-shaped crook of its handle. He spun it in his hand, and tapped the ground. Once. Twice. In time with his pace, like a cane—but not like Claire's. The umbrella was just for show. Cameron didn't have anywhere to be, but Hazelhurst was stifling and the ladies were stifling, too. It didn't matter if they meant well. Hell, didn't everybody mean well?

Maybe not, he considered darkly.

Come to think of it, maybe not even *them*.

2

STATE ROAD 177

Radio static fizzed back and forth across the closing bars of "Aqualung," so Titus leaned forward and fiddled with the knob. It didn't work. The static stayed, and the music went away entirely. He swore out loud and pressed the seek buttons right, then left, fishing for anything other than the station playing Sunday worship music—the sole broadcast survivor in a wasteland of poor reception.

Melanie leaned her head against the passenger-side window and blew a little cloud of fog on the glass. "That's why they call it 'Bumblefuck.'"

"We can always plug in my phone. I pulled my whole music collection off the server before we left."

"Why'd you do that? I thought the whole point was—"

"I remember, I know," he headed her off. "I only brought the music for the drive out, and the drive back. Up until now we had good radio. So we didn't need it."

"So . . . you're not going to keep checking your messages all week, are you?"

"First thing every morning, but that's all. I'll even leave the charger in the car, if that makes you happy."

She frowned. "Why would that make me happy?"

"It's a *gesture*." He squeezed the steering wheel. "You know I have to check in for work, but Pete said I could do it once a day, and that would be fine."

"On our goddamn honeymoon."

"How else do you expect me to pay for it? Come on, don't . . . don't be like that. It'll be fun. Me, you, and the new canoes."

"I hope we brought enough bug spray."

"About a gallon ought to be enough. It's in the back with the rest of the gear. This was *your* idea," he reminded her. "You were the one who said we should go ahead and do this."

"I say a lot of shit."

That one was low-hanging fruit, so he let it go. "We're going to have a great time." He said it like a mantra. "This will be fun. The cabins are pretty cool, according to my brother."

"At least we won't be in a tent."

"No tents," he vowed for the umpteenth time. "Cabins, with electricity and plumbing. Like civilized people."

"I'm sure it'll be fine. We'll be fine." So they both had mantras. "How much longer till we get there?"

Titus pulled his phone out of the cupholder and checked the GPS. "We're practically in the swamp already."

"How far to the cabins?"

"Farther than I thought," he muttered.

"Are we lost?" She peered through the window in time to see a sign that read SR 177.

"No. We're not lost. We're just coming at the park from the wrong direction. The main entrance is on the east side, and we're coming from the west. If we'd gone down to Jacksonville first, this would've been easier."

"I told you, I don't want to go to Jacksonville."

"Yeah, so we didn't." He'd never met anybody who went to such great lengths to avoid her own perfectly nice mother. "Now we're spending a little extra time in Bumblefuck. That's the trade-off."

She settled back into the seat. "Totally worth it."

Without the music, they fell into silence—watching the small road wind through the south Georgia woods that were rapidly morphing into swampland. Their tires chewed over a wood-plank bridge that crossed a stream, or a tendril of current, or just an exceedingly deep puddle of brackish water, marking an official change in scenery from the drier pines and whatnot they'd been passing for the last hour. Here was the outer edge of the Okefenokee, wet and dark; here were cypress knees poking through the surface and patches of cattails, milkweed, and other damp-loving flora waving in the lazy, warm breeze.

"What if there are alligators?" Melanie asked. Her voice vibrated along with the SUV, as it creaked and rumbled the final length of the rickety bridge.

"There will definitely be alligators. You know that already."

"What do we do if we meet one?"

He sighed. "We leave it alone, and it'll leave us alone. You act like you've never seen one before."

"They don't have any in Nashville."

"They have them in Jacksonville, I bet."

"Never seen one there," she said with a sulk. Titus couldn't tell if she was glad she'd missed them all, or if she was disappointed to have never spotted one in person. "Do they run fast? Do they ever eat people?" She pulled out her phone like she might be able to look up the answers to these questions, but there wasn't enough signal to bother. She put the phone away again.

"No," he answered broadly. It wasn't entirely true, but she didn't know that, and she didn't have any Wi-Fi to prove him wrong.

"What *do* they eat?"

"Everything but people. Fish," he added fast, before she could accuse him of teasing her. "And birds, and snakes. Frogs. Small-ish living things, mostly. In some places, they get a taste for dogs."

"Yuck."

"They also like marshmallows covered in peanut butter."

"You're shitting me."

He shook his head. "Nope. When I was a kid, my uncle used to—I mean, it was a bad idea, but he was a dumbass—he used to stand on a bridge, like one of these," he gestured at the one up ahead. "And toss them on down, marshmallow by marshmallow. The big kind you roast around a campfire, you know. The gators loved it. They'd all gather around in the water with their mouths hanging open."

"Did we bring any peanut butter or marshmallows?"

Through his teeth, he said, "We aren't going to *feed* them—"

"Not for fun, but in case of emergency. We could keep some gator treats in the canoe, and then throw them, and run the other way."

"Run in a canoe?"

"Paddle faster, then." Melanie shrugged. "Whatever."

"You won't out-paddle a . . . you know what, never mind.

Alligators don't want to eat people, and I'm pretty sure it's illegal to feed them peanut butter and marshmallows, or anything else. Even if it isn't illegal, it's stupid. Now I wish I hadn't said anything."

"Breakin' the law, breakin' the law . . ." she sang under her breath.

"Babe, if you feed them, they'll just follow you around. Like *Jaws.*"

"Gatorshark. Is that a Syfy movie? They should make it a Syfy movie."

It wasn't the worst idea she'd ever had. "If it isn't a movie yet, it will be soon. I bet."

The SUV rattled over another sad sack of a bridge. It had already cleared several others, each one more wobbly than the last. But this was a state park, right? The government maintained these bridges, didn't it?

Somebody had to.

Titus believed that about as strongly as Melanie believed in gatorsharks, but he didn't want to give her one more thing to complain about, so he kept his mouth shut. He had a feeling that much of his foreseeable future would be dedicated to keeping his mouth shut. He didn't like how he felt about that feeling.

He slipped her a little side-eye. She was staring out the window, looking for alligators or something else to gripe about. He realized he was bracing himself, waiting for it, when she said, "It's going to be hot."

He clenched the wheel, wondering if he could accidentally break it. "No hotter than Valdosta."

"Wetter than Valdosta. More bugs."

"Are you trying to tell me you want to go home?"

She didn't look at him. "I'm sure it'll be fine."

"This was *your* idea."

"No," she snapped. She put her feet up on the dashboard. "Stop saying that. You always put words in my mouth."

"You said we should canoe the swamp."

"No, I said I'd never done it before, but when you talked about doing it as a kid, it sounded like fun. *You* were the one who decided this was going to be our honeymoon. You booked the trip, because you weren't listening."

"I *was* listening. You don't like Florida ever since your mother moved there, so I couldn't take you around my old stomping grounds in Highlands Hammock. That's why we agreed on the Okefenokee. It was closer to your comfort zone."

She sniffed disdainfully. "My *comfort zone*, what a stupid way to put it. I like room service. That doesn't make me a fucking princess."

"Then why did you even agree to this, if you hate the outdoors so much?" he asked, glimpsing another sign up ahead. Something about another bridge.

"I don't hate the outdoors. But swamp-swimming ain't my idea of a relaxing vacation."

Titus ran his fingers along the steering wheel's ridges, over and over again, counting the indentations while he counted his breaths. "This is supposed to be a fun week, doing something together."

"It'll be fine. We'll have fun."

"This was *your* idea."

"You're just gonna die on that hill, aren't you." She slipped her feet out of her sandals and pressed her toes on the underside of the windshield. "Same as always: You decide what you want, and then you decide that I want it, too. Who booked these plans? Who went out and bought all the gear?"

"I did. You know I did. You said I should do it, because you didn't know what we needed."

"That part's true," she granted.

"I don't remember you pissing and moaning when I said you should pick out a new bathing suit. Jesus, Mellie. Don't fight with me, please? If you want, we can call the whole thing off. Turn around, go get a hotel, I don't care."

"You know good and well I didn't say that, either. You're doing it again. Putting words in my mouth."

He released his grip on the wheel and smacked it in frustration. "Then what *are* you saying?"

Louder, matching him now, she responded in kind. "I'm saying it'll be fine! I've never done this before and I don't know if I'll like it, but I'll be doing it with you, and that's the whole point of a honeymoon, right?"

"You aren't even going to *try* to like it. You're going to complain the whole goddamn time. You're so fucking scared of anything new, anything different."

"If that's what you really think, then do it—stop threatening to call off the honeymoon and turn us around."

"You'd like that, wouldn't you?" He knew it was a dumb thing to say, even as it flew out of his mouth. Now he was stuck, halfway between wanting to bail before things got worse, and wanting to punish her with a week of swamp-swimming for being such a pain in the ass.

"I'd like for you to quit yelling at me!"

He stopped himself before he could shout a response.

She was nervous, and he was nervous, and this whole "getting married" business was looking less and less like the good idea it'd seemed at the time, but they'd already filed all the paperwork and everything was legal. They were Mr. and Mrs. Bell.

He counted to five, fondled the steering wheel some more,

and flashed a glance at the silent radio. "I'm sorry I yelled at you. I didn't mean to yell."

"I forgive you."

He wished she hadn't said it out loud. Somehow it made things worse, like she wouldn't even take *part* of the blame. He let it go anyway. High ground. High road. Inhale red, exhale blue. Is that how it was supposed to go? Or the other way around?

"Good. Then . . . from here on out, for the whole week—let's see if we can do it, okay? No fighting. I won't put words in your mouth, and you'll make an honest go at having a good time. And if you don't enjoy yourself," he added as it occurred to him, "we can pack up and call it early. We'll go back to Valdosta and get someplace with room service."

"You swear to God?"

"I swear to God. But you have to *try*."

"I will. I said I will."

"Okay."

"Okay," she said, crossing her arms like the conversation was finished.

New subject. He asked her, "Hey, did you see that sign?"

"Which one? The one about the bridge?"

"No, the one about the park. It's three miles up ahead, and then we just have to take the one road—straight out to Stephen Foster. We'll go right through the swamp. It'll be cool."

"This isn't the swamp, already?"

He looked back and forth between the road, and out his window. "I mean, we'll be inside the state park. That part of the swamp."

"Is that the entrance, up ahead?" she asked. She held a hand over her eyes as if to shield them, even though the late-afternoon sun was shining behind them—highlighting the swamp's blacks, greens, and grays with iridescent orange.

"What? No, I don't think so. It's just another bridge. There's about a million of them, I swear."

"It's not wide enough to be a bridge. Look, it's only got one lane."

Titus slowed the SUV to a crawl, and then to a stop. "Holy shit, you're right."

"I'm right all the time. There's no reason to cuss about it."

"Now you're just trying to pick a fight."

She sighed. "No, I was making a joke."

"Okay then. Sorry. Hang on," he said, pulling off to the shoulder—such as it was. The SUV leaned precipitously toward a ditch, but clung to the edge of the road. Titus rolled down his window and hung his head out. "I don't hear any other cars."

"Me either, but I can't see across to the other side, can you?"

Long tresses of Spanish moss draped down from tree limbs, and thick foliage crowded out the view of the bridge's other end. It might be a long haul, or it might be a short sprint. There was no telling from where they were parked, idling, squinting at the only way forward. "No. It's kind of overgrown. Stay put a second," Titus urged. "Let me go take a look."

Titus opened the driver-side door with difficulty, since the vehicle was leaning down to the right. He pushed it, shoved it with his foot, and heaved himself onto the roughly asphalted road that was utterly unmarked except a dotted yellow line painted down its middle.

The world was dark and wet around him, the air heavy and buzzing with insects—ringing with the calls of unseen birds. Overhead, the sun was high enough that the overgrown scenery was brighter than black, and dusted with gold—for the afternoon was tipping from early to late, and their plan had been to arrive by dark.

They'd make it, with room to spare. Even with this tiny interruption.

It didn't feel tiny, exactly.

It felt like time stopping, though Titus couldn't put his finger on why.

The swamp sprawled out for miles to the east, and the line between water and earth was broadly smudged. He could hear it, running and dripping, swirling someplace down below the bridge, and alongside it. The road itself wasn't damp. It hadn't been raining. The road was only narrow, and narrowing even more, down to a sliver of a single lane up ahead—pinched as if corseted by the wood-slat bridge that didn't look sturdy enough to hold a bicycle, much less a vehicle.

This couldn't be right.

Beside the bridge, he saw a sign half covered in moss and mud. He approached it, and moved a handful of foliage to read the black letters on a civic-yellow background. "'Caution, one-lane bridge. Watch for oncoming traffic,'" he said under his breath. "No kidding." Under the main sign was a smaller one that said, SPEED LIMIT: 5MPH.

From inside the car, he heard Melanie's voice. She was yelling a question, he could tell that by her tone . . . probably asking if he saw anything on the other side of the bridge.

He waved one hand in her general direction but didn't look back. He was staring ahead, trying to see past the moss, the shadows, the looming shrubbery, and the interlaced canopy of the trees.

No matter how hard he squinted, he couldn't tell what awaited over there.

The bridge's far-side landing was distant and overgrown, and the scenery wobbled and wavered. It must have been the sun, streaming through the layers and layers of leaves. It must've been the breeze. It must've been a trick of the distance—an optical illusion, like a weird spot on a rural road where you can put your car in neutral and it'll roll up a hill. Or that's what it looks and feels like.

He could see his side of the bridge just fine; he was practically standing on it. He could run his eyes along the boards, to the weird, raised ridge in the middle, and over the water. But about midway, his eyes lost the thread and everything fluttered. The air moved like gasoline simmering around a car's tank. Like heat rising off a summer sidewalk.

He took a step forward, then another. When he reached the spot where road became bridge, the word "trestle" sprang to mind. It made sense, didn't it? This wasn't a modern, metal bridge made for cars, and with that ridge . . . no, two ridges . . . right down the middle, like tracks . . .

Behind him, he heard the electric hum of the SUV's window descending. Melanie hung her head out and yelled, "What are you doing?"

Over his shoulder, he yelled back, "This old stone bridge used to carry trains. You can see where the rails used to be."

"What?"

"It's made for trains, not cars!"

"Then why are we driving over it?"

An entirely reasonable question. "Because this is where the road goes." Then quieter, so she couldn't hear him: "This is where the road *ends*." It didn't really end, and he didn't want to scare her. He didn't know why it might scare her. He didn't know why he was scared.

He put a foot on the bridge, as if that'd be enough to test it. It felt solid enough, so he jumped up and down, and then strolled a few feet onto the main structure. It was old—surely older than the road, except that the road must've been train tracks at some point, too. He looked back at the strip of asphalt, but didn't see any hints left over. Any old tracks had been pulled or paved years ago.

So why hadn't they replaced the bridge, while they were at it?

"You're going to get hit by a car!" Melanie shouted.

"There aren't any cars!" he shouted back.

He didn't hear any cars. He didn't see any cars, either, but he couldn't make out anything at all on the other side, and that was stupid—the bridge wasn't that long, surely no more than a dozen car lengths—and there wasn't any fog, or smoke, or anything else obscuring his vision. But no matter how hard he stared, all he saw was that curtain of deep-green plants, vines, mosses, and tree trunks that all ran together in a pattern. If there was anything coming from the other side, maybe it couldn't see Titus, either.

"This thing is a lawsuit waiting to happen," he muttered.

Down below, something splashed and swam away. He looked over the edge and saw nothing but a trail in the water where a tail might've vanished, or a snake might've gone for a dip. The water itself was brackish and thick, more sludge than spring, and it pooled rather than flowed. Vivid yellow algae broke up the darkness, decorating the fallen logs and spattering the water's surface with flecks like pollen, or tiny petals.

He put his hands on the rail and tried to rattle it, but it wouldn't budge. Old shit was built to last.

One last time, he looked out to the other side. One last time, he saw only the swamp, clotting the view in a way that wasn't quite right, but was quite complete.

"Fuck it," he declared, and stomped back to the car.

"What?" Melanie asked through the window.

"I said, '*fuck it.*' Let's go. There's nobody coming—and if we do manage to hit someone, it'll be the slowest crash ever. It'll be like bumper cars. Everything will be fine."

"What if the other car isn't going slow? What if we get smashed head-on, and we drive right off the bridge?"

"Have a little faith." He climbed in instead and started the car again, then pulled back onto the road at a slow crawl. He kept the crawl rolling as he approached the edge of the bridge. He tapped the brakes for one final hesitation and pushed one toe onto the gas pedal.

"Here goes nothing," his wife breathed. She tested her seat belt with one hand, and clutched the oh-shit bar with the other.

She was overreacting, that's what Titus wanted to tell her. But he didn't, because if he'd been the passenger, he would've done exactly the same thing. He tried to reassure them both when he said, "The bridge used to carry trains. It can carry us, just for . . . for however long it takes."

They drove at a creep. A tricycle could've passed them on the left.

It still felt too fast.

When all four wheels were on the bridge and past the yellow-lined road, everything seemed very loud. The tires grumbled a loud echo, and the engine strained at a higher pitch. Every sound was vivid in their ears: every bird caroling overhead, every hard-shelled beetle bouncing off the windshield. Every creak and moan of the bridge itself, straining under their weight.

Titus held his breath and tried to keep from blinking.

The stone sides of the bridge were so close to the SUV doors that he was half convinced they'd lose a side mirror at any moment. If he hung his hand out, he could brush the guide rails as he passed. If he sneezed and tweaked the wheel, they'd jump the side and land in the swamp.

No. Old shit was made to last. That could be a mantra, too. If he said it enough times, it would magically become true.

He refused to fantasize about that last option and instead stared straight ahead, his eyes watering and fingers clenching, unclenching, on the poor abused steering wheel.

"This is weird, isn't it?" Melanie whispered.

"It's definitely weird." Maybe it was a fog, or some peculiar swamp miasma—some haze that kept him from seeing whatever was waiting on the other side. "It's just swamp gas," he explained, as if that wasn't total bullshit. "Swamp gas" was the go-to excuse for strange lights and hauntings since time began, or since scientists came up with the term. Jesus, was there even any such thing?

The air vibrated before him, as he propelled the SUV board by board across the bridge.

"How long *is* this damn thing?" he asked aloud, and wished he hadn't, because it only meant Melanie would answer him.

"Really long, I guess."

He let out a small, choked laugh.

She beat him to the punch. "Please don't say, 'That's what she said.'"

"I wasn't going to." But he'd been thinking about it. "Do you . . . can you see anything? Is anybody coming, can you tell?"

She shook her head. "No . . . it's just . . . all I see is the trees, and the air. You know what I mean? You can almost see the air."

"Yeah, I know what you mean."

"You're not going to tell me it's stupid?"

"No. I can see it too. Swamp gas, that's all," Titus repeated, but it could've been chem trails from a UFO for all he knew. He swallowed and gave the vehicle a little extra nudge of fuel.

Threat of collision be damned, he wanted off that bridge. He wanted it long gone in the rearview mirror, and when they reached the campground, he would drag out a map and pick out a different route for the return trip—because he couldn't stand the thought of driving over this damn thing for a second time.

"I think we're almost there," Melanie said. She sounded hopeful, but not certain.

"We'd better be. How much longer can this thing . . . ?" he started to ask, but the clatter of the boards beneath the wheels was loud, and the air was thick with swamp gas, since that's what he'd decided to call it—and he was sticking with it. "This bridge. It can't go on forever," he concluded.

"We have always driven on the bridge," Melanie intoned, undoubtedly quoting or parodying something Titus wasn't familiar with. She did it all the time. He hated it, because he didn't know when she was letting fly a thought of her own, or when she was deploying a line from some movie she expected him to recognize.

"Shut up. Don't say that."

"I was only—"

"I don't care." He chewed on his lip and blinked away the water that'd collected in his eyes. "I don't like this. Something's not right."

"It's just a bridge!" she said, but her pitch was wrong, too. It was almost high enough to call "shrill."

The timbre of the rumbling shifted, and the boards that passed for a bridge lane seemed wider—the shape of them sprawling, spreading, expanding. The noise of the wheels changed, from a raucous vibration to a low-frequency hum—or not like that at all, Titus thought. It wasn't exactly a hum or a rolling thud like thunder; it was more like the sound an animal might make. A huge animal. An angry animal, cornered or hurt. Maybe hungry. Maybe hunting.

He shook his head, trying to chase out the idea of it. He wondered anyway, *What kind of animal? If it is an animal, what does it want?* His mind wandered away from the whiteness of his knuckles on the wheel, the noise in his ears, his foot on the gas pedal, pressing harder.

He was going faster now. Faster than five miles per hour, that was for damn sure. Fast enough that the engine whined and the slats on the guardrail were a blur.

Melanie said something. He didn't hear her. She said it louder, and he didn't understand her.

For the first time in his life, he properly understood the term "tunnel vision"—unless this was something else, and he'd had it all wrong, all these years. Through the windshield he saw only a fixed point somewhere directly ahead, a vague circle with no details, no colors. Only motion, and everything around the point was in motion too. A tunnel, yes. For tunnel vision. A rotating tunnel, like you'd find in a funhouse—but it wasn't any fun at all.

Titus took a deep breath.

Melanie was still shouting, unless she was whispering.

He took a second deep breath. His eyes didn't just water. They burned.

He closed them.

3

INTO TOWN

The main road was barely a road and it wasn't "main" to anything except the old town square, a ways to the north. Cameron walked it anyway. If the road had a name, he'd never learned it. It hardly seemed worth the trouble. After all, it only had two lanes, and the line that should've gone down the middle had faded into a light yellow smudge that came and went from mile to mile. It scarcely had a shoulder, and in places, it lacked a full complement of asphalt. On both sides of this lamentable strip, grasses and shrubs, tall and short, lined the way—all of them waving in the damp wind as if the main road were a parade route.

And Cameron was a majorette.

He turned left, raising his knees, one-two, one-two, dodging a high patch of stickweed. His sneakers sank into sandy gravel. He pulled them out again fast; he wasn't wearing any socks, and he didn't feel like walking to town with a shoe full of grit—so he decided to walk in the right lane when there weren't any cars.

Mostly, there weren't any cars.

During Cam's walk, he saw three in total: Mr. Abernathy's Bondo-mobile shaped like a pickup truck, headed south toward the dump; Rick Holmes going north in a white Crown Vic that used to be a cop car; and Mrs. Mary Meyers in her red convertible with one yellow door, and her dog sitting in the passenger's seat, his floppy tongue licking at the sky.

As Cam got closer to town, the soggy woods beyond the stickweed and poison ivy gave way to a few buildings here and there, and a cross street or two. Most of the buildings were empty. Most of the cross streets didn't connect to anything, or lead anywhere anymore.

He didn't see any more cars, but off to the right he passed the dollhouse—and up ahead was the auto body shop that was mostly a junk shop, with a scrapyard the size of a big city block out back. He waved at the body shop as he strolled on by, in case there was anyone inside. If Quincy was working, he'd wave back and come say hello. If Jason was there, he wouldn't.

No one responded, so Cam kept moving.

On the next corner camped a gas station, with one working pump out of six and a refrigerator case inside that usually held a few Coke products, and not much else. Through the clear glass door he saw Mrs. Fulker sweeping slowly, bobbing her head along to the radio. Cameron reached into his front pocket and found a crumpled wad of bills—the leftovers from last week's allowance. His walk had warmed him up. The bills in his pocket were dank, but they'd spend.

He crossed the road with half a dozen quick steps, on the off chance any cars might appear—and he navigated the tiny forest of gas pumps, wondering which one worked today; but Mrs. Fulker hadn't put up a sign, so the identity of the functional pump remained a mystery. The label on the door said PULL but he pushed it, and it opened.

"Hey Mrs. Fulker."

She nodded outside of the music's beat, just to say she'd heard him. "Hello, Cameron."

There wasn't any music, really. The radio was stuck, alternating back and forth between the fizzy words of a broadcaster offering the news, and some shouting salesperson-speak that sounded like a commercial for mattresses.

"I'm just grabbing a Coke," he told her.

"Throw your money on the counter. I'll get it later."

"Yes ma'am." The cooler was in the back of the store, and it was so dark that it looked broken. One light out of three worked, and all the lone bulb illuminated was a row of bottles, a stack of cans, and a chilly, dusty shelf. When he opened the door, he got a whiff of old bugs and mildew—a thick smell that was cool but not clean. He swiped a bottle and wiped it on his pants.

"Just a Coke, you said?"

"The last vanilla one, so you know." The trip back to the register was straightforward, but it always felt like walking a deserted labyrinth. On either side of the aisle, oversized shelves reared up—rusting and sparsely populated, most of the way to the ceiling. The overhead lights worked about as well as the cooler lights, except that they flickered. They flashed. They hummed along to the radio static.

Upon reaching the counter, Cam straightened a single dollar bill and coughed up two quarters to keep it company. "I'm leaving a buck fifty," he called out.

"I owe you two pennies."

He cocked a thumb at the NEED A PENNY? TAKE A PENNY cup. "Keep 'em."

She wasn't looking at him, but she nodded again anyway, out of time with whatever was playing in her head, and not over the speakers, not from the fluorescent lights with their cracked plastic shades mounted flush on the ceiling.

He left her that way, swinging her broom back and forth, from aisle to mostly empty aisle. She collected the corpses of cockroaches, and the peeled-off labels of soup cans. She pushed around the remains of a busted bag of chips, and the salty, gritty contents. The broom didn't swish or swipe. It scraped.

Back outside, the sun had come out despite the sprinkles, but it immediately went away again—ducking behind a big gray cloud shaped kind of like a hand, and leaving the town a touch too cool again. That was fine with Cam. He'd rather wear his jacket than carry it, any day of the week. Another five degrees, and he'd have sweat stains peeking through his underarms before he made it home.

But heading home was somewhere at the bottom of his vaguely defined agenda. He'd only just escaped it. "Out of the frying pan . . ." he started to say, then shook his head. No, home with Daisy and Claire was never a frying pan, and it'd hurt their feelings if they heard him say it.

For that matter, Staywater wasn't a fire. It was more like a tide pool.

The town square was just up ahead, but it wasn't anything to write home about. Anyone could've told you that. Like the rest of the town it was three-quarters abandoned, and even the occupied spaces were more vacant than bustling. But at the end of the main street—which surely had a name, and it surely wasn't Main Street—the courthouse reared into view.

Built in 1840, the Kirklin County courthouse was the largest building for a good number of miles. It'd been built with logging money, and taxes from the sawmill workers . . . plus a generous grant from Zenas and Zeboim Childress, the brothers who owned and built the mill on the far side of town. They wanted the town to look official, they said, and not like some swampy Southern wide-spot-in-the-road. Staywater was the seat of government, and it deserved a spot on the map. It deserved a touch of grandeur.

All right, then—the courthouse was grand, if there was nothing else of note to be said about it. Huge, columned, and brick, it stood out in no way whatsoever from a thousand other courthouses built in such a fashion, around such a date. Cameron figured that sometime in the past, "official" must have equated with "uniform," or else so many of these little old backwaters wouldn't look so damn much alike.

Not that he'd ever seen any others, except in books and *Southern Living*, which Daisy and Claire devoured each month upon the magazine's arrival. The closest he'd ever seen to his home town on television—and Claire had told him it was nonsense, but he stood by his assessment—was a PBS piece on Detroit. He'd been fascinated by the subject, at this great city which had been home to millions a few decades ago . . . and hosted only a fraction of that, now.

All those buildings, derelict. All those empty places, between where the folks who remained worked and lived, or squatted and camped. All that infrastructure, lost or crumbling or nonexistent in some other way.

Large scale, small scale. Look close, or stand back. The pattern was the same.

For all that it intrigued him, Cam didn't like the comparison any better than Claire did, so he'd quit insisting on it. Besides, she'd been right: There were plenty of differences between a former powerhouse of industry up north and a small mill town down south. For one thing, Detroit was making an effort to pull its ass out of the fire.

Yeah, for one thing.

On the Staywater town square there were four corners' worth of storefronts: a hardware store that still opened its doors a couple of days a week, or by appointment; a drugstore that hadn't been open in anybody's recent memory, with a fading stencil sign advertising STAYWATER DRUG CO.; a photo studio that went under before digital cameras were even a thing; a bookshop that was either in business, or it wasn't, and there was really no telling; a barbershop with two chairs and no waiting; an old clothing store with window mannequins wearing dresses from 1979; several assorted offices that were so empty, there was no way of knowing what had gone there in the first place; and the pizza-joint equivalent of a dive bar, called Paulie's.

The actual dive bar was called Thirsty's, but everyone called it "Dave's" because Dave was the guy who owned and operated it. Dave's wasn't on the town square; it was located out closer to State Road 177, which was *really* the main road if Staywater actually had one. And it didn't.

But SR 177 at least went back and forth between Forto and the swamp, and the swamp was a state park . . . so it drew a steady trickle of outdoors enthusiasts from out of town. Or "tourists," if you liked that better.

As far as Cam was concerned, tourists were pretty much the worst. Everyone else would've agreed with him. Except Dave, maybe. And Maude, who ran the only hotel—a bed-and-breakfast, she called it, when she wanted to sound fancy.

Everybody else, though.

A smattering of cars were parked here and there around the

square, occupying the faded parallel lines in front of the court-house and the pizza place. None of those cars had been made in the present century. A couple had crumpled hoods from where they'd met a deer on the road and kept on driving, because nobody used the auto body shop if they could possibly help it. If you were lucky, your car would disappear into the wasteland of rust and steel out back—"Six Flags over Tetanus," as Daisy called it. And if you weren't?

Cameron shook his head.

Quincy and Jason were all right, but you really had to keep them at arm's length.

He swigged from his Coke and made for Paulie's, but changed his mind. It still wasn't raining and he still wasn't hungry, and he only had ten bucks left of his allowance. Another cash infusion wouldn't come down the pike until the weekend arrived, so he had to save it.

It'd be better to head someplace where he couldn't spend it, but that'd been the plan lurking in the back of his head all along. It now came forward to nudge him over to the next cross street, where the square worked like a roundabout. Or that's how it *would* work, if there were ever more than two or three cars trying to navigate it at the same time.

There were no working stoplights in Staywater, just a blinking red light hanging over that interchange where the asphalt tributary of SR 177 emptied into the main loop around the courthouse. A pea-green sign that used to be Kelly green called the outgoing road DUBOIS STREET. Everyone pronounced it "doo-boys," which drove Claire and Daisy up a wall. It drove Cam up the wall by proxy, but he turned right on it anyway—then walked another half mile until he hit Maude's.

It was only another couple of blocks to Dave's parking lot, where four whole cars were lined up by the side door.

Hot damn. It was practically a crowd.

He dodged an old Chevy that was halfway parked in the road. He pulled Dave's door open with a latch that was always loose, and threatened to fall off at the first strong drunk who gave it a good yank. The door creaked out, scraping on the threshold where water had swollen the small wood landing. It let the boy inside, even though he wasn't particularly welcome there.

Dave's was dark but the sky was overcast, and inside, the lights were low and small—except for the big, bright bar up against the easternmost wall.

The bar wasn't fancy. Its enormous mirror was chipped and cracked, and the shelves were propped up with books, bottles, and at least one cracked cinder block. Not old enough to call vintage, and not new enough to look nice, this bar fit in beautifully with the rest of the furnishings—which ran the gamut from "Sears catalog 1982" to "curbside find."

Cam grinned when Dave flashed him a fast wave from behind the counter, even though it was almost an outright dismissal. He watched while the bartender swabbed the grody deck with a rag that almost certainly had been a cloth diaper, once upon a time, and he kept on smiling because it wouldn't be polite to cringe. Claire and Daisy said diapers were good for dusting and polishing once you washed them hot enough, but Cam couldn't get past the idea that food and drinks were served up on a changing pad.

He hit up a back table, a small one that would've sat two people if one of them was a toddler. It was *his* table, if you asked Cameron. It was the kiddie table, if you asked anybody else.

He surveyed the room.

Six people occupied the bar apart from Dave and Cam, and Cam only recognized three of them. One was a woman who worked at the courthouse, and sat at the bar when she wasn't filing papers or issuing license plates. If she wore fewer clothes, you'd probably call her a barfly. One was a guy who worked at Paulie's, and might be old enough to drink, maybe—if Dave didn't squint too hard at his license, and that didn't seem very fair. (Cam didn't have a license to squint at, real or fake. Maybe that was why he couldn't get a beer.) And one guy was wearing a shirt from the auto body place—its real name C&H Garage, though much like Thirsty's, no one ever called it by its proper name. Cam knew the guy on sight, but couldn't think of his name and couldn't see the badge over the uniform pocket that would've revealed this bit of information, not that it mattered any. He knew better than to talk to the auto body guys, except for Jason and Quincy, and even them . . . only out of politeness, and only when necessary.

The other three folks could've been anybody, so they must've been out-of-towners. A white man and woman in their forties, who looked like a married couple. A stray dude with a face full of hair like Wolverine and a death grip on a pint glass. Cam guessed him for one of the sawmill guys, out of work but too hopeless to go hunting a job elsewhere. He had that stink about him.

Cam was about to open his mouth to ask where Jess was, but he was spared the effort when the kitchen door smacked open and the object of his affection emerged—bearing a tray loaded with onion rings, dipping sauce, and a short stack of extra napkins.

"Hey Jess," he said brightly, waving a little too cheerfully for anyone's comfort, much less his own.

She looked his way and smiled. Professionally? Genuinely? "Hang on, sweetheart. I'll be with you in a second." She deposited the onion rings in front of the ex–sawmill worker, if that's what he was. Then she asked across the tables between them, "Or do you just want your usual, water with a wedge of lemon?"

"You know me so well." He couldn't stop grinning. He wished he could stop grinning.

She said, "I know you're broke but kind," and she tacked another smile onto the end.

He'd take it. "And a terrible tipper!"

"As long as you don't cause any trouble, it's all right." She set the tray on the bar, bumped Dave out of the way with a hip-check that sent a Roman candle of envy up Cam's spine, and grabbed a glass. She jammed it into the ice bin under the counter. "What's the trial today, kiddo?"

Kiddo. She couldn't be more than a few years older than him, like *that* would matter in another decade. "Gardening. Miss Daisy was stabbing things with a spade, and Miss Claire's knitting needles were giving me a headache."

"Truly, yours is the patience of a saint." She filled the glass from a tap, stabbed a lemon with a toothpick, and dropped it in.

"Oh, it could be worse."

"It could always be worse," she agreed. "What about last week, when they had you hauling groceries on your bike?"

He nodded solemnly. "A terrible affair."

She ducked past Dave again, who muttered something Cam couldn't hear. She elbowed him gently. "Or before that, when they spent the afternoon teaching you how to make decent iced tea that wouldn't embarrass a guest."

"Hours of my life, and I'll never get them back."

Jess Thurman stood before him, one hand on her hip, the other holding his water with a skewered wedge of citrus. Brown hair down to her chin, a wisp of loose bangs dusting her eyebrow and cheekbone. Tight, dark jeans with the hems rolled up, revealing a tattoo with a heart and a banner, and a name Cam could never make out. Tank top that said, DAYTONA BEACH: 1998 but might've come from Urban Outfitters, for all he knew.

There was one in Valdosta. He'd seen it advertised on the TV in Dave's.

There were places other than Staywater. There *had* to be.

She put down the water, then slapped a coaster beside it and relocated the beverage accordingly. "Don't take this the wrong way, but you really ought to stay in more. Or get out more— *way* out, and not just 'out' as far as 177."

"What do you mean, stay in?" He pulled the water forward and barely lifted it off the table, to give it a dainty sip. His eyes hinted hard.

She took the hint, and handed him a straw. "You need a TV, or some internet. Or you need a road trip, I don't know. But it's a shame, is all I'm saying—you spending so much time alone, or with the ladies."

"I don't have a computer and my cell phone is smart, but not smart enough to grab much reception all the way out here. The only TV at Hazelhurst is in Daisy and Claire's room, where it mostly shows *I Love Lucy* and *Perry Mason*. You'll have to forgive me . . ." he said as he tapped the straw out of its wrapper, and jabbed it through the ice with a splash. ". . . if I don't spend a whole lot of time indoors at Hazelhurst. Smells like menthol and mothballs. The whole house does."

"Those old ladies love you."

"And I love *them*," he said earnestly. "Can't imagine my life without them, but some days, I can't imagine another afternoon with them, either."

"It's a shame there aren't more boys your . . ." She hesitated, and said, "age."

Cam wondered what other word she'd been thinking of using. He didn't ask. "Well, the town's dying. You know it, I know it. That dude over there knows it." He pulled out the straw and used it to point at the pizza guy. "But until it goes all the way belly-up, your TV is the only TV I can watch."

Dave laughed.

Cam frowned. "What?"

Dave shook his head, and stuffed the diaper rag under the counter, onto a shelf. "Like you come around here for the TV."

"What do you care? I'm a paying customer."

"I *don't* care," Dave assured him, and he sounded like he meant it. "Believe me. I do *not* give a single little round shit." The phone rang back in the kitchen. Jess glanced that way, but Dave was already leaving the bar.

Down to Cam, Jess said, "Never mind him. He's having a *day*."

"Isn't he always?"

"Oh, stop it. You know good and well he's not an asshole. He could've kicked you out of here long ago, and maybe he should have—for your own good."

"Aw, don't talk like that." He hoped he sounded charming, and self-deprecating. "Dave's cool, and I appreciate him. When I have some money, if I'm still in town, I'll come here and spend it all."

She rolled her eyes. "Jesus, don't say that." She leaned down to the table and put her hands on it, right across the place where two jerks named Vanessa and Cooj had carved their initials, along with the unlikely vow of "4evR."

It gave Cam a direct line of sight down her shirt, but he was strong. He held eye contact. "But . . ."

"No 'but.' Listen to me, sunshine: If you ever see a dime—whether you earn it, or steal it, or inherit it from the Spratford ladies, I don't care—but if you find yourself with enough money for a car or a train ticket, I want you to take it. Take it and *go*."

"Just a minute ago, you were saying I ought to stay inside . . ." he protested weakly.

"You know what I meant, but forget I said it if you're only gonna twist it. Go out and see the world, Cam," she said with finality. She stood up again, and straightened her apron and turned to go.

"*You* left to see the world," Cam said quickly. "But you came back."

Jess stopped and narrowed her eyes. "Who told you that?"

He shrugged. It'd been Dave, but Dave had been drinking, and he probably didn't remember having blabbed about it. Cam hoped Dave appreciated what a stand-up guy he was, not ratting him out or anything. "I heard it somewhere. I heard—"

Dave whacked the kitchen door open again. It knocked hard against the wall, loud as a gunshot.

Everything went quiet, even the televisions. There were two, neither one of them any newer or better than the one in Daisy's room. They were showing a basketball game—and that was cooler than *Perry Mason* any day of the week. At least the commercials were better.

But the TVs went quiet and their pictures went blurry, then stripy.

Dave looked at the nearest screen. Jess looked at Dave, and looked at the front door—but no one came inside.

Cam looked at everyone else, all of them as silent as the game being broadcast at each end of the bar. The televisions struggled, and the players darted back and forth. There was a hum, and the air changed . . . something like the way it gets dark and heavy right before lightning strikes, but not quite like that. Maybe not like that at all, except Cam's ears popped, and his eyes watered, and the bar filled with a smell like electricity running on old wires through old walls. Fabric burning. Air sizzling. Something else, too. Something tangier than copper on the tongue.

He swallowed hard and his ears popped again. He reached for his drink, but his hands weren't working like they ought to, so he let them lie splayed on the table, the straw sticking out from between two of his fingers like a cigarette.

Someone inhaled sharply—Jess? The woman at the bar with her husband? One of the two. Someone moaned, and he thought it was the sawmill man with an empty pint glass broken on the floor beside his seat.

When did that happen? Cam wondered. When did anything happen?

Behind the bar, the mirror cracked—bottom to top, the opposite of lightning and nowhere near as loud as the kitchen door, but it cracked. A neon sign advertising Blue Moon Ale sparked and exploded with a poof of smoke and a fizzy whine, and so did the big lamp over the single pool table, back in the farthest corner.

The room was dark, until it wasn't again. The bar was quiet, until the TVs found their footing and the basketball players and their shoes dashed and squeaked; the audience roared, and the ball hit the court floor with a sound like bongos, and whatever had happened . . . had happened.

Cam looked to the nearest TV, or the one best angled for him to see it. The ball went *bang, bang, bang,* with a note of bass to it. It bounced from the player's hand to the wood and the painted lines on the floor, slamming down between nimble feet on squeaky shoes.

Bang. Bang. Bang.

Claire's needles went *click, click, click.*

Daisy let out a low whistle. "Well, shit. Here it comes again."

Her cousin sighed, but without the musical note. "It was bound to. Only 'mostly safe,' remember?"

"The timing's just about right."

"It always is. Thirteen years—not clockwork exactly, but calendar-work." Claire's project grew row by row, by row, by row . . . spun by her knobby fingers that weren't arthritic at all, even if everything else was. "If anything, it's overdue."

"We should do something."

She snorted. "You can't hardly walk, and I can't hardly see. Last time we met it . . . that was *our* last time. We knew it then, but I'm saying it now: We're too old, anymore. We did our part. It's no fault of ours, if it wasn't enough."

"You think we could leave the rest to Cameron?"

"I think there won't be time," Daisy said sadly. "I think it's too late already. I think it's here, and it'll take what it wants—from Staywater, or from elsewhere. This next one . . ." She watched her godson as he sat transfixed, his hands splayed on that tiny, ugly table. His eyes on the television screen.

Claire finished for her. "Just like the last few, this next one's on us."

4

WIDE SPOT IN THE ROAD

Titus lay on his back. The sky was very white above him, except that it wasn't—it was black and green and brown, and gray where the fluffy, fat locks of moss dangled into view. His eyes adjusted. The colors came back. The sun was still up, though a faint tint of orange was just now wafting up from the west horizon.

A chime pinged, over and over and over and over.

A song. He could almost hear the words, even if he couldn't quite figure out the voice. All he knew, was that it wasn't Melanie's.

The things I take . . .

A second and a half between sharp digital notes. Too annoying to block out and ignore. Too irritating to sleep through, no matter how badly Titus wanted to close his eyes again and sleep some more. He'd only been asleep. Only for a minute.

. . . are mine to keep . . .

No. He'd been driving.

He sat up straight, fast enough that his head swam and his vision fluttered.

ping . . . ping . . . ping . . . ping . . .

The SUV was fifty feet behind him, both driver and passenger doors hanging open. The pinging noise was prompted by the vehicle's alert system, loudly complaining that everything was ajar.

"Shut *up*," he commanded. His mouth was dry. His throat was dry. His *teeth* were dry. "Melanie, shut the doors!"

The relentless chime didn't pause. It overpowered everything else, an ice pick jabbed repeatedly into his head, blocking out all the bugs, all the wind, all the drizzling, running drips of water in the surrounding swamp. Titus put his hands over his ears. It didn't help. He gave up, put them down on the ground, and pushed himself up.

He staggered to a standing position, wobbled, and steadied himself. His legs shook weakly, his feet parked on a yellow dot in a yellow line, in the middle of a two-lane road—one lane going east, one headed west. There were no other cars in sight, not in either direction.

"Melanie?"

He didn't hear the music anymore. If there'd ever been a voice, it was gone.

He turned a full circle. The SUV, the swamp, the road, the swamp, the SUV. No, that couldn't be right. There'd been a bridge. The memory of it was sharp, sharper than the ice pick of the door chime—which was very close to driving him crazy.

He stumbled toward the SUV and kicked the driver door shut; he smacked his hands on the hood and used it to support himself as he walked around the vehicle toward the passenger door. The hood was warm. The engine was off. When he reached Melanie's side, he saw that the keys were still in the ignition.

He reached over the seat, past the gear shift. He twisted the keys and yanked them out, silencing the hideous warning. They jingled in his hand, replacing one irritating noise with another until he crunched them in his fist and muffled them.

He withdrew from the cab.

His legs felt like jelly, and he didn't know why. He leaned on the open passenger door and stared at the spot where his wife ought to be. He said her name again, more quietly this time.

She wasn't there. She wasn't going to answer him anyway.

At least there wasn't any blood—that's what he told himself, but he would've never said it out loud. That was the kind of thing a murderer thought, or someone who watched entirely too many cop shows. But there it was in all its glory, the relief of that ugly thought: *At least there wasn't any blood.*

What he really meant was, *At least she isn't hurt.* Not that she couldn't be hurt without bleeding, but it felt like a good sign. It dialed his panic down from eleven to maybe a nine. Still plenty of panic to go around, but at least he had some semi-concrete sign that she wasn't hurt or dead.

Why would there be any blood? No reason at all. His wife had wandered off. She hadn't been jumped by an axe murderer or seized by a hitchhiker with a claw for a hand. No. This was a case of his wife leaving him lying in the middle of the road, un-conscious, and probably moseying off down that same damn road in search of help.

Except . . . she would call somebody first, wouldn't she?

Shakily, he reached back inside the SUV and pulled his phone out of the cupholder. The screen was hard to read in the tilted angle of late sunlight, but he saw two bars in the corner. Sure, the signal was feeble, but it offered plenty of juice to make a phone

call. Even if Melanie didn't have any bars on her own phone, his cell was left out in plain view and she knew his passcode—he'd changed it to their anniversary, right in front of her.

Titus didn't see her phone, so she must've taken it with her. Wherever she was.

Maybe that was it—the simplest answer was the right one: She might've gone down the road to see if she could get a stronger signal. She was on foot, and God knew she was on no great terms with the great outdoors. She wouldn't go any farther in the humid, mosquito-infested open air than she absolutely had to.

He shut the door and stood on the slender gravel shoulder. He went around the back of the car, hugging it close, to keep from falling into the squishy puddles of swamp grass and mud. Now that the door wasn't making so much noise, he could actually listen.

He looked back to the west. He stared hard at the place behind him, where there wasn't any bridge. Then he looked forward again, to the car, to the road, to the yellow dotted line that glistened faintly with thick reflective paint.

"Hello?" he called out, in case there was anyone other than Melanie out there. A bird answered. A splash from a frog or a snake or a turtle answered. "Hello? Can anybody hear me?" He unlocked his phone and pulled up the GPS. "Where the hell am I, anyway?"

The syrup-slow signal gave up the answer: He was maybe half a mile from the edge of the park, if the blinking blue dot could be believed.

"If I were Melanie, looking for help . . . which way would I go?" he mumbled to himself, still staring down at the phone. It showed him no sign of civilization any closer than Forto, really—or the other side of the swamp park, perhaps. There was no obvious spot to go seeking help. They'd stopped in the geographic center of nowhere.

"The fuck is going on here?"

A distant bird said something very loud, but it didn't help.

He tried again, with more volume: "Hello? Mellie? Anybody? Hello?"

He tapped the phone's button to darken the screen; it only had about half a charge, and for some reason he felt the sudden urge to conserve it. Usually he'd let a battery bleed out all the way, then plug it in and forget it, but not now. Something was wrong, and the phone was his lifeline, crappy two-bar service and all.

He tucked it into his back pocket. Still no cars. Still no sound of a human being, and no matter how hard he looked, there was no sign of the bridge, either.

The bridge was the last thing he remembered—a too-long stretch of tires trundling over old boards, rattling so hard that the whole thing felt like it was shaking, and maybe it was. One lane on a trestle, still wearing the scars of old railroad tracks, a bridge to nowhere—or to here, if this was any better. It'd taken forever to cross the span, from one side of the state road, across that too-tight pinch that would only hold one car at a time. It'd taken so long that he'd fallen asleep.

Asleep at the wheel? He'd done plenty of stupid shit in a car, over the years, but falling asleep was a new one. It hadn't felt like sleep. It hadn't been warm and drowsy and welcoming, it'd been a sick, drugged-up heaviness. It'd been unwanted and inescapable.

Now the bridge was gone, and Melanie was gone, and the SUV was still there—thank God or whoever—but Titus was all alone and he wasn't sure where he was, GPS be damned.

"Melanie!" He screamed her name as loud as he could, again and again, until the last syllable scratched his throat like a nail.

A bug flitted behind his ear. He smacked it until it stopped and his ear was red. He walked to the center of the road, thinking it was worth it to get a full perspective on the scene—the vehicle, the road in both directions, the place where a bridge ought to be. He turned in circles, eyeing the nearest swampy flora and the lanky, knobby trees beyond the soggy edges where asphalt met sand, and sand met mud, and mud met the thick black eddies of the Okefenokee.

He stood on the spot where he'd awakened, but looking down, he saw nothing. Not a bloody head print, not a weird outline, or any wreckage of his clothes. He was entirely unharmed, and he knew it—even without feeling himself up and down to check for scrapes and bruises. Even his hands and his knuckles were unscathed, showing he didn't put up a fight.

Against anyone. Or anything.

He could always call the police, couldn't he? But if he did, would they yell at him? Did this situation *technically* qualify as an emergency—or would he look like one of those assholes who calls 911 when he can't escape a corn maze?

Furthermore, what if they arrested him? They could do that, if they thought he was wasting their time.

But Melanie was missing.

Just thinking the word, "missing" . . . it frightened him. It wasn't true, anyway—she was only gone, and she'd only been gone a few minutes, if his phone could be believed. Last time he'd looked, before they'd been ensnared on the bridge ("ensnared" was another anxiety-prompting word, but that's what sprang to mind), it'd been 6:09 P.M., he remembered that much. Now it was 6:30, so it'd been about twenty minutes since he'd lost touch with . . . with the bridge. Or reality.

He wiped his forehead with the back of his hand, and smacked another winged nuisance, this one at his neck.

The keys to the SUV were in his front pocket. He pulled them out and let them jingle, dangling between his fingers. Before he called the cops—*if* he called the cops—he should take some time and go looking for Melanie himself. Just watch, the moment he got on the phone with dispatch, she'd come strolling down the road like nothing was wrong. Just watch.

A weird, sour feeling in his stomach spread out through his chest.

Just watch.

He held the phone in one hand. Keys in the other. He'd dared the universe before.

No. No magical thinking, no fantasizing yet about reaching the police and immediately hearing his wife holler his name. No fantasizing about the relief, coupled with anger at her and embarrassment for himself—feeling like an idiot for overreacting.

First, he could drive around a little. The sun was still up. He had a good hour before it really started getting dark.

He went back to the vehicle and let himself inside. He climbed behind the wheel, inserted the key, and breathed slowly, heavily, trying to calm himself . . . lying with each breath, mentally assuring himself that this was silly, and it was something he'd be laughing about come dark. In another hour, he and Melanie would be in a cabin a few miles to the east, cracking into that bottle of prosecco they'd brought in a cooler full of blue chill packs and ice.

He'd try not to be angry. He'd go ahead and laugh, just as long as she showed up in one piece. If she offered up a perfectly reasonable story to go along with her disappearance, then so much the better. Maybe he really *wouldn't* be mad. Maybe he'd feel nothing but relief, the moment he spied her walking down

the gravel shoulder, holding up her phone, hunting for bars and not paying a lick of attention to anything else.

Probably, she'd jump with surprise when he honked the horn.

Probably, she'd grin and start swearing.

"But she left me there," he said to himself, as he cranked the engine. "In the middle of the goddamn road." She might've tried to wake him up. She might've failed, and gotten scared, and gone looking for help without thinking first. "But she could've used my phone. My phone had bars. She knew where it was. She knows the passcode."

New mantras for a new situation.

He put the SUV in gear and on second thought, rolled down all the windows before he pulled back into the lane. With his head hanging out, he drove slowly, looking from left to right and back again—scanning the scenery in every direction.

Looking for his wife. (Looking for that bridge.)

From time to time, he'd shoot one eye at the odometer; and when he'd gone two full miles east, he stopped and attempted a two-point turn. The roadway was so narrow and the shoulder was so thin, the turn had more like five or six points by the time he was finished with it—but he got the SUV turned around with a minimum of spinning tires, and called it a success.

He still hadn't seen another car. He tried to laugh about it, but he couldn't even scare up a smile. "Everybody's been raptured but me." Nope. Still not funny.

The two-mile mark was kind of arbitrary, but he figured Melanie couldn't have possibly gone any farther than that. Now it was time to try two miles in the other direction. If he didn't find her, maybe he'd find the bridge. He didn't particularly want to see the bridge again, but he needed to. He didn't know what he'd do if he found it; it wasn't like he could confront the damn thing.

He couldn't ask it any questions, or demand to know what it'd done with his wife. But it was in his head all the same.

Just one more stupid thing to think, in a whole afternoon of stupid thoughts.

"Goddammit, Melanie."

More miles passed, and he turned the car around again—then pulled it off the road roughly where he'd begun. He was pretty sure, but not 100 percent confident. It was hard to tell. The whole swamp looked more or less the same. There were hardly any signs and there was virtually no change in the scenery.

But that was okay.

He was back where he began, and this was where he'd lost Melanie—or where Melanie had gone off and gotten herself lost. He'd been in Boy Scouts for a couple of years, back in the day. One of the only lessons he remembered was the admonition to stay put, when you're lost. You'll only end up running in circles, that's what the scout master had told him. Stay where you are and wait for help.

There was no getting around it. Waiting for help meant admitting his own helplessness, and dialing 911.

It wasn't very hot, but his hands were slick with sweat. So was the steering wheel. So was the phone. It was slippery in his hands.

A dispatch woman answered. "Nine-one-one, where's your emergency?"

"I don't know. I'm lost," he began. It sounded terrible, so he tried again. "My name is Titus Bell, and I'm somewhere on State Road 177, and something's happened . . . my wife is gone. I crossed this bridge, and I think I passed out, or something."

"Sir? Are you in need of medical attention?"

"I don't think so. But my wife is gone."

"What happened to her?"

"I woke up lying in the road, and she was . . . she was *gone*. Please, can you send somebody? I'm not sure where I am, but can you . . . can you trace my cell or something?"

"Not exactly, sir. But State Road 177 is a start. Where were you coming from?"

"Valdosta. My wife and I . . ." He swallowed. His hands might've been wet, but his mouth was impossibly dry. "We were headed to the Okefenokee, for our honeymoon. We're staying at the cabins. Now I can't find her."

The woman on the line paused. "Sir, did she assault you?"

"What? Jesus H. Christ, no. I didn't assault her, either!"

"Please stay calm, sir."

"I'm staying calm. Perfectly calm. Completely calm."

"I believe you."

"No you don't," he argued, and he heard the high note creeping into his voice, but he couldn't do anything about it. "And you shouldn't, because this is crazy, and I feel like an asshole for calling you, except that I've driven all over looking for her, and it's like she vanished into thin air. Please, I need . . . a search party, I guess. A stray cop or two, at the very least."

"I'll see what I can do about finding a stray cop, sir. Please remain where you are, and I'll have someone out there as soon as possible. State Road 177, you said—can you give me any other point of reference?"

"Point of reference?" He shook his head, like she could hear it rattle. "Lady, I'm in the swamp. It all looks like swamp."

"That's not very helpful, sir."

"Well, okay, wait. I'm not actually in the swamp proper, not yet. I didn't see a sign or anything. Actually, I'm just outside it, that's what the GPS said. I'm sorry, I'm not thinking. I'm sorry, this is . . . this is too crazy, I'm sorry."

"So your phone's GPS says you're just outside the park?"

"Maybe half a mile. I should've said that first. I'm sorry."

"It's all right, sir. I'm sending . . . one moment please." As promised, a few seconds later she added, "I'm sending someone from the Staywater PD—that's the closest precinct. He's leaving now, and he'll probably catch up to you in fifteen or twenty minutes."

"Fifteen or twenty minutes? What if I was drowning or something? What if I was bleeding out?"

"Then you'd be drowning or bleeding out in the middle of nowhere, and there are only so many police to go around. Sir. We aren't even certain where you are, just yet. We'll do the best we can."

"Sorry. Yes. Thank you. I'll . . . I'll keep my eyes open."

"You do that."

Titus hung up on her. He didn't know if he was supposed to stay on the line or not, but he didn't feel like listening to her anymore, and anyway, he wasn't drowning or bleeding. If Melanie was drowning or bleeding, nobody was going to do a thing about it—that much was clear. Not the dispatch lady, and not the cops. Not him, either. He didn't know where he was, and he didn't know where she was. He was entirely useless.

The dispatch woman didn't call him back.

Titus stayed there in the cab of the SUV with the door open, and his legs hanging out, feet tapping on the step. He drummed his damp fingers on the steering wheel, on his knees, on each other, and he stared nervously up and down the road, back and forth, looking and listening for Melanie—who was bound to turn up any damn second.

She didn't turn up, but a cop finally did.

He looked like an oversized middle-schooler but the name

tag over his breast pocket said PICKETT, and he identified himself as an officer. Despite the baby face, Titus could've figured
out that part by his uniform, his posture, or his patrol car with
its STAYWATER POLICE DEPARTMENT decal emblazoned on
the side.

He kept the shitty attitude to himself, just this once. He'd
already been a dick to the dispatch lady, and it wouldn't do him
any good to spread the love around any further. He hadn't meant
to do it in the first place. He was scared, and confused, and it
shouldn't have mattered. He shouldn't have been an asshole.

"Officer Pickett," he repeated the guy's name, and started to
shake his hand. But his was still sweaty, so he wiped it on his
jeans first. "I'm Titus Bell, and I hope you can help me. My wife
has vanished, right out of the car, and I've been driving around
looking for her for . . . for probably half an hour, now."

Pickett accepted the freshly wiped handshake and took out a
notebook. "All right now, Mr. Bell. How did your wife leave the
vehicle in the first place?"

Titus would've given his eyeteeth for someone with a little
more authority than this kid, but this kid was all he had, so he
told him the truth. "I don't know. We were driving toward the
park." He cocked his thumb in the general direction of the Okefenokee. "We crossed that bridge—that weird little stone bridge,
with just one lane. It looked like an old rail trestle. And something . . . something happened. I think I passed out. I think I fell
asleep at the wheel."

"Sir, have you been drinking?"

"No!"

Pickett held up his hands, notepad dangling from one, pen
from the other. "I have to ask, you understand."

"Yeah, but I'm not drunk, and I'm not on any prescription

meds, or anything like that. Or whatever you were going to ask me, for a follow-up. Look, I wish I knew what happened. You have no idea how *bad* I wish I knew. But all I can tell you is, I woke up in the middle of the road—"

"I'm sorry, come again?"

"The middle of the road," he repeated with emphasis. "I was lying there, about . . . right over there, I guess. And the car door was open, and my wife was gone. Her phone's gone, too. Maybe you can track it . . . ?"

"Maybe." The young officer nodded. The kid was lanky and angular, with glasses that kept sliding down the slope of his nose. "We'll have to get you back to the station for that, but it's worth a shot, sure thing. First, I think, we should run you by the hospital in Forto and let them run a few tests."

"A few tests?"

"You fainted, you lost some time, and you lost your wife."

"I didn't say I fainted."

"So you passed out?" Pickett suggested. "Or you got any better ideas?"

"I guess I *don't*," Titus said, deflated.

"Junior" (as Titus had ungraciously come to think of the officer) radioed back to Staywater and summoned another officer, a guy named Matthew Kemp who was no great prize either, but he was at least reassuringly old. Kemp was short and thick, with the shape and demeanor of an aged pugilist, but he talked like he knew what he was doing, and he gave orders like he was used to having them followed. And he didn't want Titus to get back in the SUV. "I'll get a tow, and have it brought back to town," he said firmly.

"You're impounding my car?"

"Call it what you like." He shrugged, those beefy shoulders

shifting with apathy. "But if we do open a missing person ticket on your wife, we'll look like dipshits if we didn't collect evidence."

"Evidence? You . . . you think this is a crime scene? You think somebody took her?"

He shrugged again, and Titus wasn't so sure it was apathy. It might've been a good poker face. "Couldn't say. But if it turns out she *didn't* just wander off and get lost, we have to cover our bases. You know how it goes."

"I . . . um . . . if you say so."

"Come on, now. I'll get hold of the sheriff's office and have them start a search. It's getting dark, Mr. Bell. We'll run you off to Forto for a checkup, and then I'd like to ask you a few more questions."

"You want to interrogate me."

"Son, listen to what I'm saying—not what you *think* I'm saying: Nobody said nothing about an interrogation. You called us for help, remember? So let us help. We can't do too much looking around ourselves, not at this hour, so we'll let the county boys pick up the search while we let the doctors take a look at you."

"But I should stay here. In case she turns up. She might hear me, and she'll know my voice . . ."

"She's not a cocker spaniel, Mr. Bell. If she's lost, anybody's voice will bring her around. Have you gotten any supper yet? We could get some food into you, on the way to the hospital. Can't hurt. Might help."

"How do you figure that?"

Kemp was calm, level, and firm. "You think that *maybe*, you passed out. If that's the case, then it could've been low blood sugar, or plain old hunger. When's the last time you ate?"

"I don't know. It's been a while. Lunch," he corrected himself quickly. "A little after noon."

"A good six hours, then. Food will clear your mind. Might even replace some of your 'I don't know's with a 'Hang on, now I remember.' Pickett." He waved the kid over. "You got the sheriff on the horn?"

"He's on his way out with Betty and Boomer." Then to Titus, he said, "Boomer's the best tracking dog you'll find for a dozen counties, and Betty's his wrangler. If anyone can find your wife, it's the pair of them."

"What about helicopters? Searchlights?"

The cops exchanged a look that said plenty, none of it to Titus. Cool as could be, Kemp put a big, heavy hand on Titus's shoulder. "This ain't a crime scene, right? Far as we know, your wife took off on her own, and she'll turn back up that way."

"That's what I've been telling myself."

"And you may be right. But for now, it's too soon to call her missing or endangered. We don't have a helicopter any closer than Valdosta, and the big city ain't likely to let us borrow it on a 'just in case she's out there' basis."

Titus wanted to cry. "But she's in the swamp! There are alligators, and . . . and alligators."

"And snakes," Pickett offered helpfully.

The other officer glared him down. "Come on, now. Don't rile him up. Yes, Mr. Bell, there are snakes. Yes, there are alligators. But neither one of them things opened your car's door and yanked your wife out. She left on her own, and this is a free country, Mr. Bell. We can't call in the National Guard because a lady went for a walk unaccompanied."

"This is bullshit," Titus whispered, as he let Kemp lead him back to Pickett's patrol car. "This is bullshit. She's out there, and she might be in trouble."

"She's out there, or so you've told us. It's true that she might be in trouble, but then again, she might be fine." Kemp ushered him into the backseat of his own vehicle and closed the door. The patrol car's window was half rolled down. Through it, he asked, "You got a sweater or something, anything that might belong to her?"

"There's a gray hoodie in the backseat. That's hers."

"That'll do. I'll save it for Boomer. It'll give him something to track."

Kemp relayed this information to Junior, then talked quietly with him—just out of earshot. Titus heard murmurs and the intermittent buzz of their radios chattering back and forth with someone back in Staywater.

"Staywater," Titus whispered. He hadn't seen it on the map. He hadn't seen it on the phone's GPS, either—but then again, he hadn't been looking for it. He'd been looking for himself, and the state park, and his wife. Must be a real wide-spot-in-the-road, as his dad would've put it.

Kemp came back over to the car. "Come on, now."

"I'm not ready to leave without my wife."

"Too bad, son—because we're leaving anyway. Forto General's expecting you."

5

The hospital in Forto was small but clean, and not terribly busy. On the way through the ER lobby Titus passed two kids with sniffles, one guy who was holding a bloody towel wrapped around his arm, and several old people who were watching the TV in the corner. The old folks weren't in any obvious distress. Maybe they were waiting on somebody. Maybe they didn't have a TV at home.

Titus was ushered back to an examination room by a nurse named Anne, who took his temperature and blood pressure, and disappeared with a clipboard. Ten minutes later, she came back with a doctor—a woman with a blond pixie cut and a butterfly tattoo on the underside of her wrist—along with Officer Matthew Kemp.

Kemp carried two to-go cups of coffee. He offered one to Titus.

Titus took it, even though he didn't want it. It was warm and distracting and it smelled good. It gave him something to do with his hands.

Anne left again, and the doctor performed a perfunctory examination, shining lights in his eyes and asking questions about Titus's diet, his general health, and his drug and alcohol use. When she was satisfied that there was, as she put it to Kemp, "Not a damn thing wrong with him, as far as I can tell," she excused herself—leaving Kemp to ask the rest of the questions.

He pulled out a voice recorder, and set it on the examination table. The recorder's green light blinked cheerily. Obnoxiously. Titus tried to keep from looking at it, but his eyes kept wandering back.

Mostly Kemp asked the same questions he'd asked before, out in the middle of the road near the Okefenokee, past a bridge, and before the state park.

Since the questions were the same, Titus repeated himself.

And repeated himself.

Again and again, he offered essentially identical answers to queries that were only marginally rephrased. No, he didn't know what happened. Yes, when he came to, he was lying in the road. No, he wasn't hurt, even the doctor had told him that. No, his wife wouldn't have slipped him a mickey, even if she'd had the opportunity. Yes, they were happy. No, there weren't any problems. Conjugal bliss, and all that happy shit.

(He almost convinced himself it was true. He must've convinced Kemp. Unless he didn't, and he couldn't tell.)

No, there was no good reason for Melanie to take off like this. They were on their honeymoon. Everything was peachy. Just peachy. I told you already, it was fucking peachy.

"Peachy," repeated Kemp. He fiddled with the voice recorder. The happy green light shut off, and a faint red one replaced it, then faded away.

"Are we done?" Titus asked. He clutched the coffee cup between his knees. It was full. The beverage had cooled to match his body temperature. "Can I go home . . . or, not home. Somewhere else? Somewhere I can wait for news, or . . . wait for my wife?"

"We're finished here for now. Are you saying you want to just pack it in and head back to Valdosta?"

Yes, in truth he would've given almost anything to head back home and fling himself into his own bed. He was exhausted and confused, but he couldn't imagine going anywhere without Melanie. "Of course I want to go home, but I *have* to stay here. I have to find my wife. Can you take me back to 177? I could help with . . . what were their names? The woman and the dog."

"Betty and Boomer don't need the help, and you can join the party tomorrow—assuming your wife doesn't turn up between now and then. We'll find you a place to crash around here, and we'll all keep looking until we find her. Does that sound good to you?"

No. Nothing sounded good. He sighed deeply, heavily. He turned his lungs inside out. "Sounds good enough. Could you take me to a hotel?"

"We could, but what about the Okefenokee cabins? Isn't that where you were headed?"

He shook his head and squeezed at the coffee cup, almost hard enough to pop the lid off. "I don't want to go there. Not without her."

"She might go to the cabins, looking for you."

The thought made him laugh, but it was an ugly, unhappy

laugh. "She wouldn't do that. She'd park herself at a hotel and start calling around to find me."

"Then why were you headed for the cabins?" Kemp pressed.

Titus was tired enough that he ran out of patience. "*Fuck the cabins,* all right? This was all a bad idea. It was *my* bad idea."

Kemp eyed Titus with interest. "She's not a big camper?"

"I thought she might enjoy it, if there was plumbing. But I'm an idiot, so . . ."

"So. I'll send word out to the campground, in case she wanders out that way after all. Meanwhile, I'll go ahead and take you back to town. Maude can put you up, for a few days at least. She's got this bed-and-breakfast. You'll like it. It's . . . well, it's not a shithole, and she'll feed you twice a day. You can probably still catch supper."

"Nah."

"You're still not hungry?"

He'd passed on the Burger King offer, on the way to town. "Still not hungry," Titus assured him. "The idea of food makes me want to barf. But I could go for a drink."

"Maude's is around the corner from a bar. The bar *is* a shithole, fair warning, but there's beer and whiskey and whatever else you like. Whatever makes you happy," he added, still watching Titus a little too closely for Titus's comfort. "Or whatever keeps you occupied, while the uniforms are checking the waterways tonight."

Titus sagged out of his chair, leaving the untasted coffee beside the blood pressure cuff. "That's the best offer I'm going to get, isn't it?"

"Oh, you never know. Your wife might turn up and offer to get that honeymoon back under way. But other than that, yeah. This is as good as it's gonna get."

On the trip to Staywater, Titus sat in the front seat.

He rode the first few miles in silence, wondering how far it was to this fabled burg, which wasn't on a map and was allegedly smaller than Forto—a town which amounted to a single exit off a two-lane state road. But apparently Staywater had a bed-and-breakfast, so it had to look something like civilization. Right?

"It's about fifteen miles from here," Officer Kemp said, when Titus finally broke his silence and asked. "Sounds like a long way, but it's still in the swamp. Right at the edge of it, anyhow. It used to be a logging center, back when companies harvested cypress around here. That was a long time ago, though. Before everything belonged to the park."

"If they don't do much logging anymore, what's in Staywater now?"

"Now? Not much. Technically it's the county seat, but it's basically a post office, a bar, and a gas station—plus or minus some old houses and Maude's place. We do get a few campers, hikers, that kind of thing. People show up with canoes and cameras from time to time, and then there's the bird-watchers and the ecology students, counting critters in the water. That's how Maude pays her bills, mostly. Critter-counters."

"Sounds like a nice place," Titus exaggerated, trying to be polite. Since snapping about the cabins, he was feeling penitent. And guilty. And worried. He needed to get a grip. He needed to find his wife. Being a dick wasn't going to help either of those goals, but every time he was scared he went into dick mode. He needed to rein it in.

"Staywater ain't a shadow of what it used to be, but it's got what you might call 'charm.'"

"What else might you call it?"

Kemp thought about it. "Let's stick with 'charm.' Those of us who still live there . . . we stick together and look out for one another. It's an odd little place, but it isn't bad. I think you'll like it. You'll like Maude's, at least. It's a roof over your head, and it's got plumbing. Wait, you're the one who liked camping, right?"

"Not that much. But about the bar . . ."

"Yeah."

"I like drinking better than I like camping. Forever, from here on out. Swear to God, when all of this is done, I'll never go camping again. I'll swear it off forever, if Melanie is okay and we can just . . . go be married. I want to get back to our real life. I want to know what happened, but if she shows up and doesn't remember anything any better than I do, I'll accept that. I'll accept it, and throw her into the car, and drive as fast as we can—back to the city. Nothing personal."

Kemp accepted this and said, "I hear you. You've had a shit day, and there's no hard feelings. Places like Staywater aren't for everyone. Hell, they probably *shouldn't* be. Hang on, and I'll show you the bar when we pass it."

The rest of the way, Titus stared out the window at the nighttime nothing of the swamp and listened to the static and chatter from the police radio—most of which came from a woman at dispatch called "Jeannie." She and Junior had a friendly, flirty banter going on, so either they were sleeping together, or it was never going to happen for the young cop, and he hadn't figured that out yet.

Kemp chuckled. "Pickett, he's got it bad," he confirmed. "Still not sure he's gonna work out, but you never know."

"How's that?"

"Oh, he's only been on the job for a few weeks. He met Maude on a camping trip. Stayed in her hotel, you know? Fell in love with her on the spot, and didn't much care how it didn't go both ways. Took him a couple of days to figure out that Maude's 'no' means 'hell no,' and now he's moved on to our dispatcher."

"Jeannie?"

"You caught that, huh? Yeah, that's Jeannie. If she doesn't work out for him, I think Pickett will probably leave. Jean's the last woman anywhere near his age between here and Forto. Except for Jess, and she's taken."

Just then, he pointed out a bar called Thirsty's. Before Titus had time to ask who Jess was, or even get a good look at the place, the car pulled up to Maude's. It was a little before nine o'clock, and Titus could hardly believe it'd been so long since everything in his life had gone to absolute shit.

It hadn't felt that long? Or did it feel even longer?

There'd been so many questions, all that time sitting in the hospital, all that time in the car. So fine, it was nine o'clock at night, and here he was at Maude's, and there was a bar about a block away.

Maude's was a mid-century strip motel with a neon sign that was half broken, but you could still make out that it meant to say "bed and breakfast" with "cable TV" underneath and a "vacancy" light that was altogether shot. The light didn't so much as flicker or buzz when Titus got out of the police car and stood underneath it, looking up. Moths and mosquitos fluttered in the gum-pink glow of the few letters that still worked. Crickets chirped in the distance, and frogs went croaking after the crickets. Barely within earshot a jukebox was playing, over at the nearby bar.

This boded well for booze, but not for sleep. As if Titus had any hope of sleep.

Kemp rolled down the passenger window and leaned across the gearshift to keep eye contact. His face was a weird shade of orange with flickers of blue, illuminated by the dashboard lights. "You got some money?"

"Yeah, I do. And my phone, wallet. All that stuff." He had a bag, too, the big gray duffel that held all the clothes and toiletries he'd planned to need for the week. Everything else was still in the car, which had either been towed or impounded, depending on how you looked at it.

"All right. You've got my card?"

"That too."

"Good. I'll be in touch. You be in touch right back, if you feel the need; but stick around, would you? I'd hate to have to chase you all the way back to Valdosta."

"Yes sir. I mean, no sir. I won't go anywhere. Not without my wife."

"If she shows up, you let us know."

"I'll do that."

Kemp rolled up the window and the car rumbled out of the small parking lot, leaving Titus alone beneath Maude's iffy sign, standing with the bugs, the frogs, and everything else that was still awake in Staywater, Georgia.

It was not an auspicious welcome. At the far-right end of the strip was a main office that looked like a bedroom with a counter in it, from what he could see through the glass door. When he pushed that door open, it squealed against the floor, knocking against a string of jingle bells that dangled from the ceiling on a dirty shoelace.

"You need a room?" He heard the woman before he saw her, but she ratcheted into view when she stood up. There was a TV hidden behind the counter, and she'd been sitting there on the bed, watching it.

"Yes ma'am, I do." He leaned forward on the counter, partly because he was tired, and partly because he was curious to see what was on the other side. A bed, yes—and a chest of drawers with a mirror. Weirdest hotel lobby he'd ever seen.

As for Maude herself, she was about Junior's age, thin and

pretty. She was wearing a set of pajamas with elephants on them, and holding a half-smoked, snuffed-out cigarette between two fingers. "Good. Because I've *got* a room."

Titus figured she had more than one available, since he only saw two cars in the lot, and there were at least nine doors with numbers on them. "I'll take whatever's available."

"You want a queen? Two doubles? Honeymoon suite?" She looked pointedly over his shoulder, at the absence of anyone else—then down at the wedding ring on his hand.

"I don't care."

"Just passing through?"

"I don't know. I might be here a few nights."

She frowned and set the cold cigarette down in an ashtray. She pushed the tray away, and leaned forward on her end of the counter, so their faces were hardly a foot apart. "What for?"

"Does it matter?"

"I saw Kemp drop you off, and I want to know why. Are you some kind of criminal?"

Titus retreated and crammed his hands into his pockets. "Look, my wife went missing this afternoon, and we're all trying to find her. I'm staying to help look."

"Missing? How's that?"

"We had some car trouble out on 177, so I pulled off and popped the hood. I looked up a minute or two later and she was gone. I don't know what happened to her. I don't know where she went, and I don't know why she went there." It was a shitty effort at a cover story, but it made sense—and he was something worse than tired. He wanted a drink more than he'd ever wanted anything in his life. He *needed* a drink.

He lost his train of thought.

Maude didn't soften. If anything, she went tense—and this swing in attitude wasn't as open and easygoing as her naked curiosity had been. Now she was stiff and wary. "I hope . . . I hope your wife gets found." She swiped a key out from some nook in the counter that Titus couldn't see. It was an old-fashioned key, not a card or a digital fob. It even came attached to a diamond-shaped plastic tag.

"Thanks."

"Cash or credit card?"

He forked over a Visa.

"Just so you know, it's twenty-five ninety-nine a night, plus tax."

"That's fine." She collected the card and swiped it on a cell phone square. It took a couple of tries. The signal wasn't much better at Maude's than it was anywhere else at this end of the swamp. When the charge finally went through, she handed him the phone so he could sign with his finger.

The end result looked like a streak.

Maude took the phone back. "Breakfast runs from six thirty to nine, and that's an extra ten-dollar charge. Same goes for supper, and we do that from five to eight. Food goes down in the recreation room, down at the other end of the building."

"Got it."

His duffel bag felt a lot heavier than when he'd packed it twelve hours ago. It sagged down his shoulder. He shifted its weight and hefted it higher, where it didn't hurt his back so bad. He fiddled with the plastic key tag. It said "4" so he walked to the corresponding door and let himself inside.

There were no surprises.

The queen-sized bed was covered in an ugly polyester comforter, and when Titus flipped on the light, he saw that it used to be green with red and purple flowers. Now the colors were faded, but the blanket wasn't stained and nothing stank. He threw the duffel down on top of it, and was rewarded with a stale puff of air that suggested the room hadn't always been the non-smoking sort. Maybe it still wasn't. Come to think of it, he hadn't asked.

He didn't smoke, but he didn't care. If he'd had a pack of cigarettes, he would've given them a try on principle. Didn't they calm you down? Weren't they supposed to help you focus?

He dropped his bag on the bed and looked around. None of the furniture matched, but none of it was dusty. A pair of matching cup rings marred the leftmost nightstand, but that was the worst of it. All in all, he'd stayed in worse, dirtier, and sketchier places by far.

In the bathroom, a basket on the back of the toilet held sample-sized bottles of shampoo and conditioner, and a round bar of soap wrapped in soft, thin paper. He picked it up and sniffed it. It smelled like a crayon. He put it back down.

At the foot of the bed, on top of the dresser, a fat CRT television with a screen the size of a dictionary squatted like a toad. The remote control was sitting on top, along with a very short list of channels that only technically qualified as the "cable" foretold on the sign.

Titus didn't bother with it.

If he stood real still, and listened real hard, he could just hear the jangly music from the bar, somewhere to his immediate west. He patted his wallet in his back pocket and his phone in a front pocket, just to remind himself that they were there. He locked the door and set off on foot.

He should've asked Maude which way the bar was, and he thought about stopping back by the office to ask if she could point him at it. But the music was clear enough and there were only so many directions he could go, so he followed the tune down a cracked sidewalk illuminated by the very spottiest selection of streetlamps. The first one flickered and went out when he walked underneath it. The second one held, turning the walkway a watery yellow.

Ten yards forward, and the music was loud enough that he could tell the song was a country tune, which was annoying but inevitable. Ten more, and it was definitely Johnny Cash—but something lesser known, not "Folsom Prison" or "Ring of Fire." Whatever the song was, it ended right as Titus strolled up to the parking lot where a tall, rickety sign dubbed the place THIRSTY's.

This sign wasn't as nice as Maude's. It was painted wood, with a single functioning spotlight (out of three) to illuminate it for the masses.

But Jesus, he was thirsty. The mother ship had called him home.

He climbed a couple of wood steps, up to a building that might've begun its days as one of those temporary classroom structures that often become permanent in poor county schools. It felt like a double-wide, but Titus had been promised there was liquor in there, so he lowered his expectations below rock bottom, and shoved open the door.

The next wave of music hit him in the face, along with the smell of stale beer, cheap perfume, and something sharp that was either turpentine . . . or the worst-ever gin made in the dirtiest-ever bathtub.

Once he adjusted to the smell and the sound, he saw that Thirsty's was populated by about eight or ten people, most of whom were keeping to themselves. Two women at the bar seemed to know one another. One kid at a two-man table was dressed like an old man, but he looked like he wasn't even old enough to drive. One older guy was tall and skinny, with a cane and a floppy hat—sitting alone at the farthest end of the bar, looking like he'd stepped out of some older, more dignified century. Probably not the twentieth.

Everybody else was middle-aged and heavyset, and doing the nineties lumberjack thing unironically.

"What can I get you?" the bartender asked. He was one of those tall, lean guys who would've played baseball a hundred years ago. His age was hard to guess. Maybe forty-five. Or less than that, Titus thought as he came up closer. A really wrung-out thirty-five. The kind of thirty-five that's seen some shit.

Titus tugged a barstool out a few inches and slid onto it like a pro. He ordered a double of Jack, because that sounded safe enough—even in a place like this—and the bartender served it up in a jiff. Titus downed it in a heartbeat. "Another, please." The bartender made himself Titus's new Favorite Person in the World when he just slid the bottle over and said, "Keep it."

"Thanks, Thirsty."

"It's Dave." The correction was listless and only moderately invested in being heard. Dave kept looking at the TV with the shit reception. It flickered and fizzed, and showed part of a baseball game that must've been showing in recap-form on ESPN or something. Titus couldn't tell what was so interesting about it, so he pulled out his phone and checked that, instead. The bars flickered between one and two, and LTE. There was signal, but like everything else about Staywater, it was none too exciting.

No messages. No missed calls.

He looked up and down the bar. The old guy at the end was gone, but a full shot and a glass of water were left behind, beside an ashtray with an unsmoked cigarette.

He popped the phone back into his jacket pocket and poured another drink. He couldn't feel the first one. The second one was hardly more than a hint. The third warmed him up enough that he thought he'd check his phone again, not that it told him anything new.

"Waiting for a call?" asked one of the women at the bar. Her

friend gave her a smirk, but Titus couldn't read it. "From your wife, maybe?"

"From anybody." He put it away.

"You're new," her friend observed.

"I'm temporary."

Dave was close enough to overhear. He snorted. "Then you're lucky."

"Hey now," the lone waitress said. She ducked around the counter with a tray full of empties, then swiped them all into an oversized garbage can with a big black bag. "Some of us like it here."

"Incorrect!" the chattier of the two barflies protested with a laugh.

Her friend added to the waitress, "Nobody stays here, or comes back here, if they've got any other choice about it."

The waitress was cute and brunette, wearing a name tag that identified her as "Jess." She said, "Just because it's a small place, that don't mean it's not worth living in."

Titus didn't think she was converting anyone, and maybe she wasn't even fooling anyone. Herself included. She hardly looked like the bluebird of fucking happiness. "I never implied otherwise," he said, hoping it sounded friendly more than miserable.

"But you're new and temporary," said the drunk friend. "Give it a chance to disappoint you."

"It's already frustrated me, and freaked me out, too. Does that count?"

Dave leaned back against the bar's rear shelves, arms folded. Jess took a little extra time wiping down her tray, pretending that she hadn't started listening. The barflies leaned in.

Great. Now Titus had everyone's attention. All he'd wanted was a drink.

"What happened?" Jess asked, her voice half an octave too high for the casual air she was clearly shooting for.

"It's my wife . . . she's missing. We were on our way to the park. We were going to stay in one of the cabins." He yanked his wallet out of his back pocket, and with a little fishing, he turned up a picture of them both. It'd been taken at the engagement party she'd insisted upon. They looked pretty happy, he guessed. "This is what she looks like. Has anybody seen her? The police are still out there looking, but they told me to pack it in for the night. It's not like I can sleep, so . . . yeah. Here I am."

Jess leaned in to take a good look at the picture. "How did she disappear?"

"We had car trouble . . ." He repeated the same bad story he'd offered up to Maude, deciding that it wasn't bad enough to abandon. "I pulled over to lift the hood, and she got out to stretch her legs, I don't know. Then she was gone. I've been looking for her all afternoon. Me and the cops. They even called out some woman and a dog."

"Betty and Boomer," said a couple of people at the same time.

Everyone inside Thirsty's had come up close to Titus now, crowding around the photo to get a gander at the missing lady.

Everybody except for one woman, who was older than the rest. She hung back, staying at her table but eyeing him warily.

"Yeah, Betty and Boomer, that's what they called them," he mumbled. He cleared his throat, then passed the picture to his right, to let it finish the circuit. "If anybody sees her, if you see this woman . . . her name is Melanie Bell. We're supposed to be on our honeymoon right now."

The first and closest barfly gave him a one-handed shoulder rub that was supposed to be soothing but felt invasive and creepy. "I'm sure she'll turn up, baby."

Titus gently shrugged out from under her. "I hope so."

But from that sinister far table, the distant woman said, "Yeah, but she *won't*."

Everyone turned to see her, but she didn't look like she cared. She sat there, legs crossed, arms crossed, and stone-faced. She was probably the oldest person in the bar, but she didn't dress like it. She wore tight jeans and heeled boots, and big hair that humidity had knocked a little flat.

Dave said, "Netta, not now."

"Why not now?" she asked, like there could be no better time, ever. "He may as well know sooner, rather than later. She's *gone*, honey. Let me guess, she went AWOL somewhere out on 177, didn't she? And don't let them feed you no line about a serial killer. Everybody knows there was never any such thing out here."

"Netta . . ." Dave warned again.

She ignored him. "People go missing, right before you get to the park. Ain't no human on earth had anything to do with it."

"Serial killer . . . ? Nobody said anything about—"

"There's no serial killer," Dave said flatly. "Forget she said it."

Titus didn't forget anything. He started to stand, but the press of the small crowd made it awkward, so he stayed where he was—but he swiveled his seat around to face her. "We were on State Road 177. That's where we stopped."

"Wasn't no car trouble, though. Was it? You made up that bit, thinking it'd make more sense than what really happened. The truth is, you don't know what really happened, but that's not what the police want to hear."

The waitress, Jess, tried to intervene. "Aunt Netta, please. Don't do this. Not here, not now. You're gonna get the man all worked up."

"He's plenty worked up already, like he damn well ought to

be. Something's out there. Something that takes, and takes, and takes . . ."

"Ma'am, I'm trying to work myself *down*," Titus said, more loudly than he meant to. He wiggled his elbows out away from his torso, demanding more personal space. The barflies moved. The lumberjacks did too.

Jess gave him a little more room to breathe, but she didn't leave him. "Is this *really* the best place to do that?"

"Maybe not, but Maude didn't have anything to drink." Not that he'd asked her. He poured another slug too big to call a shot and downed it in a couple of swallows. "But I would very much like to hear about anybody else who went missing on 177, ma'am. Miss Netta." He called her by her name, since everyone else had used it already.

Jess finally left Titus's side to run interference. She went to her aunt—unless Netta was the kind of "aunt" who doesn't really belong to anybody by blood—and softly told her to cut this shit out, please, because it wasn't helping anything or anybody.

Dave took the bottle back. He poured Titus's glass about half full, leaving the bottle more than half empty. Then the bartender leaned in and told him quietly, "Netta Greely isn't a bad sort, but she's crazy as a snake-fucking rabbit. Spent some time in Chattahoochee, a few years back. Don't listen to much of anything she says." He slid the bottle back a few inches, into Titus's reach. "She means well, but she talks out of her ass a lot."

"That didn't sound like ass-talking."

Dave sighed. "You want me to lie?"

"Isn't that your job? That's what bartenders do, isn't it?"

He shook his head. "Nah, man. It's my job to sling drinks. I'll lie if you want and say it's all some misunderstanding, and Kemp'll turn up with your lady in the backseat any second now. But that's probably not the case, and you don't need Netta to tell you that. Your wife will probably turn up, but it won't be until morning, at soonest. That's the best-case scenario, man. People get lost out there . . ." He waved vaguely toward the heart of the swamp, or toward some other direction. Titus was too turned around and now too thoroughly buzzed to know the difference. "They walk in circles, and then they find a road and sit there until they're found."

Titus looked over his shoulder at Jess, who was whispering furtively to Netta. "Is that what always happens?"

Dave said, "Often as not."

"So it happens *often*?"

"Man, I didn't say that. You always jump to conclusions like this?"

"Okay, but it's happened *before*?" Titus pushed.

"Sure it's happened before. People come here to camp and hike. Campers and hikers get lost, sure as the pope wears a funny hat." He took his rag, which looked suspiciously like an old cloth diaper, and used it to wipe the damp off the bar. "Then they turn up, looking like they shared a sleeping bag with a raccoon. Everyone feels silly about it, and everyone leaves with a story to tell."

"Unless they get murdered."

"There's no serial killer, I'm serious. Nobody in Staywater has ever died of anything half that interesting. Here, man. Let me get you some fries or something."

"I don't need any fries."

"You're getting some anyway."

Titus wanted to protest the entire conversation in a hundred different ways. He wanted to say that they hadn't been camping, and they hadn't been hiking. He wanted to ask if Dave was lying or not, because he couldn't tell. He wanted to blurt out everything about the bridge, and ask if anybody had ever seen it, or knew what he was talking about. But he hadn't had quite enough to drink to make such a spectacle of himself, and he decided on the spot that even if he finished the bottle, he'd keep that bit to himself.

He didn't want to look like Netta, who'd done her time in Florida's loony bin.

So instead of all that, he said something to the tune of, "I bet you're right. You're probably right." He slowed down to a sip, but ten minutes later he'd put away everything in the glass— and when the French fries came, he ate half the basket before staggering back to Maude's in the dark.

6

THE PARKING LOT

Cameron had waited, lingering and smoking a cigarette from a pack he'd swiped from a drunk lady at the bar. Karl had given him the stink eye over it, but Karl was dead and what was he going to do—tell Daisy or Claire about it? Nobody ever saw Karl hanging out anyplace but Thirsty's, and neither of Cam's intensely virtuous godmothers would set foot in the place even if their lives depended on it.

Maybe they'd smell the smoke on him when he got home, maybe they wouldn't. But he couldn't just lurk outside the bar doing nothing, or he'd look like a creep. He didn't want to look like a creep.

He just wanted to creep.

How else was he supposed to talk to Jess alone? On second thought, he wouldn't call that creeping at all. It was something else. He couldn't decide what. Courting. That's what the ladies would call it.

One by one, the patrons left. They staggered to their cars, or staggered to the road, or staggered over to Maude's down the street to sleep off the evening's drinks. While the Thirsty's sign was lit, the lot was washed in a feeble orange-and-white light; but when Dave flipped the switch to turn it off and call the day "done," there was nothing left but the ambient glow coming out the windows.

Cameron could still see the flicker of the TVs inside. Then Dave turned those off, too.

It was darker than the devil's asshole out there. Cameron lit another cigarette even though the first one wasn't finished, just because he wanted the light to see by.

Sometimes, Jess left work before Dave. Sometimes, she would walk back home—to the little house she and Dave rented, a mile or so away. Sometimes, he could walk with her part of that way. At least back to the town square, and there they could part company. Then he'd go left, and walk the rest of the way to Hazelhurst. Jess would go right, heading behind the courthouse and up the hill, back to her place.

It was Dave's place too, but Cameron didn't like to think about that. So he didn't.

Cam had a very bad feeling that he wouldn't get to walk too far with Jess tonight, because she'd driven in to work. Probably, Dave and her would leave together, and she'd drive them both home. But maybe she'd leave early and trust him to hoof it after she was gone. She might leave the Jeep for him, if he had extra work to do. She didn't mind walking in the dark.

He was tying himself in logic knots, trying to imagine a scenario where he got to spend just a few minutes in her company without her longtime boyfriend.

Cam checked his watch. It was a few minutes past one in the morning.

By the time he got home, Claire and Daisy would surely be in bed. They were never up long past nine, and if one of them was sitting up waiting for him (which had never happened before, but there was a first time for everything), he'd accept whatever hollering or punishment resulted. He could make up a story on the way home. If it was good enough, they might let it slide. If it wasn't, he'd only make things worse.

The truth sure as shit wouldn't help. He knew how they felt about Jess. He didn't understand it, but he knew it. They hadn't exactly kept it a secret.

He coughed and squeezed the cigarette between his first two fingers—hoping that was how you did it right. Jeez, Louise. Jess was really taking her time.

He heard footsteps, coming up from the direction of Maude's. They wobbled and crunched in the loose asphalt. Cameron thought it might be the out-of-towner, come back to see about another bottle; but when he heard the voice, he knew he was wrong. It was much worse than a stranger passing through. It was Netta Greely, the town nut. The best-known town nut, at any rate. There were others, but none of them were quite so outgoing.

"None of this will do you any good," she said. A little drunk. Hoarse, like she smoked a whole lot more cigarettes in an hour than Cameron could steal all night.

She approached him. He squinted at her, but couldn't make out any details. The nearest working streetlight was almost a block away. He heard a pop and a fizz, and that one went out, too. Almost like she was doing it on purpose.

"Miss . . . Miss Netta?" He took another draw on the cigarette. The ash had grown so long that it fell off like the joint of a mummy's finger. It landed on his shoe. "What're you doing out here, at this hour?"

"*You're* the one who don't belong out here. You're too young to be inside Dave's, much less hanging in the lot, mooning over that awful woman who won't have a thing to do with you."

He flushed, and thanked the darkness for keeping that secret. "Jeez, Netta. She's your own kin."

"Look at you. Out here and smoking, like a fool. I can see the coal glowing and my nose ain't broke, so don't make up no story."

His eyes were adjusting to the shadows. Netta was there, wearing a shirt that was white, or some other pale color. It wasn't buttoned up all the way. Her hair was in its usual state of chaos. A sliver of moon shone through the wild, dyed locks, and they waved back and forth as she walked toward him.

He took a step backward and met the bumper of Jess's Jeep. He sat on down on it. It was either that, or take off running. Cameron didn't run from barflies. Not even Netta.

She came up close enough to take the cigarette away from him, but she didn't. She turned around and sat beside him, instead. The Jeep sagged on its back tires, creaking and flaking rust. "Did you feel it?" she asked him softly. "Earlier today, the *jolt*. You know what I mean. You were sitting in the bar, and the TVs went funny, and the world . . ." She held out her hand flat, palm down. She tipped it to the side. "The world went off-kilter."

"Yeah, I felt it."

"You ever feel it before?"

"No, but I heard about it. Something about the . . ." He hesitated. "There's something in the swamp around us."

She agreed. "Something in the water. Something about the planes, coming and going from the military base off to the west. Something about the currents, and electromagnetic energy. Something about ley lines, or the stones between the trees."

"What's a ley line?"

She let out a small laugh—so small that it sounded grumpy. "Nothing anyone's ever seen, so it might not exist, for all I know."

"I've never seen any stones in the swamp, either. Between the trees or otherwise."

She turned her head and looked him right in the eyes. Hers were shiny, and the whites were the only things he could really see. "I could show 'em to you. Stacked up like a bridge, except it's not a bridge. When you're not looking, they pile up on top of each other. They build themselves up like an old stone gate. Yeah, I could show you. If you wanted."

"No ma'am, I don't want to see anything like that."

She relaxed, and stared into the darkness in front of her again. "That's the right answer, boy. That's the only answer that makes any sense at all."

"Then why would you bring it up?"

"I just wondered if your god-ladies had ever said anything about it. If you'd ever heard them talking."

"The push?" he asked, and almost wished he hadn't. "The push," he said again, since that particular cat was out of the bag. "If we're talking about the same thing, that's what *they* call it."

"Well, they would know."

"What's that supposed to mean?"

She snorted. "Exactly what you think it means. Those old ladies have been here longer than anybody else who's still alive. If anybody knows what's going on, it's the pair of them. Or maybe one of the ghosts, but mostly them ghosts don't talk."

"Ghosts," he scoffed. He thought of Karl.

It was almost like she could hear him thinking. "Not the old man in the bar. He's different." Netta went quiet, then went dark. She said, "You know, everything's a ghost story, eventually."

He coughed, and then sighed. "You're full of shit, Netta."

She acted like she hadn't heard him. "You need to tell those ladies," she said so low it was almost a grumble. "Tell them to get off their little old asses and *do something* about all this."

"Do what? About what?" Cameron wanted to know. His cigarette was almost dead so he dropped it, and stepped on the coal to snuff it out.

"Do whatever it is they done before. They interrupted it, once before. They came close to stopping it, but something happened and it didn't stay stopped."

"They stopped the push?"

Netta leaned in closer—so close he could feel her breath on his neck with every hard consonant. "They stopped the *thing that pushes*. They took away some of its power, but not all of it. They won't tell me how, no matter how I ask, or how many times I ask. But times are changing, Cameron. People got cameras these days. People got police, and they've got television. Even out here in Staywater, where we're all part of a ghost story too. It's playing in slow motion."

"Leave me alone," he said with more complaint than force. "Get away from me."

"You're the middleman, boy. You're those ladies' last tie to this dying place. They'll keep you here as long as they can. They'll use you up and send you on your way, nothing left except a husk or a shell. Or a ghost."

"I *said*, leave me alone." He pulled himself off the bumper of Jess's Jeep.

"You ask them—you ask them like *I've* asked them, a hundred times before they went to hide in that corpse of a house where they raised you. *You ask them*," she demanded, still coming forward. Her finger in his face. "What happened to my Jimmy. You tell me what they say. Maybe they'll tell *you* the truth."

"You're crazy."

Her hand snapped forward, invisible in the bleak parking lot where not even the signs, not even the distant streetlights were bright enough to show Cameron anything he needed to see. She seized his arm and clenched it tight. She lowered her voice, like she was half afraid someone inside the closed bar might overhear. "Take me home with you. They won't let me past the driveway, not by myself. They won't let me come up close to Hazelhurst anymore, not since last time when we struggled about it. I just want to know where Jimmy is, and how he got there. They can give me back his bones. I deserve my son's bones, don't I?"

Cameron writhed free and stumbled backward, all thoughts of waiting for Jess gone out the window. "Don't touch me. Don't *ever* touch me. I don't like it when people do that."

Still, she stalked toward him. "They've lied to you, boy. They've let the world call me all kinds of names, when they've known the truth all this time. They might've even *chosen* Jimmy. For all I know, they offered him up to whatever dead, terrible thing lies out in the water."

"They wouldn't do that. They wouldn't hurt anybody."

She laughed, and laughed, and laughed.

He turned his back on her, circled briefly and blindly, and knocked his elbow on the Jeep as he did his best to put it between himself and this cackling drunk witch who'd lost her mind ages ago. A streetlight flickered and popped to light—blinding him, just about—but he took it as a sign.

The road was right there.

He could see it now. He could see everything.

In a flat-out footrace, he could outrun Netta. She dressed like a slutty kid, but she was probably old enough to be his grandmother and how fast could she really go, in those teetering heels?

Maybe he ran from barflies after all. First time for everything, and all that. He twisted on his heel and took off full tilt down the road toward the town square.

Netta was right behind him, despite her high heels and the half-paved gravel of the lot, and then the uneven asphalt of the road that led to town if you went one way, and out to State Road 177 if you went the other way.

Cameron didn't know what Netta planned to do with him, if she caught him. Maybe she'd wring his neck, or shake him like a can of soda, or beat him to death. A lot of people said she'd killed her son Jimmy, back in 2005. A lot of people whispered that she'd dumped him into the water, and told the world that something had dragged him down into the swamp.

A lot of people said a lot of things.

God only knew what they said about Cameron, but he said he didn't care, and he pretended it was the truth. Right then, he cared about one thing and one thing only: getting clear of Netta and her acrylic nails, and her wild eyes with hair to match. When he looked over his shoulder, he could hardly see her. She was backlit by the lamp behind him, a woman-shaped shadow that any drunk would mistake for a wraith or haint. She had become something wrathful and insane, an urban legend waiting to happen.

All it would take is one car to come up behind them. One pair of headlights, one young driver with a good imagination and a cell phone to catch a fleeting, blurry snippet of footage. What would it look like? He wondered as he ran, one foot grinding into the chewy black road after another. It'd look like a teenage boy about to be murdered by a swamp witch.

He ran, and she ran, and the distance between them stayed about the same.

He was almost out of light. He was hoping he could keep

his lead when the light was gone, when there were no more streetlamps to conveniently lead the way—when one up ahead fizzled and cracked to life. It wavered and wobbled, then stayed at half illumination.

One more, another block away. Pop, spark, and glow.

"Thanks, Miss Daisy," he murmured, because he knew better than to believe in coincidence. No matter what she hollered at him when he got home, he was going to thank the living daylights out of her. He didn't know how she did it, but he knew it was her.

Claire would definitely be asleep by now, and it was usually Daisy's job to be the avenger, the rescuer. The savior.

Netta was wheezing behind Cameron, but she wasn't slowing down.

He could hear his heart banging around in his ears, and his lungs itched with sharp prickles of heat. He couldn't keep this pace up. He was younger than Netta but he'd been smoking like a fool, and he was a thin guy—but that wasn't the same thing as being in good shape. Too much lounging around, sipping lemonade and Jack. Too much soda and too little action.

He'd be out of light again, in a matter of seconds.

Off to the left, another lamp exploded to life. But this one wasn't the main drag. It wasn't the way home. There was only one thing of note, on that block apart from the square. Only one place to hide, if it came to that. You turned left at the dog who liked to sit in the tree, and then you'd see it.

The dollhouse. Speaking of ghosts.

It wasn't exactly a museum and it wasn't exactly a home. It wasn't exactly abandoned, but nobody lived there and nobody took care of it. But once upon a time, Miss Joanna Lee Kiser had a built up a collection, and she'd needed a place to put it.

Cameron had met her once, before she finally died. She'd

been a friend to Claire and Daisy—the kind of friend who almost made his godmothers look ordinary. She was a wiry, hunchback woman with arms that were always too long for her sleeves and lipstick too bright, applied too unevenly. Her hands were quick and bony. Her eyes were sunken but bright.

He'd been a boy. She'd been a hag. He'd kept his distance, but he'd listened when they talked.

"It's called 'the uncanny valley,' where the sense of un-person-ness lies. Something so close, something intended to imitate, but merely offends." She'd waved a cigarette holder like a silent film star. She'd used it to draw letters in smoke. *"You can dig such a valley, if you like. It can be done."*

"We've enough valleys here, in the foothills. No need to go making anything stranger," Claire had chided her.

"I do what I want."

He shuddered at the memory. He trembled on his toes, but the streetlight was a command and he couldn't disobey. He'd done enough of that already. His knees wobbled; his lungs were officially on fire.

Netta was still coming. Cameron was still running. Daisy was showing him the way.

He took a deep jagged breath, and took a leap of faith. He didn't look up in the tree to see if the dog was watching, a small black-and-white shih tzu instead of a Cheshire cat. He jogged to the left, and took the turn to the dollhouse.

Miss Kiser's Uncanny House of Replicas and Playful Imitations had no such sign, but everyone knew that's what it was called. It had a door, but no locks. It had many windows, all

covered with thick and dusty curtains to keep the light out, or keep the dark inside.

The house itself was unusually large, but otherwise unremarkable. It was covered in the standard Staywater-issue peeling paint and flanked with chipped columns that were meant to look like limestone. It was not uncanny from the sidewalk, and not uncanny from the steps.

Cameron paused beneath the sagging porch ceiling, knowing it was haint blue without being able to see it. The color did nothing to keep anything from coming or going, and was mostly a fashion statement that went out of style a century ago.

Behind him, Netta hesitated.

She stood at the edge of the cross street, whatever it was. She watched him with those gleaming black eyes, her hair a fiery halo. A threat. A signal from someplace else, or one of nature's vivid red displays that warned of danger.

"You get back here!" she whispered fiercely, as if she had any power there, in that place. "You don't know what's inside!"

He tried the knob and it turned as easy as the one on his bedroom door. "Go to hell, Netta, or go somewhere else. Just leave me alone."

Before he could talk himself out of it, or Netta could take another shot at changing his mind, he flung himself into the door and followed it inside, into the murky, damp blackness of the dollhouse. He shut the door and sat against it. He closed his eyes to keep from seeing any of the other eyes, brightened and glistening from the small wisps of streetlamp that fought past the curtains.

He counted to a hundred, panting between every number.

Netta didn't come any closer; he listened for her footfalls on the steps with every intake of his breath.

The dolls didn't come any closer either, not this time.

They stayed where they were, shifting on their shelves—the foam mannequins, the headless Barbies, the porcelain-faced babies with straw-stuffed bodies and missing limbs. They angled their ears to the boy whose back was pressed against the big oak door, and they listened for every scrape of his foot. Every tremble of his fingers. Every dry swallow down his throat.

This time, they didn't say a word.

When he opened the door again and peeked outside, Netta was gone and the streetlamp was still lit. The shadows were long and crooked, and the spaces between them were too white, all washed out from the lightbulb's phony punctuation.

He slipped onto the porch and drew the door shut with the softest click he could muster. It was hardly a noise at all. He barely felt it, the spring and click of a metal latch somewhere inside the frame. He barely heard the dolls inside Miss Kiser's place, grumbling darkly about what Cameron could expect from Miss Daisy when he finally did make it home.

He tugged his light jacket closer around his shoulders and squeezed them as he ran, as fast as he could.

Going, going.

Gone.

7

THIRSTY'S

Closing time rolled around at long fucking last. Even the new guy, Titus, had staggered back out the door, into the night, and off toward Maude's—or wherever. Dave had turned all the lights up, turned off the TVs, and pulled the plug on the jukebox before it could play even one more note of anything by Hank Williams, Jr.

Thirsty's was a ghost town, or a ghost joint on a ghost exit *to* a ghost town. The door was locked, and now there was only Dave and Jess, unless Karl was still hanging around at the end of the bar. Sometimes he stayed. Sometimes he didn't. Nobody knew where he went, when he wasn't there.

He'd never tell, if you asked him. He'd just wink and flash you a grin.

"Karl?" Dave called, watching the old man's seat at the counter.

He didn't appear. Dave didn't hear footsteps, or catch the smell of fresh cigarettes, so he scooped up the shot glass and water, and dumped both. He emptied the ashtray, even though the single cigarette had never been lit. "All right, then," he muttered. "Until tomorrow night."

Generally speaking, the 1:30 A.M. cleanup was a quiet, tired affair, whereupon the last tables were wiped as clean as a dirty rag would get them, the glasses were all piled up in the dishwasher, the taps were all secured, and the alarm was set before the place was vacated entirely.

Not tonight.

Jess retreated to the kitchen with a tray, and Dave followed her.

"You wanna tell me . . ." he began.

"Tell you what?"

"What the hell is going on around here." He was not so much accusing, as weary and resigned.

"Not sure what you mean." She unstacked the last dirty dishes into the sink, because the dishwasher was full. They'd wait for tomorrow. Almost everything would.

"Yeah, I think you do."

She sighed and turned on the faucet. "Well then, you'll have to be more specific. There's always something the hell going on around here. Or nothing the hell going on, depending who you ask."

"I'm asking *you*, and you know the answer already, so stop fussing around."

"You mean about the TV going weird?"

"I mean, about the whole world going weird. Right here, earlier tonight. Everything . . ." He leaned back against the wall, realized he'd put his shoulder against something sticky, and moved over a few inches. "Everything just stopped for a few seconds. Maybe half a minute."

She started to lie. She turned off the faucet and turned around, opening her mouth and then closing it again. He knew that move. It never once came before the truth.

He didn't want to hear her lie, so he kept talking instead. "It was like a weird . . . pulse, or pause, or . . . something. Like . . . the fabric of reality hit a snag. Goddammit Jess, what *was* it? What did it mean?"

"Why would you ask me?" She wiped her hands on the ragged dish towel that had been collectively approved as "clean."

"Because I want you to explain! Everyone acted like nothing had happened, but something *did* happen. Something like . . . it was like . . . I don't know. It was like nothing I've ever felt."

"Not *ever*?" She cocked her head, both eyebrows lifted half an inch.

"No, not ever," he replied crossly, not certain if she was playing around or not. He felt like she was expecting him to say something, or maybe just wanting him to. Waiting to see if he would.

She crossed her arms. "We both know that's not the first weird thing you've ever experienced here."

"Obviously not, but it *is* the most recent."

Water dripped down into the sink, slipping past the dishes and down the drain. Jess uncrossed her arms like she was buying time. She leaned her ass up against the edge and braced herself with her hands. Slowly, she said, "Around here they call it 'the jolt,' sometimes. Sometimes they call it 'the push,' or 'the pop.' It *could* mean any number of things."

"You've felt it before? Everyone else in Staywater—they've all felt this before?"

"Why would you assume that everybody has?"

"Because I'm the only one who got freaked out about it."

She didn't exactly relax. Her arms went loose, and she let her head hang. It looked more like a half-assed surrender. "Okay, fine. Yeah—it's something everyone here feels, every now and again. Once every ten or twelve years." She returned her attention—or half of it—to the sink full of glasses, plates, and cutlery. She stared down into the dirty water and battered the barware like it might give her an out, but it didn't. "Whenever it happens, it usually means someone's gone missing."

"Holy shit. What are you talking about?"

She turned around again and finally met his eyes. "That new guy, the one who showed up and drank himself dry again. Netta was right about one thing: His wife isn't coming back."

Dave was confused. "But that guy showed up a couple of hours after the . . . after the thing."

"And before that, his wife went missing. It happened right when the TV blipped. I bet you a million dollars."

"If you had a million dollars, you wouldn't be here."

She shrugged. "Then I bet you a blowjob. That dude's wife is gone for good. They'll never find her, and no one will ever really know what happened to her."

"How do you know that?"

"Because." She picked up her tray again, and left through the swinging door—back into the bar. "They never do."

He left the spot where he'd plastered himself to the wall and followed behind her, smacking the door as he stomped in her wake. "What do you mean, they never do? What about *me*? Is that the sound . . . the same *thing* everyone felt, when I almost . . ." He knew the word he meant, but he couldn't bring himself to say it. He said, "Left, and didn't come back?"

Jess shook her head. "You were different. You hadn't gone anywhere yet."

"*Did it happen back then?*" He sounded desperate, and he hated himself for it.

"*I don't know*," she replied in kind. "I wasn't here in town. I was out *there*." She waved vaguely toward 177. "That's how I found you."

He'd heard the story a thousand times. Jess used to tell it to him over and over again, like a mother whispering to her child the story of how he was born. But Dave wasn't born on State Road 177; he'd died there, and he came back to life when he opened his eyes and saw a brown-haired girl in cutoff shorts and a tank top, her face red from giving him mouth-to-mouth.

He woke up with dreams of hungry things with tails and hands.

He'd asked her about that day a thousand times. He'd spent thirteen years trying to milk some new detail from the narrative, some new angle, where she could give him one more hint that would inch him toward an explanation of where his time had gone—a lost hour on a narrow road. He'd never been able to account for it.

But Jess wasn't going to give him anything new tonight. He could feel it, so he let it drop. "Then what happened to that guy's wife?"

"How should I know?"

"Somebody has to."

"Wrong, dude. Very, very wrong. Maybe the wrongest thing you've ever said." She laughed, but there wasn't anything funny to go with it. "Try asking Karl, and if you ask him right for once, he might tell you. If anybody knows for sure, it's definitely the dead."

"I've asked him. Either he doesn't know, or he'll never say. I can't tell which."

"Maybe Miss Claire or Miss Daisy. Ask Cameron. Maybe he can tell you, if the ladies won't."

"Now you're just fucking with me for fun."

"No, I'm telling you the truth as close as I can figure it. Can we . . . can we *not* fight about it tonight?" She threw her damp, dirty rag against the bar mirror. It left a grimy splat and smear, and slid down to the counter to rest atop a bottle of gin. "I'm tired, and it always goes the same. Can we just skip it? Go home, and call it a night?" She glanced at the crooked clock on the wall. "Or call it a morning, I don't care."

Outside, he could hear somebody talking.

It sounded like two people arguing. He thought he recognized Netta's voice, but he didn't check out the window to see. Whatever she was doing, he was best off not knowing about it and staying far the hell away from it. Once upon a time, he thought, maybe she knew what she was talking about. Sometimes, when he'd been very drunk, he thought she was the only one who ever did.

But those days were over and even if Netta *could* help him out, she probably wouldn't.

Dave gave up. "We can call it a night. If that's what you want."

Back in the kitchen, he rinsed the sink's dishes because it gave him something to do with his hands, and set the washing machine to run while they were gone.

Jess leaned her head through the swinging door and jangled her keys. "You ready?"

He nodded. He rechecked the lock on the front door, then set the alarm. "Let's go."

"Hang on."

"No, hurry up. We only have thirty seconds."

She ran up to him, her almost-forgotten sweater slung over one arm, and her purse on the other. "I'm here. Let's go."

Thirsty's was as secure as Thirsty's ever got, and the road leading into Staywater was as silent as a tomb. Jess had driven them to work, so they climbed into her rattling gray Jeep Cherokee, buckled in, and rode home without talking.

They only passed a couple of oncoming headlights on the way to the north side of the town, where they shared a squat, mid-century rental house that had never been updated, not once. It was a wonder that it still stood, and an even greater wonder that anything inside it worked.

But everything did work, and the roof didn't leak—never mind the persistent smell of mildew and the old single-pane windows that fogged up no matter the weather. The window AC units were both quiet, for the wee hours of the morning were cool enough to leave them idle.

Dave almost pressed the button on the nearest one out of plain old habit, but caught himself.

Jess's warning came too slow. "Don't do it. We'll freeze to death."

He was already walking toward the bathroom. "Fat chance." Nothing ever froze in that house. Not even the stuff they used to leave in the freezer, with a hope and a prayer. But yes, the night had gone cool, and yes, he was anxious, and he had the shivers. "I'm gonna throw myself in the shower."

He didn't shut the door all the way but he turned the water up as hot as it would go and stripped down, kicking his jeans against the cabinet. They fell in a pile. His wrinkled boxers made for a dull white cherry on top.

Into the tub he climbed, and let the water hit him in the face. He liked the feel of it, hot and clean. It didn't feel anything like the dank, dirty air in the swamp, or its tepid water the color of stew. It didn't feel like tree roots shaped like fingers, grasping for what they were owed.

For what they were promised. For what they'd been given.

For what had been taken away.

8

MAUDE'S

The phone rang at 8:03 A.M. and Titus thought about not answering it. He wasn't awake yet, and he had a halfway dreamsick idea that the message could just go to voicemail, and why hadn't he thought to turn the ringer off before calling it a night? But the phone kept ringing. It wasn't his cell phone, that's why the sound was so unfamiliar and difficult to ignore. It was the hotel phone. It was relentless. He couldn't shut it up with the press of a button.

He rolled over and stared at the ceiling. Sunrise was squeaking around the polyester curtains, turning the room yellow without really brightening it much. Neat trick.

The phone's tinny jangle made Titus's teeth grind together. How much did he drink the night before? He couldn't

remember, but he was thirsty as hell. His face felt swollen, his head hurt, and his eyes felt like they were full of gravel.

He swung one arm over the side of the bed, and whacked his wrist on the nightstand. He swore and swung again—this time catching the old Bakelite handset with the back of his hand and knocking the receiver loose. It tumbled off the side, dangling and bouncing by its curly pink cord. It reminded him unpleasantly of a pig's tail, dirty and bent with kinks. He didn't want to touch the receiver, but someone's voice was coming through it.

Before he could even get his ear into position, he recognized the sound of Junior's drawl. Or Officer Pickett's drawl. Whatever.

". . . have reported back for duty and are ready to take another crack at 177 if you're—"

Titus smushed the phone against his face and tried not to notice that it smelled like a hobo's ashtray. "Wait, sorry. What? Come again?"

"Betty and Boomer, they—"

"Did they find anything last night?"

Pickett paused. "If they had, they wouldn't've come back around this morning, now would they?"

He rubbed at his eyes and tried to keep from sounding too hungover or pissed off. "I didn't hear that part. I . . . I dropped it. The phone. I'm sorry, but I dropped the phone when I picked it up. Just . . . could you start over, please?"

"Yes sir, what I said was: Betty and Boomer are ready to get back to work this morning, and Sergeant Kemp thinks maybe you should join us, out at 177. Show us exactly what happened, while we've got the dog on hand, you know. Run through the story again."

So Kemp was a sergeant. In Titus's head, he'd either been

"officer" or "mister." He wondered what the hierarchy was. Was there a captain someplace? How many cops would a place like Staywater actually employ? Who was sitting at the top of the food chain?

He exhaled and tasted last night's whiskey and a faint hint of freezer-burned French fries. "Sure. I can join you. What um . . . what time? I'm not up yet. Need to . . . got to . . . my teeth. Brush them. Get some food, I think Maude has . . . breakfast. When will you get here?"

"I'm outside in the parking lot right now, sir."

Of course he was. Titus staggered out of bed. He struggled upright, and stumbled to the window. When he tugged the curtain aside, he was greeted with a faceful of infuriating sunshine. His eyes adjusted, and yes, there was the Staywater patrol car with Officer Pickett—one hand holding a cell phone to his head, and the other hand waving a chipper greeting.

"You've got to give me a minute, man."

"Yes sir, you can have a minute. But Sergeant Kemp and Betty are waiting, sir. Tell you what: I'll grab some pastries off Maude's counter for you. A blueberry muffin, or something. I'll get some coffee, and you can get your teeth brushed and your face washed. I'll be back in a few minutes, but do me a favor, please? Get a move on. We haven't got all day."

Titus hung up before Junior could hear him mutter, "I don't see why not."

How many crimes could possibly happen in a given afternoon in Staywater? He hadn't seen much of the town so far—just Maude's and the bar down the road—but if these were the highlights, there couldn't be much else going on within the city limits.

He dragged himself out of bed and ran through the motions of morning hygiene. Inside his duffel bag he had a change of

clothes that looked more or less just like what he'd been wearing already, but at least the fresh cargo shorts and white tee were
clean. By the time he was adding a finishing touch of deodor-
ant, Junior was knocking on the door.

"I'm ready, I'm ready," Titus insisted wearily as he opened it.
"Let's go do this."

Junior handed him a to-go cup of coffee that smelled strong,
if not particularly good. "Here you go," he said, and added a little
paper bag to his offering. Inside the bag were several napkins
and a plastic stirring stick, as well as an assortment of sweeten-
ers, sugar packets, and tiny tubs of creamer.

Titus wanted to say more than "Thanks," but that was all he
could muster at first. It seemed insufficient. He was genuinely,
even pitifully grateful—and so moved by the small gesture in
the midst of a terrible hangover that he added, "I . . . uh . . .
man, this is great, thanks. I mean it." On the spot, he decided
to quit thinking of the young cop as "Junior." With this small,
above-and-beyond gesture, he'd officially earned the title of "Officer" in Titus's book.

He took the bag and clutched it to his chest as he climbed
into the passenger side of the patrol car, careful not to spill his
coffee. It was only kindness, but it was important. Even if it kind
of made him want to cry.

If Pickett noticed his passenger's rheumy eyes or shaking
hands, he was too polite to say anything. "You'll like Betty and
Boomer," he said. "Everybody does."

Titus fastened his seat belt and fumbled with the contents of
the paper bag, picking two packs of yellow sweetener and the
stirring stick, and getting to work. "I like dogs. And um . . .
people who like dogs. I'm sure they're . . ." He tore the packet
with his teeth and emptied the contents. "I'm sure they're lovely."

The young cop chattered happily and idly as they left the

parking lot, passed the bar, and headed back out onto the main road. Oh yes, Betty and Boomer were just the *best,* and Sergeant Kemp was the best too, if you gave him a chance. Sure, he seemed a little distant, but he'd been a marine before he was a cop, and he just had that way about him. Cold at first, but then friendly. Not always, but more often than you'd expect.

Titus gave the coffee most of his attention; with whatever was left, he tried to answer using the appropriate grunts and agreements while he stared out the window.

Trees raced past. Water filled spaces between them, or else it didn't—and there was nothing but mud or grass or dirt. Cypress knees still jutted from the swamp here and there, so the trees were bouncing back from the old logging days, he supposed. A few metal signs whipped by. They described the landscape, offered warnings, and reminded drivers which road they were on.

Otherwise there was nothing to see but the swamp edge bucking up against the seams of 177.

There was no sign of Melanie Bell, and no hint as to what might have become of her.

Titus tried to keep from thinking about what the barfly Netta had said. Everyone knew she was crazy. Nobody took her seriously. Even a newcomer could see that much.

Eventually they pulled up to a place that might've looked familiar, if it'd been any different at all from anything he saw on the ride there. But Sergeant Kemp was parked off to the side of the road, and a late-model Chevy SUV was drawn up behind the patrol vehicle. Even before Pickett stopped the car and pulled up third in the row on the gravelly shoulder, Titus could see noseprints on the passenger-side window. Noseprints the size of handprints.

Boomer looked like some amiable mix of Saint Bernard and yeti—thick and hairy, and mostly white and gray, with black ears and feet. His tongue hung out from the side of his mouth; and when Titus got out of the car the dog stood up on its hind legs, placing its paws on his shoulders.

"Hey there," he said uncertainly, rubbing its head. Since it was right there, at eye level and everything. Anything less would've seemed rude.

Boomer approved, hopped down, and strolled over to his handler. Betty was a black woman in round red sunglasses. She was about sixty years old and ninety pounds, maybe five feet tall in heels. Her hair was a perfect helmet of graying curls. Her handshake was firm to the point of being aggressive, but her smile was big and she wore an air of efficiency that Titus found reassuring.

"Hello there, Mr. Bell—I'm Elizabeth Harrow, but you can call me Betty like everybody else. I see you've met Boomer," she said, with a little flick of her finger to indicate a string of dog drool on his shirt. "He's a big boy, but a good boy, and I trust him with my life. We're doing our best to canvass the area for your wife, but so far we're not meeting with any luck."

"That's what I hear. Maybe now that I'm here . . . I don't know. Maybe I can help. I hope I can help." He stuffed his hands into his pockets and stood there awkwardly, sadly. "I just want my wife back."

She gave him a look that said she wanted to squish him in the world's smallest bear hug of sympathy, but she only patted his arm. "I know, sweetheart. I know."

Sergeant Kemp closed out a call and put his phone in his shirt pocket. "Now Mr. Bell," he began, his big round voice a match for his big round belly, which leaned over the edge of a put-upon belt. "This is the vicinity of your . . . accident, or whatever it was. Correct?"

Titus looked around at the road, its gritty shoulder, and the swamp beyond it. He looked as far as he could—he shaded his eyes against the morning sun, and squinted back and forth, both directions. There was no sign of a mysterious one-lane bridge. "I guess? It all looks alike, if you stare at it long enough."

"Ain't that the truth," the sergeant agreed with a swing of his head. "But this is close enough to get started, don't you think?"

He closed his eyes and rubbed them, pretending it was only the sun. "Yeah, this is close enough. What do we do? Where do we start?"

Betty answered faster than Kemp. "Boomer and I already checked up and down between here and the next two mile markers, in either direction. My boy here, he didn't offer up a single hit." She looked down at Boomer. Rather, she gave him a low-slung side-eye. His head was almost on level with her shoulders. "And we can't get too far off track in either direction. His nose is the best in the Okefenokee, but there's only so much he can do, out in the swamp. The best bloodhound God ever made can't sniff his way through the water."

"I understand." Titus wasn't looking at her. He was still staring as far west as the road and the trees would let him.

Kemp prompted him. "So here's what we're going to do: We're going to take it from the top. Walk me through it. You had some kind of episode while driving . . ."

"An . . . episode. Sure. I was driving across . . . there was a bridge." He didn't sound very convinced about the bridge, not even to himself. But it was true, wasn't it? The more time passed, the less he was sure. The more he turned it over in his head, the less sense it made to him.

"Which bridge was it, honey?" Betty asked.

He concentrated, mining his recollection for any details at all. "It was just a single lane. There were warnings posted. You couldn't see the other side; the whole thing was overgrown."

Betty and Kemp looked at one another. The woman looked confused. The officer looked doubtful.

Young Officer Pickett arrived from around the front of his car, and joined the circle. "What are we talking about?"

"A bridge. I swear to *God,* there was a bridge. But when I woke up, it was gone. I mean," he corrected himself quickly, "I couldn't find it. I drove around, looking for my wife . . . and looking for that bridge."

"A one-laner," Kemp said coldly. "Overgrown. Says he couldn't see the other side of it. You know of a bridge like that, anywhere along this road?"

Pickett was a moment too slow to shake his head. Titus saw it. He also saw the way the young man moved his eyes to look west—only for an instant. "Naw, I never heard of anything like that. Not on 177. Maybe you were on another road? We've got a lot of little ones . . . running through the park and around the edges."

Betty nodded. "They're not all marked, or not marked well. You might've gotten turned around."

"I *didn't* get turned around."

"Well, this is roughly where I met him, after he called for help," Pickett contributed. "It was right around here someplace."

"I'd been driving back and forth, up and down on this same road. This *exact* same road." Titus knew he sounded like he protested too much, but it was true, and the truth was all that he had so he leaned on it, as hard as he could. "There *was* a bridge."

Betty cleared her throat. "We'll take your word for it, just for now. But the swamp is a confusing place. Even the best of us get a little lost sometimes. Even this guy." She cocked a thumb at the dog, who didn't argue. He didn't look like he ever argued with anybody. "We'll go ahead and take it as a given: there was a bridge, and something happened to you there."

He tried to agree, to take the generous out that she offered. "All right, okay then. The last thing I remember was driving over the bridge, and I had an episode, like you said." He directed that bit at Kemp. "Then after . . . it couldn't have been more than a few minutes . . . I woke up, because I heard the car door chiming. You know, like it was left open while the keys were still in the ignition."

The sun on his face. The hard road under his back. The digital bell, clanging in his ears.

He paced around while he told the story again, for what felt like the thousandth time in twenty-four hours. He struggled for still more particulars, and he answered with as much patience as he could rally when Kemp's attention would snag on a certain point—and he'd ask another question, from another angle. It didn't matter. The answers were always the same. They couldn't trip him up, whether they were trying to, or not. There was no lie to trip over.

But he was starting to worry. He began to have doubts.

Every time he played that afternoon in his head, every time he recounted it aloud, it moved just a little farther out of his reach. The bridge and the car and Melanie became just a little more vague in his head, a little duller. A little darker. Like every

word drained the memory somehow, and it leaked away drop by drop. It would leave him altogether if he didn't somehow plug these holes, he knew it.

He just didn't know how to fix it.

After an hour of this slow leak, Betty took pity on him. "How about this, hon. Let's go to the last bridge back. You remember the last one, don't you? It's a regular two-lane thing—one coming, one going—and made out of concrete, sometime in the Eisenhower administration. It's not much to look at but it's a bridge, and you *definitely* crossed that one if you made it this far."

Kemp wasn't so sure about it, but Pickett was down for a change of venue. He was sweating through his uniform, his forehead as slick and shiny as a puddle of cooking oil in a pan. "Let's try that. It's not exactly overgrown, but it's got more shade than this stretch over here. Maybe you're just remembering it funny, because of your episode."

Titus couldn't argue. He couldn't remember the other bridge, not specifically, but he did remember there were other bridges between the interstate and the place where he woke up with his head lying on the faded yellow strip of a dotted line that marked the middle of the road.

Betty and Boomer piled into her SUV, Sergeant Kemp took his patrol car, and without any better ideas—Titus got back into the passenger side of Officer Pickett's ride. When the doors were closed, the AC was on, and the caravan was headed back east on 177, the silence began to feel suspicious.

"You, um . . ." Titus began, not sure of what words to line up next. "The bridge with just one lane."

"No such thing. Not on this stretch."

"That's what you said. That's what everybody says, but, I got a feeling . . ."

Pickett kept his eyes on the road. "What kind of feeling?"

"A feeling like . . . you kind of knew what I was talking about."

"But I don't."

"Are you *sure*?" Titus tried not to sound too pleading, too pathetic. Not as pathetic as he felt.

"I've never seen a bridge like that." It was a stubborn reply. A careful reply.

"Have you ever *heard* of one?"

Pickett took the bait, or else he just surrendered. "Heard of a one-lane bridge? Yeah, of course."

"An overgrown one, really long. Here in the swamp. A bridge so long, that you can't see the other side. There were warnings, these old rusty signs . . ."

The cop took a slow, deep breath. "Look, people talk about a lot of things, but that don't make them true. It don't mean there's anything strange, when people go missing around there."

It was barely a crumb, but Titus seized it. "People go missing? At the bridge?"

"It's not a real bridge. It doesn't exist, except around campfires and fairy tales when local folks get too much bourbon in 'em. They're nothing but stupid stories."

"So tell me a stupid story. Seriously, I want to hear one."

"No time for that. Here's the *real* bridge," Pickett said fast, and pulled off the road to park on the shoulder. "The one you definitely crossed." The tires sank, and the engine complained before it was cut off. The cop was out of the car before Titus had a chance to ask any more questions, and it might've been just as well.

Melanie was missing, and that wasn't a fairy tale. A fairy tale wasn't going to save her, or him, or anybody. But Titus still wanted to hear it.

Sergeant Kemp hauled himself free of his vehicle and shut

the door with a smack of his hip. "All right, gentlemen . . . and Betty. Gentlepersons, whatever you say nowadays in mixed company. Let's give this another shot. Mr. Bell, could you kindly join me on the bridge, over here. It's a little elevated, relative to the road. You can see farther, if you stand beside me. Tell me if anything looks familiar, or if anything jogs your memory."

Titus grimly obliged, stepping up the slight grade to the faint arch of the old bridge. It'd been built for duty, not art, and it did its job just fine for all the hairline cracks along the thick rails. Or were they rails? He thought they were more like bumpers—stubby walls to keep cars from launching off the side and into the water below.

He planted his hands atop the nearest one, and hung his head over the side.

He didn't know what he expected to see.

Boomer trotted up to hang beside him, even propping himself up on his massive paws so he could look out over the water, too.

"Mr. Bell?" Kemp called.

"I'm thinking, I'm thinking." He wasn't thinking.

He was gazing down at the brackish water that pooled and streamed beneath his feet, too murky to show a reflection. Grass jabbed up in clumps, and baby-green algae floated on the surface, coiling in small eddies and currents. Tiny plants the color of limes and mushrooms drifted along, leaf by leaf, bouncing against the cypress knees and the bobbing cattail fronds; clumps of moss tangled on thick white fingers with curved sharp nails, before ducking beneath the oily surface and disappearing.

He blinked.

He blinked again.

Boomer let out a low growl, and dropped back down to all

fours. Grumbling all the way, looking over his great and hairy shoulder as he went, he returned to Betty's side. Then he changed his mind and hid behind her, hunkering low and still rumbling his displeasure.

"What is it, boy? Come on, Boomie-butt," she cooed. "What's the matter?"

Titus looked again. His eyes watered. A second hand, not exactly white like bone and not exactly green like something bleached and drowned. "Is that . . ." He looked back to the cops, and to the small woman with the large dog. "Do you see this?"

"See what?" All three walked toward him.

But down in the water there were no more arms, no more claws the shape of talons. There was surely no long plank of a head with a devil's black eyes, sinking beneath the sluggish current.

"I saw . . . I thought. I thought I saw something. But I guess not."

Boomer quivered, coiled and whining, as his person walked away. He rose up to intercept her, trying to push her back. She told him to quit it, but either he didn't know that command—or he didn't see the sense in following it.

He kept her there just long enough for the policemen to beat her to the low wall that separated the bridge from whatever was beneath it.

"I don't see squat," Kemp griped. "What are we looking at?"

"I don't see anything, either," his junior officer said, a wrinkle nested upon his gleaming, sun-pinked brow.

Betty had her hands on her hips. The dog had his mouth around her belt, and was tugging at her, trying to draw her back away from the edge. "Goddammit, Boomer. What's gotten into you?"

Titus couldn't breathe, except in small sips. He felt light all over, and the edges of his vision sparkled. "There was something in the water. He must've seen it, too."

"Something belonging to your wife?" Kemp guessed.

"Yes. No. I don't . . . God, I hope not." His voice was hardly a whisper. Barely more than a breath with consonants. "I can't do this. I need to sit down. I need to go."

"Hang on, now," Kemp said, pulling him away from the bridge's edge. He put his hands on Titus's shoulders, trying to straighten him out or hold him up. "Get yourself together, son. Is this what happened last time? When you had your episode?"

"Stop calling it that. I didn't faint. I didn't have a seizure."

"Then what *did* you have?" Pickett asked.

"A . . ." He floundered for a word. "Spell. It was some kind of spell. Nobody . . . none of you saw that? Down there?"

"Saw what?" asked Betty, now hanging over the edge, since she'd wrestled away from the dog. "All I see is a nasty-ass swamp full of snakes and gators."

"That must be it. I saw something move, and it must've been an alligator," he lied. He knew what alligators looked like. Something big splashed below, and he jumped.

"Have you ever seen one before? In real life?" she asked.

"No," he lied again.

"There you go, then. First time you see one of those things, it can give you a real thrill. They're positively *primordial*," she said with something akin to glee. She scanned the water again. "The way they move, the way they hunt. They outlived the dinosaurs, and they'll outlive us, too. You can count on that."

"Do you think one of those things . . ." he began to ask, but his throat was too dry. His head felt too flushed. "What if . . ."

"What if an alligator got your wife?" Kemp finished the

hypothetical question for him. "Then we won't find much to bury, I hate to say. We might find bones, or clothes. What they do, see—"

Betty cut him off. "Jesus fucking Christ, Kemp. *Don't*." Then to Titus, she said, "Sweetheart, nature is red in tooth and claw, and don't we all know it. Let's focus on finding your lady alive. She's only been gone overnight. There's still plenty of hope."

He was going to be sick, he just knew it. He tasted bile and sweetened coffee in the back of his throat. "I'm going to throw up."

"Here you go, just lean over the side . . ." Pickett suggested, but Titus pushed him away.

"No, not that. No, I can't."

He couldn't stand the thought of looking again, and seeing the sinking, slithering shape that moved half under the water. It had tripped some uncanny dissonance between his ears; it was something about the not-rightness of its color, its motion— even seen in flickering fragments between the dark currents all streaked and mottled with green.

"Get him into the shade, and sit him down," Betty commanded.

Was there shade? Some. A little.

A couple of tall, leaning trees heavy with moss hung over the north edge. Titus let them lead him there, and he sat down with his back against the concrete wall. It was warm through his shirt, but not as warm as the asphalt on the bridge.

"Mr. Bell, you've got to pull yourself together."

"Oh, stop it, Matthew. Look at him, boys—he's white as a sheet. Like he's seen a ghost."

Sergeant Kemp loomed over him, all folded arms and blank cop face. "Did you?"

"Did I what?"

"See a ghost? Is this where something bad happened, to you or your wife?"

Titus shook his head, and the whole world rocked back and forth. "No. Nothing bad happened. Not here. I don't know. But not here. We drove over this bridge. This one, right here." He struggled for something solid, and the bridge would have to do. He gestured weakly down the road. "We were listening to the radio. It didn't come in very well. We were talking. Then there was a bridge with one lane and it went on forever. I got tunnel vision. Everything was dark and loud."

His companions listened closely, except for Boomer, who had retreated to the SUV and was curled up against the back right tire, still growling to himself.

"I felt dizzy and I closed my eyes, for just a second."

"Just a second." The sergeant wasn't really asking.

"And I woke up in the middle of the road, back there, where we started. Melanie was gone. The keys were in the ignition. The door was open." The story had distilled itself to these bullet points. He fired them out in a list, one after another. "I got up and walked around, looking for her. I didn't hear or see any sign of her. I got back in the car, thinking she went looking for help. I drove back here, to this bridge—and I drove up there," he gestured west again, "to the next one. Then I went back to where I started, and I called nine-one-one."

He coughed. It smelled like yellow packets and caffeine.

"That's it, that's all I've got." He leaned back, and looked up at the sky. Mostly he saw three faces staring him down. One was worried, one was confused, and one didn't necessarily believe a goddamn word of this, but there was nothing Titus could do about that. "Please, I need to lie down. Take me back to Maude's, before . . ."

Any threat would have been empty, even the one that was less a threat, than a promise.

". . . please, take me back to Maude's before I have another spell."

9

THE LADIES

The Spratford cousins never merely sat on their front porch. They occupied it like a fort. They claimed the space as if they were camped there in protest.

Claire's knitting clacked a rhythm on some new project that might've been another baby blanket or another scarf, neither one of which would ever see a baby or a neck. Daisy flipped through the pages of a *Better Homes and Gardens* that was published within the last six months or so. It was practically new. She'd only read it twice already.

A small transistor radio sat on the porch rail, its crooked antenna pointing compass-needle north. Mostly it played static. Sometimes it played snippets of NPR, where some host or another was discussing great engineering disasters of the 1970s.

Neither one of the ladies was listening. Daisy was narrating something else, something only she could hear. "That missing woman, she's made the news. Local stuff, out of Forto. They're talking about it now."

Claire clucked her tongue. "Good Lord help us all, if it makes it to the national news. We'll be overrun."

"If it doesn't happen this time, it'll happen someday. It's bound to."

"Don't be such a pessimist."

Daisy let the magazine fall into her lap, open to a page about restoring and using old shiplap. "Why not? We killed it, for the love of Christ. We killed it, and it *still* won't stop killing. If that's not something to be pessimistic about, then I just don't know."

"Well, the damn thing certainly slowed down a lot. Now he only takes one or two, once every now and again. It sure beats the bad old days." Her knitting became more measured. She counted stitches, mouthing a few like she was reading with her lips moving. Then she found her groove again. "Anything would beat the bad old days."

"These *are* the bad old days, dear. We're the tail end of them, you and I—and when we go, then there will be better days someplace, for somebody. Not here, though."

"You don't think?"

Daisy nodded solemnly. "We will die, and the town will die, and then maybe that ghost will starve to death when there's no one left to snare."

"Then what happens?" asked Claire.

"Whatever happens to things like that, on the other side of death." Daisy retrieved the magazine and pretended to read it while she listened to the smatterings of radio fuzz.

"Maybe *that* will be the end of it."

"I doubt it. It'll find some other place to haunt. Maybe it'll

keep on eating, until it's strong enough to come back to life. If that's the way it works."

Claire frowned, and dropped a stitch. "Why would *anything* work that way?"

"I don't know, and by the time it comes to that, I won't care. Neither will you. We've done the best we could, haven't we?" Daisy asked.

"That's the question of the century, isn't it? Or the question of last century? I can hardly keep up anymore."

For a minute or two, neither one of them brought up their godson. Then Daisy said, "We *will* have to do something about Cameron, one of these days."

Claire snorted. "Do something? Like what? We've already snuck a charm into every shoe heel, jacket seam, and pants cuff where he might not look. Safest boy in the county, if magic's what matters."

"Magic will only keep him so safe. We could talk to him, though. Even try to send him away, that's what else we can do. And if he means to stay here, we can arm him with information and the shotgun—but we shouldn't encourage him to do that. No matter how badly I want to keep him close. This time, this new woman who's gone missing . . . it makes me so scared for him. He's *got* to leave here, eventually—and when he does, he needs to go farther than the last bridge. He'll have to go to a real school, someday. We can call him homeschooled all we like, but God knows if he'll pass a GED."

"We should've worked harder on that. Ever since Miss Lisa passed," she mused, meaning the tutor they'd paid until she'd died when Cameron was twelve, "we've really fallen down on the job."

"She taught him good, though."

Claire's eyebrows knitted, lower and slower than her needles.

She frowned down at her work, not up at Daisy. "Good enough to get him gone, do you think? Good enough to set him up someplace else?"

"I hope so. Once we're gone, there's nothing for him here. If he stays, what if he's the next to go?"

"He won't be."

"You don't know that." She clenched the edges of the magazine's pages, rumpling them in her fist.

"As far as we can tell, he's not from around here. He'll be fine," Claire said to the needles, or to the blanket-in-progress, if that's what it was.

"The last few haven't been local folks, except for Netta's boy. That old rule must not apply anymore. Nobody's safe, coming or going. Cameron needs to leave and stay gone, as soon as this whole mess with the newest missing lady dies down. We have to talk to him. We'll use the news story as a way to begin."

"All right, if that's what you want. He'll be grown up soon enough, anyhow." She paused to pick out a stitch that didn't suit her. "But Lord help us, if this woman turns out to be any more newsworthy. Can you imagine if she makes it to CNN? Fox News? Staywater will be crawling with reporters, and rubber-neckers, and researchers, and heaven knows who else."

"So what? Let 'em come."

"So what," Claire muttered back in mockery. "So what, if we get out-of-towners who don't understand a thing about how the world works, down here. So what, if more of them go missing. So what, if we get overrun by police and FBI and whoever else. Is that what you want? What do you think will happen if authorities find that thing? What if someone figures out the truth—that there's never been no natural floods that take us by the dozen, and there's never been no serial killer, neither? You're daft. Everyone will think so."

"It runs in the family, or so I'm told." Daisy folded the magazine shut and listened to the crotchety transistor radio. NPR was running on about some terrible trestle failure that killed thirty people. She ignored that part. Closing her eyes, she folded her hands on the glossy cover in her lap and listened. "This woman was young and pretty, and probably white. People are getting interested in what happened to her. It sounds like they think the husband did it."

"Oh, that poor fellow. I wish there was something we could do for him."

"Like what?" She sounded honestly curious.

"I haven't the foggiest, unless you want to stuff a gris-gris into his pocket while he isn't looking."

"They've got him here in town someplace. The police didn't arrest him, but they told him to stay. I expect he's holed up at Maude's. Not like the town's overflowing with better options. Or any options."

Claire harrumphed and cast a scowl off the couch, down the steps, and all the way to the edge of the property where the dirt drive met the side street. "I expect you're right. Hey, look who's here."

Daisy followed her cousin's gaze and saw Netta Greely, spindly and haggard. She looked like the kind of woman who was rarely awake before sundown, all disastrous hair and smudged makeup. All clothes made for someone half her age, twenty years ago. Gleaned from the thrift shop in Forto, as likely as not. Her scuffed red heels sank into the sandy dirt at the driveway's end. She clutched herself like she was cold.

Netta didn't speak. She didn't wave. She didn't come closer.

"She won't do nothing," Daisy said. She knew it for a fact. She'd laid down the wards herself.

"She ought to know better by now. It's been long enough. She ought to move on, and go home, or just go someplace else."

"All it took was a little taste of the truth to send her around the bend," Daisy said with a sad shake of her head. "We should count it all as a lesson learned. We tried, but we couldn't help her. And after how she acted . . . she doesn't get any more help."

"You're right, and I've well and truly learned my lesson. If she comes near Cameron again, so help me Jesus she will live to regret it. She must've really scared the daylights out of him. You said he went to the dollhouse?"

Daisy nodded. "Desperate times, desperate measures. It worked out all right, though. I didn't even have to ask them to let him alone. I ought to send them a little gift, something to say thank you."

"That would be nice. What do they like?"

Claire considered her knitting. She set it aside and reached into the bag that held her extra needles and yarn. "Well, the big blond one likes bows. I could crochet her something. Maybe make a whole batch of bows for her and the rest of them, so they can share."

"You're always so thoughtful."

"Don't I know it." She gave Netta one last glance, and resolved to ignore her. She plucked a pretty ball of lavender yarn from the basket and held it up to the light. "This will be good. This will work just fine."

They let the subject drop and in time, Netta left. But the quiet that fell between the two cousins wasn't peaceful.

Eventually, Claire's hands stilled and the yarn sat limply in her lap. "Could be, it's something to do with us," she said softly. "Not just Staywater, and not just the swamp."

Daisy sighed. "Oh, sweetheart. Of course it is. I assume, it always has been."

10

PAULIE'S PIZZA

Only one piece of pizza remained on the scratched-up metal plate between Dave and Jess, and she wanted it. He waved to signal that he was finished, and she could have it. It wasn't very good, but it wasn't very bad, either, and it was the only pizza in town—so it was the pizza they ate at least three times a week before opening the bar every afternoon except for Sunday, on account of the old blue laws.

The pizza also wasn't very expensive, so that was another thing going for it. Most days, they could buy a medium pie for whatever was lying around in the bottom of Dave's tip jar.

Sometimes Jess picked up the tab, for show. The money all came from the same place, and it all went to the same places. It never really mattered who left the wad of small bills on the table.

"You know what we should do," Dave said, wiping his mouth on the brown paper towels that served as napkins.

"Go home and take a nap before opening the bar today?"

"Nah, not today. Today, we should do something productive." He tapped the folded-up newspaper lying beside the plate. The paper was provided by Paulie's Pizza, which kept a small stack in a wire rack beside the front door. It only had maybe ten or twelve pages. Not much went on in Forto, which was the nearest town big enough to produce any newspaper at all.

In Staywater, the town's tiny newspaper had gone out of business thirty years ago, so when it came to print information, you took what you could get.

"You want to . . . take up paper delivery?" she asked him, uncertainty all over her face.

"I want to help look for this missing woman." It wasn't precisely a lie. It was more like a test. He watched Jess closely, while trying to pretend he wasn't doing exactly that.

She used a shrug to limply toss her hair over one shoulder. Her eyes grazed the newspaper, whose front-page stories included a tax hike on waste pickup services, a mysterious power outage, and the suspicious disappearance of a woman named Melanie Bell. "Why would you want to do that? It says . . ." She ran through the scant lines that said very little, very briefly. "They've got Betty and Boomer on the case. And Kemp and Pickett, too. That's everybody who's qualified to go looking, right?"

"Maybe they need people who aren't so . . . *officially* qualified. They could probably use some extra hands. We know the area pretty well. If she wandered off and got lost, we might have better luck than the regular parties."

"What area?" she asked. "She disappeared miles from here."

"A couple of miles. Maybe three or four, I don't know—but it wasn't *that* far away. Someplace out on State Road 177, near the campground. But you knew that already. Her husband Titus said so, when Netta suggested it."

Jess sighed and pushed the paper away, toward the edge of the table—in case the lone server would pick it up with the rest of the trash. "Now I get it: You want to go out there because it sounds like the spot where I found you. Give or take."

He didn't argue with her. "Well, it's a coincidence, isn't it? I've been there a million times without finding anything. Maybe a million and one is the charm."

"When did you go without me? We've only been out there once or twice."

"I go every now and again. When I'm bored and sober." She almost always refused to go along with him, anytime he suggested it. He'd tried and tried. He'd given up.

"I don't know what you expect to find," she lied. She knew good and well what he was looking for. They both did. "Maybe this time, things will be different? Is that what you think?"

"Don't make fun."

"There's nothing fun about it," she complained. "Why can't you just let it go."

Dave shook his head and sat back in the ratty booth. The tears in its red vinyl were patched with duct tape. He picked at one curled edge without looking at it. "Because somebody attacked me, and I'd like to know who. I want to know why."

"That's not what you really think. You've made that pretty clear."

She had him there. He admitted as much when he said, "It's the only real answer, though. The only one anybody wants to chase. If I escaped a serial killer, hey, great. That's something you can sic a cop on."

"They did sic the cops on it. All of the cops in the county. But you didn't remember what had happened, and there was never any proof." She folded her arms and leaned back, mirroring his pose except for the tape-picking. "That's what you've always said, and I heard what you told that guy. You meant it, when you said there was no such thing as a Staywater serial killer."

"Yeah, I meant it. And I *do* remember bits and pieces. Scraps of things. Moments."

"Every time you talk about it, you say it different. You remember it different."

"No, I only talk about it different."

"You were hit on the head," she reminded him for the hundredth time. The thousandth. "You can't trust your memories. God, don't you remember?" she asked, as if she hadn't heard anything she'd said so far. "They thought you were the killer at first. Or they wondered if you might be."

"But then when Jimmy up and disappeared the next day, and I was still in the hospital."

She let out half a laugh that sounded wholly insincere. It sounded like some kind of deflection, but Dave didn't know what it meant. "That was thirteen years ago. It's *always* thirteen years between them, the people who go missing. It's been happening forever."

Dave frowned. "Christ, I guess you're right. I *have* been here that long. It was just supposed to be a week. Just another camping trip through the park."

Jess batted her eyelashes. "But then you met me."

He nodded. "Then I met you." He rose from the sticky seat and recycled one of his own tips, leaving a couple of bills on the table. "You don't have to come with me, if you don't want to. I didn't mean to badger you about it. You could go home and take a nap—if that's what you really want. I can drop you off."

She waffled uncertainly. "No . . . you don't *have* to go alone."

"Are you afraid I'll find something cool without you?"

"No, don't be silly." Jess made up her mind. "Forget it. I'll walk to the bar. You go do . . . whatever you want. Same as usual." She turned and left, letting the glass door swing shut behind her with a squeak and a click.

Paulie leaned out of the kitchen. "Everything okay out here?"

"Great." Dave took one last swig of his Coke and abandoned the red plastic glass on the table. "Just fucking great."

If Jess really hadn't wanted him to go poking around SR 177, she would've just taken the Jeep. Dave fished his keys out of his pocket and climbed up inside it, then sat in the driver's seat and banged his forehead gently on the steering wheel. He was tired. He was sober.

And something was wrong, whether or not his girlfriend wanted to talk about it.

He felt it all the way down to his toenails—and it had something to do with the pulse of energy that rattled the bar the day before. What the hell had it been, that earthquake or thunderbolt? That glitch in the matrix? What had it meant?

Deep down, he felt the answer so hard that he couldn't ignore it, not for trying. It was the sound of something breaking open, somewhere out on State Road 177 where somebody went missing, about once every thirteen years.

Dave jabbed the key into the ignition.

So he'd go and take a look. It wouldn't be like the first time. He wouldn't wake up in the road, with Jess right above him, pounding on his chest and breathing into his mouth. None of that would happen, because this time, somebody was already taken. The danger had passed, or so he told himself.

"There's a window to it," he speculated out loud. It wasn't terribly cold, but his breath fogged anyway. The chilly humidity of the persistent, annoying rain made everything feel more frigid than it was. "Whatever happens, there's a window . . . at least twenty-four hours. Maybe forty-eight."

He didn't know what time he'd passed out on the road. He didn't know what time Jess's cousin had gone missing. But the overlap couldn't be more than three days, max. Could it? He could always ask Netta. She'd know. She'd obsessed over the case for years, struggling to get justice for her son, or if nothing else, to find some sign of him.

Nah. He knew better than to ask that woman anything more in-depth than her drink order. All other queries led to straight-up madness.

He threw the Jeep into gear and pulled out into the town square, then took the turn to bring him back to the main road.

The state road.

There wasn't even a stoplight to mark the turn—just a sign saying that he should yield, if he knew what was good for him. He didn't bother. Nobody was coming, not in either direction. He could've thrown a picnic on the center line, and nobody would've been the wiser.

He leaned his foot on the gas, worked up to the forty-five-mile-an-hour speed limit, then crossed it. He cracked the windows to keep all the glass from going hazy, because the heater wasn't working very well. It didn't help much.

The forestry morphed into swampland gradually, then thoroughly—mossy oaks and maples thinning as the earth got wetter, and then the cypress took over. Mostly it was pond cypress, not bald cypress. Not much else could grow out there without succumbing to the damp and rot; and most of the trees that remained these days were newer, planted or recovered after logging stripped the rest out.

Here and there, an old giant would rear up above the canopy.

Here and there, something that seemed to be floating was swimming, and hunting.

Dave felt his blood pressure creeping upward. His face was flushed, and he was starting to sweat through his shirt. It was a concert tee from a band that broke up a decade ago, and he'd thrown a plaid flannel over it. The flannel under his pits was getting damp, too. But he was freezing. He could hardly feel his fingers, clenched around the steering wheel.

But this was just the same old road, two lanes, going east and west. He'd driven the strip a hundred times, a thousand times. A million, he'd told Jess. He'd stopped and gotten out of the vehicle and gone looking around, poking at the edges of the road as if the sandy gravel might tell him something.

The radio spat static, and he jumped.

The volume was turned all the way down. It shouldn't have made a sound. He hadn't even known it was on. He reached for the knob to punch it and turn it off. The static popped again and he hesitated, reaching instead to turn the volume up. The old-fashioned dial wasn't digital, and all you had to do was bump it to kick it off the station.

That's what must've happened, because it wasn't set to either of the two stations that came in clearly. One played all country all the time, and one was usually tepid Christian music. If you pressed the AM button, you might get talk radio. Then again, you might not.

The static's tone changed, and the little orange line that marked the dial's position slipped incrementally to the right.

Dave looked down at the radio and looked up at the road. The orange line wasn't really moving. It couldn't move unless the dial did and the dial wasn't moving. He watched it hard, three seconds at a time, his eyes jerking back and forth from the windshield.

The static found words, garbled and low. The words dragged

and stretched, broken down to their most basic parts. Consonants, sharp and clunky. Vowels, heavy and resonant. The line moved. It went past 92.3 and crept toward 93.0, then it slipped beyond that.

Dave wasn't sure what he was seeing, but he didn't doubt it. He could believe his own eyes, and his own ears, too. If he couldn't, he was no less crazy than Netta—who they'd kept at Chattahoochee for two whole years before cutting her loose and letting her straggle on home to Staywater.

The words sharpened. He could almost understand them.

A car horn approached loud and hard, reminding him that he was on the goddamn road. He grabbed the wheel and jerked it far enough to pull him out of oncoming traffic. The Jeep veered, swerved, and settled in the appropriate lane.

Dave's heart lurched, his throat dried up, and he gasped, "Betty." The dog was sitting in the passenger's seat, his great shaggy head hanging out the SUV window.

The search must not have lasted very long. Maybe they'd found the woman. Her body might have turned up, bobbing gently against a cypress knee. It might've been just a piece, just an arm or a leg. Alligators make gruesome meals, and a serial killer might've chopped her up to hide her better.

In years past there'd been talk of such a killer, lurking in the swamp at the edge of the park. It was the first thing Kemp had suggested all those years ago, when Dave sat shaking in the tiny police station, trying to explain that he had been driving . . . and then he *wasn't* driving. He was almost dead on State Road 177 when a waitress from a bar he frequented had appeared like magic, pushing on his chest and breathing for him, when he couldn't breathe by himself.

He'd known her face. It'd taken him a second or two to remember her name.

She was so pretty and so frightened. He was so grateful.

She'd picked him up and taken him into town, to the police station. She'd held his hand in hers for hours, sitting beside him in room after room. He'd barely known her at all, and in a single afternoon she'd become the most important person in his life.

Later, she told him that she'd loved him for ages, but it couldn't have been more than two or three ages. He'd only passed through a couple of times before he came to Staywater, lost an hour, nearly went crazy, and stayed. Had she flirted with him, when he'd asked for a drink and some onion rings? Or had she only been polite and hunting for a good tip?

If you asked Jess, it'd been love at first sight. If you asked Dave, he would've set the timeline a little later.

He would've called it love, though. There were lots of different kinds of love.

Sergeant Kemp's patrol car followed behind Betty and Boomer. Kemp was alone in the vehicle.

But behind him, maybe a quarter of a mile, was Pickett with a passenger. In the short flash before they passed one another on either side of the dotted center line, Dave saw the guy from the bar the night before. He looked like he was about to puke his guts out—or else he'd just finished doing so.

The radio hummed. It coughed.

Its static left the console and rose up like a cloud. Dave saw stars. They crowded into his vision until he let his foot off the gas and traded it for the brake. The Jeep spun in a ragged 180, stopping halfway on the shoulder and halfway on the road—facing back the way he'd come.

He fought to catch his breath and shake the stars away.

The radio didn't have any music. It only had a voice, whispering harsh and slow.

. . . the things I take . . .

Dave flailed for the knob, but it moved under his fingers like a planchette on a Ouija board. It found the spot it wanted, and it spoke again.

. . . are mine to keep . . .

"But you didn't take me. You didn't catch me. You didn't keep me," he said to the radio, or to whoever was speaking through it. Whatever was speaking. He didn't know if he was right or not, or if the speaker could hear him, but he swore at it anyway. He threw the Jeep back into gear and said, "Fuck this."

But as Dave sped into Betty and Boomer's wake, back toward Staywater, the voice rasped again. *The things I take are mine to keep.*

Then the signal was lost to the swamp, drowned along with everything else that got too close to the water.

11

THE STATION

Titus sat with his head in his hands, staring down at a stainless steel table in Staywater's three-room police station. There was alleged to be a police chief somewhere, or a sheriff, or however it worked in little out-of-the-way places like these; but Titus hadn't seen anyone except for Kemp and Pickett, who treated him with cautious politeness and referred to their absent superior only as "the boss."

Pickett was on the phone to a reporter from a newspaper. Titus didn't know which one. Did Staywater have a paper? Surely not. It barely had enough occupants to support a bar.

Kemp was sitting across the table from him, sighing heavily and filling out paperwork with a number-two pencil that'd been sharpened so many times, it was hardly as long as a cigarette. When he got to a stopping place, he put it down. It rolled toward the table's edge, but he caught it and set it into the crease of a folder, where it stayed. "Listen, son. I don't know what happened back there, and you don't seem able to tell me. But if there's anything you want to say about your wife, and what happened . . ."

"I've told you everything." His voice echoed back at him, bouncing off the metal. It was roughly polished. It showed him a vague reflection: the loose oval of his face, and dark spots where his eyes ought to be. "I don't even know how many times."

"More than a couple. Hey, I forgot to tell you: Your mother-in-law called us back this morning."

"Melanie's mother?"

"You said she lived in Jacksonville, and you didn't have her number. It wasn't that hard to get," he said. "Three seconds on Google turned her up. Retired schoolteacher. Widowed. Volunteers as a secretary for the local Methodist church."

"Yeah, she's . . ." He'd only met her twice. "Lovely."

"I got the impression that she and your wife weren't very close. She didn't use the word 'estranged,' but I could almost hear it in her voice."

"That's fair. Melanie found her . . ." This time he picked a more accurate word than "lovely." "Stressful. She's a nice lady, but spending time with her is kind of like dealing with a big toddler. You know what I mean? Always has to be the center of attention. Always has to have her way."

"Did Melanie take after her?"

"What? How do you mean?" Titus looked up, and let his hands drop to the table. It was cool under his palms. Halos of fog and sweat appeared around his fingers.

"Was your wife like a big toddler? Did she need to be the center of attention?"

"No, she wasn't like that. She was pretty easygoing." He realized he was using past tense. Kemp had started it. "I mean, she *is* pretty easygoing. Hell, she was game to spend our honeymoon paddling around in the swamp. Does that sound like—" He laughed briefly and uncertainly. "Does it sound like somebody who's high-maintenance? Because she's not."

"How long have you been married, Mr. Bell?"

"Please, stop doing that. Just call me Titus." It finally occurred to him to ask, and this was as good a moment as any. "Wait. Do I need a lawyer or something?"

"We're just talking. But if you want a lawyer, go ahead and call one. It's up to you."

"But do I *need* one?"

"Did you do anything that might require a lawyer to defend you?"

He shook his head, and it swam. "No, but I've told you that, too."

"Then we'll just keep on talking, if that's okay with you. Now tell me, son: How *long*," Kemp asked again, "have you been married?"

Titus gave up. It wouldn't hurt him to answer, and it couldn't help them find Melanie—but he was out of ideas. She'd vanished into thin air, wherever that was. "Only a week. We got married last Sunday."

"Fancy event? Her mother said she wasn't invited. She didn't even know you'd tied the knot."

"Nobody was invited. We went to the courthouse and made it official. We'd been together for a long time. It'd been . . . long enough. We didn't need an audience. We told a few friends, but only after the fact."

The old cop nodded. "You finally hit that point, eh? Had to either get married, or break up?"

"Pretty much."

"How long had you been together?"

"We were on again, off again for a couple of years. Before we really settled down together." He flapped one hand sadly. "You know how it goes. It took us a while to make it stick, so I guess it depends on how you count it."

Kemp moved the pencil and opened the folder that'd been sitting next to his paperwork. "But you've been together since before February of two years ago. Isn't that correct?"

Titus was confused, but only for an instant. He knew where this line of questioning was about to go, and he felt his face go hot with embarrassment. "Since before that, yeah. We were living together by then."

"You two had a little incident in Nashville, didn't you?"

What they'd had was a screaming fight. Melanie had broken every wineglass they owned. Titus had thrown every book and broken a few CDs when he flung them at the wall. "Don't say it like that. We didn't try to stab each other—we just had an argument, and the argument got loud."

"And your neighbors called the police."

He took a deep breath and let it out into his hands. He put them back down on the table and met Kemp's eyes. "She threw her purse at me, and I ducked. It hit the TV, and the TV fell off the wall. Look, our downstairs neighbors were nosy as shit. We couldn't walk in the front door without them banging a broom handle on the ceiling or calling the building managers to complain about us."

"I've had neighbors like that," Kemp confessed. "Were you and your then-girlfriend noisy, or did you try to be considerate to those who lived around you?"

"It wouldn't have mattered. We were considerate," he amended. "We tried to be, at first. After a while we kind of gave up. They were going to complain anyway. So, yeah—we got into a fight, and the people downstairs called nine-one-one when they could've just come upstairs and knocked on the door. By the time the cops showed up, we were two drinks into an apology. We were online, looking up new TVs when they knocked on the door."

"What was the fight about?"

"I honestly don't even remember." It'd been about her ex, Gary. Or else it'd been about Titus's ex, Tamara. Those two people were the main reason for all the "on again, off again" in that first year or two. It'd dragged into a third year, but they'd always pretended that it hadn't.

Kemp kept pressing. "Melanie told the officer on the scene that you'd been arguing about her ex-boyfriend."

"Jesus, somebody wrote that down? Okay then, I guess that's what we were fighting about."

"Did you fight about your exes often?" He retrieved the pencil, but didn't start writing. He twirled it between his fingers, and tapped the eraser on the steel table.

Titus nodded tiredly. "We used to. But we're over it. We've been over it for ages. That's why we went ahead and got married. Fresh start, and all. We were finished with all the old bullshit."

"So things were good?"

"We were newlyweds. Things were great."

Behind him, Pickett hung up the phone and said, loud enough to signal that he wished to be heard, "Welp."

Kemp looked over Titus's shoulder and asked, "Who was that?"

"The Forto paper again."

"What'd you tell them?"

He shrugged. "I told them we haven't found Mrs. Bell, or any sign of her. I said it about fifty different ways, and I still don't think they were satisfied."

Titus knew the feeling. "What do you mean, it was them *again*?"

"Oh, they call every other day, just about. Sniffing around for stories. They've got this reporter named Leslie, and she gets on the phone, and she calls everybody for fifty miles to see if anyone, anyplace, has any news worth printing." He put his phone in his pocket, and patted it like he was sending it to bed. "Leslie's relentless, she is. She does good work."

"You told her about Melanie yesterday?" Titus asked.

"Uh-huh. I told her we had Betty and Boomer on the case."

Titus sighed. "For all the good it did us."

Kemp frowned. "Hey now. Don't give them two any grief. I'd bet money on that pair, against any big-city K-9 unit."

"That's not what I meant. I'm sorry," he apologized quickly—so quickly it probably sounded like he was lying, but he wasn't this time. "I only meant, they didn't find anything. I feel like we wasted their time."

"Oh, you didn't waste Boomer's time. He's always happy to be on the hunt, whether he finds anything or not. And if Boomer's happy, Betty's happy. They'll try again, later this afternoon and tomorrow. They want to see your wife found. Not as much as you do, I'm sure, but they're a dedicated team."

"Nobody wants her back as much as I do." He poured every ounce of sincerity left in his body into it. Jesus, he meant every bit of it.

Titus would have given literally anything—anything at all—to have her walk through the door of the Staywater Police Station, complaining about a headache from some crazy swamp gas that knocked them both out. She could say she'd been wandering around, lost and confused. She could tell them she'd been abducted by aliens, and they'd left Titus behind while they probed her on the mother ship.

She could say anything, as long as she showed up and *said* it.

He would leap out of his chair and run to her, pick her up,

spin her around. He would be a real husband, a better version of himself. He'd listen and learn, he'd negotiate and compromise. He would do it all right, and do it all forever.

If she would just come back.

She'd been gone a whole day, almost—but only a whole day. It was two days, wasn't it? *48 Hours,* that's what the TV show was called. When somebody goes missing, you have about forty-eight hours to find them. After that, their odds of turning up drop to slightly better than "none."

Titus felt sick. He and Melanie were supposed to be in a cabin, drinking wine and fucking and watching TV—if the cabins had TVs in them. They were supposed to have TVs, he thought. Some of them, at least. He'd reserved the nicest kind of cabin they offered. He thought it'd look like civilization to Melanie.

He knew better, when he made the booking. He knew she didn't want to do it, even though it was her idea. He even knew that it wasn't her idea, not really. It was *his* idea. It was something he'd wanted to do, and he thought he could convince her to like it, if she'd give it a chance.

He was a selfish shit. Now that he could admit it, he could hate himself for it. He'd probably never deserved her in the first place, and he just couldn't stand to lose her like this.

"Mr. Bell?" Kemp asked, watching his face intently.

"I'm sorry, I'm having . . . not a spell, don't worry. But I feel like I'm going to puke again, and I just want my wife back. Why can't we find her?" he asked plaintively. "Where the hell could she have gone?"

"Son, if I knew that, we wouldn't be here."

"I know, I know. I can't . . . I can't even figure out what a clue would look like, if it was staring me in the face. I don't know where she could have gone, and I don't know why she would've gone there. I don't know what happened."

"Now you're just saying the same thing, over and over again."

"What else *is* there to say? Did you guys even talk to the park rangers? Is there any chance she showed up at the cabins?"

"We've been in touch half a dozen times since you called us yesterday. They've got people combing the park for any sign of her, you can rest assured of that."

"Right now I can't rest at all. Can't sleep, can't hardly eat. Oh shit," he realized. "I should probably eat something. All I've had today is coffee, and a little bit of muffin. And I puked up the muffin on the side of 177, so I don't know if that counts."

"You mostly got it out the window," Pickett said. "I appreciate that."

Titus sighed and tasted half-digested blueberries in the back of his throat. "I'm still sorry about it. You should let me help clean it up."

"No, no. I've got it. You know, we've got a pizza joint a couple blocks that way." He cocked a thumb. "Paulie's."

Titus turned the idea over in his head. He couldn't tell if the idea of greasy mom-and-pop pizza sounded amazing, or if it might kill him. He could get a soda, though. That would be something. "I could go for some pizza. I think. So . . ." He looked back and forth, between the two officers. "Is that it? I should go and get some pizza? You're letting me walk out of here?"

"You're not under arrest," Kemp said drily. "You can come and go as you like. We'll keep up the search for your wife, whether you're here or there, or at Dave's, or Paulie's, wherever. We've got your number."

Titus was confused, wondering about his cell phone. Oh

yeah, it was in the hotel room. He'd forgotten it, in the rush of getting out the door while successfully wearing pants. "You've got it, but my phone's back at Maude's. I'll grab it and keep it on me." Something popped into Titus's head. "Speaking of being out and about—where's my car?"

"It's in Forto, at the impound. We don't have a tow truck anymore, so they had to take it," Pickett explained.

"But when do I get it back? And um . . . do you guys have a map, or something? Of the town? I know it's not very big, but I don't know where anything is."

Kemp said, "I'll get somebody to drive the car back down today, if they're done processing it. If they're not, I wouldn't get too worried about it. You can walk to everything in Staywater. Here, I'll draw you a map myself." It only took a minute, as he wrote on the back of a blank intake form. "Here's Maude's, and here's Dave's—right down the street, but you know that already. There's Paulie's, if you want pizza. This is the station, right here. . . ." He labeled it accordingly. He noted a few other points of interest. "Don't tap on the windows at the department store; those old mannequins are weird as shit. Turn right at the dog in the tree, if you get lost and want to go back toward the town square. His name is Chuckie, and he's blind as a stone. But he likes to climb for some reason, and nobody stops him."

"A dog . . . in a tree . . ."

"Shih tzu, or whatever. Fluffy white-and-black son of a bitch. He won't bother you if you don't bother him. Like I was saying, if you're lost, face the tree and go right. You'll wind up right back here on the square." He circled the courthouse. Then he said to Pickett, "Go ahead and run him back to his room so he can get his phone. Drop him off at Paulie's, and come on back to the station. We've got work to do. As for you, Mr. Bell . . . we will be in touch."

Titus accepted the offer of a ride, swung by Maude's to get his phone, and climbed out of the car at Paulie's Pizza—where he was released on his own recognizance. He didn't know what to do with himself, so he followed his grumbling, sour stomach and ordered a couple of slices. Plain cheese. That's what sounded safest, and it was the only option that didn't make him want to puke all over again.

The pieces arrived on a metal plate, with a roll of brown paper towels to serve as napkins. He stared them down and sipped gingerly at a Diet Coke, trying to find the will to eat. He hardly noticed it when the door opened and a woman stepped inside.

He saw her out of the corner of his eye, and thought she looked familiar. Upon a second look, he remembered her from the bar.

She didn't wait for an invitation. She approached his table, tottering on red heels and weak ankles. "I'm Netta Greely. Remember me?"

"Yes ma'am. From last night."

She seemed pleased. "Good. Has anybody warned you about me yet? I mean properly warned, not that half-ass finger-wagging at the bar."

"What? Who? No. Should they?"

She slid into the other half of the booth. "No, but I thought they might. Kemp don't think too much of me, and the feeling's mutual."

"I'm sorry, do you . . . are we . . . ?" He stalled out. "I'm just trying to eat."

"It's been a hard day for you, I can see it. A hard night last night, too. I don't want to upset you or worry you any further, but you might as well know: It ain't going to get any easier." She pulled out a cigarette and bounced it on the table.

"Can you . . . do you smoke in here?"

She put it on her lower lip, where it stuck like magic. "Paulie won't stop me."

He tried it another way. "Do you *have* to smoke in here?"

She stared at him, a green plastic Bic in hand. Her eyes were green, too. The remnants of silver-gray eyeshadow still dusted the lids above them. "I won't light it, just for you. How about that?"

"Thank you."

"But I won't leave, either. That's the deal."

He picked up one slice and thought about putting it in his mouth, but didn't. "So what do you want?" He took a chance, and took a bite after all.

"I want you to know: They're not going to find your wife."

He stopped chewing. The crust had turned to putty in his mouth. He swallowed it anyway. "You said that last night. Why would you go out of your way to say it again?"

"Because it's true, and it's not right to let you think any different. They won't find her, and you already know it—somewhere in the pit of your stomach, or the back of your mind. Wherever you feel things like that. I usually feel it somewhere in my throat, but that's just me."

He sucked some soda through the red-and-white straw. It struggled to wash down the lone bite of pizza. "But I *have* to find her."

"Or what? Don't look at me like that, it's a serious question. I asked it myself, for years and years after my son went missing. What's the worst thing that will happen, if she never turns up? Oh, there could be lots of bad things, I know that," she answered her own question. "The cops might decide you did something to her, and arrest you. They won't find a body so you probably won't go to jail, but that's a cloud that will hang over your head . . . and oh, honey. It'll follow you all of your life."

"Stop talking."

"No, not yet." The cold cigarette bobbed with every twist of her lips. "Something else that might happen—it happened to me, and it's happened to other people—is that the grief makes you crazy, and they'll send you away to get better. It won't work, but you'll learn how to get along and act like you've got all your marbles together, even though that's not what they had in mind when they put you there. Then again, maybe you won't go through all that. Maybe you just lost the love of your life, your one true soul mate, the light in your darkness, forever and ever, amen. If you've got a gun, you can do it quick. If you've got pills, you can do it sweet."

"Jesus Christ, lady . . . I'm not—"

"But I'll tell you what the worst of it is, if you want to hear it. Shit, I'll tell you even if you *don't*. The worst part is that *you're never going to know*. That's what really does a number on your head. In the end, that's what will send you to the bullets or the bottles."

His protest was weak and soft. "They're going to find her. *We're* going to find her."

Netta barely heard him, so she pretended she hadn't. "If there's any truth to find, you'll never catch more than a glimpse of it. You'll find pieces, here and there, if you look long enough and hard enough. But if you've got any sense, you'll ignore those hints. You'll pack up your shit and leave, as soon as the police'll let you. Don't wait until it feels decent to give up the search. Just *go*, get back to your old life before this place gets its hooks in you. Run, before you get stuck here like me, or like that poor bartender."

"The . . . the bartender?"

"David has a story to tell, if you can drag it out of him. Lord knows I've tried, for all the good it ever did me. He was almost one of the missing ones—but something happened. Somebody saved him, or something changed its mind, and took somebody else. I told you, you'll never know the whole truth. But something happened to him, like I bet it happened to you."

"What do you know about what happened to me? I didn't tell anyone but the police, unless Pickett told that woman at the paper in Forto."

"Leslie? Oh, he gossips with her like they're a couple of old hens."

"Oh . . . okay. Wait. Did they print anything in the Forto paper? About Melanie and me?"

She snorted, and the cigarette bobbed free. She caught it before it hit the table, snatching it between her fingers. "They didn't say jack shit about *you*, darlin'. They didn't say much about your wife, either—except that she was gone. That's not how I know you crossed the seventh bridge."

If Titus had been working on another bite of pizza, he would've choked on it. Instead he gagged on the idea, on the words that now hung in the air. He coughed, and coughed again. "What? Jesus, what?"

"The *bridge*, dumbass. It caught you, didn't it?"

"There was . . . there was a bridge, yeah."

"There are a lot of bridges," she scoffed. "*You* crossed the bad one."

He racked his brain trying to figure out how many bridges they'd driven across before the strange one with a single lane and a warning sign.

Netta did the math for him. "If you take State Road 177 from east to west, you'll cross six bridges between the interstate exit and the park entrance. If you're going from west to east . . . once in a while, you might cross seven. But you better hope not."

"That doesn't make any sense. That can't be true."

"It is true. There's a little bridge, and everyone who crosses it pays a toll." She popped the cigarette back into her mouth, and flicked the lighter, even though she'd told him she wouldn't. She held the flame-tip up to her mouth and said, "Trust me, it's happened before. Now finish up your pizza. I'll take you to the library, and show you."

"I don't want to go anywhere with you."

"Well, you're *gonna*."

12

Cameron moped and moped hard. He moped like nobody else would do it right.

He lay on his back on his bed, staring at the ceiling with its water stains and cracks, not looking for patterns or answers. He stared because he was grounded, and it wasn't very different from not being grounded, to be honest—but when he wasn't grounded he could leave the house, and that was something. He could go to Dave's and lovingly pester Jess. He could go to the town square and buy a slice of pizza, or get a soda. He could find a copy of the Forto paper and see what was happening out there in the big wide world. Or within a fifty-mile radius of the small narrow one.

He knew that *something* was going on out there. He'd heard Daisy and Claire talking about it downstairs over knitting and tea, and he knew it involved that lady who'd gone missing. He'd asked them about it, and they'd told him to go back upstairs and think about what he'd done. News was for the ungrounded.

It had something to do with what had happened the night before, when he was at Dave's. The *push* had happened, and then later on, that man had arrived. His wife was missing, and he wanted to drink.

It was all related, Cameron just knew it.

He knew it because when he mentioned it, his godmothers had clammed up and shooed him off. "*Post hoc, ergo propter hoc.*" That's what Claire had said. It meant, "After this, therefore because of this." It was a fallacy, that's what they'd told him.

Now they were outside, working in the garden again.

He could hear them out there. Daisy digging in the dirt, squirting aphids off her tomatoes with a spray bottle full of soap water, and stabbing small pink things with her spade. Claire sitting on the porch in her sun hat, even though it wasn't remotely sunny.

Their chatter drifted up to the second floor, to Cameron's room. It wafted through the window, cracked halfway open to catch the breeze. (Even in the damp chill, the room felt stuffy. It was either open the window or suffocate.) He heard about one word out of every three, but he could tell they didn't know even that much was reaching him.

They were talking about him. They were talking about the missing woman. They were talking about the push.

Absolutely mad with boredom, Cameron rolled off the bed and stepped softly to the window, to see if he could hear them any better. There was virtually no difference, so he gave up and wandered out to the hallway, taking great care to keep from hitting any of the squeaky floorboards.

If they caught him, he'd just say he was going to the bathroom.

He passed the bathroom on the right, and kept going.

At the end of the hall was Claire's old bedroom. Five or six years ago, she'd moved downstairs to share the big master with Daisy. Call it arthritis or call it old age, but she had trouble getting up and down the steps. Now she almost never came up there anymore. It was too much trouble.

Cameron stopped and listened. Daisy laughed, and Claire said something in response. They hadn't budged from their preferred spots outside.

He'd been inside Claire's old room before; he'd helped her relocate everything she wanted, when she made the big move to the first floor. But now the door was always closed. He supposed it was full of "everything that was left over," or just storage for all the stuff they couldn't stand to throw away.

He wouldn't go so far as to call the ladies "hoarders," but that was mostly because there was no place to shop, and they weren't terribly mobile. If they'd been able to go out and find things to squirrel away—or if they'd had the internet, and a reliable postal service—the place would've surely been packed from floor to ceiling with magazines, knickknacks, mildewing books, candles, doilies, and all the other things that tended to accumulate in the corners.

". . . you know where Netta went."

His ears perked up. He held very still.

". . . poor man. . . . make it worse."

Netta's son had gone missing, too. It was a long time ago. Cameron had been a little thing, three or four years old, but he still had dim, anxious memories of the big fight. He remembered Netta coming to the Spratford house and screaming until Daisy'd cocked a shotgun and blown a hole in the porch roof to chase her off. Cameron had covered his ears and closed his eyes, and he screamed even louder than the madwoman who'd surely come to kill his godmothers.

In retrospect, he doubted Netta had ever intended to kill anybody. She was batty, but she was harmless . . . which didn't explain why he'd run from her, when she cornered him at Dave's. When Claire and Daisy had asked him why, he didn't have a good answer for them.

It could've been the good answer was simple: Cameron dimly remembered a big fight and a shotgun, from when he was very small. The old recollection had tickled the back of his brain and he'd panicked, that was all.

Now that he thought about it (for the first time in a decade, at least), he wondered what that fight had really been about. It must have happened right around the time of the last push. Netta must've thought the ladies knew something, or could help her find her son.

He wondered why they hadn't. Maybe they'd tried, and Netta simply hadn't liked their answers.

Next time he saw her, he could suck it up and ask her. Sometime at Dave's, in broad daylight, in front of God and everybody. Or . . . surrounded by people, if not during the day. Dave's didn't open until four. Not that he was afraid of crazy old Netta.

Fine. He was a little afraid of her. Crazy, sad, or grieving, you couldn't tell. There was just something about the woman. He was trying to figure out what it might be, when inside Claire's old room, something rustled.

He heard it like a murmur, a whisper spoken through paper.

It came and went.

There was a cadence to it, like someone was singing or calling in the distance. He thought about Jess, calling the stray cats behind Dave's—gently whistling and clucking to lure them out for scraps. It had the rhythm of that friendly, helpful noise.

"Probably a rat," he mused. But rats didn't softly summon, did they?

If he'd honestly thought it was a rat, he would have never taken those extra steps forward—still artfully dodging the squeakiest of floorboards. If there was any chance it might be a rat, he would've gone back to his room and shut the door, his heart pounding. He'd feel stupid for doing that, but that's how it would go.

He hated rats, and was scared to death of them. He was a little afraid of snakes, too, but Freddie-under-the-porch ate rats. Freddie was okay, as far as Cam was concerned. He was practically the patron saint of Hazelhurst.

The knob on Claire's former door was a round metal bulb with an ornate lock plate. He touched it, and swiftly drew back. It was so cold that his fingers nearly stuck, like a tongue on a winter pole. They left behind prints of dark, frosted smudges.

He put his hand inside his sweater pocket. Using the wool for a mitt, he tried again.

It wasn't locked. Nothing was ever locked in the Spratford house, because no one ever opened doors when they shouldn't. No one ever trespassed, and no one ever snooped. Not on the Spratford cousins. Not even Cameron.

Usually.

"It isn't rats," he reminded himself as he turned the knob. He could face literally anything but rats with calm confidence, he was sure of it.

The ladies remained outside, chattering about an old recipe in *Good Housekeeping,* or whatever it was they chatted about when they were finished gossiping about the scant remaining residents of Staywater.

He pushed the knob, and the door creaked open six or seven inches until he met resistance. Something faint but firm was pushing back. Definitely not a rat. Unless it was an enormous rat, and Cameron didn't believe in enormous rats. He simply refused to.

He put his head up to the opening and looked inside.

The room was packed. It overflowed with furniture, paperbacks, Christmas ornaments, commemorative plates, monogrammed dish towels that matched nobody's initials, stacks of mail that had been opened but never discarded, sets of sheets and blankets still wrapped in plastic, small pillows, drinking glasses with logos from gas stations, novelty ashtrays, and so many big-eyed ghosts that Cameron couldn't count them all.

The dead were crammed shoulder-to-shoulder, chin-to-neck, elbow-to-ribs.

The room wouldn't have held six living people standing shoulder-to-shoulder in the piles of junk, but it must have held at least thirty-five or forty specters—all of them a soft, milky gray except for their eyes. They were crammed together, overlapping like shadows that bled together, one into the next. Their eyes were all a few shades darker, just sooty pits in the middle of their faces, and they stared back at Cameron from every corner.

When he craned his neck to look behind the door, he saw at least three more spirits squished together, pressing against it and preventing him from coming inside. They must have had some density after all, though not very much.

"Oh shit," he exclaimed with as little volume as possible.

Slowly he attempted to withdraw and shut the door, but a spectral hand pulled it open away from him. The ghosts moved aside somehow, making room for the boy to enter.

The pale hand waved him forward.

Cameron did as it suggested, and the ghosts closed the door behind him with the same quiet caution he'd used to open it.

He couldn't hear Claire and Daisy anymore. His ears didn't have room for anything except the pounding throb of his heart, which was beating so hard, so high, that it felt like he'd only just swallowed it a minute ago—and it'd stuck in his throat.

He'd seen ghosts before. Everybody in Staywater knew at least a couple, and most everyone was on friendly terms.

This was different.

These ghosts were not clear enough to be mistaken for the living like dear old Karl, who haunted Dave's. These ghosts were pale and feeble, wearing old clothes like the ones he'd seen in *I Love Lucy* reruns on the old black-and-white TV. Men in hats, ladies with tiny waists and full skirts.

No. Not all of them.

Upon a closer look, there was more variety than he thought. He couldn't place the ladies with the small hats, or the men in large fur coats. He didn't know what uniforms a couple of the fellows were wearing—if they were from the army or navy, or what war they might have fought in.

"What . . . what are you doing here?" he asked the assembled group in a baffled whisper. He tried not to move. He didn't know where the loud floorboards were in Daisy's room, and he didn't want to give himself away.

Meeting.

Conspiring.

Hiding.

He couldn't tell who was saying what. All of their mouths moved, but none of them spoke out loud. He heard them between his ears. "I don't understand," he said.

A tall, thin woman in a kimono blouse and a soft wool cap came forward. She held out her hand, like she wanted Cameron to take it, and he tried—but he felt only the slightest resistance, as if she were made from puffs of air. He let his fingers melt through hers, and then he let her guide him to a box beside the abandoned bed. All the other ghosts recoiled, making room. He didn't know why they went to the trouble. He could've dashed through them all as easily as the paper banner at the end of a race.

They were only being polite, he supposed. He could be polite in return.

He knelt beside the box and lifted the lid. A wisp of dust rose up, accompanied by flakes of mold and a whiff of mothballs. "What's this?" he asked them. He looked around, and met their pallid faces, but nobody spoke again. "It looks like old paper. Like . . . newspapers and stuff."

The woman in the cap nudged his shoulder, and pointed at the papers.

"Okay, I'll . . . see what we've got here. These are from . . ." He picked up the top edition of *The Forto News Report*. "The late 1970s, I guess. Great pants, dude," he said to a man on the front page, who wore big, swinging bell bottoms. According to the caption, he was a hiker who'd narrowly survived a terrific flood back in '66.

"Flood?" He picked up the paper, and scanned the first paragraph. In 1979, four people had gone missing, even though there wasn't a flood that year. "Well, this is all before my time." The second paragraph went on to bemoan the event, which had become a bit of a tradition—prompting fears of a spree killer on the loose. But if there was a single bright spot to be noted, it was how low the body count was. This time.

"This time?"

Another woman came forward—this one with long, straight hair and jeans like the guy in the news photo. She wound up her hand, like she wanted him to keep reading.

"Okay, I'll keep . . . going. . . ." His eyes were already getting ahead of his mouth, and the third paragraph referenced a flood in 1966. This flood had killed eleven people. At this point, Cameron couldn't exactly skip the fourth paragraph. It went on to cite massive swamp overflows that went back to the nineteenth century, killing over three hundred people in total. At least. Before that, nobody knew. It wasn't until 1849 that people had started to write about it.

"No white people around, I guess," he mused aloud. "Probably the Indians knew. They always know the important stuff before the white people." He looked up, and didn't see any Native representatives of the afterlife. "Unless they left? Before the white people got here? If I knew the place was going to flood every few years, I sure as crap wouldn't live here. Man, this is weird. How come I never heard about any of this?"

"Because some things are best forgotten." Daisy stood behind him.

Cameron had never heard the door open, but it was open all the same. He froze, the old clippings rustling in his hand.

Daisy looked around the room. The ghosts all nodded, and she nodded back. "We thought it was safe to forget. We thought it was *better* to forget. But we've been wrong before, haven't we?"

He couldn't tell if she was asking him or the assembled spirits—so he didn't respond. He only said, "I'm sorry. I didn't mean to snoop, but I heard a noise . . . they called me in here."

"I know. Or I believe you, anyway. I've been trying to ignore them for the last couple of days. Well," she said loudly, dramatically. She followed it with a deep breath and a deeper sigh. "You'd better come downstairs, Cameron. Get the bottle of Jack you pretend you don't sip out of, and join us on the porch. We're a bit overdue for a talk."

13

THE NOT-A-LIBRARY

"I don't have a car, and Kemp didn't put the library on the map . . ." Titus protested.

Netta shook her head. "You don't need a car, and we ain't got no maps. What map are you talking about?"

"Kemp drew me one, so I could find my way around . . . see the sights. You know." He left a couple of dollars on the table and wiped his hands on the last clean paper towel of the roll.

"That was nice of him. What he put on it? Thirsty's, Maude's, this place . . ."

"Pretty much. There was something about a dog in a tree, too."

"You mean Chuckie." Netta pushed the door open and stepped out onto the sidewalk. "There's not a lot to see out here.

If I'd drawn you a map, I would've left the library off, too. It's not even really a library anymore."

He followed in her wake. "Then . . . what is it?"

"A dark building with a bunch of books rotting inside it. Come on, I'll show you. It's right over here." She gestured broadly at the far side of the square, where most of the shop fronts were empty, and there was nobody else on the street.

Titus didn't have any better ideas, so he followed Netta out the door.

She led him past the courthouse and around the next block, where a scrapyard looked as abandoned as everything else—but a dozen cars sat rusted and rotted beside a small building.

Next was a department store window that was so fogged over with dust that the mannequins within looked like ghosts from the 1970s. The dresses reminded Titus of the flowy, lacy Gunne Sax things his mom liked to wear when he was a kid. He'd seen her in pictures, looking like she lived on a prairie and churned butter for funsies.

Netta saw him looking at the window and paused to squint through the gunked-up glass. "Oh, that's nice."

"What's nice?"

"The one on the left, there. She's got the purple dress on, again. She likes that one."

He didn't get it. "What? Does someone change their clothes? They look like they've been that way for years."

"The shop's been closed since 1979. Mona's son went missing, and she cracked up. Closed the store one day and went home."

"People go missing here a lot, don't they?"

"They used to." She peered wistfully at the three woman-shaped bits of plaster in their vintage garb. "People used to think we had a serial killer. That's what they tried to tell me, when I spent so long and tried so hard to find out what became of my

Jimmy . . . before I learned enough of the truth to quit trying so hard. Poor Mona." She shook her head with sympathy. "I don't think anyone's seen her since my Jimmy was a baby."

"What happened to her?"

"Like I told you: She went home. Far as I know, that's where she is today. Probably dead by now."

Titus was appalled, and he didn't care to hide it. "Why doesn't someone go check on her?"

"People tried, at first."

"Why only at first?"

"Because she had her dead husband's guns, and she liked to use them to chase people off the porch. The first folks who tried to bring her casseroles or comfort . . . they got shot at for their trouble. She holed up, and told everyone to leave her alone. After a while, that's what they did. It's a matter of self-preservation, is all. Let her mind her own business, I guess."

"Even if she dies? Alone in an empty house?"

"That's up to her now, ain't it? Anyhow, the store's been just like this, ever since. Except sometimes the ladies swap out their clothes. This one here, her favorite is the purple dress. That one there," she indicated the middle, "usually wears these goofy yellow pants, but I guess she felt like a change. The one on the end, she's an exhibitionist. Once in a while she puts on panties, but otherwise she'd rather go stark."

"Who does that to them? Who changes them out, if the shop's been closed for so long?"

She scoffed at him, like she couldn't imagine fielding a dumber question from anyone, anywhere. "Nobody does. Those girls are on their own."

Maybe this wasn't such a good idea, Titus considered. Well, she'd asked aloud if anybody'd warned him about her. Maybe this was her special brand of crazy, something past the acceptable bounds of ordinary small-town Southern madness. He made a conscious decision to shrug it off—yet remain wary—and then he let it go. Netta was already finished thinking and talking about the mannequins, so Titus followed behind her as she walked away.

He threw one last glance at the mannequins, but saw nothing to make him think they came to life when no one was looking.

Of course he was looking. Of course he wouldn't see anything.

Great. The place was starting to wear off on him.

Behind the block with the peculiar department store, veritably buried in the trees and assorted overgrown greenery, was a single-story structure about the size of a convenience store. It was overrun with creeper vines and palmettos. Dull black mildew covered it like a rash.

"It looks like it's closed."

"I already told you it was closed."

"Oh yeah. I forgot." He frowned at the gloomy exterior and a sign out front that said St . . . wat . . . Branch Public Libr . . . The rest of the letters were obscured by moss that had fallen off a precariously leaning tree. "Wait . . . I don't think you said it was *closed*, exactly."

"You weren't paying attention." She strolled to the front door and used her shoulder to shove it open. It stuck and grated on the peeling linoleum on the other side. "Come on in."

"But it's closed."

"Don't be stupid. It's been shut up like this for a decade, and nobody cares if anybody comes and goes. Same is true for half of Staywater, if you think about it. More than half of it, if I'm honest. Everybody's leaving and the town's dying. Another thirteen years and the damn thing will starve."

"What damn thing?" he asked.

"You already know. Don't bore me, and I won't bore you."

"Okay . . . ?" In truth, he didn't want to think about it. He didn't want to go inside, either, but this woman was the closest thing to a clue he'd found so far. If she could be called a clue. She was more like a sign, really. Maybe a portent.

But his wife was still missing, and that forty-eight-hour clock was counting down by the minute. If Netta knew anything that could help him find her . . . anything at all . . . he told himself that it'd have to be worth it.

Wouldn't it?

He trailed behind her, before the door could creak shut and leave him alone on the cracked sidewalk beside the dirty library that wasn't a library anymore. The only thing worse than being in Staywater was being alone in Staywater.

Even if that meant being in Staywater with Netta Greely.

As it turned out, the Staywater Branch Public Library wasn't any more promising on the inside than it was outside. Inside, it was gloomy and damp and it smelled like the swamp, if someone had thrown a bunch of old books into the water and left them to molder. The only light came straggling in through the windows, which were blurred by the same mildew that marred the stucco.

Titus's eyes adjusted, and in a few seconds he could see a long desk with a rotary phone, a very dead tree in a pot, a set of cabinets that might have held a card catalog, and fifteen or twenty bookshelves that still held about half of their original contents. The remainders were scattered on the floor, or stolen, or eaten by rats.

"Back here." Netta guided him past the shelves. Some of them looked perfectly normal, and the books appeared untouched by time. Others held bricks of wet paper that had melted down to mush. When she saw him looking at the ruined novels, she explained, "There's a leak in the roof. Probably a lot of leaks."

"Nobody ever fixed them?"

"Who would fix them?" she asked in response. "Nobody even locked the doors when the last librarian quit getting paid, so she left. Nobody cares, that's what I'm telling you. Nobody gives a shit at all."

"When did it close?" The space grew darker as they retreated from the windows, toward a series of doors at the rear of the building.

"A month after my Jimmy went missing."

"Your Jimmy? You keep saying that."

"He was my son." She opened the middle of three doors, and to Titus's surprise, it was brighter in the room it revealed. A window ate up most of the western wall, and even though it was every bit as filthy as everything else, it let in enough light to see by. "He disappeared thirteen years ago, this week."

Titus stopped in the doorway. He watched her go to a row of boxes that were stacked on a table. They weren't regular boxes. They were extra sturdy, the kind you used for legal files and folders. "Your son went missing, too?"

She nodded. "Why else you think I chased you down?"

"I thought you were homeless or something, and you wanted me to buy you a slice."

"I got a home." She pulled down a box from a rickety, leaning shelf made more of rust than metal at that point. "But not a son. Not since the thing under the bridge got its claws in him."

"Jesus, why would you put it like that?" He shivered. The library wasn't that cold. It was muggy and mild, like the weather outside but without the fresh air. Titus shook anyway, and struggled to keep from remembering the white thing with thick hands and sharp black nails like volcanic glass.

"I think it actually has claws. I don't see why it wouldn't. Monsters usually do."

Titus felt fresh pizza coming back up against his gullet. He swallowed it all down by force. "You think there's a monster . . . what? A monster alligator?" He recalled something rough and pale swimming, wallowing, slithering in the water. He swallowed that down, too. "Something like that?"

"I don't know what it looks the most like. Alligator's a good a guess as any, but even if that's right, it's only part of it. The thing under the bridge—"

"You're making it sound like a troll."

"I've never seen no troll under a bridge. Seen plenty of gators."

"But you haven't seen . . . it? Whatever lives underneath the seventh one?"

She looked up from the box. "It? Him? I think I got a glimpse, once. I went looking for the bridge a thousand times, and just once . . ." Her voice faded. Her gaze drifted back down to the papers, and rolled slowly across them. "Right after Jimmy was gone. Right after I went to those women." She dug her hand into the box, wormed it beneath the things she didn't want, and shortly found the thing she *did*. "These women." She held up the front page of *The Forto News Report*. "See them? Look at this." She stabbed the corner with her index finger. "October 22, 1966. There they are—Claire and Daisy Spratford."

He came closer, near enough to see the headline, even in the low, murky light. "'Spratford Cousins Found Alive,'" he read. "'Eleven others perish in flood, trapped in swamp.'"

"They never found all the bodies, but they shouldn't have expected to. That's not how it works. That's not how it ever worked."

She offered him the paper, so he took it. He carried it to the window, for what extra illumination it could offer. He scanned the lede and got to the meat of what Netta wanted him to see.

"'Daisy and Claire Spratford, having left the safety of the Staywater courthouse to offer aid, were initially lost in the flood's aftermath. But yesterday morning, they were spotted in the swamp off State Road 177, lying unconscious among debris and cypress knees. They were taken to Forto General for treatment. A source at the police department told reporters that both women were cryptic, when they awakened. Daisy Spratford told first responders only, "From here on out, he'll take no more." Her cousin's statement was similar, and equally enigmatic. She said, "He'll keep no more." Both women were treated and released.'"

He handed the paper back to Netta. "I don't get it."

She sagged, like she was a little disappointed in him. He thought she was about to say he was stupid again, but she didn't. "I don't either. I was hoping you might see something I don't."

"But I'm not from around here. I don't know these people."

She put the brittle old pages back in the box. "I thought it might make the difference, having an outsider take a look at what I've got, and know what I know. I've been acquainted with those women for most of my life, and I'll be damned if I could ever figure out what they were up to. But I tell you what, those women did *something.* I don't know what, and they aren't telling. But I know it. They know it. I used to think maybe that boy they take care of knew it, too, but I talked to him the other day. Now I think maybe he doesn't. Maybe they never told him."

Titus sighed. "Lady, you've lost me. I'm sorry. I wish I could help."

"And I wish I could help *you.* I thought maybe between us . . ." But she didn't finish the thought. She started fresh on another one. "See, after that flood in '66, they acted like our troubles were over. You should've seen them, prancing around town like they'd saved us all, with whatever bog-witchery or granny magic they rustled up between themselves and the thing under the bridge. But they were wrong. . . ."

"So . . . was there a flood in 1979, or not?"

She shook her head. "No, not a flood. It didn't rise up and take a bunch of folks in a batch, not like it used to. It only took a few people, that next time. Whatever those ladies did, they took the edge off it, at least. I'll give them that much. In '79 . . . or was it closer to '80? I don't know. A policeman or FBI fellow or whatever—somebody came down from the government, trying to see if we had a killer in our midst. Like they were ever gonna find it."

"You mean . . . the thing at the bridge?"

"I do. Then in 1992, two people went missing. And in 2005, just the one: my son, James Arnold Greely. He vanished into thin air. Most folks here will tell you I went full-on crazy, gone right around the bend. It's possible that I did . . ." she quietly considered. "But I came back again, and I started asking questions." She nodded to herself, and to the box on the table before her.

A cockroach scuttled across the desk, and a daddy longlegs strolled along the windowsill on needle-thin stilts. A line of ants wound along the wall—arriving via a crack at the baseboards, and disappearing into a crack on the ceiling.

Very, very quietly, Netta said, "I've always figured, and never wanted to say out loud . . . I think my niece might've had something to do with it. She's no monster under a bridge, but she's a monster of another sort. Selfish and cold, grown up too pretty in a town full of ugly. She got herself a crush on the bar-man, David. I think . . ." Her voice got even lower, even softer. Titus had to strain to understand her. "I think she would've done anything for him, back then. Even though he barely knew her name."

After that, she went quiet.

Titus didn't have anything to add, so he stayed quiet.

Nothing else moved, not even the cool, thick air that was charged with dust and mold and the sawdust of old books being chewed apart by vermin. Titus and Netta were running out of things to say. There was nothing else in the box to share.

"I'm sorry about your son," he said.

She nodded. "I'm sorry about your wife."

He rubbed at his nose, fighting the urge to sneeze. "Netta?"

"Huh?"

"What do I do now?" There was no one else to ask, and she seemed like the one person on earth who might be likely to know.

But Netta put the lid on the box before lifting it back into place. She wiped her hands on her skirt. "Oh, honey. I wish I had the slightest idea."

14

DAVE'S

By the time Dave made it back to the bar, he was feeling a little better. A little clearer. A little less like a guy who wanted to either run and hide, or puke all over himself.

He pulled up into the gravel lot beside the rickety building and threw the Jeep into park. The door was locked, but when he got inside, he saw that Jess had already been there. The register was open, he could hear the dishwasher running, and the TV was on.

"Jess?" He shut the door and locked it behind himself. It was only three thirty. He had half an hour to get the kitchen ready before the first of the regulars straggled in. "Hey Jess? Listen, I'm sorry, okay? Fighting is stupid. Come on."

It hadn't really been a fight. Dave and Jess never really fought. They just tap-danced around whatever was bugging them and

hashed it out like passive-aggressive kids. It wasn't ideal, but it worked well enough that neither one of them had ever tried to do anything about it.

As far as relationships went, Dave'd had worse before, and at least he knew how this one worked. They hung together from affection and old habit, and it worked out all right. "Old habit" always sounded better than "laziness."

But she wasn't there.

It only took a few seconds to check around the bar and kitchen. She hadn't left a note or anything, so he had to trust that she'd be back. It wasn't like she had another job, or anywhere else to be.

He went ahead and turned on the fryers and the oven, and rummaged around in the freezer for everything that would eventually go inside them. Then it was back to the bar, and to the boxes of booze behind it. He refilled the things that needed refilling and tossed all the empties into a box.

He picked up the box and backed out the door, ready to chuck all the bottles into the dumpster outside—just as Jess was walking up the steps.

"Hey," she said.

"Hey. Um . . . give me a second. I've got to . . ."

"Yeah, toss the empties." She moved aside and let him down past her, then went inside.

Dave heaved the box and all its contents into the great metal dumpster with a clank and a crash. By the time he got back inside, the clock on the wall said 3:57 and Jess was behind the bar. She tied an apron around her waist, picked up her order pad and a couple of pens, and jammed them into the pockets.

"Hey, I'm sorry about earlier," he said.

She picked up the old diaper and wiped down the counter for invisible spills. They both knew it was clean. Nobody had touched it yet. "It's okay. I'm not mad." She dropped the rag into a bucket that had a mixture of hot water and cleaning solution.

"We could talk about it."

"I don't want to talk. Forget it. Let's just open up shop. I saw Tim and Pete drive around the block a minute ago. I bet they're right outside by now."

"If that's what you want." He went to the door and unlocked it. Tires were already grinding in the parking lot, so Jess was right. The first of the usual suspects were pulling up.

Thirsty's was never really hopping with more than a dozen or so people, but it reliably held that many—even on weeknights. Of those dozen, probably ten were folks that Dave and Jess knew by name, and one more was somebody they knew on sight. The last one was inevitably somebody headed for the park, just passing through.

So it was more than a little weird how there were about twenty people hanging around by six o'clock, the majority of them never-before-seen out-of-towners.

"What the hell is going on?" Dave asked Jess, as she stopped at the bar with another drink order.

Jess leaned against the bar, and Dave leaned in close so he could hear her better. "See the table back there? The one with all the women trying to get a signal on their smartphones?"

"Yeah."

"They're journalists, looking to cover the story of Melanie Bell."

"Was that her name? I forgot." Dave eyed the table in question. The women were all young and smartly dressed, with messenger bags instead of purses. "And I mean . . . are you sure? They could be . . . on their way to a conference or something."

"No, I heard them talking. They're *definitely* looking for her. They're trying to find the police station or a local newspaper, so they can get someone to give them quotes. They're trying to find directions on their phones, the poor dumbasses. Like Google Maps has been through here, or something." She laughed and turned back around, ready to visit the next set of new customers, a man and a woman who looked like they worked together, but probably didn't sleep together.

The woman had a large bag sitting on the floor beside her. Dave thought it might hold a video camera, so the pair might be a tiny, low-rent TV crew. He wasn't sure how he felt about that, and he wasn't super thrilled when the guy came up to the bar, acting casual. It was a contrived kind of casual. A forced, polished casual. A salesman's brand of casual, that's what it was.

"Hey there, buddy," he said for an opener, confirming Dave's worst suspicions. He was probably twenty-five, right out of college. First real gig. A good-looking guy in a Sears-catalog way—an inoffensively bland everyman, perfect for the five-o'clock news in some small town within a few hours' drive. Valdosta? Jacksonville? Did Lake City have its own local affiliates?

In return to this uninspired greeting, Dave said, "Hey."

"Listen, I'm new to the area. Me and my friend over there. Great little bar you've got here—we're really enjoying the drinks and the scenery. But listen, I was wondering . . ."

"I just bet you were."

"Come again?" He looked confused. "Wait, let me start over. My name is Ryan Bennett, and I'm a reporter with Fox News, in Valdosta."

Dave offered his bartending poker face. "Okay. What do you want?"

"We're doing a story on the woman who went missing yesterday."

"Already?"

"Her mother made some phone calls."

"Wow," Dave marveled. "You people move fast."

"We're competing with the internet, so . . . yeah. We *have* to move fast. Let me ask, did you know Melanie Bell?"

"Nope." He withdrew to begin pouring the beers requested by Jess's most recent order. "Never met her. Never even heard of her, until yesterday."

"Did you know her husband?"

He tugged the tap lever. Blankly, noncommittally, he said, "They weren't from around here. Nobody in Staywater knew them."

"Uh-huh, uh-huh," said Ryan, bobbing his head. "But the husband is supposedly here in town somewhere, because the police are keeping an eye on him while they continue the search. The mother-in-law is making a stink. She thinks the husband did something to her," he said, calling all the players by their roles, and not their names. He talked about them like they were pieces on a board.

"That's usually what the police think, when a woman goes missing."

"Statistically, it's the most likely answer." Ryan shifted on the stool, leaning in across the bar. "What do *you* think happened to her?"

"Fuck if I know. Excuse me, man. I've got drinks to make." He slapped two uncapped bottles and two full pints onto the bar. "I can't help you."

"But if you think of anything, could you maybe point us in the right direction? Do you know where the guy's staying?"

"Nope."

"Has he been in this bar? Have you talked to him?"

"Nope."

Ryan sighed and thanked him. "All right, man. I appreciate your time. Hey, when you get a minute—me and my camera girl, we could each use a Bud Light."

Dave cocked his head at Jess, who was bound to clean up in tips tonight. "Tell Jess. She'll start you a tab, and I'll put you in the queue. It's just the two of us, tonight. We don't usually get this kind of traffic. You'll have to be a little patient with us."

"Of course, of course. Sorry about that." Ryan slid off the stool and slunk back to his table.

Not ten minutes later, the door opened and Titus Bell dragged himself inside.

Jess was unloading tips from her apron pocket and shoving them in the jar on the bar to make room. Dave grabbed her by the arm. "Do me a favor, would you?"

"Okay . . . ?"

"See who just came in?"

Titus's eyes were bloodshot and his shirt was dirty. He looked around for a table, but they were all taken—so he made his way toward the bar.

"Isn't that—?"

Dave whispered: "Yeah. But don't tell the reporters it's him. He's had a shitty enough couple of days. Help me give this guy a break, for once."

She looked back and forth between Dave and Titus—who picked a stool at the end, near Karl's spot. Karl wasn't there yet. He usually didn't show up until nine or so. "He looks like he's been ridden hard and put away wet."

"I feel sorry for him, so please. Don't feed him to the wolves."

"I won't," she promised. She held out her pinky.

He took it with his, hooked it, and let go. "Thanks." When that was sorted, he finished up the order that was in front of him and went to attend his newest customer.

Titus looked up, and looked miserable. "Hello."

"What can I get you?"

"Jack and Coke?"

Dave asked, "Are you sure? That's a lot tamer than your last pick. Took half the bottle, didn't you?"

"My stomach's not behaving. You got anything to eat? Something I might not puke all over my shoes later on?"

He slipped him the brief, greasy menu. "No promises." Dave kept his hand on the laminated piece of paper and leaned over, close to Titus. Close enough to make himself quietly heard over the TV that was hanging right over their heads. "You see all these people?"

Titus looked around in confusion. He wouldn't have known who was a regular patron and who wasn't, so Dave clued him in.

"Most of them are reporters, come in from all over the place. They want to do a story on your wife. They're looking for you."

"Shit," he mumbled, and started to stand up.

The bartender caught his hand. "You don't have to go. I won't tell them, and neither will Jess." He flashed a glance at the waitress to point her out. "Nobody else knows. Most of the usual guys left when this crowd came in. All the new blood made them uncomfortable."

"Thanks," he whispered back. "Thank you, man. Seriously."

"No problem."

"But why . . . ?" he wondered aloud. "Why would you do that for me?"

"For one thing, I don't think you hurt your wife. For another, we've got something in common, me and you."

Titus brightened. It was pitiful. "You mean, what happened to you? Out on 177? Holy shit, man. We really need to talk," he insisted. "Netta said we should."

For a split second, Dave regretted his decisions to speak up

and look after this guy. "Christ. Netta? You been talking to her?"

"She showed me things."

"You can't . . ." He put his elbows down on the bar and came close again, pointing down at the menu so it looked like he was explaining the particulars of the potato skins. "You can't just take every word she says at face value. She's crazy. Not the cute, quirky kind, either. She's straight-up mad as a hatter."

"That doesn't mean she's wrong. She showed me things," he protested, and it almost came out in a whine.

"Fine, I believe you: She showed you things. But we can't talk now, so it'll have to be later. Right now, all I can do to help you . . . is keep my mouth shut. Wait until these people have gone, or wait until closing time. You think you can stay awake and drink that long? Or do you want to come back later, instead?"

"I'll stick around. I'll try. I can give it a shot."

"Then do that. Hang around and I'll grab you when the coast is clear. Maybe we'll hit a lull."

For the next hour or two, Titus took it easy—drinking more soda than booze, and ordering some French fries to munch on, since he'd kept those down the night before. He ate them slowly, but the bartender didn't see him run off to the bathroom to chuck anything up, so he must've kept these down, too.

Later, Dave shot him a look to see how he was doing, over in his little corner.

Karl had appeared a little early tonight. The two men were talking.

Titus surely didn't know that Karl was dead, and he'd been dead for years. Nobody ever knew, unless someone pointed it out.

Dave was glad Karl had showed up. Maybe he felt sorry for Titus too; at least he was keeping him company. Hell, there was always the chance that Karl could help. He had been a kind fellow, in life and death alike. Wise, too. Blunt as a motherfucker, with the patience of a saint, that's what everyone always said. Dave believed it, too. He'd never known him in life, but he was a perfect bar patron in death.

Dave dropped in briefly on the conversation, in order to hand over the traditional offering of whiskey and a cigarette. "Hey Karl. Sorry I'm late, but you sneaked in a little early tonight."

"Aw, son. Don't worry about me," he drawled with a smile that lifted his salt-and-pepper mustache. "I see you've got yourself a crowd tonight."

"Somebody's gone missing, and somebody else made a stink about it."

Karl jutted a thumb at Titus. "This guy's mother-in-law."

"You told him?" Dave asked quizzically.

"I figured he wasn't a reporter."

Karl laughed, and Dave shrugged. "Yeah, you can tell this guy anything. It's safer than talking to a priest, and twice as much fun."

The bartender left them to chat and went back to filling the orders. They were slowing down as the evening wore on. The reporters went looking for someplace to stay, and a few probably found lodging at Maude's. The rest would have to hit the road and go back to Forto. If Maude's was full, they were shit out of luck, unless they wanted to break in to one of the many abandoned houses in Staywater and camp out there for the night.

Dave had a feeling that sort of thing wasn't on the table for this high-heeled, skirted, pleated-pants, manicured crowd. Call it a hunch.

By midnight, the bar was back to normal—only Titus and six of the usual guys remained, several of whom had crept back

around as the reporters had wandered off. Titus got up to use the restroom. When he returned, Karl was gone.

Titus looked back and forth at the ashtray and the drink, both untouched. He looked up at Dave. "What happened to Karl? Did he leave?"

"Yeah, he left," Dave said simply.

"He didn't finish his drink. Or . . . or light his cigarette."

"He comes and goes like that. Don't worry. Don't be offended, either. It doesn't mean he didn't like you, or he won't come talk to you again. He just has places to be. If anything, you should be flattered. He doesn't chat with just anybody that long. What'd you talk about?"

"Melanie. My wife. What happened." Titus pushed the half-picked plate of fries forward. "And thanks, man. That's all the damage I could do."

"No problem." Dave took the plate with its remnants of crumbs and grease. He put it in the busing bin, and came back. "It looks like Jess has the bar situation under control, now that everybody's mostly cleared out. You want to take a minute outside? Join me for a smoke?"

"I don't usually smoke, but if you've got a pack, I'm happy to make an exception." He glanced over at Karl's untouched Marlboro, but Dave headed him off at the pass.

"No, that one's Karl's. Leave it there."

"Will he be back for it?"

"One way or another." Dave took off his own apron, loaded down with tips, cigarettes, and a bar rag. "Come on. I've got some menthols, and I'm willing to share."

"I've never had a menthol."

"You're in for a treat. Sort of. Not really." He pushed open the door to the kitchen, where Jess was loading the dishwasher. "Hon, would you watch the bar for a minute? This guy and I are going out for a smoke."

"Sure." She eyed Titus up and down, like she was still deciding how she felt about him. "Don't leave me all night, though."

"I won't." To Titus he added, "Come on, there's a back door."

The back door led to a landing too small to call a porch, and down a couple of steps into grass and gravel. About twenty yards away, there was a big metal dumpster. The streetlamp was on the other side of the building, and so was the half-lit sign that advertised the bar—so the shadows were thick. You could see your hand in front of your face, but just barely. If you wiggled it.

Titus tripped on the bottom step and caught himself.

Dave told him to watch his step about three seconds too late, and passed him a cigarette. He lit his own, and then handed over the lighter, too. "So. You've been talking to Netta."

Titus accepted both. "She's been talking to me. I was down at Paulie's trying to keep down a piece of pizza, and she made herself right at home in my booth. She said that you and me should talk, because we've got the bridge in common."

Dave caught the bit about the bridge, but for the moment, he let it ride. "You know, she's my girlfriend's aunt."

"Then you must know her pretty well."

"Nah. Getting to know her is more trouble than it's worth. There's too much bullshit to sort through. Jess puts up with her, and serves as a buffer between us. That's our deal. Netta can drink in my bar, but she can't be crazy in there. This place is sacrosanct for every drunk within fifteen miles. That's why we shut her down when she started getting weird last night."

"She seems pretty . . . um."

"Crazy. You don't have to hunt for a better word than that. It's the right one."

Titus nodded. "Crazy or not, she found me and took me to the library."

"Library's closed."

"Wasn't locked."

Dave sucked on his cigarette, and light from the coal lit up his face. "All right, I'll bite. What'd you find there?"

"A box of old newspaper clippings. There used to be a bunch of floods around here, did you know that?"

He nodded. "It's the only thing this town was ever famous for, apart from the cypress logging and a hypothetical serial killer who nobody ever caught. Hell, nobody even proved he existed. But anyway, all of that stopped happening back in the late sixties."

"Why?"

"Nobody knows."

Titus shook his head vigorously. "Somebody has to know. Netta told me about a couple of people, these two women named Daisy and Claire . . . they survived the last flood. Netta thinks they know something."

Dave laughed, short and sharp. "Whaddaya know, a broken clock's right twice a day. Yeah, she's right about the Spratford cousins. They know something about everything, but here's the catch: They don't talk. To *anybody*. They live alone on the other side of town in a big old house that's falling apart, right out of a Faulkner story. The house even has a name: Hazelhurst. Who names a house these days, seriously?"

"That does sound kind of gothic."

"*Super* gothic. They've even got an orphan kid who lives there. *That's* how gothic the place is. I think somebody dumped him off, and they took him in. He was in here last night. You maybe saw him. He's our only regular who isn't old enough to drink."

"I saw some kid in the bar, yeah."

Dave smoked and sulked. "If it were up to me, he'd get out and stay out, until he turns twenty-one. But Jess puts up with him, and the old ladies don't care if he wanders down here to hang out. He mostly comes to watch TV and watch Jess. I feel sorry for him, and I'm a little bit afraid of his godmothers. Those old witches have never bothered me before; shit, I've only ever met them a time or two in passing. But there's something strange about them, and everybody can smell it from a mile away. I wouldn't want to fuck with them. Nobody in their right mind would, so I let their kid hang around."

"You don't mind him staring at your girlfriend?"

He smiled around the cigarette. "Jess and me have been together . . ." He almost said thirteen years but changed his mind. It sounded unlucky. "For ages. I'm not worried about some dumb boy who's got nothing better to do than bat his eyelashes and make awkward small talk. Christ, she's almost old enough to be his mom, but he doesn't know it. He thinks she's like . . . barely old enough to drink, just because she's so baby-faced. I don't know if he's ever even seen a girl his own age. He probably wouldn't know one if it bit him."

Titus took a drag and coughed. He took another drag anyway. "So if anybody here knows anything, it's those old ladies."

"With regards to any given subject in the county, I'd say yes."

"I should talk to them. They might know what happened to Melanie."

"Good luck getting anything useful out of them." Dave leaned against Thirsty's wall and folded his arms.

Titus joined him. "What about the kid who lives with them? Does he talk?"

"About everything and nothing. I promise you: He doesn't know shit, or I would've heard it by now. The kid's got no filter. Learned how to talk from watching 1950s sitcoms and listening to NPR, so he likes to practice his chatting skills when he gets out of the house."

Then they smoked in silence, until they didn't.

"What happened to you?" Titus asked him. "Out on State Road 177. I don't want to rush you, but my wife's been gone for a day and a half now, and you know what they say about forty-eight hours."

"No, what do they say?"

"After forty-eight hours, your odds of finding a missing person go to shit. That's what they say. I don't know if it's true or not," he backpedaled. "But come on. I feel like the trail is getting cold. Just tell me what happened to you, so maybe I can figure out what happened to *her*."

Dave closed his eyes and leaned back, bouncing his head gently on the wall. "Fucking hell, I wish I knew." He slid to the ground and sat there. After another minute of sitting and smoking, and letting the ash grow long, he opened his eyes.

He said, "I used to be super fit, can you believe it? I was into rock climbing for a long time, then hiking and camping. Then I got into canoeing, and sort of . . . fell in love with the swamp." He laughed to himself.

Titus asked, "What's so funny?"

He flapped his hand, like he was about to say, "Nothing." Instead he said, "I haven't been to the Okefenokee in . . . a couple of years, I guess. Haven't done much except drink since I came here to stay."

"Where'd you come here from?"

"Valdosta. Used to drive out here once a month or so, bringing all my gear strapped to the roof of my station wagon. It wasn't the world's coolest ride, but it held everything I needed. I got in this real nice rut," he said with a hint of a smile. "I'd come down, stop at the same place as always to get gas and a couple of lottery scratchers. Then I'd come by this coffee shop that used to be near Paulie's—let's say, it was halfway between Paulie's and the bar. Jess worked there. I think she might've been the only employee, except for the owner."

He took a drag on the cigarette, and let it sit on the edge of his mouth while he tucked his hands into his front pockets.

"I stopped there oh, maybe . . . eight or ten times, over a year or so. Jess was always so sweet, and I guess I flirted with her. I guess we kind of knew each other, but not very well. I always looked forward to seeing her. I liked the routine.

"Anyway, about a dozen years ago I was headed this way like usual, and things went sideways. I'd just left the coffee shop and hit 177. I remember driving with the radio on and the windows down. It was a nice day, real warm and clear. Real bright, too. I had a pair of sunglasses . . ." He retrieved his cigarette and used it to gesture at his temples. "Kind of expensive. I'd picked them up at an outlet someplace, I don't remember."

Titus could relate. "I never spend more than twenty bucks on a pair. I lose them too often."

"Me either, usually. So it was a nice day, and the radio was on, and I was driving over these bridges, like you do when you're passing through. I never counted them before, not until that day, and I don't know why I did it then—but once I crossed the sixth one, I had it in my head that it was the last. After that one, I was in the home stretch before hitting the park. But then I saw another one, up ahead . . . a little one, and I didn't recognize it. I was trying to figure out if I'd ever seen it before; I was starting to wonder if I'd fucked up, and taken a turn without meaning to. How do you get lost on 177, you know? There's nowhere to turn, nowhere to go. . . ."

He cleared his throat. He knocked his cigarette ash loose with a flip of his knuckle. "This bridge was real narrow, maybe a single lane. It was stone, not concrete and metal like the rest of them. It looked old."

He stopped talking.

Titus gave him a minute, then prompted, "And?"

Dave shrugged. "And nothing. That's the last thing I remember. I heard something weird on the radio—a voice, and I couldn't really understand it. Then I was on the ground, staring at the sky, while this waitress from the coffee shop in Staywater was beating on my chest like a drum."

Titus's cigarette was mostly burned down, and barely smoked at all. He'd all but forgotten about it. "What about your car?"

"Cops pulled it out of the swamp a week later. No signs of foul play, that's what they said. I must've passed out at the wheel and driven off into the water. Pure dumb luck that Jess came along, or so they told me. And now . . . now you know as much about that day as I do."

Dave jammed his cigarette against the wall until it was just a smudge of gray. He went back inside, and left Titus out by the dumpster to think.

15

DAISY AND CLAIRE'S

The rain had started up again, just loud enough to sound pleasant on the metal roof of the backyard shed. It beat a tinny time to the clicking of Claire's knitting needles, and to the creaking rock of Daisy's chair as her foot lifted and fell, pushing herself up and down. Cameron sat at their feet, the bottle of Jack open beside him. Each one of them had a glass filled up with two or three fingers' worth of whiskey.

The ladies both said it was okay if he had some, too. He was probably going to need it.

Cameron wasn't entirely sure how he felt about this. On the one hand, they were letting him into the booze stash—no subterfuge required. He was thrilled! On the other hand, they clearly knew he'd been helping himself all this time, but he'd been right when he'd assumed that they didn't much care.

On a third hand, if they were willing to get him lit before they even started talking . . . this must be extra, *super* serious.

"Daisy, do you want to begin?" Claire asked, counting stitches with one eye and watching her godson with the other. "Maybe you could start with the floods."

"All right." She nodded. Her ankle worked the porch floor, nudging the rocker a little harder, a little faster than usual. Was she nervous? Cam had never seen her nervous before. Neither one of the ladies ever wasted any time being nervous. In his experience, they preferred to make other people nervous. "My dear boy," she said, "I don't know how much you know already, but Staywater used to be famous for its floods."

"That's a shitty thing to be famous for."

"Shitty and deadly, too," Claire interjected. "Dozens and dozens of people died, over the years. Probably hundreds."

Daisy said, "Definitely hundreds. This area's been flooding for centuries. The native folks knew better than to live here—and they were kind enough to warn the first dipshit white people who set up homesteads. Every thirteen years, they said. The waters come around."

Claire chimed in again. "But they didn't exactly mean 'waters.'"

"No, they meant the creature that *brings* the waters. Or else he comes along with it, I don't know." Daisy paused to take a deep swallow from her glass, lowering the level by almost half. "Don't ask me its name, because I don't know that, either."

"Nobody does."

"If the Indians had a word for it, they never passed it along; or else, nobody who spoke English ever wrote it down. Over the years, we've read everything we could find about floods and the creatures what cause them. There are lots of cultures out there, with monsters that sounded almost right . . . but not quite."

"There's a thousand and one sea monsters, lake monsters, and swamp monsters, for example. Some are more famous than others, but none of them are exactly like the thing we've got here in Staywater."

Daisy shook her head. "No, nothing like what we've got, God help us. Near as we can tell, we've got something unique on our hands."

Cameron sipped his drink. He didn't know how much they would let him have—was this small helping his entire serving, or were they planning to kill off the bottle between the three of them? "What does it look like?" he asked them.

Neither one answered right away. Claire knitted. Daisy rocked, as she stared off into space, like she was thinking about how to respond.

He tried again. "Have either of you ever *actually* seen it?"

"Oh yes," they said together, um-hmming and heads bobbing.

Daisy took the reins again, having found a way into the explanation. "We've seen it," she said slowly. "We've seen it up close and personal, probably better than anybody else who's ever lived to tell about it. I don't mean to get all coy and quiet with you, Cam. It's hard to explain, that's all."

"It wants you to think it looks like an alligator," Claire said cautiously. "A pale, strange one. And it *does,* but only at first. Only if you're looking right at it. If you see it from the corner of your eye, or if you stare at it too hard, too long, the costume starts to waver."

"You start to see past it. You get a glimpse at the thing underneath. It's not exactly a man, but of course it's not. It's something much older, and it's not of our world."

"You're losing me," Cameron confessed. "If it's not from our world, then where did it come from?"

Daisy sighed. "God only knows, but it's another place that's very close to this one . . . close enough that sometimes the walls between our world and this other thing's world grow thin—for just a little while. Sometimes, they're so close and so fragile that it can reach right on through. That's when it brings the waters."

"Every thirteen years." He hung on to the only detail that made sense.

She smiled, like he was finally getting it. "Every time it can, it takes every *one* it can. That's what it's always done."

Claire stabbed her needles into the yarn ball, setting aside her project in favor of her glass. "Well, that's what it used to do."

"That's what it still does," her cousin argued. "Just not as easily as it did before. Now it only snares one or two people, here and there, and you can thank us for that. We're the reason it doesn't eat half the town anymore, once every generation or so. We took the fight to the bridge, back in 1966. We showed it who was boss, didn't we?"

"Sure did, but it was nearly the death of us."

Cameron was lost again. "How? What did you do?"

The ladies took simultaneous swigs. Daisy reached for the bottle and said, "That thing, what brings the water and takes the people. Whatever its name is. We killed it."

"We murdered it dead, before it could come back for more, and we saved our town from ruin. Or that's what we thought . . . until the next cycle rolled around."

She topped herself off, and set the bottle back down on the porch floor, between her and the spot where Cameron sat cross-legged and rapt. "It was 1979. That's the first time we felt the *push*. The creature wasn't strong enough to pull the worlds apart anymore. It's dead now, the ghost of something that never lived—or never should've lived *here*. All it can do anymore is set a trap, and see who takes the bait."

"The trap sits open for . . ." Claire's hands wobbled up and down as she guessed an estimate. ". . . A couple of days? No more than that, I don't believe. But that's all it needs. It always catches somebody."

"Then it goes away. Back to wherever it came from . . . wherever ghosts of its kind find themselves, when they've been beaten by two old ladies."

Claire protested. "We weren't old, not back in '66!"

"We weren't spring chickens, either. We were two spinsters with shotguns, granny magic, and no goddamn plan. That's how it almost got us." She drank again, and settled back in the chair. Her foot slowed, and the rocking all but stopped. "Do you want to know how it happened? What we did?"

"If you don't tell me, I'll probably explode."

"Then dump out the last of the bottle. Split it up between us."

His eyebrows lifted. "You're going to let me keep drinking?"

Claire laughed. "Baby, I want to get you so liquored up you can't leave the house for the next two days. I want you staying right here, and a formal grounding will only keep you so close. I know how quiet you sneak, and how well you climb."

Cameron didn't care why they were letting him indulge, he was just happy to take advantage. "Hang on. I'm going to go get a Coke from the icebox. I want to mix it up, and make this last awhile."

When he returned, he sat down on the swing beside Claire and her knitting. He already felt a little fuzzy and very confused, but that was fine. The world was strange, and his godmothers were stranger. He had a drink, right there in the comfort of his own home—even though that jerk Dave would never serve him. What did Dave know, anyway? Not a damn thing. "Okay, let's do this. Tell me what happened in 1966."

"You do it," Claire suggested to Daisy. "Your memory's sharper than mine."

"All right then, I will. You stop me, if I get something wrong."

"I'll keep you in line. You just start."

Daisy took a deep breath, and let the jelly jar she was using for a highball glass rest on the arm of her chair. "It was early October, and we knew the flood would come any day, because it hadn't come yet and the year was almost out. We were as prepared as anybody was ever going to get.

"So we waited for dawn, when it'd be nice and quiet out on the water. We took a little canoe to the edge of the park on the first day that the water started rising, and we made ourselves easy marks—trying to draw the thing out."

Claire said, "We used ourselves as bait!" just a tad too gleefully for Cameron's taste.

Daisy elaborated. "So there we were, every day for a week at the ass-crack of dawn, hoping to find a monster. Boy, we had no idea what we were in for.

"It was cold that week, those mornings. Cold for here, I mean. I remember we put on our sweaters, and I had a little wool hat that I liked a whole lot. We used gardening gloves on our hands, to keep them warm and to give us some grip on the oars. We moved through the swamp real slow, real cautious; and it was so damn dark under the trees, between the canopy and the water. Even when the sun came lifting up, and it cut through the moss so sharp that sometimes it would blind us. Still somehow, it was terribly dark. But that was good. That's how we first saw it, moving in the ripples up near a bridge we'd never seen before."

Claire made approving noises. "We'll never see it again, either. Not in this lifetime."

Daisy paused, and her eyes went dark. "That's the truth of it. But seeing it once was enough, I tell you what. Even at a distance it was a creepy thing, made of stone and very small. More like a gate than a bridge, that's what it looked like from the canoe. Underneath it we saw a thing moving, a pale, weird creature in the shadows. An alligator—an albino one, that's what I thought. It's funny, how your brain tries to tell you that you're looking at something normal, when you're not. Like it's trying to protect you from your very own self."

Claire murmured her assent. "I was thinking the exact same thing, when I looked it in the eye."

"You couldn't look at it for more than a second or two without feeling like you were going mad. The thing had arms and legs, but its hands and feet were rough toes with dark claws. Its head was flat and long, and it had the dead-shark eyes of a gator waking up in the spring. Maybe it always had those eyes, and that's why it picked the disguise. It might have seen the gators sliding around in the swamp. It might've seen something of itself in those ordinary beasts.

"We snuck up as close as we could, and we got closer than you might think. There's plenty of noise in the swamp each morning—the bugs, the fish, the snakes, and the birds. . . . sometimes you can hardly hear yourself think. But close wasn't close enough for a surprise attack. It saw us, and I . . ." She put a hand to her chest, like the memory was enough to take her breath.

Claire swallowed hard, and then took a swig. She swallowed that even harder, and took up the tale from there. "It saw us, and it stood up in the water—on all fours, at first. The water came up to its knees and elbows, if you could say it had such things. Then it rose up on its hind legs, so smooth and naked and white. Its skin was like milk, spoiled and soured when the power goes out and the fridge goes warm. Its face was long and smooth, and again—at a glance, you'd call it an alligator. But the longer you looked . . ."

"Yes, the longer you looked. It *wasn't of this world,* Cam." Daisy's eyes were still dark, and the line of her mouth had set hard. "It came for us, slow and steady. It wanted us to see it, to get a long, hard look at it. It wanted for us to be afraid."

"That son of a bitch got what it wanted, too. I nearly shit myself, right there in the canoe."

Daisy nodded hard. "If I'd had anything in me but coffee and a couple of smokes, I'd have lost my lunch. But I stood up too fast, and the boat rocked. I fell right into the swamp, but it weren't too deep, not where I landed. I caught myself on my hands and knees, and somehow Claire kept the boat from turning over altogether. She climbed out into the water after me, but she did it right, without tipping anything. She had a cigarette hanging on the corner of her mouth, bobbing with every move she made. Lord Almighty, Claire. You should've seen yourself: up to your thighs in the swamp, while I was elbows-deep and struggling to find my feet."

"You lost a glove in the mud, I remember."

"I surely did. But not you, though. You held up the shotgun and let both barrels fly. I never been so proud in all my life. And I never been so sure that we were about to do some good and kick some ass."

Claire held up a finger at Cameron. "But it wasn't so easy as all that. I missed the bastard with my first shot, and only winged it with the second one. That's where *she* stepped in." She pointed at Daisy. "She pulled herself together, reached into the canoe for the second gun, and just as that goddamn thing was rushing up to us—she caught it point-blank in the chest. Blew a hole right through it! I could look through its ribs and see the bridge on the other side of the water."

"And that's all it took?" Cameron asked, not sure which parts to believe, and which parts to call bullshit.

Both ladies laughed. "Oh no, honey," said Daisy. "That was just the first round. It was stunned, and it was hurt . . . but mostly, it was *pissed*. It took hold of the prow of the canoe, and with one hand it swung the damn thing like a baseball bat. Caught me in the chest and knocked me off my feet. I flew smack into the nearest tree, then fell down on a cypress knob and fractured my collarbone. Knocked the wind out of me. I almost passed out cold."

"But she didn't! And meanwhile, I was reloading," Claire declared in a happily sinister voice. "I had the shells in my pockets—"

"And I had some too, but mine were wet by then. Besides, I didn't know what'd become of my gun. I dropped it when I hit the tree so I was on my own, except for the hunting knife I'd put in my boot."

Cameron gave her the side-eye. "You didn't mention the knife, not when you started telling this story."

"Well, I'm mentioning it now. I never did hit the swamp without a knife—it's just not smart. You never know when you'll get snakebit, or find yourself caught up in old fishing line, or something. You know I put my faith in a shotgun, any day of the week and twice on Sunday—but every girl with an ounce of granny magic knows it's true: Things from other worlds don't like iron."

"I bet your knife wasn't iron. I bet it was steel."

"They don't like steel, either, you smartass." Daisy grinned, and then the grin waned as the memories unspooled. "But after it threw the canoe—as easy as a child throwing a toy—it turned to Claire. It roared with this awful sound, like a train throwing on the brakes. Almost more of a squeal, don't you think?"

"It was the loudest, most awful *squeal* you ever heard in your life, yes. That's a good way to put it."

"You wouldn't think anything on earth could make that sound with its mouth, but I heard it with my own two ears. It was stumbling toward Claire, making that noise, and it wasn't watching for me. It must've thought I was done for, but I was harder to kill than *that*. Busted collarbone or no, I splashed right back to it and I swung the knife."

"It was a big ol' knife," Claire added. "Thick like a Bowie blade."

"My daddy used it for hunting. He left it to me and said I should always carry it, if I found myself out in the trees or on the water. Thank the good Lord for it, and thank Him also that it was the left side of my collarbone that got smashed up—so I could still swing with my right arm. Did I ever tell you I played baseball, when I was a girl?"

"Don't believe you ever mentioned it." Cameron had forgotten about his glass. An hour before, he would've sworn that such a thing was not possible. He could never forget a drink without finishing it. Daisy could've never played baseball. Claire couldn't never been a shotgun-toting spinster. Monsters from other lands could not reach across the worlds to kill with claws and floods.

"I mention the baseball now, so you know that I had a good arm and I could swing a knife real hard. I got my feet tangled up in the water and mud, so my swing went wild—but as I went down I caught it in the back of the leg. It hurt, I know that much. I know because it screeched some more, and a long spray of black blood came flying out. It splashed me right in the face, and for a minute, I couldn't see a thing. But for a minute, the monster staggered—"

"It reached for her, but she slipped and fell down flat in the water again, and it missed. That was all the time I needed to finish reloading."

Daisy picked up the story again. "The next barrel caught the side of its head. Half its skull was hanging open, and that long, narrow head was wobbling on its neck. Its skin wasn't that milky white anymore—it was turning gray. All that black blood was everywhere, staining the water and getting in my hair—"

Excitedly, Claire said, "I ran up closer for that second barrel. I didn't think I'd get another chance, and I'd lost half my shells out of my sweater pocket."

"Together we closed in on it," Daisy said, using her drink and her free hand to mime the scene, and how the two women had maneuvered. "Me with my daddy's knife, and Claire with the last shot we were likely to get. The creature, you gotta understand—it was a whole lot bigger than us. Half again as tall, with limbs so long and thick, with that tail it lashed around like . . . like . . ."

Victoriously, Claire cried, "Like a tentacle!"

"Or a whip! Or something like that, you know. But it was hurt bad, and between the two of us, we hurt it a whole lot worse. She used that last shot to get in close—right up against its throat—and boom!"

"Its head came clean off! Almost!"

Daisy was quick to say, "But not quite! I had to cut it the rest of the way. Even then, its body didn't want to stop moving. We hacked it and hacked it, and took it to pieces—one chunk at a time. Until nothing was wriggling, wobbling, twitching, or blinking." Daisy twitched her eyes for emphasis.

Cameron thought it was creepy as shit.

"Don't think it had any eyelids," Claire mused.

She considered it. "Now that you say so, you're probably right."

"You're sure it was dead? One hundred percent sure?" Cameron asked, hoping and praying that the answer was yes.

They nodded intensely. "Very dead. *Totally* dead." In her

enthusiasm, Daisy splashed a little bit of booze out of her glass. She shook it off her hand. "Once we'd finished cutting—"

"And it took us half the damn day."

"Oh yes, at least that long, and I was nursing a broken collarbone that hurt so bad, I halfway thought I was gonna die from the pain of it. The worst thing was, even though the damn monster was dead . . . the water started coming up anyway. It was like we were sitting at the bottom of a mostly empty pool—and someone tossed in a hose. It didn't come as bad as the years before, but it was bad enough. We were caught out there as the waters rose."

"We ended up in a tree, hanging on for dear life. When the waters went down, rescue crews finally found us and helped us get back to earth." Claire finished the contents of her glass and set it aside. "Then a few days later, when Daisy was out of the hospital, we went back out there to double-check for ourselves. But we couldn't find no sign of the bridge. Not a stone, not a pebble. It's like it never existed.

"We found parts of the monster, though. Not all of it, but enough big pieces that we could weigh them down with rocks and sink it all in the swamp. We left bits of it here, there, and everywhere, scattered to the distant corners of the Okefenokee. We patted ourselves on the back for a job well done . . . but then thirteen years down the line . . ."

Daisy sighed. "A couple of people went missing, right on cue. The rains didn't come and the swamp didn't rise, but people still vanished."

"So we went back, to make sure we hadn't screwed up something, and let it live—let it recover, and get back to its awful business. We fished up a few of the parts we'd sunk, and they were still there," Claire confirmed. "Rotted away to scraps of skin and soggy bones. We had definitely killed it. We did a damn thorough job."

Daisy sighed. "But it wasn't enough, now was it? Thirteen years after *that*, when another couple of folks went missing, we went back to look again. This time, some of the bits were gone, and some were just wisps of tissue. But the bones were still there, soggy and splitting, as fragile as a mummy's. It's *dead*, Cameron. I want you to know that. Believe it with all your heart, because it's true."

"But some things are so awful that they don't quit, just because you've killed them." Claire put her needles aside. Scraps of yarn spooled across her lap, unmoving.

Her cousin agreed. "The dead in our world linger, don't they? Why not the dead from someplace else?"

Everyone went quiet. Cameron remembered his glass, and, sobered by this thought, he finished most of what was in it. "You know what," he said. "It's this place, Miss Claire and Miss Daisy. It's right there in the name, 'Staywater.' Nothing ever really leaves."

The two ladies exchanged a look, and then gave Cameron a glance before gazing away.

"Oh, my sweet boy. Don't talk like that." Daisy closed her eyes, leaned her head back, and started pumping her foot to move the rocking chair again. "Because sometimes, I'm afraid you're right about that. Sometimes, I'm afraid that nothing really *can*."

16

TITUS'S PLACE

Titus hung out by the dumpster for maybe five minutes, finishing his cigarette and staring into the darkness on the far side of the parking lot. It didn't tell him anything.

Dave had told him plenty, not that it helped. God only knew how much of it was true, versus how much Dave believed was true.

Even if half of it didn't matter, it'd given him a lot to think about.

It also gave him weird dreams, when he finally hiked back to Maude's and turned in for the night. He dreamed of strangely shaped limbs that were so utterly translucent they could scarcely be seen, writhing in the water. He dreamed of an old stone bridge with a single lane, and no beginning, and no end. A bridge that wasn't a bridge, and never had been. And something lived beneath it.

He awoke to a fast, hard rapping on the door.

The knocking wasn't any better or worse than waking up to the ringing phone, the day before. Both were terrible. Either one was extra awful when it was barely dawn, as he realized when he opened his eyes and made a halfhearted effort to roll out of bed.

Yes, it was only barely dawn—not *even* dawn, he might've argued. Still half purple outside the curtains, as he could see through a narrow slit where they weren't quite shut all the way.

A realization fired a jolt of adrenaline up his spine: It must be the police. There must be some news. They must have found Melanie.

He flung himself to the edge of the bed, where he had pants and shoes waiting. He successfully got the pants on, decided this much was sufficient, and ran to the door. There was a peephole, but he didn't bother with it. Whoever was on the other side was still knocking. They weren't going away. They must have news. The kind of news you didn't deliver over the phone, good or bad. You did it face-to-face. You needed to look somebody in the eyes when you said your piece.

He sucked in a hard breath and grabbed the knob, pulling the door open. "Hello." He hoped he sounded awake, alert, innocent, and prepared for the best or the worst.

"Hello, Mr. Bell."

He blinked. He sagged. It wasn't Kemp or Pickett; it was some old lady. She was thin and bent, with snow-white hair and bright green eyes. "Hello?" He asked it like a question, this time. He wished he'd grabbed a shirt or something to go with the pants.

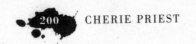

"Mr. Bell, if you want answers, you don't have much time left to find them."

He crossed his arms across his chest and squeezed his own ribs. He wasn't just embarrassed and deflated. He was cold. "I'm sorry . . . come again?" The adrenaline evaporated, and exhaustion settled in its place. Then it flickered—a match struck in the dark. His mind matched up this face with another face, one from a long time ago, in black and white. "Wait, are you—"

"I'm Daisy Spratford. I expect you've heard my name by now."

"Um, yes? I have? Could I ask you—"

"To come inside?" she stopped him. "A few questions? Anything else? No, and no, and no some more. I don't have time for that, and neither do you. There's no telling how long the window will stay open. Hell, it might've closed already. Anyhow, I just came by to give you this." She offered him a piece of paper with an address. "I put some directions on the back."

He turned the paper over and tried to parse the information. "Thank you?"

"That's where David lives."

"David? Oh. You mean Dave. Right? We um . . . we talked last night."

"Yeah, I know. Call him what you want, or what he wants—it's all the same to me. Here's the thing, Mr. Bell: He needs answers, too. I don't know if either one of you will ever get them, and it probably won't be safe for you to try. But you should see it for yourself, if you're able. Not everyone can live with not knowing. Now get off your ass, pack up your shit, and go get David. See if you can get his attention without rousing his girlfriend. I swear to Kingdom Come, that woman is a special kind of trouble."

"She seemed . . . nice?"

"A lot of things seem nice, but they're not. So don't you go alone, into the swamp. Once you've got David, you head back to the water, to 177 where you both met something that's not of this world. Get off the road, get in the muck, and go find whatever's left of that bridge. Find your wife. Dead, alive, I don't know and I won't make you any promises, but I'm finished lying and hiding, and misdirecting. All I can do now is point you all in the right direction and wish you the best of luck."

With that, she turned on her heels and walked away.

Titus looked at the address, then looked at the directions.

He was beat, and his stomach was growling instead of sour. He hadn't slept ten hours in the last two nights together. He still didn't have his car back.

He shut the door slowly and stepped back inside the room.

According to the clock on the bedside table, it was 6:47 A.M., so Maude ought to be serving breakfast by now. He could grab some grub, collect some coffee, and go see about getting Dave.

Then what? Tell him that Daisy Spratford said they had to go find the bridge.

Would it work? Even in his bedraggled, groggy state, Titus remembered the specific awe with a hint of fear in Dave's voice when he'd talked about the cousins. So. . . . maybe.

He shut the door and finished getting dressed. Once his teeth were brushed and his face was washed, he was as awake as he was going to get—and he knew for a fact that he couldn't go back to sleep. Not without another bottle of something hard, and a handful of Valium to chase it. Like it or not, want it or not, happy or not. He was awake.

Dave had closed the bar down at the usual time, Titus assumed. The odds were good that he wasn't a morning guy. The odds were likewise good that his girlfriend, that waitress, wasn't

a morning person either. Nobody at the address on the little scrap of paper would be delighted to see him.

But even if Daisy hadn't hammered home that time was of the essence, he felt it somewhere deep in his chest. It was lurking right alongside all the fear and confusion he'd been harboring since he'd arrived.

The police would come back soon, with more questions. His mother-in-law would show up one of these days and she'd have questions, too. Titus hypothetically had a life to get back to in Nashville; he only had another two weeks of vacation time before he was damn well expected back at work full time, and he hadn't checked any of his messages since he'd arrived—despite his promises to the boss about keeping loose tabs on work while he was on his honeymoon.

It was a stupid thing to think about, and he knew it. In the scheme of things, his missing wife was vastly more important than a job in another state that he didn't really like.

But without that job, he'd run out of money and then what? He couldn't live at Maude's forever. She'd throw him out when he couldn't pay. Then where would he go? Would he squat in one of the abandoned buildings he'd seen—one of the haunted storefronts, or collapsing businesses? One of the decrepit houses like Hazelhurst with no batty old ladies living inside them, spooking bartenders and delivering odd portents at dawn?

Jesus, what would he do?

Staywater struck him as one of those places where you were born there and you lived there forever, or else you left when you could and you never went back. It wasn't a place where people came to stay and live out their days.

Unless you were Dave. Had anyone else come to Staywater in the last fifty years? Twenty?

In the last thirteen?

The thought of remaining there forever pushed Titus perilously close to a panic attack, but how could he leave without Melanie? They'd only just gotten their shit together and tied the knot. They'd only just agreed to take a real, serious shot at being together and building a life—a *real* life, not the half-assed on-again, off-again nonsense that had gotten them nowhere but angry and jealous for the last four years.

It was supposed to be a fresh start but it'd turned out to be a false start. He hoped to God it wasn't the last start, but with every hour that went by, even that slim hope lost a little of its grip.

What hour was this, now? It hadn't been forty-eight yet, but you could see it from here. It'd come by lunchtime, give or take. Or a little later than that, yes. A bit after lunch she'd have been missing for forty-eight hours, an arbitrary finish line that didn't mean anything at all but felt like a terrifying finale all the same.

The police would come, whether or not there was any news. They'd bring the FBI—isn't that who you called, when people went properly missing? Not just wandered-off missing?

"Fuck it," he said, throwing on his jacket. There wasn't much left to lose.

He locked the door and went to Maude's lobby, where he picked up some toast and juice, and crammed it all down without tasting a bite of it. Into a bag he tossed an apple and a couple of muffins. He added a paper cup full of coffee that was strong if not terribly good, and he set off for Dave's house.

The house was along a rise too small to call a hill, back behind the library and the courthouse. It was within spitting distance of the police station, but Titus went out of his way to avoid that particular landmark. He'd prefer to keep Kemp and Pickett from spotting him.

He saw a light on inside and one patrol car parked, but no other signs of life.

If they saw him skulking along in the early-morning hours, toting food and swilling coffee, they might be crazy enough to think he was trying to skip town.

How would he do that? With no car, little money, and no sign of Melanie?

God help him, if he became one of those living ghosts who haunted Thirsty's, always hoping for some news, or some change, or some scrap of information that never comes. He hated the thought of it, almost as much as he hated the thought of leaving the swamp forever and never getting any answers. Never seeing his wife again.

He reached Dave's house in ten minutes or less, but only knew it for certain by the Jeep parked under a rusting carport. The house itself was wildly overgrown like everything else. It had that almost-abandoned look that the rest of the town wore like a uniform. He didn't see a street address, not even on the mailbox that leaned toward the road like a hitchhiker seeking a lift.

There were no lights on. The curtains were drawn and the porch was dark.

Titus climbed the step up onto the porch and thought about knocking. He thought about trying to peek in the windows, in case he could determine where the bedroom was. Should he throw pebbles at the glass?

No, that was stupid.

The door was covered in flaking paint that used to be red, and now was the color of somebody's tongue. He lifted his fist and knocked quietly. He was working himself up to try again, harder and louder, when he heard a chain slide back and the door opened wide enough to see the man on the other side of it.

Dave was red-eyed and unshaved. His hair was flat on one

side, and crazy on the other. He was dressed, if you could call it that, in a stained gray tee with a flannel pulled over it, and a pair of sweatpants that he'd probably slept in.

"Jesus, fuck," he said. "You again?"

"Me again." Titus nodded wearily. "You were already up?"

"Couldn't sleep. What do you want, man? How did you even find your way here?"

"Daisy Spratford showed up at Maude's, to wake me up and be weird at me. She gave me your address and told me how to get here, and she said that we have to go looking for the bridge. We have to do it now, while the window's still open. Or something. Don't ask me. I'm just the messenger."

"You're a little more than the messenger, dude." Dave opened the door a little wider, and leaned on the frame like he honestly couldn't hold himself upright without it.

"She said I shouldn't go alone, and that you needed answers as much as I do."

"You don't have a car," he observed blearily, with a faint slur that said he was either hungover or still a little drunk from the night before.

"It's still in the impound lot in Forto. Or if it's not, I haven't seen it." Titus wished he had something to sag against. "Do you want to know what's going on around here, or not?"

Dave closed his eyes and tightened his grip on the frame. "I don't even know, anymore."

"*Please* help me. I can't do this by myself."

The bartender opened his eyes and looked back into the house. Whatever he was listening for, or waiting for, he didn't hear it. He sighed heavily and said, "If we go, you can't tell Jess about it. You have to leave her out of this."

"Works for me," Titus agreed immediately. He didn't mention what Daisy had said about her.

"All right, give me a minute. Stay out here. It's early as shit for me and her, but she doesn't sleep that hard. If we wake her up, we'll never hear the end of it." Dave shut the door and left Titus on the porch, where he dutifully stayed.

It was more than a minute. It was enough time for Titus to stand there and eat both the apple and one of the muffins; and then, when Dave emerged looking exactly the same except for a pair of jeans and sneakers, Titus offered him the other muffin.

Dave waved it away. "No thanks. I can't eat this early."

Titus didn't have room for it, so he stuffed the now-empty coffee cup into the bag, rolled it all up, and looked for a trash can.

"Give it here," Dave suggested. He took the brown paper bag and launched it into trees behind the house.

"What was that for?"

"The raccoons, I guess. Nobody lives back there, and I don't feel like taking your shit back inside." He pulled the Jeep's keys out of his front pocket. "Get in. Let's do this."

"We need to get a boat or something. Don't we?"

"Water's not that high right now. I'm willing to get a little wet if you are."

Titus threw a glance into the backseat before opening the passenger door and letting himself inside. "How about weapons?"

"Do you have any weapons?"

"What? No. I came here to go camping like a civilized person, in a cabin."

Dave slid into the seat behind the wheel. "Then I guess we're not going armed. I don't have a gun or anything. Well, I've got a hatchet in the back," he remembered. "Pocketknife, rope, duct tape. That sort of thing."

"So if we want to kidnap somebody, we're golden."

He put the key in the ignition, but didn't turn it. He gave

Titus one hell of a side-eye. "That's a fucked-up joke, man. What with your wife missing, and all."

Titus snorted at the thought. "You and me both know that nobody kidnapped her. But I wish we had some guns."

"It's just as well we don't. We don't want to be those idiots who go into the swamp and shoot each other, thinking we're gators."

"You put it that way . . ."

"Besides, we're looking for a bridge. Can't shoot a bridge. I mean, you *can* . . . but fat lot of good it'll do you." Dave started the Jeep and put it in gear, then looked back at the house. "Shit, I hope she's still asleep."

"We'll be back before she's ready for breakfast."

"Your lips to God's ears." Not seeing any curtains move, or any other sign of Jess in pursuit, Dave took the Jeep out of the carport and put it on the road. Quietly, slowly, until he made it to the side street that would take them downtown, and past Thirsty's, and onto State Road 177 where they might find six bridges going one way . . . and seven going the other.

17

DAISY AND CLAIRE'S

Daisy and Claire were up and around, and putting away the breakfast dishes while Cameron slept upstairs. "We should save him some coffee, at least," Claire suggested. "We're the ones who got him liquored up, after all. He might not want food right away, but he'll want something hot to take the edge off the hangover."

"I'll leave the pot on. How long do you think we should let him sleep?"

"For the next few days." Daisy washed the last toast crumbs off the last plate, and set it on the rack beside the sink to dry. "The longer the better. Keep him here, until the window closes—and everything goes back to normal for the next thirteen years."

"We'll never see the next round. I won't, anyway."

"I doubt I will, either. I can't decide if it's a relief, or a worry."

Claire leaned on her cane with one hand, and used a damp cloth to wipe the table down with the other. "We've told Cameron enough to keep him safe. And you told that poor man where to look, if there's ever going to be a trace of his wife. Maybe he'll find a shoe, or some hair. A sweater, I don't know. Some proof that she existed, and she's gone now."

"We sent him on a wild-goose chase. That's what it feels like. I'm not sure if it was kindness, or not."

"It *was* a kindness." She nodded certainly. "If he doesn't go look now, he'll never know. He'll linger and wonder. He'll stick around this godforsaken place until the gate swings open again, waiting for another chance to get a glimpse of her—and I don't know about you, but I wouldn't wish that fate on anybody. Wild-goose chase or not, it's the only answer he's ever going to get. He can take it, and he can go back home, to wherever he came from."

Daisy looked up, and out through the window. "But what if the thing takes him, too? We can't run around playing God."

"Who's playing God? Don't assume the worst, and don't beat yourself up about it. You were trying to help." Claire paused. "Do you hear that? What's that crunching sound?"

Daisy craned her neck to look down the long gravel path that led up to the house. "Someone's coming up the drive. Well, son of a bitch."

"Who is it?"

"Bet you can't guess."

"Is that . . . Netta's niece? You can't be serious." Claire's eyes narrowed. "Well, I never."

"Never what?" Daisy asked.

"Never did care for that one, that's what. Not once I realized what she'd done."

"She don't look happy."

Claire put the rag down, and stomped the floor with her cane. "You hold her off. I'll get the shotgun."

"She don't look armed."

"Even better."

"Claire, honey, you can hardly hold that big old thing anymore. See if you can't talk to her for a minute—keep her on the porch—and *I'll* go get it."

Daisy left for the utility closet down the hall, and Claire went to the door. She yanked it open just in time to see Jess standing there, hand raised, ready to knock. "What the hell do you want? And who do you think you are, coming up here like you've got something to say? We've heard it all already."

Jess dropped her hand, and put it on her hip. "Nice wards you got out at the property line. They don't work for shit, though. If you know how to kick 'em over."

"You dumb little witch, *you're* not the one we're keeping out. Maybe I should've put in something stronger, if I'd known you'd storm up one day. Honest to God, I thought you had better sense than that."

"Well, it's too late to beef up security now, ain't it? Now what the hell did you tell Dave?"

"I didn't tell him a goddamn thing. Neither did Daisy." Claire planted her feet on her side of the door, and got a better grip on her cane. "Why? Did something happen?"

"He's gone, and so's my Jeep. That means he didn't just pop on down the street to get some coffee. Did he go back to the road? Did you send him looking for that goddamn bridge? He's already looked a million times, and he's never found a thing."

From behind Claire, the unmistakable sliding clack of a shotgun joined the conversation. "Watch your fucking mouth, girl."

Claire stepped aside.

Jess stayed where she was, her toes inches from the threshold.

Daisy stepped forward. "You know good and well why he's never found anything, or else you wouldn't be worried just now, ain't that it?"

Jess didn't flinch. She hardened. "Tell me what you've done."

"Don't mind if I do." Daisy adjusted her grip. The gun was heavy, and her arms weren't as strong as they used to be, but she didn't let it droop. "Nobody talked to your boyfriend, but I had a word with that fellow whose wife went missing. I suggested David might help him go looking for his wife, so if you've got something to say, you say it to *me*. But mind your goddamn manners," she said. Her eyes stayed hard on Jess's, nothing but a few feet and the gun's barrel between them. "Because I don't need your bullshit today."

"That's not playing fair, you with a gun and a line of nails." Jess glared down at the round metal heads that stuck out just barely along the porch floor, a tiny row of soldiers protecting the house.

"If you didn't come here with ill intent, they don't mean a thing."

"Ill intent? I came to you asking for help!" She was growing shrill. Her hands clenched, unclenched, and looked for something to hold. "You've sent my fiancé off to get killed—him and that Titus fellow, alike! Why would you do that?"

"He's a grown-ass man, allowed to come and go as he likes. And since when a fiancé? He's never given you any ring that I ever heard of."

Claire harrumphed and folded her arms. "You been mooning over him since before he came to stay. We *all* know good and well what hand you had in *that*."

"I didn't even know him, until I found him."

Daisy and Claire both laughed out loud, and now the gun's barrels bobbed.

Jess rolled her eyes. "Fine, I'd seen him before—when he passed through on his way to the park, but I didn't *know* him."

"You only wanted to, real bad. Is that it?" Daisy asked. "That was a neat trick you pulled, yanking him free. I don't know how you did it, I'm big enough to admit that much."

"And I don't know how you killed it," she said in return, offering a smidge of respect, clearly on the off chance it'd help her case. Then she added, "I don't know what Dave will find out there. I don't know if it'll remember him, and try to take him back." Tears welled up in her eyes. They might've been genuine. You never do know. "You know what it always says—the things it takes, are its to keep."

Daisy sat down in the nearest dining room chair. The vinyl seat cover squeaked beneath her rear. It wasn't a dignified noise, but she couldn't stand with the shotgun any longer. She let it fall across her lap, but left her hands poised ready to lift it again. "Don't get all weepy on us now. *You* chose who to hurt, and who to keep. *You* could've told him yourself, at any point in these last years. But you didn't. You let him wonder, and halfway remember things he can't understand. If he's taken off in search of answers, that's on you. Not us."

"You went out of your way!" she hollered at them both, openly crying now. "You sent that man to our place, and Dave was too kind to send him off alone!"

"Tell yourself whatever you want," Claire said. "Whatever lets you sleep at night, after what you did to your own flesh and blood. But get yourself off our porch, before the haint blue gives you a burn that stings for a week."

Jess looked up and saw the pale paint overhead, covering the porch ceiling. "That don't bother me at all, you with your silly little charms." But she scratched at her neck, and her nose twitched like it was ready to sneeze. "I'll go, but not because I have to. I'll go because you won't help me."

Claire corrected her. "*Can't* help you."

"Wouldn't if we could, and that's God's own truth. You've made your bed, and you can lie in it." With that, Daisy rose again and went to the door. Using the shotgun as a lever, she smacked it shut.

Claire and Daisy stood very still, not quite holding their breath. They listened, hearts beating too loudly, as Jess made a frustrated growl and then stomped back down the steps, off the porch and back down the drive. The rough rumble of her feet in the gravel was loud, then softer, then quiet. Then gone altogether.

Daisy put the shotgun down on the table, and exhaled so hard that she almost gave herself the hiccups. "I *knew* we should've refreshed those wards, out by the road."

"She's gotten stronger, as she's gotten older."

Daisy took a seat as well, then pulled it up to the table. "Yes, that's usually how it works."

"Not us. We've come over that hump and down the other side. We're slipping."

Claire considered it. "We're out of practice, that's all. We've become so . . ." Her eyes darted to the stairs, and her thoughts flitted to the boy who was sleeping off a hangover at the top of them. "Domestic." Firmly, she decided, "We need to *un*-domesticate ourselves, as soon as possible."

"What's the point of that? Leave the lot of them to their fates—we've done our part to help, and then some. Maybe we shouldn't have said a thing to that poor widower, but we were trying to give him aid, and we've kept Cam safe. That's all that could be asked of us."

Claire didn't exactly agree. "But nobody ever *did* ask. We took it upon ourselves, and we might take on more, if time allows."

"What if it doesn't?"

"Then we won't. Now, I think I heard Cam stirring up there. That woman must've woken him up. I hope his head don't hurt too bad."

Daisy put the shotgun back in the utility closet. She tucked it back behind some old umbrellas and raincoats that nobody ever used or wore. "I hope it hurts bad enough to teach him that drinking is no easy way to avoid anything. I hope he's learned that it's not a habit to pick up, and I hope he stops stealing sips from the decanter downstairs, for a little while at least."

"I just hope it keeps him home. For now."

"Yes. For now."

But upstairs, Cameron was standing at his bedroom window. He'd heard the last bit of the argument, bits and pieces of swears and threats and challenges. When it was over, he'd watched Jess leave—stomping back to the side road that led back to town.

His pulse was throbbing high and hard in his temples, and his throat was burning like it was about to bring up something from his stomach, but he couldn't look away. Not until she was gone past the old gate that never closed, and the fence that was lying on the ground. Then she was lost to the trees, and the road, and the things beyond it.

18

OUT

Cameron paced back and forth, his brain banging around in his skull, and his throat so dry he was spitting cotton. He tried to decide how to play this: He could be upfront with Daisy and Claire, admit that he'd overheard their argument with Jess, and ask them what the fight was about . . . *or* . . . he could climb down the drainpipe and go chasing after the object of his affection, and find out that way.

The quaking of his hands and the wobbling of his vision suggested an obvious course of coffee and breakfast, then maybe a nap—but this was *Jess*. She'd fought with his godmothers, and she was gone, and his gut said she wasn't headed for Thirsty's.

It was only—

. . . he poked his head out into the hall and squinted at the grandfather clock . . .

—ten thirty in the morning.

Jess wouldn't have gotten home until maybe three thirty in the morning. She shouldn't be up at this hour. She and Dave usually rolled out of bed and back to the bar much later in the day. And no, it wasn't weird that he knew this much about her routine.

Was it?

Well, if it was . . . who cared? He loved her, desperately and stupidly. Did anybody ever love anyone else, any other way? If he'd learned anything from the old romance novels he'd read on the sly through the years, picked from Claire's discards and stashed beneath his mattress, the answer was a concrete *no*. That's how he knew it was true love.

He felt just like the girls in those books felt.

No, he wasn't a girl, but it must've gone both ways. He'd read *Romeo and Juliet,* too. Boys were just as bad. *He* was just as bad.

He couldn't just let her go, not like that. Not when she might be heading into some kind of danger. All alone. No sign of Dave. No one to rescue her, if it turned out she needed rescuing.

His stomach lurched, and the idea of climbing out the window lurched, too.

The bathroom was only a few steps outside his bedroom, so he made it to the toilet in time to feed it everything he'd swallowed for the last two days. Two weeks. That's what it felt like, when the puking just wouldn't stop.

Sneaking anyplace was no longer an option. The ladies surely knew he was up by now. Loggers in the next county knew it. The song of his puking had been positively resonant, and had no doubt carried for miles.

Somebody knocked softly on the door. "Cam, baby . . . how are you doing in there?" It was Daisy, of course. Claire couldn't have climbed the stairs that fast.

"I've been better, ma'am." He'd certainly sounded better. His voice was all acid and exhaustion and regret. "But I'll be all right."

"You want some breakfast?"

He gagged, swallowed, and tasted whatever he'd eaten last. He couldn't remember what it was, and he didn't recognize it now. "No . . ." he said firmly, if weakly. "God, no. I don't think I could keep anything down, just yet."

"What about some coffee? Or maybe a glass of orange juice? Something for the taste, Cam. Orange juice will wash it right out of you. You finish up whatever you've got to do in there, and come on downstairs."

"I might . . . brush my teeth." He cleared his throat. The smell of vomit went up his nose, and lingered there. "And take a shower, if that's okay. I feel too gross. I'm . . ." He picked a phrase he'd heard from one of them, at some point over the years. "I'm not fit for human company. You ladies deserve better."

She laughed, short and sympathetic. "You take your time, and do whatever you need. We'll be waiting for you."

He listened for the patter of her feet retreating, and when he was sure she was gone, he stood up and splashed water on his face—then turned his chin up under the faucet so he could swish out his mouth with something fairly cool, and fairly clean. It tasted like old pipes and sulfur, but it beat the taste of his own puke.

Barely.

His toothbrush was in the medicine cabinet, so he took advantage of that, too. The toothpaste mint cleared his head a little and perked him up.

He cupped his hands and drew himself more cold water to sip. When he was finished, his stomach made gurgling noises. The water made him feel better, and almost made him think he could take some food or juice or coffee after all.

He'd bought himself some time when he said he'd take a shower, but he was still wearing the clothes he'd gone to sleep in. Or the clothes he'd passed out in, as the case may be. He only vaguely remembered climbing the stairs to go to bed. He'd gotten up once to pee and hadn't washed his hands, he remembered that, too. He'd tried to turn the sink knob and just couldn't make it work, so he'd given up. He remembered the smell of his pillow.

And morning. And Jess. And a fight that he wasn't any part of.

Upon inspection, his clothes weren't that dirty. He hadn't even gotten any puke on them, so Jess wouldn't care. She probably wouldn't even notice. She'd notice how determined he was, when he went after her. She'd remember his dedication, and his commitment to making sure she was okay. Not everyone fought with his godmothers and lived to tell about it. Not everybody just walked away from them, he knew that, now.

He needed to follow Jess. He needed to find out what this was about.

When he stood up straight, his vision did not swim. His head hurt, right behind his eyes, but he could work with it. He could ignore it for the sake of true love.

The hot-water knob in the big claw-foot tub was tight, and it squeaked. Cameron drew the shower curtain around and tucked it in, to keep the water off the floor. He twisted the lever to send the water from the faucet to the shower head. He gave the cold knob a turn, so that the water would be hot enough to steam—but not so hot that nobody would ever bathe in it.

This needed to look legit.

These small plans, these small details . . . they wouldn't matter in the long run. This wasn't a grand conspiracy, designed to fool secret spies. He was just trying to stall a couple of old ladies, old ladies who would never *dream* that he'd do such a thing.

Even Cameron was thoroughly astounded that he was, in fact, preparing to do such a thing.

This was a way to stall, and to gather his wits—such as they were. He wasn't afraid of them, exactly, because he didn't believe for one hot second that they'd ever harm him. He didn't want to hurt them, and he was loath to disappoint them, and he couldn't imagine successfully lying to them. He would fling himself upon their mercy, when he got back.

There. He had a plan.

He washed his face. He drank a little more cold water from the sink faucet. He ran his hands through his hair, so his damp fingers made it lie down in loose waves. It popped back up again. He smoothed it again, it fluffed up again, and he gave up on it.

As the pipes warmed up, they creaked and moaned. You could hear them all over the house. The ladies would definitely assume that he was showering. They'd have no reason to think otherwise, unless they were Watching him.

He knew they sometimes Watched him. Sometimes, it was helpful—like when he'd gone running from Netta. Sometimes, it was annoying—like when they peeked in on him when he was hanging out at Dave's. At Thirsty's, whatever. All he could do was cross his fingers and hope they had no interest in watching him struggle with the hangover.

He wasn't a little kid anymore. They didn't need to hold his hand when he stepped over the tall lip of the old tub. They didn't need to hold open the towel to catch and swab him.

The little memories hit him one by one. Little darts of guilt stabbed him, but didn't really slow him down. He'd beg forgiveness later. He'd apologize until he was hoarse, and never do it again. Oh, the promises he was prepared to make, upon his return with Jess—safely in tow and grateful for his company.

On tiptoes he left the bathroom and closed the door until it clicked very softly behind him. It didn't lock. He wouldn't lock it; that was just one crime too far. Daisy would curse his name if she had to break the door down to turn off the water. He only wanted to rebel and rescue a maiden. He didn't want to be rude.

Back into his bedroom he sneaked, avoiding the squeaky boards.

He opened the eastern window and leaned out with his left foot leading—straining and stretching—to finally brace against the rickety drainpipe. Just this once, he thanked his lucky stars that he wasn't a big guy. He'd wasted too many prayers asking for more height or more muscles, so maybe someone was listening when his petitions were never answered. The drainpipe would hold a skinny kid, and not much else.

It groaned softly, but it didn't pop loose. Cameron gripped it with his right hand, turned his body, and used his inertia to swing out for the elm. He caught it, fell against the trunk, and held on for dear life.

Then he began a slow but steady descent, branch by branch, until he'd reached the last one that he could stand on with any real confidence. He sat down, scooted forward, and went over the side—holding on by his hands, while his feet dangled in midair.

He let go and fell to the ground about eight feet below. His shoes and knees took the brunt of the impact, and he staggered, caught himself on one hand, and shakily stood up again. When he listened for all he was worth, he could hear the pipes creaking and the shower running. He had to trust that he was—only this one, precious time—half a step ahead of his godmothers. If he wasn't, he'd never make it to the end of the driveway.

But nobody stopped him when he threw one foot in front of the other. In a stumbling run, he left the house, and dashed through the grass beside the driveway because it would make less noise.

He didn't feel like he was making less noise.

He felt like the swish of the grass against his ankles and knees was the loudest sound that anybody, anywhere, ever made in their whole life. Even louder than his puking a few minutes earlier, a noise that had seemed loud enough to drown out a hurricane.

But nobody called him, or set anything in his path to turn him back.

Past the gate that was never closed he ducked. Beyond the fence that was mostly fallen down he leaped.

He was clear.

Hazelhurst was behind him.

He didn't know where Jess had gone, but he could make a guess. She'd gone to the swamp. It all led back to the swamp— to State Road 177, where people went missing, and never got found. Didn't it? Didn't everything?

His chest went tight. Jess couldn't go missing. He couldn't live with the thought.

He'd have to save her. It was the only way.

A quarter mile down the road, it dawned on him that Jess hadn't driven to the Spratford house. She must have walked. He hadn't heard her Jeep, either coming or going. Was she trying to creep up on the ladies? Did she park at the edge of the road, and walk? Cameron knew there were wards around the house, and at the end of the driveway. Could wards pop tires like spikes? Or was that a stupid thing to wonder?

He didn't hear anyone driving now, but then again, he wouldn't. Cameron had a head start on the Spratford cousins, and Jess had a head start on Cameron. If she'd picked up her Jeep again, she would have already driven it off by now.

How big was her head start, exactly? Ten minutes? Less than that, he thought. Five minutes and change. All he could do was make a run for the main road and hope someone who knew him might be driving by and feeling charitable enough to pick up a hitchhiker.

The stars aligned in his favor, and he lucked out right away. Maude was headed west, toward her bed-and-breakfast. She leaned on the brakes when she saw Cameron waving his arms like he was trying to land a plane. She rolled down the passenger-side window with the push of a button. It jerked and dragged until there was enough room for her to ask, "Cameron? The hell's the matter with you?"

"I have to get to the park!"

"What for?"

He leaned over and put his hands on his knees. He was half afraid he was going to throw up again, but he didn't. He looked up and said, "Long story. Did you see Jess come through here?"

"Nah, I haven't seen anyone."

But she was coming from the wrong direction, if Jess had headed toward the swamp. "Good." Cameron nodded. "That's good. She's probably still up ahead. Can you give me a ride? I um . . ." He thought on the fly. "I have to give her a message from Claire and Daisy. It's important."

"Why didn't you say it was for the two of them?" She popped the locks. "Get in, would you."

It was only a few miles to the edge of the swamp, and all the way, Cameron glared out the windshield, hoping for some hint of Jess. He saw nothing and no one, all the way through town and out the other side, past the big ugly sign that had advertised Thirsty's since long before Dave took over the place.

At the edge of the park, where the swamp met the solid land as near as anyplace ever did, Maude pulled off to the side of the road, drawing up behind the only other vehicle in sight. The shoulder was damp with the recent dank mist, and her battered old Corolla objected with tires that spun half bald in the mucky sand. "Isn't that Jess's Jeep?" she asked.

Cameron already had the door open, and was stepping outside. "That's it. That's her, she's here. Thanks for the ride," he added, shoving the door shut behind himself. "I'll get her to give me a ride home, don't worry about us!"

Maude might or might not have heard him, but she left him there regardless. He scarcely heard her car leaving, turning around and aiming back for Staywater.

19

JUST BEFORE

Dave swore and waved hot steam away from his face, then wiped it off his cheeks. The Jeep's hood was up, and its engine was not technically on fire. The radiator had run dry. Everything overheated, and there was no clean water to be found, so this was as far as the old beater would take them for the time being.

"Are we stuck here?" Titus asked, shifting his weight from foot to foot. He fidgeted with his phone, looking for a signal. One bar. Half a bar. Two bars for a split second. No bars.

"Yeah." Dave adjusted the narrow metal wand that held the hood aloft. If it wasn't sitting just right, it'd slide down and close on his head, as he knew from painful experience. "Unless you've got a bottle of water that you ain't mentioned yet."

"No, but I wish I did. Maybe if it starts raining again . . ."

Dave checked the sky. It was overcast and spitting just a hair harder than a mist, and not hard enough to call it rain. "I've got a tarp in the back here, someplace. We could spread it out, I guess. Prop up the corners. Might collect a little rainwater that way. Eventually."

"By then, the engine will be cool enough to drive back." Titus wiped his phone on his shirt and held it up again—watching closely to see if any decent, stable bars would magically make themselves known. But no, they only flickered.

"You don't strike me as a car guy."

"I'm not, but I've had a few clunkers. I've picked up a few things through trial and error, and getting stranded like this."

"You're saying you've been broke."

Titus nodded, still staring at the phone. "Been a contractor or freelancer most of my adult life. It's feast or famine, and nothing in between."

"I hear that." Then Dave said, "Hey man, give up on your phone. We're right outside the park. There's no cell service in the parks."

"Oh yeah, I forgot. I remember arguing about it with Melanie, right before . . . she . . . she got lost. I told my boss back home that I'd check in with him once a day, but when I made that promise, I forgot that I wouldn't have any signal. I don't know what I was thinking." Titus tucked the phone into his front pocket. "So what do we do now? Where do we go? How close are we, to that bridge?"

"The invisible bridge that doesn't exist?"

"You know what I mean, and that makes you unique, my dude. You're literally the only person on earth who understands, just about. Please don't be a dick about it."

Great. Now Titus was sulking.

Dave sighed and used the back of his hand to wipe the mist out of his eyes. "You're right, you're right. I'm sorry, man. I'm just tired. Fact is, I don't have the faintest idea how to find the damn thing. I don't know where it is, or where it isn't. All I know is that it's got to be . . ." He squinted down the road, deeper into the Okefenokee. "That way."

"Then that's the way we go." Titus squared his feet and put his hands on his hips, like he was Peter fucking Pan.

"Like we have any choice."

He set off, his shoes crunching and squishing in the mushy shoulder. "There's always a choice. You could turn around and go back to town. You don't owe me. You don't have to help me. You don't have to help my wife."

"I don't know if anybody can help your wife," Dave said, and instantly wished he hadn't. It was true, but that didn't make it kind, or fair.

Titus kept walking. "Nobody helps anybody. Got it."

Dave hollered after him. "That's not what I said! I just think . . ." He trotted to catch up, but hung back and let Titus take the lead. "There's no guarantee *we'll* help anybody, ourselves included. There's no guarantee we'll find any answers."

"You knew that when you answered the door. So walk with me, or don't. Maybe we'll learn something. Maybe we'll find my wife. Maybe we'll die like assholes."

"Try not to make it sound so appealing," Dave griped, falling into step beside him.

"I'm a hell of a salesman."

He tried not to grin, but grinned anyway. "Hell yeah, you are. Hey, come to think of it . . . *I* got away, somehow. Maybe your wife did, too, so anything's possible." Dave pulled out a pack of cigarettes and a lighter. "Want one?"

"Except for last night, I've never smoked before."

"There's a second time for everything. Or a last time."

"I thought that was for, like, a firing squad." Titus eyed the offered cigarette dubiously.

"Is this better than a firing squad, or worse? Either way . . ." Dave popped it between his lips, and let it dangle. "We deserve one now. Come on." He foisted one into Titus's uncertainly extended hand. "What's it gonna do, kill you?"

"This is a fucking morbid conversation."

"What other kind should we have?" He gestured at the gray road, the gray sky, and the black swamp off to their right. "It's about to rain, we're walking into a swamp full of monsters, and we're looking for answers that nobody's ever gotten before. Let's smoke before the bottom drops out, and it's too wet to keep these things alight."

"Sold," Titus declared, putting the cigarette into his mouth in such a fashion that Dave was now one hundred percent confident he'd been telling the truth about having never done it before.

Dave sparked the lighter and offered it to the end of the stick. "I thought you were the salesman."

"A hell of one," he confirmed again.

Titus did some coughing, Dave did some smoking, and before long, the rain came just like the sky had long promised it would.

Titus hugged himself, his sweater getting dark on the shoulders where the rain was wetting it down. "It's too cold for this."

"This what? This search party? The one you instigated?"

"Yeah, but . . . this is south fucking Georgia, man. It's not supposed to be this cold in the goddamn spring. If I'd known the weather would have been this shitty, I would've never headed to the Okefenokee for a honeymoon."

Dave tossed his damp, half-smoked cigarette onto the asphalt, where it sizzled down to nothing. He looked for Titus's, but didn't see it. He didn't know when the other guy had tossed his aside. "Who picks a swamp for a honeymoon, anyway?"

Titus didn't answer immediately. He stared straight ahead, down the road where no cars were oncoming, and no cars were coming up behind them. "Some asshole. As it turns out."

Dave considered this, and nodded in agreement. "Some asshole."

"I mean, me. It was my idea."

"No, I got it." He marched at Titus's side, blinking rain out of his eyes as it came down even harder. It wasn't a squall and it wasn't a thunderstorm, but it was a nasty, chilly dampness that came down hard enough to be super annoying.

"It was my asshole idea. I told everybody it was Melanie's idea, and she didn't stop me, so I kept . . ." He stared at his feet, and yanked one free of a mud puddle. "I kept saying it until I practically believed it. It was bullshit, though. It was always bullshit."

Dave dodged the puddle and kept closer to the road. The swamp trees were coming closer, and there was only one bridge to go, by his best count. They'd passed at least five before the Jeep had crapped out. "Okay then, so *why* did you pick a swamp honeymoon?"

It took him a minute to find an answer, and when he did, it wasn't a very good one. "It sounded like a good idea at the time."

"A good line for a tombstone."

"Maybe it will go on mine. If I'm lucky, and anyone ever finds my body. Do you think we'll ever find Melanie's? Do you think she's dead? It's been forty-eight hours. I know it doesn't necessarily mean anything, but they say if you don't find somebody within forty-eight hours . . ."

"Yeah, you already said that. But if that's what you really

think, then what are we even doing here? Trying to join her? You could've left me out of that quest."

Titus took a deep breath, and let it out with a shudder. "I'm out here . . . looking for some trace of the woman I only just married a few days ago. Dead or alive. Obviously I want to find her alive. I would cut off my arm and wave it around to get God's attention, if I thought it'd bring her back in one piece. I'm hoping she hears us, and she comes struggling out of the swamp covered in moss and mud and pissed as hell. I don't care if she runs up to me and punches me in the face; I don't care if she's scratched up, missing fingers and toes, chewed on by an alligator . . . as long as she's alive."

"And if she's not?"

He sighed, hard and heavy. "Then I want proof. Some sign of her, anything at all. Her shoes, an earring, a sweater. Her . . ." He hesitated. "Her body, or whatever's left of it. I might puke all over, and I might start bawling, and I might even pass out—fair warning. But I need something. I can't just leave, and go back to Tennessee, and shrug it off and say, 'My wife disappeared, I don't know, whatever.' I need . . . something. Anything."

Dave grunted. He wished for a drier day and another cigarette, but his pack was probably all wet by now—or it would be soon, if he whipped them out again.

"What about you?" Titus asked him. "Why are you here with me? Why'd you even answer the door?"

"Because I don't know what happened. I might've died out here, but I didn't stay dead. If I went anywhere, I came back." He stared down the next bridge. "Somewhere just past this next bridge."

"Yeah, that's what you said by the dumpster."

"No, man. I don't think you understand. I stone-cold *died*. And Jess . . . she brought me back."

"Mouth-to-mouth, or whatever." Titus nodded. "I get it."

"No, you don't. Nobody does. Nobody ever has except for her, and nobody else ever will—unless we find your wife and she needs resuscitating. If we find her and save her, then she might get it. Then again, she might not."

Titus looked like he wanted to say something, but he didn't. He just trudged onward, staring ahead at the next bridge on State Road 177—a determined look on his face, and a slime of swampy rain across his hair and shoulders.

Dave continued. "I was dead as shit, and then I wasn't. There was a bridge." He held out his hands, like he could make some universal gesture for "bridge." He couldn't think of any, so he let them drop again. "And the world went sideways, and then dark. When I woke up, there was this girl."

"Jess. The waitress. She's not exactly a girl."

"It was thirteen years ago. She was . . . I think she was still a teenager. Maybe nineteen, maybe twenty. No older than that." He remembered her, and he remembered that day. The hard road against the back of his skull and his spine. The sky above so amazingly, impossibly blue that nothing was ever blue before, and nothing would ever be blue again. "I'd seen her before, a couple of times. She worked at this coffee shop . . . it's not there anymore. It was before the one that . . ."

"The one that . . . what?"

Dave lost his train of thought. "Check it out—this is bridge number six."

"Is it?" Titus frowned.

He frowned back. "You weren't counting? This is it, trust me. One more to go. Look, this one's normal, right? See, it's two lanes. One in each direction. The bad one just has the one lane, that's what you said."

"How much farther past this one, do you think?"

"Fuck if I know." Dave marched onward, and Titus marched with him.

The water crept closer and closer to the road's shoulder, and the trees got taller and taller. Their reach stretched over the sprawling streams, over the grimy and damp shoulder, and over the asphalt itself—vintage and gravelly though it was. They dangled pale moss and the swamp canopy above them seemed to close. Only a seam of dull gray sky reached through, following the dotted middle line right down the center.

The seam grew narrower and narrower, until it was a thin white line.

The rain dulled to thick, intermittent drops that fell from the leaves; the weather itself was filtered through the cypress branches and Spanish moss and the snakes and whatever else hung out in the trees that loomed along the side of the road. It came down more rarely, but in bigger splats. Dave and Titus didn't get much wetter, but their clothes didn't dry out and their shoes still squished with every step.

"Is it getting late?" Titus asked, shielding his eyes from the water, not the glare. "What time is it?"

"Check your phone," Dave suggested. "It can't possibly be lunchtime."

"My phone is dead."

"It just doesn't have a signal. It isn't dead. We talked about this."

Titus shook his head. "No, I mean, it's dead. It's totally dead. Look." He held it up, and showed a blank, shiny black screen. Nothing else. "This is an ex-phone. A ghost phone, even."

"Did you get it wet?"

"Probably?" He shook it, pressed the buttons on the side, and shook it again. Nothing. "Do you have a phone?"

"In my back pocket. Maybe it stayed kind of dry." But when

Dave pulled it out, he found that it was dead, too. He squeezed the appropriate buttons, wiggled it, wiped it off, and held down the power button. "Well, shit. It's either not the water . . . or we're both soaked, so maybe it *is* the water. Let's say it's the water."

Titus was quick to agree. "All right, it's the water and not some sinister force, ramping up its game as we get closer to that seventh bridge." He was trying not to sound nervous.

Dave was nervous, too. He shrugged, like this was no big deal. "We didn't *really* have phones anyway. No signal, remember? No cell, no Wi-Fi. The only thing we're missing is a watch. It's no problem."

"It's kind of a problem."

"If it was *really* a problem, it would've come up before now," he said with a shitload more confidence than he felt.

"At least my phone had . . . it had . . ." Titus waved it around some more, like that did any good. "A compass and stuff."

"What good would a compass do us?" Dave looked up at the trees, and out at the water swirling and roiling between the cypress knees and vines and logs that may or may not have been logs or alligator snouts, and there was no way to tell except to poke them with a stick. Were things moving out there? Things that weren't snakes and gators and frogs and birds? Did reptiles move at all, in weather like this, when the sun was hidden, and the air was too cool for spring?

Titus had stopped walking. He stared straight ahead. "Shit's getting weird, isn't it?"

"Shit's always been weird. We're getting closer, that's all. The question is . . ." Dave stopped, too. He looked over his shoulder; he was three or four steps in front of Titus, whose mouth was hanging open as he breathed. No cigarettes, no lighter. No coffee and no clue. "How much closer do we get? It's now or never, man. Either we keep walking, or we go back to town and call it a wash."

"Why?" He swallowed and stared straight ahead, past Dave and up State Road 177.

"You can see it now, can't you?"

Titus whispered. "Is that what I'm looking at?"

"I don't know," Dave whispered back, looking forward at the mirage of a thing in the road ahead. "What do *you* see?"

He stared, trying to figure out the details himself. He listened.

Titus talked. "I see a dark place, just over there. It's a little farther away than I can . . . than I can see clearly. It's so far away, and so dark . . . the details are fuzzy—even though it can't be more than a hundred yards up the road. It's narrow, though. It's a skinny little spot where the swamp meets the sky, and there's a little pathway through it. From here, it looks like . . ."

Dave went ahead and said it. If he didn't, neither one of them might ever do it—and he needed to give it a name. He needed to remember and recognize the thing that had taken so much away from him, all those years ago. He tried to keep his voice level, and he mostly succeeded when he said, "It looks like a bridge."

"Yeah, but it looks like . . . a pinch," Titus didn't quite argue. "It looks like a tight place, where the road narrows and the trees are too close, and the water is too high. It's a pinch in the fabric of space and time."

Dave sniffed, but he couldn't look away and he wasn't about to contradict him. "You watch too many movies."

"It's just a bridge, but it's not a bridge. *Look at it,*" Titus pressed, his voice an octave too high, and his hands gesturing expansively. "That's not a *real* thing. That's not a *real* place. That's something else. From somewhere else." He gazed at Dave harder and more pathetically than anyone ever had before, in Dave's whole life.

He pondered a decent answer and couldn't come up with one. He could only see the tiny place up ahead, that pinch in reality that didn't make any sense, and never had. "We've come this far, man. All we can do is . . . we keep going. We stand on that fucking bridge. We look out at the water and see if it has anything to say."

"But it's not the water, is it?"

Dave forced himself to put one foot in front of the other. His feet proceeded slowly and reluctantly. They went without any real determination, or goal—practically of their own volition. "Then it's something *in* the goddamn water. But we can't see it from here." Momentum caught up to his shoes and he kept going forward, a little faster. At a normal pace, almost—if you were walking someplace you didn't really want to go.

Titus got into gear, too. He didn't want to lead, and he didn't want to follow. He clearly had no idea what he wanted, and only half an idea of his destination. He fell into line. Single file. Right behind Dave, and none of this was even Dave's idea.

Together they quit worrying about the narrowing shoulder, and they quit worrying about the traffic.

In the middle of the road, they walked toward the point in the distance that was infinite, and everywhere, and no place at all. Then they saw the thin scar of a trail, leading off to the right—winding back and forth, into the swamp. Under the bridge.

20

IN THE WAKE

Beside the Jeep, a series of scuff marks looked like footprints. Is that what they were?

Cameron crouched down low and his stomach lurched, but everything stayed where it ought to be . . . or else there was nothing left to vomit. He'd seen enough old mystery shows to investigate the area like a detective, or like his idea of a detective in the 1950s.

Someone had gotten out of the Jeep, that much was clear by the marks in the gravel. The engine had overheated. The hood was up, and a thin trail of steam still hissed up slowly into the air. It smelled like grease and rust. He hadn't missed her by much.

He checked inside the vehicle and saw nothing amiss, and nothing unusual. No sign that anyone had left in haste or unwillingly . . . so this was probably exactly what it looked like: plain old car trouble. He couldn't tell if Jess had been driving alone or not. She'd left Hazelhurst alone, but she might've picked up Dave on her way to the swamp. Dave might've gone with her, and Cameron had caught his name a couple of times in the argument.

But if Dave had come along for the ride, he was gone, too. The vehicle was abandoned.

For now, Cameron would assume he was dealing with Jess, and only Jess. It was easier to keep going that way. He didn't like Dave, and he didn't like the idea of Dave being around while Cam was trying to run to the rescue. Some hero he'd be, if he found them together and everything was fine. At the very least, Jess should have the decency to be lost.

It was a stupid, rude thought to think.

He knew it as soon as it formed in his head, but he only halfway regretted it. He really didn't like Dave. Maybe that was unfair, considering the guy let him hang out in his bar, spending almost no money, ever.

But there it was.

He looked back and forth, up the road and down it. He didn't have to wonder which way she'd gone: it was either into the swamp or back to town, and why would she go back to Staywater if she'd come all this way? Ordinarily, he might assume that she walked back to town to get help with the car, but if she'd done that, he would've seen her on the ride out with Maude.

That meant she'd gone into the swamp. She'd left her car and gone along the road, as the clouds curdled and thickened above, and the trees leaned closer and closer to the shoulder with every yard.

So Cameron did, too.

He crossed one bridge and stopped at the middle—looking

over the side and squinting down into the murk. He saw water, swirling slowly from eddy to eddy. Somewhere out there, gators were masquerading as flotsam and jetsam. A snake wound its way between everything else, unmolested. It might've been the kind you'd find in the garden, like faithful old Freddie who kept watch for rats and other interlopers.

Or it might've been a cottonmouth. It was hard to say from all the way up there.

Vertigo crept up on Cam, even though the bridge wasn't very high. It was maybe tall enough to admit a man standing in a canoe, not that anyone in his right mind would do that. The bridge wasn't anything that anybody would ever jump from, in some final act of desperation. A jumper might break a leg, but he sure as shit wouldn't die.

It'd be more of a stumble than a plummet.

But the ladies had let him have so much Jack, and they'd done this to him on purpose—he understood that now. Or he remembered it now. Come to think of it, they'd warned him up front of their intentions, and he wasn't sure if that was better or worse than them being sneaky.

He closed his eyes and pretended that he'd had nothing but lemonade the night before, for all the good it did him. When he opened them again, he looked up at the sky and got a face full of chilly drizzle. It almost felt good. He almost didn't hate it, even if he was kind of cold. His sweater was wool, but it wasn't magic. It'd keep him from freezing to death, even in the damp. That was all he could ask, and the most he could expect.

He buttoned it all the way up to a spot below his neck. He wished for a scarf, and then unmade that wish. The thought of something so close against his throat made him want to gag.

He could pretend all he wanted. He had a hangover, and it wasn't going anywhere anytime soon. He wished he were a more experienced drunk, a man with some decent ideas about how to fix a hangover. He knew that some people drank hot sauce, or coffee, or ate greasy food; but Cam didn't have any of those things handy, and the cold mist in his face would have to do. It felt kind of good, for all that it was kind of annoying.

Enough dillydallying, as Daisy would say.

He pulled himself together and kept on walking to the other side of the bridge, and back to the road's shoulder—not that any- one was coming in either direction. But the shoulder narrowed into a strip that was hardly a foot wide, and his shoes were stick- ing and unsticking in the wet sand and gravel.

He trudged forward, scanning the scene for any sign of any- one. A footprint with a skid mark made him wonder if Jess had left the road, but he couldn't tell how old the print was, or what kind of shoe it came from. He wasn't even sure if it belonged to a woman or a man. Or a kid. It was just as well there were no Boy Scout troops for him to join, anyplace within fifty miles. He would've been absolute crap at whatever it was they did all day.

He was on a straight road that went directly back home one way, and into a state park the other way. There was no way on earth to get lost as long as he stuck to it—but that didn't stop him from feeling like he was, in fact, utterly lost.

Until he'd gone another half a mile. Until the something new came into view.

When it did, his stomach couldn't decide whether to sink or rise. It wanted to do something other than stay where it be- longed, that was for damn sure—and Cameron didn't have anything to wash down the taste of vomit, so by pure force of will, he kept everything in one place except for his feet, which deter- minedly, slowly, moved.

Toward whatever that was up ahead.

It was a bridge. One he couldn't recall having ever seen

before, not in any of his trips on the rusty old bicycle before it'd fallen apart, and not while riding around with Jess or Maude or anybody else. He didn't know how many bridges he'd crossed already, but he could guess the number if he had to.

He could, but he didn't want to.

The bridge up ahead was hardly a blip on the horizon. It was nothing but a small dot where the road nipped in tight to a single lane, with a vague and uncertain darkness waiting on the other side. This was where the creature lived, or where it died. This was where its ghost lingered, and lured, and killed.

Should he call it a ghost? Is that what it was? It must be.

From a certain angle, everything was a ghost eventually.

He stopped walking, much to his belly's relief. He might still have one more real good, real bad puke left in him—but God, he hoped not.

Alas, hope had nothing to do with it. His insides lurched, and he stepped off the road a little farther—to the place where the shoulder met the water. You shouldn't just barf in the middle of the road. He didn't know why he felt that way, but he felt it deeply and profoundly; if you were going to hurl, you should hurl into either a container or something wet. Preferably both, ideally a toilet. You definitely shouldn't do it out in the great wide open, where a car could come along at any minute. Even if one probably wouldn't.

Seeing nothing of the sort, he looked instead into the brackish puddle flecked with algae and grass, and he retched. Nothing came out except a filthy stink of bile, and a mouthful of saliva that he spit, and spit, and spit until his mouth was mostly dry again.

He couldn't decide if he was glad that he hadn't vomited again, or if he wanted to get it over with. If it was inevitable, maybe he ought to just stick a finger down his throat and be done with it. He psyched himself up, leaned over, and with great personal resolve and determination, raised his finger to his open mouth.

And stopped. He lowered his hand, and his extended finger pointed down at the mud beside the road. There, he saw a footprint. It was deep and sliding, as if someone had stepped down into the muck and skidded down.

He stood up straight, then stooped to take a better look.

The print had been left by a sneaker, he thought. Not a boot, not a sandal. Because it was smeared and smudged, there was no way to say how big it was. Could it be Dave's shoe? No, he didn't want to believe that. There was no good reason to believe it, not when Cameron was coming to the rescue.

Up ahead, he heard someone moving. Someone running.

He heard the patter and splash of feet moving swiftly across the damp earth. He glimpsed a flash of color, and the shape of a person beating a speedy retreat from the road. He thought he saw long brown hair. He thought he saw denim cutoff shorts, and sneakers without any socks.

Did he, though?

"Jess?" he breathed. Then, "Jess!" he called, before taking a moment to wonder if it was his eyes or the swamp or something else playing tricks on him. There wasn't any time for that. If he was being tricked, then fine—he was being tricked. But he wasn't standing still, letting the love of his life get lost in a swamp and eaten by monsters.

He staggered forward, his feet less willing to fly than his heart.

"Jess!" The word burned his throat, where the whiskey had burned it before and the vomit had burned it later on. It all felt raw, like he hardly had any voice at all—but when he shouted again the woman stopped.

She looked over her shoulder, only for the briefest of seconds.

She was so far ahead, and so far away—Cameron couldn't see for a fact that it was Jess after all. The woman's features ran together at a distance, and her clothes might have been shorts and a tee with a flannel she stole from her boyfriend; or her clothes might have been a sundress, or anything else. All the details were fuzzy and they wobbled in and out of focus, but that didn't stop him.

It was probably just the hangover. Hangovers played tricks, too.

"Wait for me!" he called, and then he coughed.

She didn't wait. She turned on her heel and kept running along the weird path, as fast as her legs would carry her. This time, Cameron told himself, she might not have heard him. She was so far ahead, by now. She might've mistaken him for someone else. Or it could be that the woman's name wasn't Jess, and she didn't want him to follow her. No, he didn't believe that.

Or it could be.

No, not that, either.

Except.

What if the fleeing figure was no woman at all? What if it was just one more wobbly detail? A figment that lied and vanished, like so many other things in the swamp?

She was going, going.

Her hair flew in an arc as she took one look back at the bridge. She disappeared into the bleak, grimy darkness.

She was gone.

Cameron took a big, deep breath, and then when it expired to the point that his lungs ached, he let it out and did it again. The third breath was the charm, and it gave him just enough gas to get him moving. He didn't run fast, but he ran—and as he drew up closer to the spot where the woman had vanished, he saw that he'd been mistaken: She hadn't darted down the bridge, and across it to the other side.

She'd left the road.

She'd jumped into the swamp before she'd ever reached the bridge.

A small path led away from the road and down into the swamp. It twisted and turned, no straight lines and no right angles, winding through the trees. It was dotted with footprints that'd been freshly shoved into the damp, sandy dirt.

"Okay," he said to the path, panting heavily and bending over double. "Okay, she didn't take the bridge." He rallied, because if she hadn't crossed the bridge, that meant there was still hope for her. Right? Was that how it worked? He *hoped* that's how it worked. If he'd known how, he would've prayed it, too.

He wiped a smear of rain off his forehead, out of his eyes. It was raining now, not just misting or drizzling. He was thoroughly wet, and not merely moist.

He looked at the trail, winding through the wet and muck.

He looked at the bridge, and he said, "Not *yet*."

21

LAST CHANCES

Daisy stopped talking and listened hard for something she couldn't see. Claire kept on talking about poor Cameron and his terrible hangover that served him right, but Daisy shushed her. She waved her hand and pointed a finger at the ceiling. "Wait a minute, honey. Listen."

"To what?" her cousin asked. "The water? The pipes? The dear boy is taking his own sweet time, but bless him, he must feel like absolute shit. Let's not fuss at him, for running up the hot-water bill. Not this month, when it's our own fault. Even if it *was* for his own good."

"No, I mean *listen*. What do you hear? I hear just the water, and just the pipes. What I *don't* hear is the creak of the tub, when he steps around in it."

"That one claw foot is a little squeaky, I'll grant you." Claire scrunched her mouth with suspicion, and looked up at the ceiling. The bathroom was directly over her head, and a few feet to the right. "He might be sitting down, resting. He might be half asleep in there. Last time I had a bad hangover, the only thing that felt good was sitting in a stream of steaming water. I bet that's what he's doing."

Daisy didn't buy it. "There's no shift in the timbre of it, when the spray hits his head or when it hits the porcelain. It's just a shower of water, pouring straight down uninterrupted."

"Your hearing is outstanding, for a little old lady."

"You're littler than I am," Daisy said. "But thank you." She scowled at the ceiling, as if she could see past it and right into the bathroom, right through the cast-iron tub. "It's not just my hearing, I'll have you to know. It's intuition, too."

"Are you using your gift?"

"Not right this minute. Don't need it, when I know the boy like I do. Anyway, the water interferes with it, for some reason. I'm just using regular old hearing, and I'm *not* hearing the sounds a boy makes in a bathroom when he feels like shit, but he's taking a shower. Something's off," she insisted. "I'd bet my ass on it. Well . . ." She rose from her chair and proceeded toward the stairs. "I'd bet *yours*."

Claire protested, "Stick to betting your own body parts, you old bat." But it took her a minute to get out of her chair and follow. She did so with a struggle and leaned against the rail at the bottom of the stairs. "Let the boy have some privacy," she hollered, but Daisy was already most of the way to the top.

"I'm not gonna beat the door down and catch him with his willie in his hand. Don't be nuts." True to her word, she went to the bathroom door and stood there, listening for motion and looking for a sign of steam coming from the crack under the door. That boy liked his baths hot enough to boil pasta. "Cameron?"

She said his name again and knocked, not too softly. She already had a pretty good idea of what she'd get in response, so when she was answered with nothing but silence, she yanked the knob and threw open the door.

The shower curtain was wrapped around the tub, holding in the spray.

Downstairs, Claire yelled something new and more insistent about not bothering Cam, but Daisy ignored her.

She yanked the curtain aside and shoved her hands into the stream of water. It was cold. "Son of a bitch," she said to herself. Then she wrenched off the water, dashed back to the top of the stairs, and said it to Claire, as loudly as she could. "Son of a *bitch*!"

"What'd he do now?"

"Guess," she said, taking the stairs back to the kitchen as quickly as she was able. "Just fucking *guess*."

"He wasn't in there?"

"No."

"Did you check his bedroom?"

"I didn't have to." Daisy crashed over to the kitchen table. She put her hands down on it and spread her fingers, steadying herself. "He left the water running and the door shut. He wanted us to think he was here, because he isn't. At least he had the good sense not to lock the door; Lord knows I'd have tanned his hide if I'd broken that knob to get inside. No, the little monster took off."

"For where?"

"For wherever he thinks that young witch has gone, unless I'm badly mistaken. He's got the worst case of puppy lust I ever saw." She changed her mind about the table and went to the radio, then turned it on, leaving the needle parked between two stations so the static was mostly pure.

"You think he's gone to David's bar?"

"I *hope* that's where he's off to, but I doubt he'd go to this much trouble, if that's all he was planning. If he wanted to run off to Dave's he might ask permission first, and if we said no, he'd strike out alone when he thought we weren't looking. That's how it usually goes. But this time . . . this time he's planning to ask forgiveness instead. That's what scares me, Claire. He's just stupid enough, even after everything we told him . . ."

"Just stupid enough to head for the water, looking for the bridge. Oh God, you don't really think so, do you?"

Daisy didn't, but it might not matter. "He's not looking for the bridge. He's looking for *her*. I don't know how much he over-heard, when she came by. Jess thinks her man went riding off into the swamp, so that's probably where she's headed, too. That's what any eavesdropper would think."

Claire pulled her chair out and struggled to return to the seat. "Get my needles. Get my knitting bag. It helps me think."

Daisy did as she'd asked, dropping the bag into her cousin's lap. She pulled up a chair and put one hand on the radio, the other on Claire's shoulder. "Get yourself going, and let's see what we can find. Let's cross our fingers and pray he's just headed for the bar. Nothing would make me happier than being wrong, just this once."

"You're never wrong by much."

"There's a first time for everything. Now concentrate," she commanded with more desperation than authority. She shut her eyes and listened to the static and listened to the needles as Claire found the start of her yarn and got to knitting. Her pro-gress came at a frantic pace, and a stitch was dropped for every two that were sound. Each flaw clacked in Daisy's head, knock-ing her off her groove. "Slow down," she told her. "It doesn't have to be fast; it just has to be right. Come on, now. You can do better."

"Well I'm *scared*, Daisy. What if he's gone off to the bridge? What if it hasn't closed down yet, and that spirit's still there? What are we gonna do? That boy is the only thing that ever grew here. The only good thing we ever tended."

"I wouldn't go *that* far," she muttered. Then she changed her mind. "Oh, yes I would. A few tomatoes and some rhubarb don't compare to that child, who was left to us for raising. It's our job to protect him. I don't know who gave us that job, and I don't know why—but I sure as shit don't plan to drop the ball now."

Claire paused to fix a stitch. "We can't let him run off and get killed, or get disappeared like the rest of them."

"We *are* doing something: We're listening. Hush up, please. I'm trying to hear. I'm trying to see." She stared at the radio speaker, at the round metal grate with a few tiny tines bent and rusted. She looked into the pattern and opened her ears. She opened her eyes.

"Do you have him? What's he doing?"

"Give me a second, would you?" She concentrated, letting her eyes unfocus and watching the speaker grate go fuzzy. "He's . . . he's feeling poorly. That's the first thing I've got."

Claire harrumphed. "I should think. He's got enough booze in him to floor a bigger man for a day."

"He's outside in the rain—wet and getting wetter. He's on the road. Headed . . . headed I can't tell just yet. So much of the god-damn road looks so much like every other part. Maybe he's headed for David's after all, looking for a little hair of the dog."

"What else, Daisy? Do you see anything to mark his position? Any milestones, or mile markers?"

She looked and looked and looked. A mile marker, yes. A sign for SR 177. "Goddammit, he's not aiming for David's. He's headed toward the bridge." She smacked her hand on the table and stood up, then shoved the radio off the counter and let it smash to the floor. One speaker grate went rolling across the linoleum; the other merely acquired a new dent. The radio was still running, though, so Daisy kicked it violently, punting it around the kitchen until it came unplugged from the wall and finally went quiet.

"So it's as bad as we thought?" Claire asked with a squeak.

Breathless and outraged, she shoved the radio grate with her foot. It scooted under the fridge. "It's as bad as I feared, ain't that bad enough?"

Claire's needles went still and her hands went limp. She let the knitting fall to her lap. "Maybe not?" she tried desperately. "If you really thought there was any danger, you wouldn't have sent that man looking for a sign of his wife there. Would you?"

"Not on purpose, but what if I was wrong? I think I was wrong, cousin. I think it's still there. I felt the black hole it leaves in the swamp, when that beast rises up and uses the bridge like a lure. Waves it around, that's what it does—like them fishes at the bottom of the sea, who have those lights hanging off their faces."

"Anglerfish."

"If that's what they're called. You've read more *National Geographic*s than I have." Daisy clenched her fists and breathed deep, trying to think—trying to find the center of the situation, and see some way past it. Somehow, she had to catch up to Cameron. The boy they never asked for, but couldn't imagine doing without.

Claire's eyes were wet when she said, "We can't do this. Not again."

"Don't say that. We're not finished yet."

"But it's *true*," she pressed. "We *are* finished, and you know it. We're too old to run off and fight like we used to. I can hardly walk, and neither one of us can drive—if we even had a car to go chasing after him. But we owe that boy. We can't let him face this alone."

"From another point of view, you could say he owes *us*." It was a weak protest, and Daisy knew it as soon as she said it.

"I wouldn't say that at all. He was a baby, and he didn't ask to be left here with us. Even if you're right, from a certain *point of view*," she added with something perilously close to a sneer. "We owe the town, too. All this time we've felt real good about saving Staywater . . . it was all bullshit. We haven't saved anything or anybody, so long as that bridge and that bastard keep coming back."

"We never told nobody that we saved Staywater."

"Word got around anyhow."

Daisy didn't quite agree. "Not the right word, because we didn't finish the job. There's more work to do here, cousin. Whether Cam gets stolen away or not, somebody else will, somewhere down the line. We fix this now, or we fix this never."

"We did the best we could."

"Only at the time. At the time, killing it was the best we could do." Daisy leaned back against the kitchen sink, half sitting on it, with her hands on either side of her hips. "And now? How do we finish it off? How do we fight a ghost?"

Claire's face went hard. She stared past her cousin, out the window, into the backyard where birds and the season's first bunnies were getting into the garden, but she couldn't bring herself to give a damn. She inhaled hard, and let her needles lie crossed in her lap atop of the tangle of yarn. "How did we fight a monster? You remember, don't you. We behaved monstrously."

"I'd argue we behaved bravely, smartly, and even heroically."

She rustled up a grim smile. "I'd never tell you different. But I think you know what I'm trying to say."

Daisy met her eyes. "Are you sure? *Really* sure? There's no changing your mind. No second chance if we're wrong, or if it doesn't work. All we have left is a Hail Mary, and who knows if it would even work."

"I never believed in Mary or most of her kin, and this *is* our second chance. We tried to be heroes, and we only made it halfway there. I'm not even sure if it counts, but we still have time to finish the job."

"We can try. We should try." Daisy sagged and gripped the sink tightly. She stared out into the yard, too. "Staywater is our garden. We're the only ones who can tend it."

"Like you always say about gardening . . . there are so many things you've gotta kill, if you want to do it right."

"But are you *sure*?"

"Perfectly." Claire nodded hard. "I mean it."

Daisy meant it too, but her part would be harder. The decision was made. She hesitated anyway. "You know . . ."

"Pull yourself together. Do what needs to be done."

Daisy Spratford nodded. She went back to the hall closet where the shotgun had been stashed. She picked up the box of shells that went along with it and returned to the kitchen, where the Formica table with old chrome trim was rusting and leaning.

Claire had put her knitting into a tidy pile within her bag. She put the bag on the floor and folded her hands. She set them on the table, like she was waiting on a cup of tea.

"Any last words?"

Her face was still hard, and still crossed with that fixed, determined grin. "I'll see you in a few."

Daisy lifted the gun. She didn't give herself time to reconsider, or hesitate, or overthink the decision. She pulled the trigger and Claire's head snapped back. Then what was left of it fell forward with a splat. Her body toppled onto the table.

Daisy's hands shook. She lowered the gun. It was too big and her arms were too short. She couldn't turn it on herself; she didn't have the reach for it. But she had a glass of lemonade, and she had some Jack left over from the night before. She mixed the two and added enough rat poison to kill a steer.

She pulled up a chair next to Claire and sat down. "All right, honey. One last round, eh? Bottoms up."

22

THE TRAIL

Titus looked toward the sky, but he couldn't see it. Only a canopy of dark, sagging branches loaded down with moss hung broadly overhead, permitting nothing but a faint glimpse of grumpy gray through the leaves. "We're lost. We're so lost," he mourned.

"We're not lost. The road is over that way," Dave said, pointing his thumb in some meaningless direction. "As long as we know where the road is, it's basically impossible to get lost."

"I can't see the road, and I can't see the bridge. I can't see anything except this trail, and I think I saw that tree over there . . . maybe ten minutes ago."

"You can tell one tree from another?"

"Not usually, but that one looks like it has a face on it. It *doesn't* have a face on it," he added quickly, lest Dave think he'd started seeing things. "It just looks like it does. See?"

Dave stopped and stared at a ragged trunk that was wet with swamp water, sap, and bird shit. "Oh, I get it. Yeah, if you look at it right. Those are eyebrows."

"Uh-huh. I saw those eyebrows earlier, and if you look . . ." Titus pointed a little lower. "Right here, it's like a little green mustache. I'm telling you, I've seen this tree. We're going in circles."

"We can't be going in circles," Dave disagreed, but he looked back the way they'd come anyhow. "We haven't left the trail."

"But don't you get the feeling . . . like it's not . . . it's not *right*?"

"None of this is right. Isn't that why we're here?"

Titus didn't know whether to nod in agreement or shake his head at the futility of it all. "None of it's right, and none of it's normal. This trail is fucking with us. It's leading us around and around and around again."

Dave hugged himself. He was wearing that flannel with a jacket over it now, but it wasn't enough to keep him dry, or warm, either. "But how? What does it want? I mean, if you want to ask what a trail wants, or what a bridge wants."

Titus was cold and miserable, and thoroughly wet. "Maybe it wants us to wander around until we die of thirst."

"Not likely. The swamp water is terrible, but you can drink it if you have to. You'll shit out worms for days, but you won't croak. Nah, we're more likely to die of a snakebite, or get snatched up for a gator snack, or . . ."

"Knock it off, man," Titus snapped. "I don't need to know all the ways we can bite it out here." He looked down at the trail, wondering if he'd spot any sign of his own footprints, having come this way before. No such luck. He gazed imploringly back at Dave. "But we can't stop here. We have to keep moving."

"If you really think you're lost, you're supposed to sit still and wait for rescue. Build a fire or some shit." Dave's teeth were chattering, and his nose was red. When he spoke, puffs of fog came out of his mouth. "That's what they tell you in the Scouts. Not that it matters, I bet. Stay or go, sit down or keep walking. Either way, we're not getting anywhere."

Titus gazed back and forth between the only guy on earth who kind of believed him, and the trail that was undoubtedly lying to him. "We can't give up now. We've been walking around for half an hour already, and when we left the road, we could see the damn bridge. I can't figure out why we can't find it now."

"Me either, but I'm about ready to give up. We should quit while we're ahead."

"You don't mean that."

"Yeah, I do. Let's call it, and try to find our way back to the road."

He was losing Dave. If Dave left him there, could Titus go it alone? He wished to God he had the balls to keep moving by himself, but he didn't. He needed a sign. Any sign. Any hint at all, that they weren't wasting their time—anything he could show Dave to prove that this wasn't as fruitless as it looked.

Then he saw the shoe.

It was wedged between a cypress knee and a ragged branch, half submerged in the thick black water. A sandal, not the sensible kind. Something entirely unsuited for hikes or camping or canoeing around in a swamp.

Titus saw it, and the wind left him all at once, and he saw stars. He thought he might pass out and he couldn't quite talk—not even when Dave took his upper arm and asked if he was okay, because he looked like he was about to pass out.

He pointed down into the water, then dropped to his knees despite Dave's best efforts to keep him upright. The soggy shoe was just far enough away that Titus got wet up to his knees as he crawled toward it, but he didn't care. He hardly noticed. The swamp water was warmer than the rain, that was the only difference.

Dave tried to pull him back, but he let go when Titus scooted forward into the water. "What the hell are you doing?"

"Look!" He found his voice, raspy and feeble though it was. He seized the sandal and held it aloft. The heel was soaked so badly that it was about to fall off, but it was still clearly recognizable as a woman's shoe. "This is hers!"

"It's . . . a shoe."

"It's Melanie's shoe!"

"Are you sure?"

He nodded so hard that the stars in his eyes cleared up, shaken away or scattered to someplace less intrusive. "I told her not to wear these. I said they were stupid, because you didn't wear sandals with heels in the swamp—but she liked them, and she wore them anyway. Just to spite me."

"To spite you? On your honeymoon?"

"No, no. I shouldn't have said that, and I only did because I was in asshole mode." He sat up, cradling the shoe. "The truth is, she liked them. She thought they were pretty. It didn't have a damn thing to do with me." He hugged the soggy sandal against his chest, where it left a shadow of mud on his shirt.

"This is good," Dave said. He didn't sound like he believed it, but he was trying to get back on board. "This is a clue. It's proof we're not going in circles."

"Kind of."

Secretly, Titus was afraid that this was just another trick, another bread crumb to keep him circling inside the trap. It had to be. He was too certain that the path was looping, and he was being played. Melanie used to accuse him of gaslighting her, and he hated it because sometimes, he knew it was true. Kind of true. Not exactly true, but true enough from a distance. Sometimes he only wanted her attention, and he couldn't figure out a better way to get it or keep it.

Now he was being gaslit by a goddamn swamp—or by the washed-out pale thing that waited underneath a bridge he couldn't find.

But he had this shoe. He held it like a lifeline, though it wasn't connected to anything at all. There was no second shoe, no matter how hard he stared down at the water and psychically commanded it to provide one.

"Hey, man. What's . . . that?" Dave sidestepped past him, a little farther down the path. "Looks like . . . it's something shiny. It's . . ." He picked it out of the mud before Titus could climb to his feet and join him. "An earring, I think. It's broken." He held it up.

Titus staggered over, still clutching the sandal. "Let me see." Dave held it up.

Titus took it and wiped it on his shirt. Then he wiped it on a cleaner part of his shirt, a part which the shoe hadn't covered with mud. It was the size of his thumb and shaped like a cicada with intense and gruesome detail, in his opinion. "This is hers," he said with pure and perfect confidence. "She bought these in Atlantic City, when we went there a few years ago. They were the cheapest, tackiest things I'd ever seen in my life, and she thought they were hilarious. They made her laugh, and she laughed when I rolled my eyes, and she bought them anyway. Where'd you find it?"

"Here, it was right here." Dave pointed.

"We wouldn't have missed this, and missed the shoe too," he lied to himself.

"But you just said—"

"I know what I said. But I'm not blind. I would've seen this. One of us would've noticed it." If he said it hard enough, enough times, he might believe it. He *needed* to believe it. If he couldn't believe in the gleaming piece of bug-shaped metal in his hands, then nothing was even possible anymore.

Titus stuffed the bug in his pocket and tucked the shoe under his armpit.

"What are you doing?"

"We *have* to keep going now. You see that, right? You understand? This is proof. She was here."

"Some part of her was here," Dave said a little coldly. "Don't buy your own bullshit. A gator could've taken this stuff. Rats could've done it."

"Or she could've lost it, as she was running away from something. Or just walking around, getting lost like we are. It doesn't have to be a fucking tragedy." Titus was working himself up to this new idea. "It could be exactly that simple. She left the road and got lost, and went in circles—that's what people do, when they get lost."

Wryly, Dave said, "Yeah. I know. We've had that conversation."

Titus ran with it anyway. "So we talked in circles, and she ran in circles, and she could be . . . she might've found the bridge, and just stayed there, hoping someone would find her. She wasn't a Scout, Christ knows. But if she got tired enough, she'd quit running around and find a place to sit down and cry. She could still be out here!" He forced himself to brighten, even as his stomach was doing leaps and twirls.

He lumbered forward, farther down the trail.

Dave hung back. "You're losing your shit, Titus." He didn't yell it. He just said it like a fact.

Titus tried to respond in tired, confident kind. "Nobody's losing any shit. I'm going to find my shit. I'm going to find my wife."

"That sounds—"

"I know how it sounds!" Titus shrieked, loping into a clumsy run. "But I'm going to find her! She's out here, someplace!"

Now Dave came up behind him, slower and less certain. Not running, but awkwardly jogging—the tree-filtered rain smacking him in the face, and his damp clothes sticking to his body. "You're losing it, man! Pull your shit together, for fuck's sake! Or for your wife's sake! For *my* sake! Do it for me, man!"

Titus didn't even look over his shoulder. "Your sake?" he shouted to the trees.

"Don't leave me here by myself! Last time I was here by myself, I died!"

"So what are the odds it'll happen twice?" He laughed, and it sounded crazy even to him. He laughed again anyway. "How special do you think you are?"

"The things it takes . . . are its to keep," Dave said quietly, like he wasn't sure Titus would hear him. Like he didn't care either way.

Titus froze, skidding to a slippery stop. "What did you say?"

They faced one another on the trail, both breathing hard. Breathing steam. "The things it takes, it keeps."

"It didn't keep *you*."

"It keeps everyone else, except maybe you—if it ever took you in the first place."

Neither man found any new words, and the swamp felt terribly, terribly close. Then they heard the shouting. A woman shouting.

"Jess," gasped Dave.

"Melanie," squeaked Titus.

Whoever she was, she was close, and she was crying. She was just ahead, unless the acoustics fooled them. Why wouldn't the acoustics fool them? Titus wondered. Everything else so far had been designed to fool them. Everything was a trick. Everything a circle, everything a lie.

Probably this, too.

It didn't stop either one of them.

Titus ran in front, but only until Dave overtook him and charged into the lead, into the trees. Into the swamp.

Going, going.

Gone.

23

THE DARK

Cameron walked into the dark, and into the darker. The sky had gone from white to gray to charcoal, and the trees were taller and closer, and the rain was steady—even when it was broken up by the leaves and the moss and whatever else hung over his head: twigs and branches and snakes and curious birds, and buzzing insects, too, even though it felt chilly enough that there shouldn't have been any bugs. There were always bugs.

It felt like late afternoon, just before sunset. It couldn't have been half past lunch.

He hugged himself and kept going. He had a path. It was kind of a shitty path, but that was better than no path at all. Right?

Except.

Down in the bottom of his belly he knew: The path could

not be trusted. He had a very bad feeling that he was being lied to, profoundly and capriciously. When he went forward more than a few yards, and then looked back—the way behind didn't look like the way he'd come. If he didn't know better, he'd think that the trail was shifting behind him. He didn't know better. He had to believe his own two eyes and his sense of direction, muddled by the hangover as these things might have been.

He wasn't crazy. He'd seen that stump before. It made him think of a very fat dog, squatting to take a poop. Something about the shape of it. If he hadn't been so miserable, he might've laughed about it. If he hadn't been alone, he might've pointed it out to someone in order to share the giggle.

The path led in a more or less straight line, if you stood still in the middle and looked down it—back and forth. But when he followed it, he traveled in circles.

He thought about Daisy and Claire, and everything they'd told him about the bridge and its dead master. If a bridge could be a trap, then a path could be a liar, now couldn't it?

Well, what did he know about paths, anyway. Maybe it was playing a trick on him. Maybe he was only disoriented, and he should've thought to bring a compass or something.

Not that he would've had the faintest idea what to do with a compass. A compass would tell him which way was north, he guessed, but he didn't know what good that was. He thought he was going west, but he might've been going east. He knew the sun went down the one way, and came up the other. But he couldn't see the sun. The sky was gray and dead. The sun could've been anywhere.

He considered other things, too.

Most of all, he considered turning around and going back home. He wasn't that lost, when he could hear a car going by, once in a blue moon. Cars meant the road was off to his left. If he could find the road, he could find his way back to Hazelhurst.

He might even make it back before the ladies knew he was missing, if fate was with him.

Fate would not be with him. Rationally, he knew that.

The way things worked, here in the real world, Daisy would have gone upstairs by now and found that the shower was running with nobody inside it. She and Claire would have sat down together to have a little scry with their knitting needles and radio static. They would realize he'd gone out to the swamp because they could probably see him there, if they looked hard enough.

Then what?

He paused, shivering. His heels sank very slightly into the wet path that was more mud than dirt.

What would they do, when they knew he was gone, and they knew where he went?

He hadn't really sensed them watching, like he sometimes could. He hadn't gotten that prickly feeling on the back of his neck and between his shoulder blades—the feeling that said there were eyes on him, from somewhere far away. He'd noticed no odd rustling through the trees, and no odd shapes in the water, tracking his progress.

If they'd looked in on him, they hadn't watched for very long. If they hadn't seen him yet, they'd see him soon. When that inevitably occurred, what would they *do*?

It had surely been decided by now. They undoubtedly had a plan under way, mid-execution. But what was it?

That's the question that niggled at him, leading him to stand there like a dummy in the middle of nowhere, all alone and chasing a phantom who might or might not be the girl he loved. It might or might not be something far worse, leading him into a trap. He didn't like that thought, so he pushed it out of his head. Still, a sick, clammy feeling spread in his chest, up into his throat.

It was only the hangover, he told himself. It was only the things he shouldn't have been drinking, not a terrible sense that something had gone wretchedly wrong in his half-formed rescue plan.

Not that he had even half a plan to work from. He knew about as much about plans as he did about paths.

He thought, as he stood there, that Daisy and Claire might call the police. They might ask Pickett for help, since they always flattered him so excessively. They liked to tease him about being young and handsome, even though Cameron thought that nobody so freaking awkward ought to be called handsome to his face. It just wasn't kind.

No, it was just a game the ladies played, pretending to flirt. It was a game Pickett played in return, pretending to be embarrassed but liking the attention anyway. No harm in it. No implied threat or danger, though Pickett surely must know they were more than the sweet little old ladies they appeared to be. He was new to town, but he wasn't *that* new.

But that's who they'd call.

Yes, that's what they'd do.

They'd call Pickett and tell him that Cameron was lost. Pickett was probably already in his patrol car, heading down State Road 177, hanging his head out the window and using the speaker to call out Cameron's name. The sound of this one-man search party ought to be ringing out across the Okefenokee by now.

Why wasn't it? Was he that far from the road? That lost? That wrong?

He held very still and listened very hard. It had been a few minutes since he'd heard a car.

Birds chirped back and forth, complaining about the weather. Fish splashed and so did snakes, he assumed. So did gators, not too far from the path that grew more narrow with every few yards. Soon it would be so thin that he'd have to walk one foot behind the other, single file. Soon it would be a tightrope.

A sharp syllable rang out—a human voice, exclaiming something.

Was it his name, shortened to Cam like people sometimes called it? Was it someone shouting for help? It hadn't been more than four letters, surely—the outburst was too short for that. Was it afraid? Angry? Hopeful?

Desperately, he wished to hear it again.

He waited, wet and clutching his own arms, his face held up to the sky like he could see this strange sound, should it happen again—like he could see its trail and follow it all the way to its source, if he looked hard enough.

His patience was rewarded when it came again, not so loud— but it absolutely came from somewhere up ahead. Someone was farther along on this faithless path that led somehow deeper into the swamp, if it went any direction at all.

"Maybe it doesn't," he said to himself, one more "maybe" in a vast and uncertain string of them. "Maybe it doesn't go anywhere but circles, around and around like . . . like . . ." He looked at the water near his feet, scanning for alligators or snakes. He didn't see either one, but the trailing eddies made him think of water circling a drain. That part, he didn't say out loud—in case the ladies were listening. He only thought it real hard, and tried not to feel it in his bones.

Nothing would have surprised him.

No, that wasn't true. Anything would have surprised him. Everything did.

He jumped out of his skin when he heard the call a third time, and when he played it over in his head, again and again in the span of a second or two, he was confident that the voice belonged to Jess. Her voice was as familiar as always; even in brief—even in a single syllable, whatever it was—he knew the same voice that offered him water with no lemon and teased him about buying tater tots that would spoil his supper.

It was her. It *had* to be.

He ran, blind and wet and forward, even though running in any direction was hard. His stomach still hurt, and it was very loud—empty except for the slosh of acid that crept higher and higher up his throat. His heart was loud, too. It banged in his ears, keeping time to the throb of the headache that had never quite left him. He was cold and he was almost completely soaked, and his jeans were heavy slabs of icy fabric clinging to his legs.

He was worried about Jess, alone in the swamp without anybody coming to save her except for him. He was worried about the ladies, too, though he couldn't have articulated exactly why.

He needed them, and he'd run from them. He'd tricked them. He'd done them all a grave disservice, he knew it from the bottom of his heart. No, someplace deeper. In the deep dark bottom of his soul, which was undoubtedly going to hell—if there was any such place. The way the ladies brought it up in their routine and copious cursing, it surely must be.

Because he'd tricked them.

They'd tricked him too, he recalled, in some slim sham of defense. *They* were the ones who got him drunk, thinking it'd keep him home long enough for the danger to pass. But their trickery was the good-hearted kind. His was the selfish kind, and he knew it.

No, his feeble defenses rallied in a small, persistent measure. His was the trickery of true love, and no one could fault him for that. Jess would understand. She'd probably even love him back at long last, too. Those were the rules, he was pretty sure. No one could fault him, not any of the poets or writers or even Shakespeare, who wrote about it all the time.

No one could possibly blame or scold him except for himself, because suddenly this wasn't the best idea in the world. He'd done too many bad things to see it through.

This might actually be the worst idea in the world, but he was eyeballs-deep in it now. Now, all he could do was chase that cry, track down that person who was surely Jess, and do it at top speed so he had something to show for this betrayal.

The path veered to the right, and something moved—he saw it from the corner of his eye, and almost tripped over himself trying to see it better; but the cry came again, and he abandoned whatever it was. The splash in his wake said that it'd been big, maybe a gator or something worse.

He didn't need to see it, and as he ran, he decided that he didn't want to know. Forward was the only way through.

The path pinched, and widened, and straightened. It was as long as a runway, a tiny landing strip in the middle of nowhere. At the end of it a woman stood, facing away from him. Watching something that flickered and darted between the trees up ahead in front of her, barely beyond the horizon where Cameron could see it.

He doubled over and gagged. Nothing came up.

He stood up straight. He wheezed, "Jess?"

She didn't turn around, but it was definitely her. He knew her long brown hair that was both wavy and limp from the rain, and her skinny jeans that she'd cut into shorts—the ones with the rhinestone design on the back right pocket. The pretend diamonds glinted in whatever light there was, wherever that light came from. They sparkled and dazzled him, the gems on this little square on her ass-cheek that he'd seen a thousand times before.

It hypnotized him, until he blinked it away.

"Jess!" he tried again. "There you are, Jesus . . ."

Relieved by the sight of her, he approached at a slow walk. He didn't want to look too eager. True love was cool, but desperation was never sexy. He might not have a proper television or the internet or anything but romance novels and two old ladies with a radio, but even Cameron knew that much. You had to take it easy. It was best to act like there was no rush, no danger.

Unless you were acting out of passion, and that was a different thing entirely. If you wanted to stop a girl from leaving, you ran up to her and kissed her so she wouldn't get on a boat, or she would get off a train and come back to you.

But this was a rescue mission. When faced with a romantic rescue opportunity, you needed to look like you were in control of the situation.

Cameron was absolutely in control of this situation.

As he walked, the rhinestones on her pocket flashed and the thing between the trees in front of her kept sliding from here to there, behind this trunk, around that one. Always glimpsed but never truly spotted. It was a shadow in front of her . . . white and opaque. It was a ghost of a shadow, and that made sense, he thought. Everything was a ghost. Everything was a ghost story.

Eventually.

Jess stood as still as a statue, and still facing away from him. She wasn't even breathing, that's what it looked like from where Cameron was, walking slow, trying to look cool, even though she wasn't looking in his direction and no one could see him unless Daisy and Claire were—

—No. He would've noticed. Probably. He always noticed. No, he often noticed. Right now, the universe was silent on that peculiar frequency where the old ladies would watch him, and think they were sneaky. Right now, no one could see him except for the thing in the trees that was just in front of Jess, who still wasn't moving, wasn't breathing, and wasn't turning around to answer him when he called her name.

And he wasn't getting any closer.

It took Cameron fully a minute to suspect it, and another thirty seconds to be confident. No matter how cool he walked or how nervously, no matter how long his steps or how short they were, he was not getting any closer to Jess—who was planted on the path like an oak.

She remained exactly as far away as when he'd first seen her. She hadn't budged. She might as well have been a hologram, or a photograph laid out as a trick of perspective.

Cameron stumbled to a stop. "Jess? Turn around, would you? Are you . . . are you okay? You don't seem okay." He wasn't okay. The swamp wasn't okay. Nothing was okay, especially not that thing in front of her—just past her, just inside the tree line. It was not shaped like a person and it did not move like a person. It slinked back and forth, smoothly and swiftly for something with such an ungainly shape.

Cameron recalled a time when he was small, and he'd been playing hide-and-seek with himself in the long venetian blinds that used to hang in the living room. He'd been charmed by the look of his own reflection, hidden but visible, a boy in stripes of light and stripes of dusty plastic that hadn't been cleaned since before he was born.

That's what the thing in the trees looked like. A reflection of something that wasn't here anymore, but refused to leave.

And that's what the trees looked like: a row of blinds hanging down on the other side of Jess, who did not move and did not speak. It was as if the path ended where she stood. Like she was stopped in front of a movie screen that stretched all the way from east to west and back again.

Or. Or something else.

He couldn't think of anything else. His brain was going at a million miles a minute, trying to parse the scene.

Jess was a doll. A voodoo doll, pierced with pins he couldn't see. She was a photograph. She was a mannequin, like the ones in the shop front downtown who never moved, but sometimes changed—a dressed-up thing that only took action when no one was looking. Always different. Never in motion.

Cameron couldn't look away. Jess was none of those things.

"This isn't right. This isn't . . ."

He broke his attention free and looked back after all. He looked forward. Something watched him in return from between the trees, but it had no shape or face that he recognized. He didn't know where to look at it, when it didn't have eyes and he couldn't see its mouth.

"You aren't Jess." It wasn't even a question. "You're . . . an illusion. A hallucination." Whichever. "This is a trap." He was certain of it, and saying so out loud made him feel no better at all, only more confident of the truth. "This is a trap, and I walked right into it. You're not Jess. I bet you're not even human."

He looked to the sky, but he could barely see it through the trees. He listened for the ladies. "Miss Daisy? Miss Claire?" Nothing responded. Nobody replied. "Oh shit. Oh shit. Oh . . . I have screwed up big."

He shook, and shook harder, and his whole body vibrated until his teeth knocked together.

"What do I do? Miss Daisy, Miss Claire . . . what do I do?" he implored, but he was alone except for the mystery beast that

slithered and climbed and crawled through the trees, and the fake woman who was not Jess, and maybe was not anybody at all. Maybe she was a ghost, too. "I have to get out of here. I have to get back to the road."

Finally the figure spoke. Its words were Jess's words, as perfectly hers as if they came from her throat, though the thing that looked like her did not turn around. It said, "There is no road. There is only the bridge." Then it collapsed, top to bottom. It disintegrated like a kicked sandcastle, and when the earth was still again, there was not so much as a pile of dust to prove that it'd ever been there in the first place.

24

THE STASH

Daisy rummaged in the hall closet while Claire tackled the storage shed.

The window was open, so they could hear each other when they called back and forth—not that their voices were loud, and not that anyone else could've heard them at all. They could hear each other just fine, and they could also hear the ghosts who sometimes hid in the old bedroom upstairs, and the spirits of the town a few blocks away. The world was filled with the whispers of the dead, and the cousins shouted over them all.

What about the shotgun? Daisy asked.

Can't hurt. I found a nail gun.

Might help.

Claire kept digging. *I didn't even know we had a hatchet. It's*

*steel. Got some rust, but close enough to iron. I'll add that to the ar-
senal. Is that what we're building? An arsenal?*

Yes, and we've got to build it fast. Daisy lifted up the shotgun.
It stayed in the closet, but she carried it away—an outline, a
memory. She held it close, a spirit of something that was never
alive. She cocked it, and it sounded like it always had. She
grabbed a box of shells the same way, and added them to her
purse, where they rattled together with the sound of tiny wind
chimes.

*See if you can find those golf clubs my daddy used to have. They're
in there someplace.* Claire hefted up a garden hoe, testing its unreal weight in her hands.

We gave them to Goodwill, I don't know how long ago. Daisy
pulled out an axe, just a hair bigger than the hatchet. She didn't
know they'd had either one, and now they had both, and that
was fine by her. It wasn't terribly large but anything with iron
would strike a real blow when these monsters were alive, so they
could do some damage in the afterlife, too. That's how she figured it.

She added it to her purse, which otherwise would not have
held much more than an overstuffed wallet, a packet of tissues,
and a tube of ChapStick. While she was at it, she stuffed in a
pocketknife and a long flat-head screwdriver with a chip on its
blade. Everything disappeared into that little crochet bag that
was hardly bigger than both her hands folded together.

Claire asked, *How will we find Cameron?*

Same way we always do. We'll look for him.

Claire came back inside the house, walking up the steps like
she used to, forty years ago when she didn't need a chair or a
cane. Her hair was darker and straighter, and curled up only at
the ends—just above her shoulders. Back in the day, she did it

with soup cans and bobby pins. Now she did it by memory. *Can you think of anything else we might need?*

Daisy was blonder and a little thicker, in a way all the men in Staywater (and Forto, too) used to call "pleasing." She wore a light blue dress she used to love, and hadn't seen since long before Cameron came along. *Can't imagine what else we might use. This will either work, or it won't.*

If it doesn't work, then we lose the boy—and we did all this for nothing.

Daisy opened her bag and pulled out a pack of cigarettes she'd been saving since the Reagan administration. *We were going to die anyway, sooner or later.* When she was alive, and the wrinkled pack was barely more than mulch at the bottom of an old purse, they would've tasted like dust. But she was dead and now everything was just like it ought to be. She lit one with a match on the kitchen counter, and it tasted like being young. It tasted like life, which was surely ironic, as if she gave a shit. *So what if we jumped the gun? If we have to throw ourselves into the void, then that's what we do this time. Wherever that goddamn monster goes, we're escorting it out. Once and for all.*

Once and for all, her cousin agreed.

While we're at it . . . Daisy put the gun over her shoulder and grabbed a pair of sunglasses that she'd found in the back of a drawer. *Let's do something about that bitch from the bar.*

This ain't her fault.

In the scheme of things? No, she said. *But this particular round, this particular mess . . . it's on her head. Cameron, and David, and everything that ever came of poor old Netta—mad as a hatter and half as useful. This belongs to her.*

Claire sighed. *If it hadn't been Jessica, and Netta, and James, who got tangled up in the thing this time—it would've been somebody*

else. But now I think about Netta, and maybe it's just because of what we did, and how I can see better now, and hear better now . . . Daisy, I wish we'd been gentler with her.

She was none too gentle with us, even when we did *try to do right by her. She came at us, like we were the ones who did something to her boy. But . . . she relented. Maybe we can do a little righter, this time. Will that make you happy?*

Yes. No. It'll make me feel more satisfied, if that's the same thing.

Daisy nodded. *That's close enough. Come on, now Cameron needs us.*

Can you see him? Can you hear him?

I can't see or hear a damn thing just yet, but if he don't need us now, he'll need us soon.

Claire steeled herself and tightened her grip on the hoe. She wielded it like Daisy did the shotgun. *Come on, then. We've gotta go find him before that beast does.*

Couldn't have said it better myself.

The ladies left through the front door and stepped into the yard, then strolled down the driveway. By the time they reached the end, they'd faded altogether—drifting by force from one place to another. Slipping from living to dead, from Hazelhurst to the Okefenokee swamp and an old stone bridge that didn't belong there, or anywhere else.

25

THE BRIDGE

Dave ran toward the sound of the crying woman, and the faster he went, the more certain he became that this *had* to be Jess. He knew that cry, the frustrated and angry sob she would sometimes do when they fought—on the few occasions when an argument went that far. Usually, he gave up long before she resorted to the waterworks. Usually, he had the good sense to apologize and let her have her way, regardless of whatever that was.

Once she was crying, they were in for the night. They were going to bed angry, like it or not.

Sure, they'd argued the day before. Sure, he'd taken her Jeep while she was asleep—and maybe she was awake, and discovered what he'd done. She could've come out here looking for him. Could she have beaten him there? If she hitchhiked, or if she got Pickett or Kemp or somebody from the bar to drive her,

it was possible. He couldn't think of any other reason she'd be out here, much less ahead of him someplace on the trail and crying her eyes out.

She must be hurt, and surely she was lost.

Yes, the cops must've given her a lift, that's what probably happened. She woke up and found the Jeep gone, so she'd called for help. Either Kemp or Pickett would have happily set himself on fire, on the off chance she might look his way, and say, "Hey, look at that dude in flames." She was the prettiest thing in the whole county, and Dave was lucky to have her.

Once in a while he forgot he was lucky, and that was his bad. He shouldn't do that. He *wouldn't* do that, not anymore. Not once he found her, and talked her off a ledge, and convinced her to come back to town, come back to Thirsty's.

He'd never forget his luck again. He promised and prayed it.

"Just let her . . . be . . . okay," he gasped between labored breaths. He wasn't a runner, and he was somehow both freezing cold and sweating through his clothes.

It was too cold for this time of year. Everybody said so, and everyone was right. Was it this cold back in town, or only here in the swamp? No, that would be crazy. The swamp was always wetter, hotter, and heavier than this. It should never feel like walking through a meat locker. Not even in the dead of winter.

It wasn't supposed to. He knew it, and he tried to ignore it. If it was true, it meant that whatever was wrong was bigger than a bridge, bigger than a missing, crying girlfriend and somebody's wife who nobody was ever going to see again.

This was nuts.

He was nuts.

Titus was nuts, too. Behind him, Titus was hollering for him to slow down—but fuck a bunch of that. They were lost and being lied to by the swamp or something in it, and if Jess was lost too, at least they could all be lost together. It beat being lost alone with some whiny dude he barely knew, and maybe shouldn't have tried to help.

But even as Titus's voice grew more distant, Jess's voice did not sound any nearer.

No matter how the trees slipped past like jagged frames from a slowing film strip, and the water between them blurred, the crying voice was always the same distance away. No, when Dave listened again he thought it was worse than that: the voice was growing fainter and farther off. Very slightly. So slightly that it might have been a hallucination, a trick of his eyes, or another hoax of the swamp.

He didn't know where he was going, but that was fine. He didn't know where he was coming from, either, and although the swamp had been leading him in circles before, he suddenly felt like he'd escaped that grinding loop.

So something had changed.

Titus was silent.

Dave looked over his shoulder. No, Titus wasn't silent. Titus was gone.

He looked forward again. Now the path was as straight as any arrow; it was flat and dry, almost a sidewalk cutting through the water and mud. Dave didn't know when it had made this stark and unsettling shift. One minute his feet were sticking in the mud, and the next he was flying, kicking up dust in the rain.

None of this could be right. You didn't kick up dust while it was raining. The swamp wasn't a walk-in freezer during the spring.

He drew up to a stop, skidding a bit from pure momentum.

His shoes scraped short trails into the dirt, and left small swoops as he turned around, then around again. He pivoted this way, and that. Titus was nowhere to be seen, and nowhere to be heard, either. Jess was still crying somewhere in the distance, but the crying was softer now. It didn't sound like crying so much anymore. It didn't sound like laughing, either. But it wasn't sorrow or confusion.

The woman's voice was burbling and low, like running water thick with slime.

"Jess?" He stared down the ramrod-straight path. It didn't disappear between the trees or sink into the swamp. It simply ended, thoroughly and abruptly, at the horizon line.

Only there weren't horizon lines in the bottom of the swamp, standing in a place so dark in the middle of the day that Dave could hardly see the sky.

He looked back the way he came. "Titus? Man, where'd you go?"

Titus didn't answer.

But he could hear Jess. She wasn't speaking, she was mumbling. No, she was singing—but it wasn't any song Dave had ever heard. It made his skin feel tight, and his cheeks go flush.

"I can't believe any of this," he reminded himself. "This place is lying. That's not Jess."

He listened, not expecting a reply and not getting one. The path wavered, moving above the earth like hot air on a summer street. If Titus was behind him, he was too far away to be heard. If Jess was in front of him, he wasn't going to catch up to her this way.

"That's not Jess, and I have to get out of here."

But there was an end to this. There had to be. When he looked back again, half hoping to see Titus crashing through the overgrowth. No such luck. Dave was standing, making a single point on a tremendous line that stretched from one end of the world to the other, and all the way around it. There was only this perfect walkway, narrow and long, without any branches or breaks.

"David."

He jumped and whipped his head back and forth. The word had been whispered close, right into his ear. It was Jess's voice. But it was *only* her voice. He couldn't convince himself it was really her. He could only admit that it was a perfect copy of her voice, if she'd ever once—in all their time together—called him David.

"What do you want?" he asked the voice.

The reply came from nowhere, from no one. "The things I took."

There was no other noise at all, that was the worst part. No bugs or splashings, not the faint patter of what little rain made it through the canopy. No wind through the branches and moss. Nothing dripping or running.

He heard absolutely no other sound, until the rocks began to move.

They ground together, big pieces and small—something moving, unearthing itself.

No. That wasn't quite right. He understood this, when he saw a shifting shadow at the end of the path, in the place where it did not end but merely stopped. The shadow expanded and adjusted, growing and assembling itself stone by stone, until it was big enough to drive under. Or over.

When the rocks quit moving and the illusion at the end of the trail had found its finished form, it was clearly and terribly the most mundane of things: a rickety old bridge, sitting atop an arc of stone.

Before Dave was certain that he'd come to a decision, he was moving forward. He hadn't commanded his feet; they worked independently of his brain, though he did not try to stop them. He knew he *ought* to stop them—he should *want* to stop them— but he steadily paced forward. What else should he do?

There was nothing behind him. (He understood that now.)

In front of him, there was only the bridge and its master, or its servant. (Whichever one it was.)

Nothing moved beneath the bridge, and no weird creatures scuttled back and forth. No pale horror only loosely shaped like a man—and more closely described as an alligator with long arms and long legs—prowled excitedly between the pillars that held up the arch, that held aloft the road someplace overhead. No skinny, dead beast with gleaming teeth the color of coal crouched low to the earth and stayed there in the grass, which did not swallow it until only the bright black eyes and the shape of its skull were visible.

"I can't believe anything I see here," Dave said to himself, in choked, tiny syllables that were cold in his mouth. They spilled over his lips like the chilly fog he exhaled with every breath. "There's no chance that anything here is true."

"That's unfair." Her voice came again, so close that he should've been able to trust her.

"You're not here at all. You've never been here."

"Now that's untrue," the voice insisted. "I was here, and I made a bargain. Come closer, dear. I can show you."

"Who are you really? Talk to me yourself—quit hiding behind her voice. Use your own, or shut the fuck up."

At this suggestion, the rocks adjusted themselves, and between the grinding noise of granite rubbing itself into sand, there was a low hiss, and a lower growl, and a tragic hum that rose and fell, but did not sound like any song, or any words.

Dave frantically looked to the bridge, and back again—where the trail was rigid and inscrutable, and Titus was nowhere at all.

Under the bridge a creature did not move, and it did not shift in the wet grass.

In Dave's ear, Jess's voice did not say, "When I spoke to you myself, you could not understand me."

"Do . . ." Dave coughed and swallowed, and the fog went down his throat. Back from whence it came. "Do you *want* me to understand you?"

"I don't care."

The last letters of the last word lingered and dragged and lured. They pulled him like a string, or like a leash. (It felt more like a leash, tugging him along by the throat.)

They drew him toward the bridge.

26

THE GATE

Titus followed Dave until he couldn't keep up anymore, and the other guy disappeared ahead on the winding path that doubled back, circled around, and didn't make any sense at all. They'd only done thirty or forty seconds of flat-out, full-tilt running, but it might have been thirty or forty minutes for all he could tell. His chest hurt, his legs hurt, and his side had a cramp, but that wasn't all. He was swiftly learning that time was not so much meaningless there in the swamp, as irrelevant. It probably was a bit before noon, but it felt like twilight. He hadn't left the Jeep more than an hour ago, but it felt like it happened yesterday.

"Dave? Jesus Christ!" he shouted with all the breath he had left. Nothing answered but the retreating footsteps of his companion crashing after a voice that sounded like the waitress, unless it sounded like Titus's wife. Except when he couldn't hear it at all.

He stumbled forward, because backward wasn't going to get him anywhere new—and if he was going in circles, then he'd wind up back where he started. Forward felt like progress, even if he knew good and well that it wasn't.

There was only one path. Dave wouldn't have left it willy-nilly. He'd have to catch up to him eventually. Hell, Dave wasn't any more of a runner than Titus was, so he couldn't have kept going all day. He probably stopped just out of earshot. He was probably out of breath, just like Titus.

But he couldn't hear Dave anymore, calling for Jess. The shouting hadn't gotten fainter and fainter as his semi-reluctant companion had pulled ahead. It had simply stopped.

Could be, he'd caught up to Jess and that's why he wasn't yelling for her anymore.

But it hadn't been Jess, had it? It'd been Melanie's voice, clear as day. What was wrong with Dave, that he'd thought otherwise? Didn't he know what his own girlfriend sounded like?

Titus knew damn good and well what his wife's voice sounded like. He would've known her anywhere, even here, where the air was cold in his throat and the trails came and went in circles. She was lost, he understood that now. She was every bit as lost as he was, and as lost as Dave must be by now. Any second, Dave would come doubling back.

Any second.

He stopped staggering forward and perked up. What if Dave had found Melanie, instead? He'd be disappointed, but he would stop yelling for Jess. It explained the sudden silence, and it explained why Dave hadn't come back looking for him yet.

It was as good a theory as any. It made him feel better and move faster. He started running again.

Jogging, at least.

He launched into that half walk-trot that doesn't really go any faster than a standard stroll, but feels like an improvement. He couldn't be too far behind them, and Dave couldn't be too far ahead—from wherever he'd caught up to Melanie.

All he had to do was catch up to them both.

"Titus."

His head jerked around, and the rest of him followed—a full circle, trying to figure out where his name had come from. He was alone, but he'd heard it right in his left ear, clear as day.

"Melanie?"

"*Here* . . ." The word ran long, exhaled slowly and finished with a faint gasp, choked off at the end.

There was a shift in reality; he didn't see it but he felt it, a drop in his stomach and a flicker of the headache that had never quite left him.

When the moment finished, the path lay spooled out before him, straighter than it was before. Straighter than it'd ever been, or ever had any good excuse to be—there in the middle of the swamp, where the cypress trees grew too close together and the water was too sprawling and deep to allow any such thing.

But there it was, as perfect as if it'd been drawn with a ruler.

"Melanie, if I find you at the end of this, I don't even care why you did it," he declared. He was walking now, heavy with the realization that something was wrong beyond any wrong thing he'd ever imagined. "I don't even care *why* you left, or if you're not lost then I don't care why you've been hiding. If it was my fault, you can just tell me. I promise . . . I promise I won't put words in your mouth. I promise I'll shut up and listen. If you changed your mind, I'll understand. We can get the marriage annulled, if that's what you want. If you want to give me a chance to be better . . . to be more *decent* than I've been so far . . .

I would really love that. Please give me a chance. Things will be different, I swear."

He felt that awful shift again, and this time it was like all the sound had been sucked out of the world. If he didn't talk, he'd go mad. "If you're lost . . . I understand. I just . . . I hope you're okay. I want you to be okay. We can . . . we can be okay together. Better than okay. Please come back to me. Please?"

He looked up but didn't see any birds.

He stared around the water and looked for gators. Snakes. Turtles. Anything.

Nothing alive moved. Now that he'd stopped rambling, nothing spoke except for the faint, horrible voice that came from no place, and no one. It absolutely did not come from Melanie. This didn't so much dawn on him, as become very obvious all at once.

"You're not Melanie." He didn't need to ask. He knew when he'd been lied to, even if he couldn't see the liar and now, he couldn't hear it, either. His ears popped, and his eyes watered.

Finally he heard some sound apart from his own voice: the grinding, crunching rustle of big rocks. It was coming from the end of the path, where there was now a bridge. It hadn't been there a moment before. He would've bet his life on it.

He shook his head, but that didn't clear it. He blinked his eyes a dozen times, and wiped them, too. That didn't change anything, either.

Right there he saw a bridge, old-fashioned and overgrown. It must have been there for a hundred years, and not ten seconds. Its stacked stone formed a large arch, and on top . . . that must be where the road was running. A single lane. He had to guess that part, without being able to see it.

He hadn't realized how far below the road he and Dave had wandered. The top of the bridge must be twenty or thirty feet above the spot where he stood.

For that matter, where the hell *was* the road? He couldn't see it. There was no break in the trees on either side of the bridge, not as far as he could tell. It was almost more like a standing building than a connective and functional piece of architecture.

It was a bridge that didn't look like a bridge. No, not at all. If Titus wanted to describe it accurately, he would have to say that it looked like a gate. The gate was something ancient and Roman, or inspired by some ruin of the Greeks. It was a relic of something older than that, even. He stared at it hard. If he looked long enough, the thing might explain itself.

Figures moved beneath it. At least two of them. One was as white as a cave fish, shaped like nothing he could describe—but he recognized it all the same. He'd seen it from a more mundane bridge, out on State Road 177. It'd been moving in the water, neither man nor monster, but a little something of both. Some dead, hideous mutation of either one.

Titus could hardly bring himself to look. His eyes slipped off the creature, unwilling to hold it for too long.

Besides, there was something else to see.

Someone else.

When he quit trying to watch the unreal thing with the long, sharp face and the thick, clawed hands, he saw that it wasn't alone. A woman stood there, in the curved shadow of the bridge. She had light hair and was wearing shorts and an oversized sweater, hugging it around herself.

He thought of Melanie's sandal, left on the trail. He looked at the woman's feet, but he was too far away to tell if they were bare.

"It doesn't matter, because I know it isn't you." His mouth was so dry that the words rasped through his throat. "Not really. Not anymore."

He came forward anyway. Slow and unsteady, but unable to stay planted on the unnatural path where he was safe. Safer.

Perhaps nowhere was safe and nothing could stop him, not even his own good sense or any force of will he might've had on some other day, at some other time. On a better day, a week ago. When he wasn't freezing and unseasonably cold, and wet, and somehow thirty feet below street level in the middle of the Oke-fenokee swamp. When he wasn't yet married, or when he'd just *gotten* married—before he'd had the dumbass bully idea to drag his wife out for canoeing and camping, when she probably would've had a better time with room service in Vegas.

Her earrings. Her sandals.

What else was left of her?

This outline? This sketch? This memory of someone who'd vanished, either for good, deliberate reason or on accident—if that's what the shadow was. He approached and she remained still, facing away from him. She was so immobile that he couldn't tell if she was breathing, if she was even alive, or merely propped there like a scarecrow meant to lure instead of chase.

He walked and walked, and at first, he seemed to draw no closer. The path was a people-mover at an airport, and he was going the wrong direction. Never making any progress, standing still while trying valiantly to proceed.

Leaning into the mist, pushing against whatever odd force both lured him and kept him at bay, he prayed to no one in particular. "Stop this. Just stop it. I don't know what's going on, but cut it out. Just let me reach . . . just let me . . . see . . . let me touch . . ."

Under his feet, the path shifted. It made Titus think of an earthquake, or the quick snap of a sheet being unfurled across a bed. He stumbled and found his footing again, and now the swamp was letting him through. The bridge (the gate) was letting him approach. He must've needed permission. He'd never asked a bridge for permission before. He hadn't even meant to do it, but if it'd worked, he'd take it.

"Melanie," he called, now that he was close enough that she might actually hear him. "Melanie, is that you? It looks like you. It has to be you." More quietly he said, "It isn't you."

He knew the shape of her shoulders, a little sloped—and the way her hair went wild in the humidity. He knew the way her knees leaned toward one another when she was cold and anxious, and the way she didn't stand up straight unless you reminded her to.

The mist was driving and sharp, and very cold. He sniffled against it and ran the back of his forearm across his face. It only smeared the wet chill everywhere.

"Melanie, if it's you, turn around."

He wasn't close enough to touch her, but in another few steps, he would be. He couldn't bring himself to take them. Stopping just outside the arch, with its shadow falling at his feet, he froze and could not come any closer.

"Turn around. Please, for the love of God, turn around. Talk to me," he begged. "Tell me I'm an asshole, tell me to leave you alone. Tell me you want to go back to Nashville and never see me again. Tell me you don't love me, and you only married me because you were jealous. Tell me whatever you want, but tell me *something*."

The woman wavered, not as though she was considering anything he said—but like a TV channel when a storm threatens its reception. She flickered. Something beside her in the grass, half in the water . . . it slithered swiftly—almost too fast to see—and ducked away.

"But you won't, will you? You couldn't if you wanted to. You're not her," he remembered. "You're not even real. I don't know why I keep forgetting." His voice clogged up and his eyes were filling with tears. "Melanie's gone."

Over his shoulder, just behind the place he could see from the farthest corner of his eye, something tall and white drew close and said in Melanie's voice, "Yeah, but that's okay . . ."

Before he could turn to look—before he could even decide to turn and look—it spoke again.

"You're gone, too."

It seized him with a strength so shocking, immense, and terrible that it hardly even hurt when the creature crushed Titus to the grass, to the water, and ground him into muddy mortar for the bridge's stones.

He barely had time to notice, much less forget.

27

A MEETING

Cameron heard hollering. One of the hollerers sounded like Dave, using the exact same voice he used when he was yelling at the bar about how you didn't have to go home, but you couldn't stay there. One sounded like that other guy, maybe—the one whose wife was missing. That guy was farther away, and harder to hear. Dave was pretty close by.

He didn't hear anybody else, and he didn't know what either man was yelling about. They might've been calling for help, or for each other, or maybe they were shouting other people's names.

Yes, that was it.

The longer he stood there, shivering and listening, the more confident he was that he heard Dave call for Jess. So that's what all the shouting was about. It sounded like he'd found her—and that could be either good or bad.

On the one hand, Cameron was cold, wet, and miserably lost; he could use the company of another person, if he was going to wander around hopeless and doomed. On the other . . . it was Dave. They weren't exactly friends. And now, instead of riding to the rescue like the goddamn cavalry, Cameron was about to become a third wheel.

Still, he was definitely an actual human being, and he hadn't seen anybody else since he'd left Maude's car at the road.

He tried to pinpoint the direction Dave's voice was coming from. He thought he'd successfully nailed it, and if he was right, then the bartender was farther down the path he was walking already. For some reason, the other guy sounded like he was off to the right somewhere. That was fine. He didn't know the other guy. He would've settled for him in a pinch, but at least he and Dave had a goal in common.

Jess.

He was confident of very few things, but he knew that much for certain.

Somewhere between the rain and the dark, dreadful day, and getting lost . . . he'd almost lost sight of that fact. It wasn't that he didn't still love her from the bottom of his cold, soggy little heart—far from it. But he was increasingly worried about Daisy and Claire and the silence thereof, and he was soaked to the bone, and he could barely feel his feet.

Absolutely every possible thing was wrong.

So he went looking for Dave, sticking to the path in lieu of any other decent options.

Dave couldn't be too far off, if Cam could hear him that easily. He picked up the pace, almost eager to find the guy—proving once and for all that there was a first time for everything. He thought of all the times he'd come into the bar and wished to see almost anybody else, doing anything at all except being Jess's boyfriend. Now with every passing, uneven, sliding step, he grew more and more desperate to see Dave's face.

Catching up didn't take long, and it didn't happen slowly. The path jogged to the left, he jogged with it, and immediately collided with Dave—who looked about as terrible as Cameron felt.

Dave was wet and wild-eyed, alone on the trail that looked much straighter over here, for some reason. Cameron hardly noticed it, and it didn't worry him. Dave worried him. Dave was someplace between collapsing and dying, and screaming his head off. He looked like he'd drowned in a pool yesterday, but somebody'd pulled him out, then shook him hard and set him upright again.

"Holy crap, man!" Cameron barked. "What happened to you?"

"What happened to *me*?" he asked in reply very quickly, all the words running together. "What happened to *you*? What are you doing out here? What the hell is wrong with you?"

"I got lost!" he said defensively, glossing over the particulars.

"Well, I'm looking for . . ."

"Jess?" Cam guessed carefully. "I thought I heard you yelling for her."

Dave looked back and forth along the trail, and over his shoulder like he was confident someone was right there—or someone had been, a minute before. "I'm looking for Titus. Me and him were out here, and we got separated. I . . ." Again he checked the path, the trees, the end of the trail where a peculiar stone bridge loomed large.

Cameron did not look at the bridge. He knew it was there, but he went out of his way to avert his eyes. He knew what it was, and the knowing filled him with dread. It made him think of the ladies, and wonder why he hadn't heard from them. Surely they knew he'd come close to this thing? Surely they were com-ing to warn him, punish him, or save him?

But the skies were silent.

Dave continued, "I thought I saw her. Heard her. I mean, I *thought* I heard her. But Titus thought it was someone else, and we . . ."

"Titus is the guy whose wife went missing?"

"Uh-huh. He thought the woman we heard . . . that it was his wife. I was pretty sure it wasn't, but now . . ." He looked back at the bridge, which was either a million miles away or right there, fifty yards off. "I think it was all a trick. I don't know if there's anybody here at all."

"Then who's that, under the bridge?" Cameron squeaked, because there it was, and he wasn't any good about forcing the idea or the horror out of his head, no matter how bad it felt. Once he looked, he couldn't not look. Now that it'd caught his eyes like a snare, and he couldn't see anything else. "Is it . . . is it even a bridge, really?"

"Of course it's a bridge," Dave snapped, but he didn't look back to make sure. Dave didn't want to look at it, either.

"From here, it looks more like an archway or something." Cameron tried to talk himself down from his rising terror. It turned out, Dave's mere presence didn't reassure him of any-thing, not at all. "Maybe it's just a weird old gate."

"That's how bridges look, from underneath. Some of them." Dave looked back after all, stared hard at the dark cave beneath the stonework. "And what did you mean—who's under the bridge? I don't see anybody."

Cam squinted. "I thought I did. Maybe I was wrong." He hoped he was wrong.

Dave asked, "Did you hear anything? Before you got here? Did you hear a woman . . . calling, or crying, or something?"

The kid shivered, hugged his own arms, and shook his head. "Sorry, man. All I heard was you and the other guy yelling. That's how I found you."

Dave's eyes narrowed, but not at Cameron. He was scowling at the path beneath them both. "You followed the trail and found me on it. This stupid trail . . . it goes around and around in circles, so it *had* to lead to me, eventually. It *had* to lead to that bridge. I've seen it before . . ." His voice went softer and rougher. "I know I've seen it before. I've been here before."

"When?" the boy asked. Then he heard a voice. He told himself it came from the swamp, but he knew better. He didn't believe himself. Deep down, he knew it was coming from the bridge. "Wait, did you hear that?"

Now they both froze, dubious and curious and very afraid.

"See? That's what I mean," Dave said, drawing closer to Cameron like they could keep each other warm. He was whispering now. "You hear it, and you follow it—you go looking for it—but this path just takes you wherever it wants. Around and around." He drew a circle with his finger. "But all roads lead to Rome, right? This one leads no place except for that damn bridge. It's not even a bridge, I bet. You might've been closer when you said it was a gate, but that's not right, either."

"Then what is it?"

"It's a *trap*. It's a lie. Everything's a lie. That voice, that bridge, this trail. We're screwed, kid. That's what I'm telling you. We're never getting out of here, alive or otherwise."

"You sound crazy, Dave. I'm just sayin'. Please, please don't be crazy."

He brightened, glad that now Cameron finally understood. "But it *is* crazy! You're completely right! And here we are, kid."

"Stop calling me 'kid.'"

"You *are* a kid." Now he sounded like regular old Dave again. "A fucking kid who's never had any business in a bar—but there you are, fawning after Jess every chance you get. You think I don't see it?"

"I don't care if you see it," he retorted. Dave was losing it, and Cam was starting to feel sorry for him. It didn't make him feel any better, though. It made him feel like he had to be the grown-up, and he didn't like the thought at all. "Jess is nice to me."

"She's too old for you. You need to go someplace where there are more kids. Any kids."

"She's not that old."

Dave frowned. "What are you, like, seventeen? She's thirty-two."

"What? She is? Seriously?"

"I know she looks like she can barely drink, but that's good genes or whatever. Let it go. She's practically old enough to be your mom."

"Barely," he scoffed stubbornly. "In another ten years, no one will care. That's why you want me to leave. You don't want the competition."

The bartender rolled his eyes. "I'm trying to help you, Cameron. Christ, if you never listen to another living soul in your life, listen to me now, please? *Leave Staywater.* Get the fuck out, as soon as you can. The ladies will let you go, I think. They'll send you off, give you some money—whatever they've got. They want the best for you, everybody knows that."

"You don't want to help me. You just want to get me out of the way."

"Can't I want both?"

Something flashed and darted under the bridge. They both saw it, and they both whipped their heads to see it better. There was light and motion. A figure walking. A woman. She was talking quietly, chattering to herself beneath the canopy of stone.

"Jess?" Dave asked, softly enough that someone so far away probably wouldn't have heard him.

"Jess!" declared Cameron with glee. He saw the woman with the long brown hair, strolling without moving. An image on a movie screen.

He started toward her, and Dave grabbed him by the collar. "Stop it—you weren't listening. That's not her. I shouldn't have called out—I shouldn't have said her name. I know it isn't her. Please, come on. Something's wrong."

"Don't be a jerk." He yanked himself free. "She's right there. She's upset. Can't you hear that?" But no, she wasn't crying, exactly. He listened a little longer. She was talking in a hushed, urgent voice.

"I hear it. But I don't believe it."

"Well, I'm going over there." But when Cam started trotting toward the bridge, he heard Dave start up behind him and he warned him off. "Don't follow me, if you're chicken!"

"Don't do it! Everything here is a lie!"

Cameron broke into a run and pulled ahead of Dave, who was clearly losing his shit in a profound and alarming way. The boy reached the bridge and drew up to a stop outside the big, dark archway. His feet scrambled backward, a brief retreat that didn't take him anywhere except back into Dave, who grabbed him around the arms—drawing him even farther away from the looming presence that seemed out of time, out of place.

Even Cameron could see that, now that he was up close. No, this wasn't a bridge. It was a monolithic creation, older than any building in Staywater and a hundred times weirder. (Which was really saying something.)

Underneath it, not quite close enough to touch, he saw Jess.

But it wasn't Jess. Not Jess *now*—both Cameron and Dave saw that much immediately. It was Jess before, years ago, when she was much closer to Cameron's age. When he might've actually had a shot at getting her attention.

The thought didn't comfort or interest him in the slightest. He was so thrown by the sight of her, that he didn't even try to pull away from Dave—who kept his death grip around his shoulders.

This version of Jess was thinner, almost skinny. She wore dirty sneakers with folded-down socks and a short dress. Around her waist she wore an apron. Her hair was in a ponytail. She was dragging something large. Some*one* large.

Relatively large, or so Cameron revised his opinion.

It was Dave, unconscious and limp. She had him by the armpits and was hauling him off the shoulder, into the road. Cam watched it like a movie, if a movie were in full 3-D and happening right in front of him. He knew instinctively that if he called her name, she wouldn't hear him.

She wasn't here, not now. She was there, and then.

Without meaning to—without even noticing that he was doing it—Cameron leaned back against Dave for support. He'd seen weird before. He'd lived in Staywater for all of his remembered life. He'd even known danger, from time to time, but that was typical of everyone who stayed in a place so abandoned and decrepit. But he'd never seen anything like *this*.

Transfixed, he watched as Jess argued with something he couldn't see.

"Leave me this one, and I swear, I swear," she gasped, dropping him into the road. She straddled him, leaned forward to listen to his chest, and smacked his left cheek, his right cheek. His head lolled back and forth, but his eyes didn't open. "I'll bring you somebody else. I won't leave you hungry. I know it's

different now. I know what the cousins did to you." She sat up and started CPR, or at least what passed for CPR if you've only seen it on TV.

Beyond the edge of anything Cam and Dave could see, something hissed and spit, and rumbled peculiar growls.

She lifted her head to look at it, or toward it. While she pumped desperately on Dave's chest, she spoke to the thing that they still couldn't see. "I promise. I swear it, and if I'm lying, you can take me, too. You know I won't lie to you. You know I keep my word. Just give him back. *Please* give him back!"

Jess stopped pounding and glared. Her eyes gleamed. "Give him back to me, and I'll trade you another. Deny me this, and I will finish what the ladies started."

A count of one, two, three.

Past-Dave's eyes shot open and he gasped.

Without looking behind him, Cameron asked quietly, "Did that happen?"

He felt Dave nod. "I woke up like that. I remember . . . that's what she was wearing."

"What . . . did she . . . " But the scene was already shifting to another day, another time of day. In the span of a few seconds the light was different, and Jess was wearing different clothes. Now she wore a pair of sunglasses and carried a messenger bag for a purse, and there was no sign of a freshly awakened Dave lying on the road. "Who did she . . . ? Who's that?" Cam pointed at a guy who was walking beside her.

Dave couldn't speak.

Cam was pressed against him, feeling the fast, hard rise and fall of his chest.

"Who *is* that, Dave?"

"That's Jimmy," he squeaked. "Netta's son. He's . . . he's her cousin."

"I . . . I never met him," he squeaked back.

Dave exhaled with a shudder. "Well, that's him. He used to work at the coffee place with Jess, before it closed. I stopped there, every time I passed through . . ."

Long-ago-Jess was staring down at the shoulder. She said to her companion, "It was around here someplace. I feel so dumb—I was driving with the window down, and my phone just fell right out. I have to find it. I can't afford another one. Keep your eyes open."

Her cousin was following her lead, eyes on the road's shoulder. "I hope it still works." Jimmy was a skinny guy with brown hair. They definitely looked related. "Are you sure this is where you lost it?"

"It might've been a little farther up. Maybe near that bridge over there."

Dave's grip on Cameron became painfully tight. He slipped one arm around his chest and drew the boy back. "Jesus fucking Christ. Look what she's doing. She's going to . . ." He turned him 180 degrees so they couldn't watch whatever was happening.

Cameron let himself be drawn away, but he looked over his shoulder. The scene under the bridge was going dark. "She's going to what? What did she do? Why would she lead him over to the bridge, if she knew what happened to you there?" He tried to come to terms with what he'd seen, and what he'd already known. He didn't want to say it out loud, but he couldn't hold it in. "Dave, did you . . . did she . . . did she *trade* him? For you?"

His voice cracked and shook when he said, "Looks like it."

"You weren't together back then, were you?"

"No." Dave kept pulling, and Cam let him. They walked backward along the trail which wasn't straight anymore. "It was . . . it was thirteen years ago. I barely knew her."

Dave stumbled, and Cam stumbled too.

Cam stepped free of his grip and faced him. "But you *did* know her?"

"I'd seen her three or four times, when I was coming and going from the park. I used to kayak and . . . and stuff. I used to be an outdoors guy, and I'd see her . . . like . . . a few times in the spring, a few times in the fall. I'm not even sure I knew her name."

"It must've been true love," Cameron mumbled bitterly.

"Is that what you think?"

"True love makes people do stupid stuff."

Dave didn't exactly laugh, but the sound he made was close enough to a chuckle to call it one. "Love me? She didn't . . . she didn't even know me." He looked down at Cameron, like he suddenly understood something he wasn't saying out loud.

"What?" Cam wanted to know.

Under the bridge, something different shifted. Cam struggled to get a good look at it, but Dave didn't bother. He took the kid's arm again and said, "Nothing, never mind. Come on. We have to go."

Cam looked back at the way he'd come. The path didn't look anything like it had a few minutes before. Now it forked and split, and there were half a dozen side trails feeding in as many different directions. "Where do we go? How do we get out of here?"

"Can you reach Daisy or Claire? I know they watch you. Everybody knows. Can you watch back? Send them some kind of message?"

"It doesn't work like that!" Cameron could see it now, this monstrous thing that his godmothers had struck down decades before. It was a ghost, any fool could see that. A ghost of what, precisely, he couldn't say. It rose up on two ghastly tapered legs with thick feet and hands, and all those claws. All those teeth in that long, ugly face.

"Cameron?"

"Yeah, Dave?"

"Promise me something, would you?"

"I'll try."

Dave swallowed hard, and took a step forward on the path, putting himself between Cameron and the creature. "Promise you'll run, and you won't look back."

"You can't—"

"*Pick a path.* Make a run for your godmothers. Tell them I gave you a head start."

"Dave—"

"Now!" he shouted, at the very instant the monster leaped forward.

Cam hesitated, but only for a moment. He didn't want to leave Dave, but he didn't want to get dragged into the swamp, either, and he was confident that Dave was right—they needed Daisy and Claire. Without them, no one was getting out of there in one piece.

So Cameron turned, and he didn't look back.

He picked a path and he didn't turn around, not even when he heard the worst wet crunch and gurgle, and he cringed as he fled, to the sound of a thrashing and then a splash, and then the grinding of bones and rocks.

He picked the trail that looked most likely to head for the road, if he was right about where he was standing—and he wasn't exactly positive of that much, but he was fairly sure it didn't matter. Dave was right, and it was all a lie. His heart banged around between his ribs and his throat felt hot and swollen, then cold and tight, back and forth, with every breath.

His feet pounded on the trail and slid around in the wet mud.

Behind him, something finished its task. It dropped back into the grass and water and cypress knees, and every turtle dived for safety. Every snake disappeared into the nearest hole, and even the dragonflies found someplace else to be.

Cameron ran and his lungs hurt, and his legs hurt, and the pathway was lying to him.

And the creature was following him. And he couldn't hear Claire or Daisy chiding him and offering guidance or assistance. No streetlights came on to guide him; no televisions broadcast helpful static; no faint voices guided him to the road and away from danger. They simply weren't there, standing between him and the thing in the water better than Dave ever could, because they'd already killed it once and it might've even been afraid of them.

But how could even his godmothers kill something that was already dead?

All of these questions flashed through his mind as he ran. They distracted him from the agony in his chest, and the blind fear that was the only thing he had left for fuel.

It was coming.

He could hear it, swishing through the reeds and moving in tiny splashes on one side of the path, and then the other. It was closing in, no matter how fast he dashed, and how carefully he placed his feet. Dave had thrown himself in front of the thing, and if Cam's ears were telling the truth, it'd finished him in a matter of seconds. If he'd been able to double back and check, he knew in the pit of his stomach that he'd find nothing but a smear and maybe a shoe left behind.

Cameron had no chance, and he knew it. He had no prayer, either, so he didn't say one.

He just kept running, on the off chance that the trail would lead him to the road and he could dash back to town, as far from that bridge as his sopping sneakers would take him.

He listened while he ran, paying attention to everything else, looking for any hint that the ladies were looking for him, and they were planning to help him. But the swamp was quiet except for the approach of the pale and terrible creature who was on one side of the path, then the other. It swept up behind him, and zigzagged around him.

It was herding him.

When the path split, it guided him. It was leading him right back around to the bridge. He knew it before he saw it come back around into view, and when it did, he knew he was sunk.

The ladies were nowhere to be seen. Dave was probably dead, and the other guy probably was, too. There was blood all around the pillars that held up the bridge. It smeared between the stones as if the rocks themselves had devoured the missing men.

All the missing men. The missing women.

All the missing *people,* like that one guy's wife, and Netta's son Jimmy, and Dave, and everybody else the ladies couldn't save when they killed the monster but didn't stop it.

Cameron drew up to a halt.

He panted, and the world swam in front of his eyes. He wanted to cry but there wasn't enough hope left. Tears were for people who might yet survive, if they still had room to beg. Tears were not for boys who were lost alone in a swamp, wishing they'd never had any stupid crush on any stupid waitress who was old enough to be his mother, almost . . . certainly not a stupid waitress who would send up her own stupid cousin because of her own stupid crush on some guy who went kayaking in the park a few times, and sometimes stopped for coffee.

Not that Cameron didn't understand what True and Stupid Love could do to you.

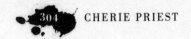

He understood it all too well, and that's why he was here, freezing and wet and hunted in the swamp. He was standing in front of a bridge that was anything but a bridge, getting ready to die for it.

Whether it was worth it or not.

28

LAST STANDS

Daisy and Claire walked down State Road 177, straight down the middle, not giving a single shit if a car was coming or not. Claire strutted like a queen, toting the garden hoe like a scepter. Daisy stalked like a soldier, the shotgun over her shoulder. The trip to the road hadn't taken any time at all, once they figured out how moving around while dead worked. It wasn't too tricky, but it took some getting used to—some hops, skips, and jumps as they decided where they wanted to be, and slipped through space to get there.

Now they'd found the road, and they had to walk it until they found the bridge. That was the iffy part.

It could be anywhere, Claire complained.

Daisy shook her head. *No it couldn't. It's always the seventh, and we just passed number six.*

I mean, it could be anywhere between here and Kingdom Come.

Yeah, but it ain't.

A car came up, going east. They didn't step aside, the driver never saw them, and the car never touched them. It moved through them like light through a windowpane, something with glass stained and colored. Whatever they were made of now, it did not flinch or flutter. They were insubstantial and inhuman and scarcely more than wisps of ectoplasm, if there was any such thing. They were more powerful now than they'd ever been in life—this was also true, and both of them felt it, even if they could not explain or describe it.

We should've done this ages ago, Daisy said, adjusting the sunglasses she'd also found room for in the bag she carried.

Maybe if we hadn't had Cameron to see to, we might have.

Don't blame him for this, she chided.

I'm not blaming him for anything. Though from a certain angle, everything is entirely his fault. Claire looked left, and looked right, and saw nothing on either shoulder of the unending road. *He appeared, and we had to look after him. Now he's run off, and we have to come after him.*

Then we should thank him for prompting us.

Claire winced and clutched at the hoe. *When we find him, we'll do just that. I hope it makes him feel better. I hope he doesn't feel too guilty about anything. Oh good Lord, I hope he doesn't go home and find us there in the kitchen.*

Of course he's going to find us, and of course he's going to feel guilty—he's going to figure it's all his fault, assuming we can get him out of here alive. He's not an idiot. But once we pull his ass out of the fire, I guess we could swing by the station and tell Kemp to go get us first.

You think he'll hear us?

Daisy nodded. *I fully expect that we can make ourselves heard.*

Claire stopped. She pointed with the hoe. *Oh shit, honey, there it is. I think we've found it.*

Goddamn.

Time to leave the road?

Look around for a path, or a trail or something. Remember? That's how we got it last time, playing its stupid little games, Daisy recalled. She went to one of the road's shoulders, and Claire went to the other. *It likes to mislead people.*

But before they found anything, they heard a man hollering his head off.

Claire planted the hoe beside her. *That's not Cameron. I think it's David, from the bar.*

Could be him, or could be that fellow whose wife went gone. Whoever he is, he don't sound happy.

The shouting ended as quickly as it'd begun. Sinister silence fell in its wake.

We don't have time to hunt and peck, even in our present condition, Daisy decided. *Let's go toward that shout. You think you can do that with me?*

I can sure as shit try.

Come on, then. Take my hand. I don't want us to get separated.

Claire obliged, and together they slipped through the trees, through the fabric of what passed for reality in the swamp near the bridge—where everything was a lie and no one was safe. They looked for a path, but didn't find one. They looked for Titus, but saw no sign of him, either.

They stopped at a sandal, wedged in the mud.

Some woman's, Claire speculated.

Some woman who didn't plan on going to the swamp—look at that heel.

That poor man's wife, then. Nobody older than that—this is a new shoe, in a new style. But there's nothing we can do for her now.

Daisy concurred. *No, nothing we can do for her. But Cameron . . . can you hear anything? See anything? Cameron!* She shouted at the top of her no-longer lungs. *Cameron, boy—can you hear me?*

Can you hear us?

If anyone could hear, no one could answer.

Where do we look next? Claire asked.

We look toward the bridge, I suppose. It'll lure him, like it lures everyone.

Just a goddamn trap, she grumbled.

Which way was it, again? Daisy stood on her tiptoes, not that it helped. She was a little taller than Claire, but she couldn't see past the trees.

Claire was more confident. *This way. It's forward, and to the left.*

They were skipping and sneaking between the mushy acres of swamp, on a beeline for the bridge—courtesy of Claire's sense of direction—when they heard their names.

Very faint. Hardly whispered. No, not whispered at all.

Prayed.

"Miss Claire, Miss Daisy . . . oh God, where are you? Can't you see me? Can't you find me?"

He's alive! Claire gasped.

He's in trouble!

We knew that already. Claire was already shifting and sliding, pushing through water and grass and trees.

Daisy caught up in an instant. The cypress trunks flew by, and past, and between. The murk of the swamp didn't bog them down or swallow their shoes. They ran and they jumped, and they listened—passingly noticing that all the fauna was silent, and knowing they must be close.

Human, living, stumbling feet were crashing and stomping, splashing on the turns.

Right behind them, inhuman limbs swished and veered, crawling and loping along the ground. The monster moved much faster than it should have been able, if judged by its shape. It was swift and wicked, like a long-limbed gator dashing low to the ground, fast enough to catch and kill anything on two legs, and many things on four.

Both boy and beast were coming right toward them.

The ladies charged headlong, and when a clearing broke, they saw the path. They saw Cameron, running for his life—soaked and panicked, the pallid and clawed creature darting back and forth across the path behind him, toying with him. Taking its time.

Daisy loaded the shotgun on the fly, her motions as smooth as any action star's in any movie that she'd never seen.

No! Claire stopped her. *The farther it gets from the bridge . . . the weaker it grows. Look, it's not moving so fast. Let it go a little more. Let it chase him until he can't run anymore.*

Daisy started forward again anyway. *It's still coming fast enough to catch him.*

Her cousin sighed and joined her, fearing she must be right. She brandished the hoe, while Daisy cocked the gun.

Cameron was coming in fast.

The ladies emerged from the swamp and threw themselves onto the path, into his way.

He saw them. Neither woman had been sure that it was possible, but he did—he saw them and he knew them. He flailed, tripped over himself, looked back at the advancing crea-ture . . . and did the only sensible thing: He jumped off the path—tucking and rolling from the relatively flat thorough-fare, into the shallow black water.

Daisy smiled down at him. *Good job, boy.*

You stay there. We got this.

The boy's eyes were enormous. He saw them, yes. But did he see two solid figures? Two specters? Did he see them the way they saw themselves in this sudden and violent afterlife, or did he see a pair of corpses—one with her head blown half apart, one blue-faced and flecked with vomit?

There was no time to ask.

The creature had slowed, too. It stopped, no more than ten yards from their feet. Its oil-black eyes were lidless, so they did not blink, but they flashed with what little grim, dirty light filtered down to the swamp floor.

It was thinking.

Remember us, motherfucker? Daisy asked. *We're back to finish what we should've finished a long time ago.*

It heard her, and it must have understood. It *had* to understand something of the way people spoke, and what they meant when they offered up a threat, or a promise. It copied them too well and too purely to be completely ignorant.

It kept its distance, while it considered its course of action.

But it was dead—every bit as dead as the women who stood between the monster and its prey to the side of the path, sunk as low as he could get in the water.

The creature flicked a glance at Cameron, then ignored him. It focused on the women.

Slowly but confidently, it rose up on its hind legs until it was straight and skinny and tall—taller than Daisy by at least two feet. Every bit of it was long: its torso, its limbs, its face, and its claws. Its teeth. Its fingers and toes that were knotted with thickened knuckles, and its skin that was waxy and warty, even when stretched tight across its warped old bones.

Claire spun the hoe around like a sword and pointed it right between the monster's eyes. *I'll bet you thought you'd seen the last of us.*

Daisy didn't bother to speak. She aimed the spectral shotgun and pulled the trigger. The blast that rang out sounded very loud, very real.

It caught the creature square in the chest.

The fiend rocked backward, stunned.

She fired again, and the second shot smashed into the spot below its shoulder that should've held a heart, if it'd ever had one to begin with. It reeled but did not go down. The shells blew skin into viscous, gummy-looking patches of hamburger, but there was nothing pink to bleed beneath, only an opalescent ooze that welled like pus.

The beast roared, and the sound was not words, not a scream, and not a howl—but it could have been mistaken for any one of those things. It spoke in tongues, and the ladies understood its gist, if not the finer details of its anguished cursing.

It was daring them. They had done their worst, it said. They could not hurt it anymore.

But the swell of shiny liquid where the shotgun landed said otherwise. *We can still hurt it,* Claire said to Daisy. Then to the brute itself, *We can still hurt you!*

Daisy growled, *You're going to find out what's on the other side of dead, for whatever the hell you are.* She reloaded.

The creature charged.

Claire pretended she was an action star in an old movie she'd seen one time. Being free of her body had its perks. She was faster than she'd ever been, and stronger than she'd ever dreamed—and she felt like a superhero when she caught the beast in the face with the rusty edge of the hoe.

It railed back and lashed out, trying to disarm her.

She was too quick. She was out of the way before it could do more than wing the edge of her blade. With a duck and a roll, she stood up to its left and brought the garden tool down on its

nearest eye, which burst like a dark grape—gushing fetid wine in an arc that sprayed across the path and into the water.

It clutched the eye and withdrew, but Daisy had fresh ammo.

She fired for its face, since it seemed to be vulnerable there. The blast took a couple of teeth; they shattered like ice.

The creature drew its hand away from the popped eye, and they saw how the orb had drained and deflated. The socket was just barely gray, emptied of whatever ichor used to pool there. Now the monster gave another roar: this one was rage and defiance, anger and vengeance.

Daisy's second shot caught it in the nose, and now dark liquid drained from that, too.

Now she needed time to reload, and that meant it was Claire's turn to step up. She swung and missed, because the thing was retreating. She chased after it and it ducked away, but she took another crack and caught it on the throat—not hard enough to break the skin. Not hard enough to do anything but make it angrier.

Get away from it! Daisy demanded. *If we can hurt him, he can probably hurt us!*

You don't have to tell him that! she shouted back.

I think he's already figured it out!

Long-limbed and slick, it lashed out with its unnatural long arms, whipping claws like a cat grabbing a mouse. It snagged Claire by the hand, and she howled when three sharp nails raked her flesh. Her skin tore open but didn't bleed. It hung ragged and gaping.

Now she was mad.

Daisy had enough time to get another couple of shells loaded, and she used them to blow the beast back away from her cousin. The shells didn't hurt it too much, but pushed it back farther on the trail, buying time for Claire to swear and return to her side. Daisy dropped the little purse. *Here. Get the hatchet. It's in there someplace. Rusty as shit. Give the thing tetanus if it comes at you again.*

Claire didn't ask questions, she just unfastened the little clasp and rooted around until she was elbow-deep, and she found the wooden handle. Out came the hatchet, and she took it with her good hand. Her bad hand was hot, like she'd been seared instead of scratched. She couldn't look at it.

Daisy dropped the next two shells, and the monster closed in—but Claire stood up and lifted her hatchet-wielding arm. She brought it up in the widest curve, for the best momentum, and swung with all her might. The blade connected under its chin, the softest spot she'd hit since she'd smashed its eye.

The hatchet cut deep and the creature lurched—so she reached up harder, at a sharper angle, and dragged it forward. Gruesome bile spurted and sizzled where it met the iron of the blade. It curdled against the rust and burned the wood like acid. It burned Claire's fingers, too, where it dripped down onto her hand.

She jerked away, just in time to miss the creature's tail.

It finally remembered it had one, or else it finally realized it was going to need it. The thick white thing swung around and smashed into Daisy's chest, knocking her back into the water—where she slid backward until she was able to stop herself. At the moment of impact she'd dropped the gun; from the corner of her eye, she saw it spin off into the freezing muddy water near Cameron, who cowered and quivered and stared, because what else was there for him to do?

Emboldened, the beast used its own torso for leverage—it anchored itself to the trail with its feet and flung that vicious tail, spinning a compass circle of heavy meat and bone. The ladies scattered, crawling away in different directions.

Claire still had the hatchet, but the hoe was broken now. She didn't know how, or when it'd happened. Everything was moving too fast. She couldn't watch everything at once, and keep an eye on Cameron, too.

Daisy couldn't either, but Daisy used to have a shotgun, and by God, she was going to have it back if it killed her. Again. She scrambled toward it, and the beast grabbed her foot—but she got her fingers on the butt of the gun. The creature yanked her back and she dropped it, but it scooted away even closer to Cameron, who remained paralyzed and hugging his knees.

Cam! she cried, in case he heard her as well as he saw her.

He gave her a funny look; her voice might've sounded weird to him, or it may have only been a whisper from a radio station that was foggy with static. But he got the idea, when he saw her grabbing for the gun that was now beyond her reach . . . and just within his own.

Unwrapping his arms from around his knees, he stretched out his fingers, fumbling for the gun. It wasn't real anymore. He couldn't touch it, could he?

He could see it. It was still real. Maybe he could touch it. Maybe he could use it.

Claire was coming around, picking herself up and testing the hatchet's weight. She ran up to her cousin, alongside the creature who dragged and pulled, and chopped down hard on its hand.

It barked in pain and let go of Daisy's leg—leaving behind a burn in the shape of its handprint, and slices from its claws. But apart from that and some skinned-up elbows, she appeared otherwise unhurt.

The monster rolled over, scrabbling and scanning the scene for a safe place to retreat.

Claire stood before her, brandishing the hatchet. She worked it like a baseball bat, leaving stripe after stripe on the beast's forearms, its chest, and the top of its knees, if those were indeed knees beneath that grimy flesh.

It skittered away from her, though the injuries looked like nothing more than large paper cuts.

It was not looking at Cameron, who drew the gun toward himself and quivered, his fingers sliding along the wet metal. It felt so real! It looked like any ordinary double-barrel, hanging on any redneck mantel. How could it be spectral? How did this work?

Daisy held her hands out, gesturing wildly. *Give it here! Hurry!*

Cameron never disobeyed Miss Daisy, not when she was looking right at him. He shoved the gun sideways. It skidded out of the mud, across the path, and into her hand. She flipped it around and fell back when the creature took her by the foot again.

As it drew her forward, she aimed.

She fired.

The first blast took it under the chin, where Claire's hatchet had already done a great deal of damage. The shell did more damage still; the beast's jaw broke and hung down low on one side—the spectral bone sticking out with a jagged edge.

The second blast. Right after the first, at a slightly different angle.

The shell didn't go right up its chin, but right up its throat and into its head.

It reeled and lurched, and fell back down until only its thick tail held it half upright. Then its whole body collapsed forward. One leg buckled. The other one locked, its knee upright. Its hands hit the ground. Its broken head hung in pieces, one eye gone and part of its elongated, toothy mouth pointing to the side.

Claire turned the hatchet in her hand, getting the best grip for murder. She jumped forward and brought the blade down on the flat white space between its eyes. The weapon cut deep, and the head went down.

By then, Daisy had reloaded. *Out of the way, Claire.*

She retreated in three long steps that put her beside Cameron, who still hadn't found his footing. He sat miserable and cold, up to his waist in murky water. His hands were scraped up and his breath puffed pale in the low, filtered light. She gave him a smile that she hoped was reassuring, and not gruesome.

He tried to smile back, but it vibrated on his face and a tear slipped down one cheek.

She smiled even harder, and wondered if a ghost could cry—because if it could, she was surely crying right back at him.

Well, a ghost could definitely die, she knew that much.

Even if she hadn't believed it, and hadn't even expected it, necessarily—even when she'd only hoped it with all her heart, because she knew that her godson was in terrible danger . . . she'd *known* it. The alternative was simply unacceptable.

When Daisy pulled the trigger again . . . once . . . twice . . . when the creature's head was blown to pieces, and its body slumped down to the gravel and sand path, and the path itself began to disintegrate in front of their eyes, she knew they'd done it.

Again.

The hatchet! Claire, take that son of a bitch apart, before the earth swallows it up!

She was right: as the little trail dissolved, the creature was sinking. If it was going home to whatever afterlife had called its name a second time, there was no good reason for it to go in one piece.

Claire rallied and began hacking at the nearest limb—the left arm, as skinny and warty and pale as she'd ever imagined an arm could be. It split easily now, since there was no more soul left to hold it together. Or that's how she wanted to think of it, as she smashed through bone, and cut through tendons.

Daisy was reloading again, and she took a faster approach. She aimed at the joints and fired, dismembering it a finger-pull of the trigger at a time.

All the while, it came apart and fell to slivers, to sludge.

And all the while, Cameron remained in the muck—where now there was no path to sit alongside, and no creature to chase him deeper into the swamp. He looked very young, as he sat there clutching himself. Soggy and frozen and filthy, he could've been seven instead of seventeen. It made Claire's heart hurt, and when Daisy was finished blowing the thing to bits—and every shell had been spent, and there were pieces of the creature no larger than a handprint left to remark upon, even in its spectral state—her heart was hurting, too.

She was exhausted, and that seemed strange, didn't it?

I'm tired, Claire, she said. She leaned on the gun, its barrel facedown against the wet earth.

So am I. But it's done now.

It's done. She looked at the boy, whose face was clean only where the tears had wiped his skin with salt water. She crouched before him and let the gun fall away. *Cameron?*

"Yes, ma'am."

You can hear me all right? You can see me all right?

"It don't look like you, exactly."

She laughed, and so did Claire. *Yes it does, baby. It looks like me—and it looks like her—a long, long time before you ever met us. We look like . . .* She looked back at her cousin. *We look the way we always felt, on the inside. What do you think?*

She stood up straight and twirled around.

He found his grin and it wobbled, but stuck. "You look like I ought to flirt with you, if you wandered into Dave's."

You're a rotten boy, and always have been, she replied with the biggest, truest smile of the afternoon.

"What . . . what *happened* to you, Miss Daisy? Miss Claire?"

Claire took that one. *We happened to ourselves, honey. We chose our time, that's all. Don't you worry about us. We're all right, here and everywhere else.*

Daisy agreed. *Never felt so free, to tell you the truth. Or I haven't felt this free in so long . . . I might as well call it never.*

"You won't just leave me now, will you? Will you . . . will you stay? Will you come see me?"

They both shook their heads. Claire sat down beside him, and if she'd been wearing real clothes, they would've gotten filthy right along with his. *We've never left you yet, and won't start now.*

Or ever.

Or ever. She patted his shoulder but couldn't tell if he'd felt it. *So for now, first of all . . . let's get you out of this place. Let's get you to the road, at the very least.*

Daisy thought to ask, *Before we go, is there anyone else we ought to round up?*

"Jess . . . she's out here somewhere. I have to find her, that was the whole point of coming out here."

Sweetheart, Claire told him gently. *We haven't seen any sign of her. If she made it out this far, I'm afraid the swamp's already taken her.*

He shuddered and looked over his shoulder, back where the path used to be. "That's everyone. There's nobody left to save."

Daisy nodded, and looked around at the encroaching water, the swimming turtles. The world was coming back to normal, but he needed a real-life way to find his way to the road. Some way without snakes or bugs, if possible. *Hate to say it, but you're probably right.*

Follow us, Claire urged. *Stay with us, and we'll find a way out.*

Cameron never disobeyed Claire, not when she was looking right at him. He followed like a duckling, and they pushed aside the dangers, just like they always had. Just like they always would.

When he found the road, it opened up to his left and right like the most normal thing in the world—without a bridge to be seen. He gasped out loud and dropped to his knees. "I'm safe," he sobbed, and the tears welled up again. "I'm safe. You did it, Miss Daisy, Miss Claire. You did it again. You . . ."

Before him there was asphalt.

Beside him there was a gritty shoulder, and a row of cypress trunks running in both directions, skirted with tall grass and shiny knees.

The ladies were nowhere to be seen.

29

JESS'S PLACE

Cameron lurched down the center dotted line of 177, praying for a ride and not getting one.

His shoes were full of mud. They squished with every step. His clothes were wet. They stuck to his body and chafed at every crevice. He listened for cars, but mostly all he heard was the faint, persistent patter of soft rain hitting the road. Once in a while, a bird would call or something would splash in the water off to either side of the road; but he was on his own, and he knew it.

Really, truly on his own.

Daisy and Claire were dead, somewhere. What would happen to him now? Would someone appoint him a guardian? Would he inherit the house? What would he do with it, if he had it? Would he stay and live there? Would he try to sell it?

Who would buy it? Nobody ever came to live in Staywater on purpose.

If he left, where would he go? He didn't have any money.

Did the ladies have any money? Surely not. Surely the place wouldn't have fallen into its present state of disrepair if there'd been any cash to fix it up.

Then again, if they had been willing to pay someone to fix the gutters, the roof, the chimney flashing, the rotting porch, the holes in the siding where Freddie missed a rat . . . who would they pay to do the work? Were there any contractors left in Staywater? Maybe there were contractors in Forto. Maybe they could find somebody on the other side of the swamp. How did you go about hiring one?

The ladies were dead, somewhere.

He wondered how they'd died. Would there be a mess?

No, he couldn't think about that. He could think about anything else, and he *had* to.

He could think about the future. He could think about getting a diploma someplace and going to college to study something. Like what? What did he want to do? What did he want to be when he grew up, like people always asked little kids? He liked to read, so maybe he'd study literature. Except, he didn't really like to read literature. He'd rather read romance novels.

Did guys ever write romance novels? Maybe he could do that.

He could always put a lady's name on the cover. He could write the smuttiest smut, with the prettiest heroines and the baddest heroes, and they'd sell a million copies, he was sure of it.

But Daisy and Claire were dead, somewhere.

He didn't know how to cook anything more complicated than scrambled eggs. He could make cereal. He could make a sandwich. He knew how to do laundry, at least, because he always helped Daisy on Mondays, when it always got done.

Daisy and Claire were dead, somewhere.
Daisy and Claire were dead.

He couldn't wrap his head around it. He couldn't imagine a world without them.

But did he have to?

They were ghosts. Strong ghosts. Ghosts who had left him at the road. Would they turn up later? Could they? Of course they would. They'd promised. They wouldn't leave him alone.

On some level, he'd always been aware that the ladies were very old, and not likely to live a great deal longer. Deep down, he'd forever known that he'd be on his own one of these days sooner rather than later. But not this soon. Much, much later. This soon wasn't fair.

But Daisy and Claire were dead, and he was so cold that his tears felt very hot as they tracked down his face. "What am I gonna do?" he asked them, wherever they were.

They didn't answer. Either they couldn't hear him or they couldn't reach him.

But they'd *promised*. Did promises from dead people count? Did they ever expire?

He took the turn that would bring him back to Staywater. On autopilot, he headed to the house, and then he remembered that Daisy and Claire were dead, and he didn't know where, and he probably shouldn't go home. He should go see Kemp and Pickett, that's what he should do. The police station was a little ways outside the town square. Just past it, by a block or two.

Then again, Dave's was closer. He could clean up at Dave's. Dave would never toss him out again, not that he'd ever done so in the first place. Man, but he'd misread Dave. Dave had been all right, and Cameron hadn't figured that out until right before the guy had died. That wasn't fair, either.

The parking lot was off to the right of the road. It was mostly rocks and sand, which stuck to Cameron's shoes because they were still wet. They would never dry, and Daisy and Claire were dead.

Dave was dead, too. That other guy was dead. It was safe to assume that his wife was dead. They'd have to quit calling the bar Dave's and go back to calling it Thirsty's.

Oh God. What would happen to the bar? Would it close? Would someone buy it?

Who?

His footsteps crunched across the parking lot, where there were already a few cars. It must be after four. It felt both earlier and later. He couldn't imagine that he'd been gone most of the day, yet he was so tired he could've gone to bed and slept all night. All week.

He dragged himself up the creaky wooden stairs and pushed the door open, then stepped inside. Jess was behind the bar, pouring beer for one of the handful of people who populated the place. She looked up when he came in.

Her hair was tied up loosely, and she wasn't wearing any makeup. She wore the same clothes he'd seen her in last, as she was leaving Hazelhurst—a plaid button-up with the sleeves rolled past her elbows, and a pair of jean shorts with the rhinestones on the one back pocket. He knew those rhinestones like he knew the back of his hand.

Jess lit up when she saw him. "Cam! Holy shit, dude. Could you um . . . could you come over here for a minute?"

He replied by doing as she asked, bellying slowly up to the bar like he meant to order a drink—almost reluctantly, like he'd been sober for a while and his wife would yell at him if she smelled the whiskey on him. Cam had spent too much time in this bar, even at his tender age. He knew the stories it told, truth and lie alike.

The stool was hard under his butt, and he left wet prints on the counter where his sleeves slapped upon it.

Whatever she'd been ready to say to him at first . . . she put that thought on hold. Instead she frowned and asked, "What on earth happened to *you*?"

I chased you into the swamp. I thought you were in the swamp, but you're clean and dry and you obviously haven't been outside for hours, like I have. I saw you there, even though you weren't there. I saw what you did. Dave's dead, did you know that? Everybody's dead except for us.

"I walked in the rain all the way here, and I slipped in the mud. I know . . . I look like crap. I look like shit," he corrected himself.

She didn't believe him. Her eyebrows said it, and so did the fold of her arms, but she was willing to let it slide. "Okay . . . ? Well, whatever. Have you seen Dave?"

He totally saved my life. Did I mention he's dead?

"Not lately."

"Goddammit. I haven't seen him all day. I thought maybe he . . ." Her gaze narrowed, and that meant she was about to lie. Why did he know that? What did it mean? "I didn't know where he went. Thought maybe he went to lunch with Titus, that guy whose wife went missing. I don't know why or how, but they kind of bonded."

"Maybe. I don't know."

"I've called him, like, a thousand times but he never picks up. I'm worried about him." That part was true, if you could judge it by how tightly her fingers were squeezing her own arms. The skin beneath them was going white. "I kept thinking he'd come home any minute, but he didn't. When three o'clock rolled around, I came over here to open up like always—halfway thinking I'd find him here, waiting for me." She looked toward the kitchen and looked toward the front door. It didn't open. If it did, it wouldn't have been Dave anyway. "I didn't know what else to do."

"Right." It was a meaningless word, but she seemed to need an answer and that was all he could think of.

She looked out over the lobby, and looked down at the beers on the tray. "So I'm kind of screwed, and I *really* need a hand. You want to help keep this place running, until he shows up?"

"I'm not twenty-one."

"I won't tell anybody if you don't. I'm *desperate,* Cam. I'll give you five bucks an hour, and you keep all your tips."

"That's . . . actually a pretty good deal." Twenty-four hours ago, he would've been floating on cloud nine. Now he was trying to look at her and not remember watching the way she walked back and forth, pretending to look for her phone; he tried to not remember how calculated she'd been, all the while knowing what she was doing to her aunt.

All for some guy who didn't even know her name.

Because True Love was bullshit, if the last day or two had taught him anything.

"So . . . Cameron. Are you in?"

He didn't really think about it. His options were few and limited, and he would've rather been anywhere but home—where the ladies were probably dead and waiting to be discovered. "Give me an apron."

"You know how this works?"

He shrugged. "I've seen you do it a million times. I'll write down what they want, then give it to you. Is that about right?"

"You left out the part about flirting for cash," she said with an effort at a funny wink.

"You're probably better at that, than I am."

"Oh, I don't know. You'll be a real hit with the ladies. Especially old ladies. They're every bit as bad as old men—always happy for attention from somebody young enough to be their kid. Or better yet, their grandkid." She put an apron on the counter. "All right, go clean up—and this will be waiting for you when you're finished."

"Okay."

He slipped off the stool and went to the men's room to tidy up.

It was dark in there, with a lot of wood paneling, doors that sagged on hinges, and a sink that only offered hot water—no matter which way you turned the lever on the faucet. He stared at himself in a mirror that was so fogged and darkened that he looked like a ghost of himself. He pulled off his sweater and threw it in the sink, and stripped off his shoes and socks.

It took some time, but he got himself presentable again. More or less.

He tried to check himself out in the mirror again, but his eyes were so dark and hollow that he suddenly understood all those movies and TV shows where a guy punches a mirror to break it.

He wasn't going to do that. But he thought about it. He *got* it.

In the corner, there was a hand dryer that worked pretty well. He used it to dry out his clothes and warm up his body. It took about half an hour, but the end result was a teenage boy who looked clean, if a little damp. It would have to do.

By the time he emerged, Jess was swamped with another half-dozen customers, and using her eyes to beg him for help.

He took the apron off the bar and tied it around his waist.

But the door opened, and Sergeant Kemp stepped inside. He was wearing his official uniform, which he sometimes didn't bother with. That meant it was serious. He was on Official Business. Before the man even opened his mouth, Cameron knew it must be about the ladies.

He couldn't decide if he was relieved or not. The inevitability of the conversation didn't make it any easier, and it wasn't like there was anything he could do to prepare himself for it. He'd already turned it over in his head a million times during the walk back from the bridge.

The one that wasn't there anymore, and hopefully, would never come back.

He took a deep breath and swallowed, and as the heavy older man crossed the floor, Cameron untied the apron and slipped it back to Jess. "I'm sorry," he said. "I think he's here for me. You've got to give me a minute."

"Okay?" She looked at the cop like she was half afraid he was there for her, and half afraid he wasn't. She clutched the apron to her chest, crushing it in her fist.

"Cameron Spratford?"

"Yes sir?"

"Son, I need for you to sit down. We need to have a word."

The old cop was a stout, short man who was at least an inch shy of Cameron's height; but something about his waistline and his age gave him the gravity he needed to lure the boy to a table in a corner. They sat down, and it was almost dark there. Almost private.

"Is this about the ladies?"

"All right," he said, and he sounded relieved. "Then you already know."

"They told me."

Kemp nodded. "They asked me to go to the house before you made it home. They said to tell you, that's why they left and let you walk back alone. They were buying time for me and Pickett to reach Hazelhurst and handle the worst of it."

Cameron nodded, too. He blinked back tears. "I was worried about that. I was afraid they'd just . . . left me for good, either because they had to, or because they wanted to. I thought they were gone."

"No, no. It's nothing like that. They came to me and Pickett, and they told us to clean up before you made it back. They asked me to make sure you're all right. They said I'd find you here."

He nodded. "There aren't a whole lot of other places I could go." Then he knew he shouldn't ask, and his curiosity waged war with his reluctance to hear about it. "Sergeant Kemp . . . sir . . . how did they . . . I mean, was it messy . . . ? Was it . . . quick, at least?"

"Oh, son. You don't really want to know the particulars. But yeah, it was quick. Neither one of them suffered much of anything."

Cam thought about it. "I guess that's something. Do I need to . . . should I . . . do I need a funeral? How do I throw a funeral? Oh God, where do I bury them?" He gave Kemp a stricken look. "Or . . . do they want to be cremated? Do they even care?"

"Calm down, now. I'm sure they'll let you know, one way or another. For now, we had to send them to the morgue in Forto. We don't have the facilities to take care of them, here in town."

"Sure, sure. I understand." Cameron stared down at the table, a scarred wood thing that was made to seat two people. Initials and curses and warnings and declarations of love were carved upon every inch. "Sergeant Kemp, sir?"

"Yes, son?"

"What do I do? What about the house, and—"

"Aw, now." He waved his hand. "Don't you worry about that, not yet. The ladies left you a little money, and the house itself. They told me that much. I know it's not . . ." He looked at the bar, at Jess, and at the door. Like he was expecting someone to come inside any minute, too. But nobody did. "It's not the way things usually work, out in the regular world on the other side of the swamp . . . but it'll be okay. You believe me, right?"

"I guess."

"Staywater is part of the world, but it's a different, weird little part," he tried to explain. He used his hands when he talked, shrugging his palms this way and that. "Things happen here that might not happen, anyplace else. We can overlook things, here. We can pay more attention to things, too. You can't just . . . well, you're not eighteen yet, are you?"

"I don't think so," he said. "Not for another few months. If I have a real birthday, nobody mentioned it. Miss Daisy said they called it September second, because that's the day they found me."

"That's close enough, but you'll need a birth certificate. I'll see what I can do about that. You'll have to get a driver's license someday, and get a job someplace that'll pay you over the counter." He flashed a look at Jess, who was watching the pair of them with one eye while she worked. "But for now, it doesn't matter."

"No?"

"Not here. Not between us. The ladies . . . all they asked me to tell you, besides 'Don't go home right fast,' is 'Get out of here, when you can.'"

Cameron thought he was going to cry again, at the very thought of leaving. "But where would I go? This is the only place I've ever been."

"No, that's not true. You were someplace else, until you were three or four years old. You can go try to find out where. Look up your real parents, if you can find them. Or if you don't care, and can't be bothered . . . go to Forto. It's not that far away, and there are a few jobs there. You can come back to Staywater any time, if it means that much to you."

"It does . . . but. I . . . I can't." He wasn't sure if it was true or not, but it felt true. "I have to stay here, for a while."

Kemp's eyes darkened. "How long is a while? And don't you tell me 'thirteen years.'"

They stared one another down.

"A while is . . ." Cameron was not about to say "thirteen years." He'd been prepared to think it very hard, very loudly. Instead he said, "'A while' just means . . . I should stay until I figure out what to do with the house, and all their stuff. Sir, they have a *lot* of stuff."

Kemp nodded vigorously. "Jesus, but they really *do.* I had no idea, until I went inside to tend to them. That place is packed to the rafters!"

"So you understand, don't you? It'll take some time to go through everything. Weeks, at least. Maybe months. I'll be eighteen by the time I'm done, I bet."

"You may well be," said the cop. "But you know . . ."

"Yeah, I know."

They sat in silence, until they didn't.

The cop cleared his throat and said, "Pickett is over at Hazelhurst, cleaning up the scene—I mean, the house—right now. The ladies made . . . a mess. I think they decided to do . . . what they did . . . on the fly. So don't hold it against them, would you?"

"I won't."

"Good. Then give Pickett an hour or two. Like I said, the coroner in Forto has already carted the ladies away, so don't worry about that. Except . . . you *will* have to ID them, at some point. I'll drive you out there, tomorrow or the next day."

"Seriously?"

"You're their next of kin, if they ever had any—apart from each other. But that doesn't have to happen right now. It'll wait."

"Oh." Cameron scratched at the plus sign in a carving that read HS + JE = 4EVR. He had no earthly clue who was supposed to be together forever, or why they decided to declare as much in a bar off State Road 177. He tried to imagine what their names might've been, but Daisy and Claire were dead and there was no room in his thoughts for anything else, no matter how hard he tried. "Will I have to look at their bodies?"

"We can do it through a window or . . . I think they may have a camera system there. You might be able to just . . . look at them on a screen. It won't be that bad," he said, but the wrinkle of his forehead and the strained look in his eyes said he might not be strictly certain. "You can do it. You're a brave kid. You're a

weird kid, and you're kind of the only kid in town, but . . . please. Listen to me, will you?"

"I can try?"

"Then listen to the ladies, if that's easier for you: Get out of Staywater, kid. There's nothing for you here. Not this bar, not that house, not that girl." He cocked his head toward the kitchen, where Jess had just disappeared. "Especially not that girl. I know a mooning boy when I see one."

"I'm not mooning over her," he said, with such sudden and intense honesty that the cop was taken aback.

"Um . . . well," he flustered gently. "I read that wrong, I suppose."

"You probably didn't," he admitted. "But things change. I'll change, too. Everybody does, right?"

Kemp gave him a dubious stare, but then softened. "Sure. Everybody does. Will you leave, though? Will you pack up and head out, when all of this is settled?"

"Sure. When everything's settled. Until then, I guess I'll . . . work here?" It was a risk, but not much of one. The cop had already hinted that he wouldn't stop him.

"If you work here, I can't hear about it. I can't know about it. You get me?"

"I get you."

"So if I see you wearing an apron in this bar, you tell me you're cross-dressing and we're all right," he said with a feeble grin. He rose from the table and sighed hard, pushing his chair under it like he was done here, and he was glad for it. "You wait a few hours before you head home. Maybe . . . wait until Thirsty's closes, even. You can walk home from here all right, can't you?"

Cameron said, "I've done it a million times. I mean . . . once or twice, if the . . . um. If the ladies sent me on an errand."

"Good boy. Stay here, and we'll wrap up what we can. I'll be in touch about the formal ID in the city, and the funerals. They left you a little inheritance, I think I said already. It's more than you'd think, but not enough to retire. They did what they could, to leave you options."

"I never deserved those ladies. They never deserved a jerk like me."

"Don't talk like that. You never deserved to get dumped on their doorstep. Everything that happened after that was up to them. They could've called child services in the next town over, and you'd have gone into the foster system someplace. But they chose to keep you, son. They loved you, and did their best to raise you. Now do them the honor of abiding by their wishes."

"When the time comes, I'll get out," Cameron promised to nothing and no one, least of all the officer across the table. It was a meaningless promise anyway. Meaningless, because it could've meant anything.

"They'll hound you all your life, if you don't."

"I'm well aware, sir."

"Lord Almighty, listen to you. You've always talked like an old man."

Cameron finally found his smile. "I was raised by old women."

Kemp smacked the table with his open hand. "That you were, that you were. So I've got my eye on you, and they've got their eyes on you, too. One way or another, we'll all be in touch."

"Thank you, sir. I'll be right here. Or at home, but not for another few hours."

"Perfect." He adjusted his belt around his big belly. Jess was back behind the bar; before he left, he flicked her a small salute to wish her well. Then he was gone, the door swinging shut behind him.

The bar went back to normal. To its new normal, if there would ever be any such thing again.

Now it was Jess back there, slinging drinks where Dave used to stand. Jess, who knew almost nothing about Cameron—and Cameron, who knew more about Jess than he'd ever cared to. Now he couldn't love her. Now there was no such thing as love at all, least of all True Love.

All that shit was nonsense, and he was going to wear an apron anyway.

He picked it up off the bar where Jess had left it and tied it around his waist. This was the new normal, for however long it lasted. Now, he could promise anything, to anyone. Even the ladies, whenever they presented themselves again. Cameron was not yet prepared to go anywhere, but he was fully prepared to lie.

The lying would get elaborate, he knew, but he had time to think of some pretty elaborate whoppers. He had a job, and he had an inheritance. He had two corpses to claim in the next town over, and a home that was a crime scene. (Was suicide a crime? It was probably a crime, but a really, really stupid one.)

He had Jess to keep in the dark, because if she knew what he knew, things would get even weirder and worse than they already were.

He knew about a creature that lived under a bridge, and there, it collected a toll.

He'd seen it rise up to feast, and go down in pieces, and disappear into the swamp—killed a second time over. But there was always the chance it would rise again. The ladies were wrong once, and if the ladies could be wrong, then anyone could be. That damn bridge might well be back in thirteen years.

Somebody had to wait. Somebody had to make sure, and Cameron had plenty of time.

Anyway, thirteen years wasn't really that long—not in the scheme of things.

Was it?

ACKNOWLEDGMENTS

I've said before—and will surely bemoan in the future—that acknowledgments are never my strong suit. Although I'm always happy to insist upon credit where it's due . . . it takes so many people to make a book happen that I live in permanent fear of accidentally leaving someone out. Therefore, my preemptive apologies to anyone who deserves a space here and does not get one. This book was written around a cross-country move; my husband and I bounced back out of Tennessee again, and moved back to the West Coast right over the due date for *The Toll*. This time, we brought two large dogs and a couple of cats with us, on a six-day drive with two cars. Those months before, during, and after the trek are something of a blur.

But here goes nothing!

For starters, this book had two different editors, due to the departure of my longtime editor, Liz Gorinsky—who I dearly love, forever and ever, and wish her the very best wherever she goes and whatever she does, until the end of time. Many thanks to her, of course, for beating this thing's terrible initial draft into something like a decent shape. Then, in the wake of Liz's exit, this book was shepherded through the rest of the process by editor Beth Meacham, a marvelous woman who helped me find the story's center when I thought I'd lost track of it for good. Huge thanks to her, as well.

Likewise, big ups to my bottle rocket of fiery justice, wonder-agent Jennifer Jackson. She's the one who managed the deal in the first place, and she's always my champion. And to the other usual suspect, thanks go to my husband, J. Aric Annear, for keeping the lights on and the pets fed as I generally lost my shit trying to close up one household and set up a new one, while I simultaneously juggled all my deadline commitments.

Also, and I realize this sounds somewhat random . . . but I want to thank a woman named Dr. Linda Jack, who—at this moment—is running for the Florida House of Representatives (West Pasco, 36th district). I've been volunteering for her campaign for months, and I don't know if she'll win in November (though *you'll* know, since you'll be reading this well after the fact), but watching her put her life on hold in order to try to establish a little bit of light in the world has given me so much hope in a time without much hope in it. As I said in the dedication: Win or lose, this book is for her.